RIPPLES

RIPPLES

JENNIFER LEW

TORTOISE SHELL BOOKS

TORTOISE SHELL BOOKS

Copyright © 2016 by Jennifer Beulah Lew

Cover design: Abram Foster. Cover illustration: Arthur Clifton Goodwin, *Customs House Tower, T-Wharf*, oil on canvas. Courtesy of the Athenaeum. Book design: Michael Foster. Author photograph: Accent Photography.

ISBN: 978-0-9973533-1-0

For Chahna, Paul and Susan, who encouraged me—and Gretchen, Dan, Kristen, Lisa and Caleb, who took care of the baby.

1

Ariella did not expect three police cars parked at crazy angles
in the road when she turned the nose of her little Mazda into
Longwood Avenue, but she should have. In her standard
scan of the morning paper she had noticed the brief front-
page story on a Brigham and Women's Hospital shooting.
Her reporter's instincts should have told her the cops would
be investigating, but she had been too absorbed in her
impending interview to think. She stared at the sea of traffic
in her path. At this rate, she should probably just abandon
her car at the curb with the police and walk.

She sighed and switched on the radio. A harp
reverberated in the car for a moment; then an announcer
launched into the top news story, the brutal murder of a
pregnant woman in Roxbury. Murder? So the poor woman
had died. In her mind's eye Ariella could imagine the
imposing brick facade of Brigham and Women's Hospital
around the corner; it lay just behind the College of Pharmacy
buildings in front of her, and somewhere in its catacombs a
woman had breathed her last. Ariella snapped the radio off;
she had heard the details of the assault before leaving the
newsroom and did not want to hear them again. If she ever
graduated from general assignment to a regular beat she
would avoid crime stories. Behind her a man in a delivery

truck was leaning on his horn, and others began to pick up the tune—typical Boston drivers.

Fishing in her purse for lipstick, Ariella tried to screen out the noise. She pulled the rearview mirror toward her face and examined it, smoothing an eyebrow with her fingertip and touching up her lips. Then she slid her fingers into her black curls to massage the scalp and rub away a little of the tension.

I don't know why I'm fussing over my appearance for an interview with a reclusive researcher, she thought. *He's probably a near-sighted introvert who finds people far less compelling than petri dishes.*

Just then the traffic began to crawl forward, and wiggling the mirror back into place, Ariella edged down Longwood again. The cars moved at a snail's pace, but she finally passed the gleaming white Children's Hospital building and turned left into an unmarked alley that Dr. Becker's secretary had described. The passageway climbed so sharply upward that Ariella paused at the base, imagining what would happen if a delivery truck came barreling down the hill at her. She would finally take part in a major news story, only not as the reporter. Shifting to low gear, she mounted the hill and with a few twists and turns found the parking lot the secretary had recommended. Grabbing her briefcase, Ariella jumped from the car, tugged her scarf more firmly around her neck, and hunched against the biting November wind ran to the massive doors of the Carver Cancer Center research labs.

A sallow security guard behind a faux-marble desk cocked an eyebrow at her as she entered. Heels echoing in the empty reception area, she stepped forward, stated her name and asked him to announce her.

"Got to sign in," he grunted, shoving a clipboard toward her. Ariella complied.

"May I just go on up to the fifth floor, then?"

"No," he barked, picking up the telephone. "Yeah, security," he told the receiver. "A woman named Richards to see ya."

"Richardson," Ariella corrected. The guard hung up.

"Go ahead." He waved vaguely to the left. Following his gesture, Ariella passed into a corridor and found an elevator bank at the end. When the elevator arrived, several older men in lab coats stepped out, deep in technical conversation. They gave Ariella a nod, and she stepped in, wondering whether she was the right reporter for this assignment. She felt very young and lacking, but she reminded herself that her mentor, David, the *Boston Times* medical reporter, had no advanced degrees in science either.

Ever since journalism school Ariella had planned to specialize in women's health, but until now she had gotten few opportunities. Fortunately for her, top management at the *Boston Times* had recently decided to give higher priority to her favorite beat, sending out a call for stories. Never one to sit still, her editor had popped into last night's meeting at the American Cancer Society to ferret out any whispers of hot research around town. The piece she had assigned Ariella to write on cervical cancer sounded too dry for the front page, but Ariella had only worked at the *Times* for a year and did not yet expect top billing, only a chance to develop a file of health clips.

When she reached the fifth floor, Ariella found herself in an antiseptic hallway with a white-tiled floor and pale blue walls running endlessly in both directions. She walked through the first open doorway into what appeared to be a secretary's office and asked a heavy-set woman with gray hair wound into a tight bun for Dr. Samuel Becker. The woman greeted her with a grimace, glanced at the wall clock, and identified herself as the grants administrator. A black name-plate on her desk read "Mrs. Fiona Doyle."

"Of course, I suppose you can't help being late what with that horrible mess out there. The police won't let any cars at all down Shattuck Street, they've closed half the staff parking lots, and I actually had to show I.D. to get in here this morning. You've heard about that shooting, of course." She wrinkled her nose. Ariella made commiserating noises and tried to steer the conversation toward the grants that funded the lab, but the woman clammed up. So Ariella settled down on the rather hard, gray couch, gathered a copy of each brochure and report on the table beside her, and began leafing through them, underlining several sentences with a yellow highlighting marker from her purse.

After a few minutes, the telephone rang, and Mrs. Doyle picked it up. "Yes, Mr. Becker, she's here." She grunted out a chuckle. "No, no horns. Shall I send her down to your office right now? All right." She hung up, gave Ariella a chilly look, and said, "Mr. Becker is ready now. I suggest you take it easy in there. He's not too fond of the press. Now just take a left and then a right at the first corner you come to. He's in room 551." Ariella smothered a smile at Mrs. Doyle's protective attitude. Becker must be one of those socially-awkward geniuses who was trying to blow himself up with a chemistry set at the age of six. She hurried down the stark corridors to room 551, where she found the door shut and knocked twice.

With unexpected suddenness the door swung open and Ariella found herself inches away from a tall, broad-shouldered man, back ramrod straight, blue eyes piercing her from above. She took an involuntary step backward.

"So," he said, "Miss Richardson." He studied her petite figure from the top of her curly head to the toes of her black boots before stepping aside to let her into his inner sanctum. Ariella struggled to compose herself at the force of his personality, but recognized defeat when he remarked, "Are you all right?"

She decided to make light of it. "Well," she answered, mustering a warm smile, "You're not exactly what I expected!"

He gave her a wary look. "I see the media hasn't given up on prejudging the world. Come in. This office is a mess; so at least that will fit your image. Be careful not to move any papers—or remove any."

Ariella was rapidly revising her assumption that this would be an easy interview as long as she could understand the technical jargon, but she had dealt with a long line of unreasonable people in her time, beginning with her mother. She sighed gently. "Look, Dr. Becker, there's no need to be hostile. This is a friendly interview. I don't want to take anything; I just want to learn about your cervical cancer research and its potential to help women."

"Okay." He sat down behind his desk and crossed his arms in front of his broad chest. "I'll tell you what; I'll make a deal with you. I can keep it very friendly as long as you agree to let me see your story before you print it, just so I can correct any errors and make sure you don't misquote me. How about it?"

"It sounds fine. I'll check with my editor," Ariella replied. "I can call you with an answer as soon as I get back to the office."

Becker raised a brow. "Good cop, bad cop, huh? Just leave the 'no' to your boss. Don't play games with me, Miss Richardson. I'm not stupid, and I know your type."

Bristling, Ariella stifled the urge to tell him off. She needed this story. "I'm sorry if you have a low opinion of the media, but you agreed to do this interview, and I'd like to begin. I'll do my best to get your approval of the finished piece, but I simply don't have the authority to make promises. That's the truth, and if you don't like it, too bad."

Mixed emotions played across his blue eyes. The two sat in belligerent silence for a moment. Ariella broke eye contact first and glanced around the room; on a shelf in the bookcase she noticed a mahogany-framed photograph of an Asian woman in a red bikini. The woman was twisting a lock of shining hair around her finger and smiling intently at the camera. Knowing how coldly the scientist would greet personal questions, Ariella subdued her curiosity and cautiously slid her eyes back to his face, saying, "Well, shall we? I can start with a very basic and unobjectionable question: shall I call you Dr. Becker in my piece, or Mr. Becker?"

"I'm both actually," he replied curtly.

"Would you care to explain?" She held her breath.

He sighed, pulling absently on an earlobe. "All right, Miss Richardson, I'll give you your interview, but only because I promised Roland Chan. You've got twenty minutes, and if I don't like your questions, you're out. And don't think I'll forget about seeing the article." The force in his stare unnerved her.

"Thank you." She smiled weakly at him, but elicited no response. "So why does Dr. Chan want you to talk to the *Times*?"

"Let's start with the first item. I have a Ph.D. in immunology, giving me the honorary title of 'Doctor,' but I'm not a medical doctor. No doubt you noticed that our administrator, Mrs. Doyle, calls me 'Mister.' Either one is correct as long as your newspaper does not imply that I have an M.D."

"Fair enough. And Dr. Chan?" Ariella slid a small notebook from her briefcase and began to scribble.

"Roland Chan is an old friend and colleague, a highly respected immunologist. He established this lab many years ago, then coaxed me here to work with him. Roland has great faith in my work and feels that we're really onto something. Unlike me, he sees benefit in publicizing the research. He's a visionary, and he feels that our preliminary findings may give hope to sick people."

"And you disagree?"

"Let's just say that I don't trust the media to get the story right, and I don't want to give anybody false hope. This research is far from complete, and I don't want our early findings trumpeted as a panacea for cervical cancer."

"And is it a potential cure you're researching?"

"No," he snapped. "It is not a cure. Be precise if you want to work with me." He stared at her, jaw clenched.

"I'm sorry," Ariella said calmly, "but I don't have an extensive scientific background. If my terms are incorrect, just tell me. Now what is it if it's not a cure?"

"At best it's a preventive measure—like a vaccination against smallpox."

"Is it a vaccination?" She noticed that despite his curtness he did keep explaining.

"No, not yet. But that's the goal. You see most experts believe that cervical cancer is caused by the human papilloma virus. In the last ten years, the study of viruses has dominated the field of immunology. As you may know, immunology research has grown enormously in response to AIDS. And in trying to understand AIDS, we've learned a great deal about viruses in general."

"So how does this relate to your research?"

"Well, as I said, most experts think a particular virus called human papilloma is at least one major factor leading to cancer growth in the cervix. I've been studying this human papilloma virus, learning how it functions and replicates, and I believe I've found a protein produced by the virus that is expressed on the surface of infected cells."

Ariella bit the end of her pen and drew her eyebrows together. "Now, what are the implications of that?"

"Well, if during the virus' attack on a particular cell, a new protein is created, then this new protein may provide us with a route by which to kill off infected cells and prevent the virus from spreading."

Ariella was staring at him in concentration, her pen moving rapidly across the pages of her little notebook. "How do you mean?" she asked.

"You see, this protein provides us with a way to identify infected cells and distinguish them from healthy ones. If we can then give people a vaccine which interferes with the production of the protein, we can stop the replication of infected cells." His voice had taken on the calm, clear tones of a lecturer.

"So what do you put in the vaccine?"

"You attach the protein I discovered to another protein known to cause an immune reaction. The vaccine would also contain adjuvants, which heat up the immune system, get it into attack mode."

She was beginning to get the picture. "So the vaccine identifies infected cells for the immune system, which then destroys them?"

Dr. Becker nodded. "Exactly. This has two benefits. First, the virus never spreads because we get rid of the first infected cells as soon as the virus invades. Second, infected cells are gone too fast to become cancer cells."

"So what is this special protein called?"

"We call it the EV2500 protein—not flashy, but it's traditional to name a substance by its molecular weight." There was the faintest touch of irony in his tone, and Ariella did not miss it.

"Okay." Ariella looked him in the eye. "So you've discovered a protein which enables you to prevent women from getting the virus that causes cervical cancer by preventing the virus from spreading in the body. So if you vaccinated women, the virus couldn't get going in them, and they would never get cervical cancer. Is that right?"

"Essentially. But don't use words like "never." It's possible that some vaccinated women would develop cancer anyway as a result of random mutations or some other cause...."

Ariella cut him off, her voice rising, "But still, if this vaccine works, you could greatly reduce the number of cervical cancer cases! This is very exciting stuff, Dr. Becker. You could be a savior to thousands of women! No wonder Dr. Chan wants some press coverage."

"Well, I appreciate your enthusiasm, Miss Richardson, but..."

"Why don't you call me Ariella? Yes, I know. Nothing's proven yet. Although you won't believe it, I really can understand subtlety. Clearly you must be sure that the vaccine works and has no serious side effects before the public can use it."

"Yes." He could not help noticing the subdued excitement glowing in her eyes. He suppressed the thought and deliberately glanced at his watch. "So, do you have a lot more questions?"

Ariella weighed how to respond. "You've given me my twenty minutes, and I'm certainly grateful, but I would love to talk to you some more if at all possible. We could make another appointment if you wish or a telephone date—at your convenience, of course."

"No, no. Better to get it over with. Look, wait here for a minute while I stick my head into the lab, and then I'll give you another twenty. I have a new research assistant, and I just want to make sure he knows what he's doing." He rose, his body dominating the cramped quarters of the small office, and stepped around the desk past numerous piles of papers strewn on the floor near the door.

In his absence she took a deep breath and studied the photograph in the bookcase. The woman in the picture looked to be in her twenties and had exquisitely fine features and a perfectly symmetrical figure. Although clad only in a bathing suit, she seemed elegant. She stood alone on a white sand beach with bright blue water in the background--Hawaii perhaps? Ariella wondered whether the woman was Dr. Becker's wife or his girlfriend. In a pose like that she had to be one or the other. The office contained little else with clues to the man's personal life, just shelves and shelves of scientific books, journals and stacks of paper. Two turn-of-the-century circus posters decorated the one wall free of bookshelves, one depicting a tiger and the other, a clown. She took the clown as a hopeful sign that the man had a sense of humor hidden beneath his gruff exterior.

2

Ariella never got her additional twenty minutes. Becker reappeared with a preoccupied look and told her that he had to return to work immediately but would schedule another appointment with her. All the same, she graciously thanked him for his time.

Half an hour later she walked into the cavernous *Boston Times* newsroom to find the Roxbury murder story on everyone's lips. The dead woman's baby had been delivered by cesarean and was hanging on, the husband still in intensive care. Ariella meandered through the maze of desks listening idly to the speculation about gang involvement, not mentioning that she had just been at the medical center since she did not want to get sucked into conversation. Then, from the opposite end of the newsroom, a lanky woman in a severe black pantsuit called out her name. Ariella picked up the pace considerably, half jogging past the scattering of desks to her editor's glass office door.

"So how did it go? Did you get anything good? And did you run into Mayor Reilly?" asked Joyce Aldrich with a raised eyebrow, waving Ariella into her cubicle.

"Mayor Reilly?"

"Yeah. He rushed to Laurie Griffin's bedside this

morning—you know, that woman who got shot—him and his buddy, the police commissioner."

"Coughlin's there too?"

"Yup. They just gave a blistering press conference: 'This crime is an outrage to all decent people, and Boston will not tolerate it! We will comb Roxbury till we find the animal that did this.'" She gave a perfect imitation of the mayor's deep voice. "Another slick move by city hall— hogging the limelight, inciting the populace and making a pitch for their favorite new issue, gun control."

"Still—it must comfort the family some to know that the mayor and police commissioner are taking the whole thing so seriously."

"Oh, Ariella, give me a break. Reilly just wants to raise his poll numbers. Now tell me about your interview."

"It was interesting. I got some terrific material, but Sam Becker isn't exactly the ideal interview subject." Ariella sank into the brown leather chair opposite Joyce's desk and pushed the murder case from her thoughts. The chair was definitely not standard issue. It had come from Joyce's home, along with the flourishing ferns hanging from the ceiling corners, and the oversized Sam Francis print, its splashes of brilliant color on the wall over Joyce's head giving her space its unique style. As always, Ariella found herself marveling at her boss' tasteful, well-ordered office, an oasis in a building teeming with messy males.

"Tell me." Joyce smoothed her auburn coif and sat.

"Well, Becker has made a very promising discovery, a vaccine that could prevent cervical cancer. It really has amazing potential. If teenage girls were routinely vaccinated with the stuff in school, we could basically eliminate the disease. It's an upbeat story—for cancer—and I got a lot of detail." She pulled out her notebook.

"Sounds great," said Joyce with a faint air of surprise; "so what's the catch?"

"What catch?"

"You're a reporter, Ariella. You know there's always a catch. For instance, why was Becker a difficult interview subject?" Ariella studied her editor's long face, bright, narrow eyes, and the small lump half-way down her nose. She had never summoned the guts to ask whether Joyce had broken it, but it looked that way.

"Well, it was partly an expectations game. I thought he would be a shy, reclusive scientist." Ariella paused and made a face. "Instead he's a big man with a powerful personality—and he hates the media."

Joyce's sculpted eyebrows rose toward the heavens. "I'd heard that. Perhaps he's a man with something to hide."

"Oh, I don't think so," Ariella replied quickly. "He gave me straight, detailed answers to all my questions once we got going. He just didn't want to speak to me initially, acted like it was a waste of his precious time and said he only agreed to do it as a favor to Dr. Roland Chan, who seems to have brought him here to Boston."

"Are there any women working on the project?"

"I don't know."

"Well, I'm always a little dubious about women's health research conducted exclusively by men." Joyce tapped on the desktop with a long, maroon fingernail to emphasize her last three words. "Despite all the wonderful medical research facilities in Boston, very few have devoted substantial resources to women's health research. It tends to get short shrift: the studies receive less funding, have fewer experimental subjects, and use too many shortcuts. And it's amazing how even now in the 1990's many of them proceed without one female on staff."

Ariella nodded. "But Joyce, my impression is that Becker is a very precise and intelligent guy. I can't imagine that he's cutting corners."

"Don't imagine. I need hard facts, not your impressions."

Ariella took the rebuke with good grace, but her gaze hardened. "Anyway, isn't his reputation on the line when he publishes his research? I mean, if he uses shoddy methods, the scientific community will call him on it—won't they?"

"They should, and eventually somebody usually does. But many doctors just accept the scanty knowledge and inconclusive research on women's health problems. After all, a lot of standard treatment for women is based on studies of men only. So, for instance, we don't really know whether women with heart disease might benefit from different treatment than men receive. And there hasn't exactly been a ground swell of support for more extensive studies of women's health."

"Well, I hadn't really thought about it from that perspective."

"Perhaps you should. I think that before we write a paean of praise to Sam Becker, you should find out a little more about him. Why is he so suspicious of the media? Get his resume, find out about his previous research, look into whether he has women working with him. And another thing—is he testing his vaccine on humans?"

Ariella narrowed her eyes in thought.

"Getting a vaccine approved for sale requires a series of steps." Joyce liked to explain things even if it meant repeating the obvious. It satisfied her need for order. "First, they test it on animals; then they test it on humans in various ways. The FDA requires a certain process to insure that the vaccine is safe."

"Sure..."

"If Becker's doing human trials, then you need to find out about his experimental subjects. They should be an ethnically and economically diverse group of women, but often researchers just use whatever they can get, which tends to be poor women who don't understand the risks of participating in a study."

"Pretty cynical about all this, aren't you? And here I thought that Sam was a genuine American hero, porcupine though he is, making a real contribution to society."

Joyce made a face. "What does he look like?"

Ariella blushed. "Definitely attractive—tall, dark and handsome, basically."

"Just don't let it go to your head. I need your objectivity." Joyce gave her a stare. "Maybe I should have given this to David, but I honestly didn't think it would go this far."

Ariella bit back a retort to this unflattering comment. That would only drive those sculpted eyebrows higher. "You're tough, Joyce, but I do appreciate the opportunity."

Joyce laughed. "I know I'm a skeptic, but that's how I got ahead in journalism. You're an excellent writer, Ariella, but sometimes too idealistic. And yet I like you that way. It's unusual—and so unlike me."

"Well, one of these days I'll turn out to be right."

"Maybe deep down I'm rooting for you." Joyce gave her patented pursed-lip smile. "I'd hate to think the world is really as bleak as it seems, but it probably is. Anyway, write up what you've got and look into those other questions we discussed. I'd like to see a draft by Thursday noon because I want to get this story into next week's Health/Science section." Just then the phone rang, and Joyce waved her out.

3

Several days later, Ariella pushed through the massive doors of the historic Massachusetts State House and stood poised at the top of its broad, stone steps blinking in blinding midday sunlight. Her frustration at a wasted morning began to seep away as she breathed the unseasonably warm air and gazed out at glorious blue sky over the Boston Common. Clumps of business people in gray suits were strolling through the park, teenagers on skate boards and roller blades careening around them, and waves of people were emerging from the underground passages of the subway, smiling at the December sun, and stripping off their coats. A school group had gathered at the foot of the steps, and a petite black woman in a trench coat, undoubtedly their teacher, was explaining that the American Revolution and the roots of our democracy could be found right here in this landmark building. Then the children began swarming up the steps; one snapping a fat gum bubble that broke into Ariella's reverie and reminded her of her hunger. She threaded her way through the children to the street below and waited for the light to change.

Crossing the street, she noticed a man in the distance, striding towards her; he looked familiar. As he came within hailing distance, she recognized Sam Becker in a spotless, navy blue suit which deepened the color of his eyes, a slight smile on his lips, clearly rapt in thought. In the instant before he noticed her, she found herself wishing that she could cause that peaceful expression on his face, or any man's.

"Ariella Richardson! What brings you downtown?"

She could not suppress a little thrill that he at least remembered her name. "I could ask the same of you! Listen, about that story on your work..."

"Oh, it's all right. Fiona—Mrs. Doyle—gave me your message this morning that it's all been pushed back a week. Fickle business, newspapers."

"Right. They ran out of room because of that big story on the space shuttle—so they're holding yours for next week's Health/Science section. But I didn't want you to think I had forgotten to get back to you..."

He broke in: "So are you working on the Griffin murder story? It seems to be the media sensation of the moment. Everywhere I turn I hear about the urban jungle and how we need to reinstate the death penalty."

She did not care for his sarcastic tone, but found herself rushing to deny her involvement. "Oh no, I'm not working on it. It's a terrible tragedy, and yes, politicians are definitely jumping on it to push their agendas. That story's too big a fish for me. I'm down here covering a health-related story at the State House. The Legislature is considering a bill to ban all smoking in public schools, and I'm trying to get a sense of what some powerful legislators think of it."

"Ban smoking in schools? Isn't it banned already? I don't remember any smoking being allowed when I was in public school." He gave her a speculative look.

"Well, it's complicated." She sighed, amazed that he

wanted to pursue a conversation with her. His gaze strayed downward, taking in her multi-colored scarf, red knit dress and black boots glinting in the sunlight.

"You look great." His mouth widened into a breath-taking smile. "But I detect a bit of frustration."

"Very good, Sherlock. How'd you know?" She wondered whether he could hear her heart pounding in her chest.

"Scientists tend to be keen observers," he said dryly, stepping closer to her. "So, do you have plans for lunch?"

"Well, I..." She swallowed her surprise. "No, I was just thinking of picking up a sandwich and eating it in the Public Garden. I can't believe it's so warm today—it feels more like April than December—I didn't want to lose the chance to be outdoors."

"It is gorgeous. Must be 65° out. Well, do you mind if I join you? There's a French bakery right around the corner where we can get some sandwiches." He raised his eyebrows invitingly. "You can tell me all about smoking in schools and what's bothering you."

"Sounds lovely, but maybe I should get back to the newsroom...."

"Nonsense. It's a beautiful day, and we should seize the opportunity. Who knows how many months it will be before we get another day like this one?"

"Are you sure?"

He looked puzzled. "Of course. I wouldn't ask you otherwise. It's not every day that I have a chance to picnic with an attractive woman in the Public Garden. And I promise to be on my best behavior."

Ariella could not help smiling at this because he had put on the wide-eyed, pleading expression of a small boy.

"All right, let's do it." She started back towards the corner, clutching her shoulder bag, dwarfed by the tall man at her side. His light-hearted mood unnerved her; so she tried distracting her mind. "And what brought you out of the depths of your lab? Must have been something important."

"Why do you say that?"

"Well, I got the impression that you're pretty single-minded about your research."

He gave a snort of laughter. "Is that a polite way of saying you think I'm a workaholic? No, don't apologize. You must have been talking with Roland. He thinks I'm incorrigible. Actually, I came down here for a meeting at DPH, the Department of Public Health. I peer-review some of the proposals that they're considering for funding."

"Interesting."

"Yes, well, Roland got me into it last year, probably partly to get me out of the lab. But I've come to enjoy it. I'm glad that I can help needed research projects get the attention they deserve and weed out some of the unsound ones."

"How do you decide what to support?"

"You do love to ask questions, don't you? Well, I look at the statistical method and experimental design, for one thing. Many doctors have a good idea for a project but only sketchy notions of how to properly design a study. They don't get enough statistical and research training in med. school."

"Really?"

"Yes, well, medicine is so complex these days that they have an awful lot to absorb to just become good clinicians. So research training gets short shrift."

They had reached the cafe, and Sam held the door for her. She hesitated slightly on the threshold; it had been so long since a man held a door open for her that she had almost forgotten how to respond. Joyce would have found it annoying, but Ariella liked little courtesies. She joined the take-out line, keenly aware of Sam's tall frame behind her. The tantalizing aroma of fresh bread filled the air of the small shop, and her hunger sharpened. Deliberately avoiding eye contact with her companion, she studied the menu blackboard overhead until the quickly moving line brought her face to face with the French-accented saleswoman behind the glass counter. Ariella ordered a turkey sandwich with all the trimmings on their special four-grain roll and a large, hot apple cider—she thought about lemonade, a favorite of hers, but a memory of the park breeze deterred her. Sam asked for a roast beef sandwich, coffee and an apple pastry. At the cash register he tried to intercept her bill, but she would not let him.

"Dr. Becker, I can't let you buy me anything while I'm still writing a story about you. Thank you all the same...."

He scowled. "At least call me 'Sam.' And I don't think one sandwich would compromise your journalistic integrity!"

Temper, temper, thought Ariella, but she did not flinch. "Come on, Sam. Let's not waste another second of this beautiful afternoon. You can buy me a sandwich as soon as I get that article in print—that is, if you still want to." She headed for the door.

Out on the sidewalk, he confronted her with a stubborn look. "Promise?"

"Sure." She nodded gravely with only the tiniest twinkle in her eye. "You can take me to lunch to congratulate me on the incredible accuracy and fairness of my reporting."

"Hah. We'll see about *that*."

They wandered along the broad paths of the Boston

Common like so many who had walked through that historic pentagonal park at the heart of the city, looking for an empty bench. At length they found a sunny spot beside the pond where, in summer, the Swan Boats would drift along, and settled down to eat lunch. Ariella retied her scarf against the breeze, but Sam shrugged off his jacket drawing her attention to his red plaid bow tie.

"Hard to find bow ties these days, isn't it?" she asked.

"My Uncle Charles gave it to me years ago," he explained. "He was a practical sort of guy and said bow ties stayed out of your way."

She nodded. "So tell me about this uncle of yours."

"Oh, he was an engineer, born and educated in England, actually. He was a tinkerer—tinkered with everything till he figured out how it worked—and sometimes drove my aunt to distraction while he was at it. But he could fix anything, make anything. He worked for the government as a bridge-building expert, but in his spare time he fixed clocks and watches for the neighbors, made furniture, repaired cars—you name it!"

"Wow! I'm pretty hopeless at that sort of thing. I missed out on the spatial gene." She was polishing off the first half of her oversized sandwich, deliberately looking down to encourage him to rattle on.

"Well, Uncle Charles had a real gift. I think I've got a little of it, but nowhere near the talent he had. But enough of your questions. I think it's high time we turned the tables and let me ask you some questions." A gust of cold air rustled through the bare tree branches, and Ariella sipped her hot cider, grateful for its warmth.

"If you're cold, you're welcome to wear my jacket," he offered. He had devoured his entire sandwich.

She wavered. "Are you sure you don't want it?"

"Not at all. I'm very warm." He stretched his arms and torso to their full length in the sunshine, oddly reminding her of a big cat, perhaps a panther. "Go ahead. Don't stand on ceremony." As Ariella drew his jacket around her shoulders, she could feel the clinging warmth of his body seeping into her bones. The intimacy of her thoughts annoyed her. "You look much better now," he remarked with a penetrating glance. He was too observant. He had certainly noticed immediately that she was cold. But he continued, "Now, on to my questions: how long have you worked at the *Boston Times*?"

"A little over a year."

"What did you do before that?"

"I worked for the *New Haven Register* in Connecticut for about two years—first the Hamden beat, basically any news from Hamden, which is a quiet suburb of New Haven; then later I was promoted to doing New Haven city politics. It was a good job—nice people, and I learned a lot there."

"So no science stories...."

"No. I did do a story about Yale New Haven Hospital once, but it had to do with a dispute between the hospital and the city over a piece of park land which the hospital wanted for a parking garage." She made a face, remembering the charming park which was no more.

"Yeah, parking is a big problem at the Longwood Medical Area too. And what did you do before the *Register*?"

"Well, how far back are we going—my birth? By the way, the city was right about that park. The area around Yale New Haven Hospital is an ugly, concrete jungle. People there had no public amenities other than that park, and today they have nothing. Look how the Boston Common has brightened our day! Doesn't everyone deserve a little natural beauty in life?"

Sam was staring into her eyes. "Everyone does deserve a little natural beauty," he agreed, his gaze wandering over her. Ariella stirred nervously, and he quickly interposed a question.

"You're avoiding my question about where you worked before the *Register*. Was it another paper?"

"No, actually. Before New Haven, for a couple of years after college I lived in New York, working as a paralegal, helping to care for my niece, Ruby, and getting my masters in journalism at N.Y.U. night school." She paused for a sip of cider, and noticing his expectant look, continued.

"Ruby is my sister's little girl," she explained. "She's five now, but she was born with a heart defect, and Nina was terrified about her that first year. She hated to leave the baby with anyone other than a family member; so I moved in and did a lot of baby-sitting. Ruby's already had three open-heart surgeries in her short life, but thank God she's big and strong for her age—so far no apparent ill effects except for a few scars."

"Sounds like a busy life you had." He was wondering about the men in her life, but did not want to ask. It was really none of his business. "What's the name of Ruby's condition?"

"Persistent truncus arteriosus. A doctor at Boston Children's Hospital pioneered the treatment she's getting. The amazing thing is that if she had been born ten years earlier she would have died...."

A shadow crossed Sam's face, and his eyes unfocused for a moment. She fell silent, watching him. Slowly he returned to the present, and his jaw thrust forward.

"So did the politicians get the better of the press at the State House this morning?" he asked, with a lightning change of topic and an appraising glance.

She grimaced. "Not exactly. But I didn't get very far. As I told you, there's this bill to ban smoking in the public schools. Currently a lot of schools allow teachers and staff to smoke in school buildings, and some high schools even let the kids do it, a holdover from the sixties."

"The old 'anything goes' attitude."

"Yeah. Only now there's more and more evidence that secondhand smoke is dangerous to your health. It's definitely bad for kids with asthma, and there are a lot of those kids in the public schools."

"I'll bet it wouldn't do much good for a kid with a heart defect either," he said.

She ignored the comment. "The bill, which a Newton state rep is proposing, would also earmark some money for 'quit-smoking' programs around the state to help those teachers and staff who want to stop. The rep had a lot of tentative support until yesterday, even some positive words from the powerful Senate President."

"You mean Mahoney?"

"Right. Only today nobody's talking. It seems as if the support is going up in smoke—no pun intended."

"When is the vote?"

"It's scheduled for Friday. But you never know in politics; they could always delay it. The worst part of the morning was just having a whole list of politicians refuse to see me. I felt like a pariah...."

"Try not to take it personally. If you're going to work in the media, you'd better get used to people disliking and distrusting your profession." His jaw had not relaxed.

"Like you, you mean." She eyed him warily, aware that the good feelings of the afternoon were evaporating, but unsure why.

He nodded. "You reporters bring far too many prejudices to your work. Maybe what you need is some scientific training—I don't know. I can see why you would favor this school smoking ban, especially with your niece and all, but don't you think that you should maintain some neutrality and explore all sides of the issue?"

Ariella shook her head defiantly. "How can you question my neutrality when you hardly even know me? Are you saying I've totally made up my mind on the bill?"

"Haven't you?"

She felt backed into a corner. "Well, I do have an opinion, but it's not set in stone; I'm open to change. And I'm a professional. I can write a neutral story no matter what my opinion. It's really too bad that you have to spoil a lovely picnic by taking that nasty tone with me. Don't you think you're the one making snap judgments?"

Across the path a small boy in a red jacket was throwing pebbles into the pond, and Ariella watched the ripples spread. She wondered why she had let this man get her goat and struggled to regain a calm demeanor. After all, Sam Becker's opinion of her made no difference in the general scheme of things—he was simply a tiny ripple which would soon fade away.

"I didn't mean to offend you, but I meant what I said, and I won't candy-coat it. If it helps any, I have a pretty low opinion of politicians too."

"Worse than reporters?"

"Worse than reporters." The awkward silence that followed was broken suddenly by a shout. A woman arose from nowhere, running within feet of them towards a blond toddler beside a bush and yelling, "Justin, did I see you put a worm in your mouth?"

Sam laughed, his good humor restored, and although Ariella's smile did not reach her eyes, she accepted the apple strudel he proffered and munched on the delectable pastry with relish. After a smattering of random remarks that never quite fused into a new conversation, he walked her to the subway entrance and watched the back of her graceful figure all the way down the steps until it turned out of sight into the underground tunnel.

4

Shoving the desk away with two hands she rolled backward in her desk chair and stared at the short stack of papers beside her computer. Several hours of computer research on Medline had yielded only this incomprehensible jumble. Half the abstracts of scientific papers were useless—written by an older California doctor, Samuel R. Becker, who was conducting scientific studies when her Dr. Becker was probably still wearing braces on his teeth. Other abstracts, although for the right Dr. Becker, concerned his theoretical immunology work as a graduate student in Wisconsin, his Ph.D. dissertation, and his post-doctoral studies—all of it over her head, at least five years old, and unrelated to women's health. She slipped off her shoes, wiggled her toes, and swung her feet up, crossing her ankles atop the frustrating pile. Six thirty p.m. Maybe it was time for a break.

Ariella was working at home, as she occasionally did to escape the chaos of the newsroom. Using her home computer and a modem that connected her to the office she could conduct all the computer searches she needed, but the very ease of working in her apartment sometimes seduced her into endless overtime. She loved digging into a story and ferreting out hidden facts. Tugging Becker's resume from the pile, she gazed at the black letters marching across the page as if force of will could reveal the secrets written between the lines. Unbidden the image of the photograph in his office sprang to mind: who was the alluring figure in the bikini? She shook her head impatiently to clear it. That kind of secret she didn't need to know.

Her gray Persian, Miranda, gave a yowl from her favorite perch—a window seat overlooking Commonwealth Avenue, where rain was pouring down in sheets—and a sudden flash of lightning illuminated the cat's yellow-flecked eyes. Ariella startled. Becker had spent four years at the University of Michigan before coming to Harvard a year ago. *So why were there no published papers from his years at Michigan?* She snapped on her computer, initiating a new search. The machine churned away for a few minutes, then reported, "No documents found." She tapped at the keys, trying several other searches. Nothing. Then she glanced at the resume in her lap, picked up the phone and dialed information.

"Hello, Immunology Department."

"Yes, this is Ariella Richardson of the *Boston Times* newspaper. I'm doing a story on some medical research in Boston, and I'm looking for a little background on a Dr. Samuel Becker. He worked for you for several years...."

"He never worked with me, kid. I don't know the name. Of course, I've only been here six months."

"Oh. Well, is there anyone there who could give me just a quick summary of his research at Michigan?"

"I'm sure Dr. Leonardi would know. He's the chairman of the department, and he's been here for years and years. I can see whether he's still here."

"Would you? I would really appreciate a minute of

his time."

Ariella waited for a long moment, fingers crossed. Then a cultured, slightly accented voice came on the line.

"Yes, Miss Richardson, what can I do for you?"

"I'm doing a story on some very promising women's health research being done here in Boston by a Dr. Samuel Becker, who used to work for you, as I understand, and I wondered whether you could tell me about his research there."

"Why yes. Sam Becker was here at the University of Michigan for four years working on the immunology of liver transplantation—to understand why so many patients reject a new liver, you see."

"Liver transplants? So he wasn't working on women's health?"

"Well, women do have livers, my dear, but it was not gynecological research, if that's what you mean. You must understand that an immunologist can easily transfer his theoretical knowledge of the immune system from one disease to another."

"I see. So did Dr. Becker publish anything on his liver transplant work?"

"No, I believe not."

"And why not?"

"The research never yielded publishable results."

"Why would that be?"

"My dear, you cannot imagine how many medical researchers in this country never reach a publishable result."

Ariella did not appreciate his slightly condescending tone, but she persevered. "And why did he leave Michigan? He doesn't strike me as a man who would give up easily."

"He eventually lost his funding. Scientists must

subject their work to strict peer review to keep the research grants that pay for their studies, you know. If results don't come in, grant monies dry up. As much as we like and respect a colleague, our department cannot afford to fund his research without some support from outside grants. But I must tell you that I have the highest regard for Sam Becker. I'm not surprised that he's doing excellent work in Boston."

"Is there anything I can read that would describe his studies at Michigan?"

"Not that I know of. But why don't you ask him?"

"Maybe I will. He doesn't seem too keen on reporters, though."

"Can't say that I blame him."

"What do you mean?"

"Oh, nothing. We researchers tend to be a bit single-minded, that's all. He probably just doesn't want to be bothered. And on that note—not to be rude—but I really must be getting back to work."

"Well, thank you for your time, Dr. Leonardi. I do appreciate it."

"Not at all, my dear, not at all." The line clicked dead, and Ariella sat twirling the phone cord in the air, pursing her lips. Joyce was right: there was a story here somewhere. Turning back to the computer, Ariella switched databases to the NEXIS information service, an archive of news stories from almost every newspaper in the country. She limited her search to the relevant years, using Dr. Becker's name and the University of Michigan. The computer hummed and gave the message, "Processing search request." Her stomach growled, and knowing how slow the computer system could be at this time of day she jumped up to start dinner. Digging in the refrigerator she found a chicken casserole from the previous night and popped it into the microwave. While it heated, she chopped spinach for a salad, humming to herself. *If Sam Becker's hiding something, I'll find it if it's the last thing I do.* Grinning at her own cliché, she flipped on the radio.

"Laurie Griffin, the pregnant Dedham woman shot to death last Sunday was laid to rest today following a funeral mass at historic Saint Mary's Catholic Church in Boston," the male announcer crackled. Ariella sighed. "Eight hundred people attended the service including Cardinal Blake, Governor Podos, Mayor Reilly, Police Commissioner Coughlin, and a number of other local officials. Noticeably absent was Laurie's husband, Brian, still in intensive care at Boston City Hospital from his wounds in Sunday's shooting. The Griffin's baby, Mary Christine, delivered by emergency cesarean section Monday morning, remains in serious condition at Brigham and Women's Hospital. And now traffic."

A woman's voice cut in. "It's quite a mess out there tonight. Storrow Drive is completely backed up. There's been a four-car accident near the B.U. Bridge, and the Boston Police are asking motorists to use alternate routes. Mass transit is running at least ten minutes behind schedule; the red line is temporarily shut down due to flooding near Charles Street..." Thunder crashed, momentarily drowning out the voice. "...and so the police are recommending that people avoid non-essential travel tonight. We've got gale force winds out there, and this storm's definitely going to get worse before it gets better." A bright flash gave the spinach in Ariella's hand a neon glow, and without warning the apartment plunged into silent darkness.

She slid the knife from her hand to the counter and took a shaky breath. The fuse box—where was it? In the basement. Sliding her hands along the counter edges on either side of her she made her way to the living room, where a pair of yellow eyes glowed in the window seat. Ariella picked her way around the furniture to the window and peered through the glass, stroking the cat's silky back.

"You're certainly taking this calmly, aren't you, Miranda? Well, the streetlights are all out. None of the buildings seem to have any light. Even the traffic lights are dead." Another thunder clap. "I guess there's no point in checking our fuses, looks like the whole neighborhood is out." Eyes better adjusted to the dim light, she wound her way back to the kitchen to pick up the phone. Dead.

She swiveled to look at the blank face of her computer screen. "Oh no. My search is gone!" Miranda watched impassively from her perch. "You think I work too much, don't you, pussycat? Well, I guess all I can do is eat some half-baked casserole and wait. That's a joke, Miranda. Half-baked, get it?" The cat yawned.

◈

Sam was pulling at his earlobe and rewriting the methodology section of the grant proposal for the third time in Roland's windowless office when the lights flickered and went out.

"Damn. Not again!" He jumped up and pushed toward the door, invisible papers crunching beneath his feet. Thrusting the door open he found the corridor almost as black as the office. Fingertips grazing a wall, he strode down the hall to his lab the tension in his limbs mounting. He burst into the lab and immediately sighed with relief to find the emergency bulb glowing and the refrigerator humming normally, his experimental cells safe from power failure. He had just completed a quick inspection when he heard some banging in the next room.

"Hey!" He knocked three times on the wall. "You okay?" Hearing a muffled curse and a clatter he stepped into the hall to investigate. "What's going on in here?" he asked, peering through the open doorway into the black hole of the room next door.

"Oh, man, my experiment's crashing as we speak." A slender, dark shape emerged from the gloom, and a young man with thinning hair emerged, rubbing his knee. "As you can see the power's dead, and if it doesn't come on in about three minutes I'm history. And since it's black as hell out the window I figure my odds are looking pretty lousy."

"No emergency generator?" asked Sam.

The thin man snorted. "I'm the new guy on the block. Rich Carruthers." He stuck out his hand. "I don't rank a generator. And who would have thought they'd lose power at this esteemed institution." He shook his head in disgust. "Sorry. I just don't know what I'm going to do. All my funding depends on this experiment, and the whole shooting match is riding on keeping the refrigerator at its arctic temperature, which is probably rising as we speak."

Sam waved a hand impatiently. "Well, let's stop talking then. I've got the lab next door, and my generator's working. We've just got to hook you into it. Got an extension cord?"

A dazed look passed across Rich Carruthers's narrow face. "I don't know. Can we really? You don't know what this would mean to me..."

"Believe me, I know. Let me get you a flashlight. And I'll go rummage around my lab and see what cords I can find." Sam darted back into his lab, pulling a flashlight from a drawer beside the sink, and handed it out to Rich, who groped his way back into his room, swinging the beam of light from side to side. Sam began pulling open every drawer in sight leaving them hanging like gaping mouths as he hunted for any kind of extension cord. He could hear banging next door. He stopped to think, wishing that he had never allowed his research assistant to reorganize the equipment last week. Beginning on the cabinets, he tried the corner farthest from the main work area and immediately spotted a thick cord coiled on the top shelf. Short, but it might have to do.

"Found something!" he yelled, moving to the generator. "Any luck in there?"

"Not yet."

"Keep looking! We may need to string several together." Sam paused, his hand suspended over the generator's controls, then turned to the nearest drawer for the manual. It wasn't there. "Time's wasting, Becker," he told himself, tinkering a moment with the wires until satisfied that he could connect Rich's refrigerator. Just then Rich rushed in brandishing another cord and a handful of adapters. Sam slipped the cords together and stretched the makeshift cable into the hallway and through the door of Rich's lab.

"It's not going to make it," Rich warned, the flashlight beam trembling with his hand, "and what if it just blows out your generator? How long can the little devil handle powering both our fridges? What if it runs out of power? Maybe this is crazy..."

"It'll work," said Sam with quiet determination, dragging the cord toward the silent refrigerator along the back wall. Rich squeezed into the small space between a cabinet and the refrigerator and fumbled in the inches behind the big behemoth to extricate its short cord from the dead wall outlet so that he could connect it with Sam's cable. In his haste he dropped the plug, and it disappeared into the blackness behind the machine. He swore and pushed his nose into the crack searching, twisting the flashlight atop his head like a cartoon mining robot scanning a cave.

"Do you see it?" asked Sam.

"Yeah, but there's no way. It's much too heavy for us to move, and my fingers will never..."

"Let me try. Hold this." Sam held out the end of the cable, and Rich reluctantly removed his nose from the crack and switched places with him. Sam stumbled back into his lab and reappeared with a thin metal rod. Peering into the crack with one eye, he swung the rod lightly until it hooked under the fallen plug and drew it gently upward and into his hand. "Got it." He reached his hand toward Rich as far as the cord would go, but it stopped three feet short, plug and socket straining uselessly toward one another.

"I have to hand it to you for trying, but this looks like the end of the road," Rich sighed, his arm slackening. "Do you want to get a cup of coffee or something?" Sam did not reply, head pivoting on his neck as his eyes scanned the darkened room. He turned slowly away from Rich, settling on the dim outlines of the window beside the refrigerator. His eyebrows rose.

"Oh no! I don't think so."

Sam gave his first smile since meeting the other man, and a mischievous look lit his eyes. "Aw, come on, what have you got to lose? It'll work fine. The distance from window to window is much shorter than going all the way out into the hall and back in here." He had already grabbed a heavy operations manual to weigh the plug down on the counter so that it could not slip back into the crack behind the refrigerator, and he was working on the rusty window locks. With a determined shake, he pushed the window open, bringing a rush of wet wind into the lab. Thunder crashed as he leaned across the counter and stuck his head and shoulders outdoors looking left; then a crackle of lightning obligingly lit his window next door.

"Would you get your head in here?" Rich rasped.

"It's only about five feet away," said Sam, complying calmly. "Here. You just sit sideways on this counter like this with your legs braced along the wall and reach out, and I'll throw you the cable." He had swung around to demonstrate, legs stretched straight out on the countertop along the back wall, his back to the refrigerator.

Rich opened his mouth, shut it, and opened it again. "This is crazy. You want to hang out of a fifth-story window in a lightning storm swinging an electrical cord at me?"

Sam jumped to the ground. "Come on!" He clapped Rich on the back. "It's going to work fine. Now get up here. How many minutes do we have left before your cells are wrecked?" He snatched the cord from Rich's limp hand and left the other researcher staring into the hallway gloom.

Back in his lab, Sam cleared the counter below the window with a swift stroke of his arm and jimmied the window open. Kneeling on the counter like a runner poised to sprint, right foot hooked over the edge, the left pressed against the sill, he leaned his head and torso outside, the cable coiled loosely in his left hand ready to throw. The rain had increased in force, and was beating against the building's brick walls. It ran off his forehead and down the bridge of his nose. No sign of Rich in the next window.

"Hey, Rich, stick your head out!" he called. After a long pause, half the narrow face slid into view, scowling. "Okay, now I'm going to swing the cable toward you, and you grab it."

"Wait a second. Now there's no current running through that thing, is there?"

"Nope." Sam eased the coil out the window, grasped one end firmly in his right fist and wound it several times around that wrist to anchor it, bracing his palm against the window frame; then he held up the remaining coil for Rich to see. "Ready?"

"I guess so."

Sam tossed the coil hard at the other window. It unrolled as it flew across the void and slapped the windowsill just below Rich, but he made no move to catch it.

"Sorry," he said. "This whole thing makes me a little nervous." The cable hung straight down from Sam's window, swinging in the rain. "Hey, are you left handed?"

"No, but this is the best angle to use. One, two, three!" Sam swung the cable in an upward arc, and Rich reached out a hand to meet it, but it never came close enough to the building. More and more of Sam's body emerged in the driving rain as he twisted his body to launch the most accurate throw possible. Again he tossed the cord upward, and Rich reached a whole arm outside, but the cable slapped him across the forehead and eluded him. "Oops. You all right?" asked Sam.

"You know I hate to tell you this, but I can't see depth worth a dime. I have double vision. They even kicked me out of Little League for it!"

Sam snorted. "Think about the grant you're going to lose if you don't catch this cord," he said, leaning further out the window for another launch. A flash of lightning illuminated Rich's nervous fingers clutching convulsively at open air as the cable rapped the wall above his head and fell away. "My fault," said Sam. "I can't seem to deliver it right to your hand. Let me try something." He swung his entire left leg out the window feeling with his toes for the ledge below. Braced against this ledge he leaned his whole body out the window, leaving only his right foot wedged over the counter edge and right palm flat against the window frame for support.

Rich opened his mouth, snapped it shut, but could not contain himself. "Who do you think you are, Tarzan?" Sam leaned even farther out the window. "Hey, take it easy, will you? I really don't want to see you fall."

"You know what, Dr. Carruthers?" Half-turning and bracing his shoulder against the glass he gently flung the cable straight up the brick wall. The end sailed right past an incredulous face through the open window to the countertop where Rich slammed his palm down on it. "You worry too much! Now hold on tight." Sam slid back into his lab, swiping at his dripping face with a wet sleeve as he slipped to the floor.

"It's connected!" yelled Rich through the wall. "Turn on the power!" Sam stepped to the generator and flipped the switch. No sound from Rich. Another thunderclap, and then a flashlight beam lit the doorway. "I don't believe it," said Rich, disentangling a matted lock of hair from his glasses. "I think you actually saved my experiment. This means the world to me. What a crazy night. And look at us. We look more like two drowned rats than two Harvard researchers! Speaking of which, I never even asked your name."

"Sam Becker." He saluted. "At your service."

"Well, you really went out on a limb for me here tonight, Sam. Literally. And I won't forget it."

"No problem." Sam grinned. "Nothing like hanging out the window in a downpour to spice up your evening. I was having a pretty frustrating and unproductive night until you came along. And I knew how you felt. I lost a refrigerator full of experimental cells at Michigan a few years back."

"Well, I really can't thank you enough. Can I at least buy you a cup of coffee to warm you up?" The slight man's gaze rested on his colleague's sodden shirt with regret.

"Sure." Leaving the generator humming quietly, they groped their way through the gloom to the stairwell.

5

The phone rang at 6:30 a.m. Ariella reached instinctively for the receiver, blinking in the gray dawn as she tried to remember why she was lying in bed fully clothed in yesterday's dress. The blackout. She remembered stretching out on the bed for a minute, sinking her head into the pillow. The darkness must have lulled her to sleep in seconds.

"Yeah—what?" she croaked into the telephone.

"I said, 'Wake up, this is Joyce.' We've got quite a little story on our hands. Do you know what your great American hero, Dr. Becker, did last night?"

"Got stuck in the blackout?" Ariella yawned.

"No, genius, but close. He was hanging out a fifth-story window over at the Carver Center building throwing wires around in the lightning storm. Some concerned citizen got photos."

"What? Why was he doing that?"

"Maybe he likes flirting with death. You know they classified that storm as a hurricane, Hurricane Edna. First genuine hurricane to hit Boston head-on in five years. Most of the south shore still has no electricity. That scientist of yours must have a screw loose."

She rolled her eyes. "He must have been trying to get

some emergency power going."

"Yeah, well, most people don't try to harness lightning as an alternative energy source. Most reasonably sane people, that is. I myself prefer to string electrical wires *inside* buildings. Anyway, I want the story today, as soon as you can get it to me. We're supposed to have an exclusive on the photos because the guy who took them has a cousin at the paper. But you'd better find Becker fast before local T.V. is all over him."

"You know, Joyce, he really doesn't like me much. Maybe you should send somebody else."

"It's not you. He just doesn't like reporters. At least he knows you. And anyway, aren't you intrigued?" Ariella stifled another yawn. "That excited, eh?"

"Sorry," she replied sheepishly, "but it is pretty early. Don't worry—I'll do it."

"I never worry," her boss responded in clipped tones and hung up just as Ariella gave an incredulous grunt. Left listening to the dial tone she let the receiver slip onto the quilt and abandoned her body to an enormous stretch reaching for the four corners of the queen-sized bed with every limb. Refreshed she groaned out the last of her protest to the empty room around her, lifted her legs straight for the ceiling, pointed her toes and contemplated her next move. Should she call or just head over to the medical area? Suddenly she remembered her abortive computer search. She should really reinstate the search right away, even if there was no time to wait for the results. At least she would have some answers by nightfall. She jumped out of bed and switched on the computer.

❧

At nine a.m. sharp she stood in front of the Carver Center's grouchy security guard suppressing her impatience as he cradled the phone under his ear giving an excruciatingly detailed description of a dishwasher breakdown. She had already tried to walk past him to the elevator bank, but he had stopped her with a sharp, "Wait a minute." Apparently the repairman on the line had a lot of questions. She considered ignoring his warning and striding past, but she knew she would not get far. Ever since the Griffin murder, the medical area had been crawling with extra security guards; the *Times* had even covered the change in a major article. On her way here she had noticed a new guard outside the Carver doors, another in the parking lot and a third in front of the College of Pharmacy.

Finally she said, "Are you going to be long?"

The guard glowered and hung up. "Whaddayou want?"

"I'd like to go up to the fifth floor to speak to Dr. Sam Becker please. I'm Ariella Richardson."

He glanced at his log. "He's not up there."

She took a chance. "How about Dr. Roland Chan?" He dialed a number and made the inquiry. She held her breath. Several grunts later he waved her toward the elevators. Exhaling slowly she thanked him with a smile.

When the elevator door slid open, Roland Chan was waiting for her. A short stocky man with an aura of authority, he inspected her without expression, then thrust out his hand as his face broke into a wide smile.

"Very nice to meet you, Ms. Richardson." He nodded for emphasis. "Right this way. You will excuse the clutter in my office." He led her quickly down the corridor she remembered. "So you're interested in Sam are you?" The question had a peculiar ring to it. "Heard about last night's heroics?"

"Last night's heroics?" she repeated.

He stopped short and swung around to look into her eyes. "That's why you're here the minute the building opens for visitors, isn't it? Let's be candid, Ms. Richardson. I'm a former military man, and I like to be direct. I can help you quite a bit if you play straight with me."

She returned the gaze evenly. "Yes, Dr. Chan. I did hear something about an incident last night—although I really don't have any details. That's what I'm here to get. Of course, I'm also working on that story on Dr. Becker's research for next week's Health/Science section, and I would certainly appreciate any help you can give me on that."

He nodded, his smile displaying broad upper teeth and a left dimple, and walked on. They stopped at room 551. As they walked through the door and her eyes lighted on the photo in the bookcase, everything snapped into place.

"So this is your office?" she said casually, more a statement than a question.

"Yes. A bit cramped, but we devote as much space to labs as we can on this floor. That's the way I like it." He pointed to the shelves. "That's my wife, Cecile."

Impressed at his perceptiveness, Ariella found herself absurdly relieved that the woman was Chan's wife. "She's the one who started this whole thing, isn't she? She met my boss at the American Cancer Society conference and talked up the wonderful women's health research going on in your lab as a great story for the paper."

"Right. Well, Cecile's on the ACS board; she's a

terrific networker and a big fan of our work, naturally."

"So what can you tell me about last night? Were you here on the premises during the blackout?"

"No. I was home. But Sam called me late at night and told me about it. You should really talk to Rich Carruthers, though. He was here."

She leaned forward eagerly. "Is, uh, Mr. Carruthers in the building now?"

Roland's eyelids crinkled with humor. "Young Dr. Carruthers, our newest researcher. Yes. I'll call him in when we're finished. Basically, Sam engaged in some acrobatics to save the last four months of Rich's research from destruction. Rich had experimental cells in deep cold storage—liquid nitrogen. The blackout knocked out the power to his refrigerator, and without electricity a refrigerator like that starts to warm up pretty fast."

"So what did Sam do?"

"Sam's lab happens to be next door, although I don't think he knows Rich. We just moved Rich in there about a week ago. He used to be in another building. Actually, that's why he had no back-up power system. Usually I try to make sure everybody has access to a generator, but we hadn't set things up for Rich yet. Anyway, Sam has a generator, and he's well aware of the danger of power failures. So he first tried to string some extension cables through the hallway to connect his generator to Rich's refrigerator, but they wouldn't quite reach. So he connected them through the windows."

"In a hurricane?"

Roland shrugged. "I've known Sam Becker for many years; so it doesn't surprise me. He's definitely a good man in a pinch. Determined."

"Determined, but maybe a bit foolish. It's pretty dangerous to throw electrical wires through the pouring rain, isn't it? Not to mention lightning!" She shivered.

"It's dangerous, but less so if you know what you're doing. He took some risk, but he escaped none the worse for wear and saved a $500,000 project from ruin. I must say I'm extremely grateful, and Rich Carruthers is practically ready to promise his firstborn. The fourth floor labs took some losses; so he knows how lucky he is. You know, Sam stepped in to help without even knowing Rich. I don't know whether I would have done that."

She could not help feeling impressed. "That's quite something. I'd love to hear Carruthers' firsthand account."

"Oh, he'll be delighted to tell you. He was in at the crack of dawn to check on his refrigerator, and he's been telling everyone who will listen about Sam's daring exploit."

"Since you've known Sam for so many years, perhaps you could tell me why he left Michigan and came here."

"Ah," said Roland, no humor in his narrowed eyes now. "Well, I'm a persuasive man."

"But what led him to leave Michigan? There's more to it, isn't there?"

"Yes, there is more to it, but only if it's off the record."

"All right."

He looked sharply at her. "I'm relying on your word, Ms. Richardson." She put away her notebook and saw a decision in his eyes before he continued: "I think I can trust you. I'm a pretty good judge of character after years in the academic jungle. Just remember that I'm a good contact to have. I know everyone at Carver—*everyone*." He paused for emphasis. "So Sam gave you a fairly hard time when you came to interview him, didn't he? It's not personal. Sam was my college roommate. You probably think he has no sense of humor, but that's recent. He's had a rough few years with his mother's death and all." Her pulse had quickened, but she leaned back in the chair so as not to appear too eager.

"You see, by the age of eighteen Sam had no family left in the world but his mother and sister, and he was particularly devoted to his mother. After college Sam got his Ph.D. in Wisconsin, did a post-doc there and got an offer at the University of Michigan. Then about five years ago his mother's liver suddenly failed and she went into a coma. Sam sat beside her hospital bed for nine straight days. On the tenth day she woke up, her mind miraculously intact. She was diagnosed with cirrhosis of the liver, not because of drinking—she rarely touched alcohol—but because of undiagnosed childhood hepatitis. She must have gotten it in utero from her mother, who was exposed as a nurse. Anyway, Sam moved his mother to Ann Arbor with him, and she began treatment and was put on the liver transplant list...."

"No wonder he wanted to do liver transplant research," Ariella broke in.

"Yes. Sam did extensive reading on liver transplantation and became obsessed with the problem of transplant rejection. He competed for a grant to study the problem and began working like a maniac on it. After a couple of years she began to deteriorate. Finally she went into liver failure and had to have an emergency transplant. I visited them a few weeks after the surgery, and she seemed to be doing beautifully, but she died eight months later."

Ariella sighed. "Transplant rejection?"

"Right. Sam was devastated—withdrew into his shell

like a turtle. Cecile and I really felt he had to get out of Ann Arbor to begin to heal. So I got permission to make him an offer. It wasn't that hard. He's very highly regarded. Then I twisted his arm. But that wasn't as hard as I thought it would be. Deep down I think he knew that he had to move on. He's been here a year and a half, and it's done him some good. The only trouble is that those years at Michigan made him a loner and a workaholic. He resented any interruption."

"You can't blame him, though. He must have felt that any day he might seize on the discovery that would save his mother's life."

"Yes. So you see why he's so private. I think he's finally coming to terms with his loss, but he's still submerged in work. Cecile and I are gently prodding him to come out, but he's pretty stubborn."

"I got that sense," said Ariella ruefully, and Roland chuckled. "Well, I appreciate your telling me the story."

"I did run on a bit, didn't I? I'm a big talker." He shook his head. "Don't ever let anyone tell you the Chinese are a quiet people."

6

The next morning when the Sunday newspaper hit her apartment door with the customary thud, Ariella jumped to grab it from the mat. She found her article on the first page of the B section titled, "Stunt Saves Cancer Research." Scanning the paragraphs she saw that in editing the piece Joyce had increased the drama, but the article remained accurate. Ariella breathed a sigh of relief. Sam Becker might not love the publicity, but he could not fault her work. She flipped on the Channel 5 morning news to check the competition. Sure enough, a few minutes later a reporter was telling of a Harvard researcher's daring escapade to save his colleague's cancer research. With no footage of Sam they had settled for pictures of the reporter outside the Carver building pointing out the window where Sam had thrown the cable and a shot of a cornered-looking Rich Carruthers exclaiming, "Why, yes, I am extremely grateful."

The phone rang.

"I really ought to string you up," said a familiar voice that sent tingle down her spine.

"Dr. Becker," she replied evenly, rolling her eyes at the cat.

"I thought we had it straight that you were going to

call me Sam."

"Sorry," she said. "But after all this unwelcome media attention, I thought we might be back on square one."

His voice became somber. "Let me tell you something, Ariella, there's no going back in life."

She thought of his mother. "I suppose not. So have you called to tell me off?"

"No, actually, I liked your piece." She shook her head at Miranda in disbelief. Miranda arched her back and stalked off waving her tail. He was admitting, "You write well. There were a few adjectives I could have done without, but..."

"Joyce threw those in," she interrupted. "My editor."

He snorted. "It's the whole fuss I don't get. That puppy Carruthers is on every network."

"Well, that's the news business. We're like sheep. If one media outlet covers a story, everybody covers it. And Carruthers seems more willing to be interviewed than you. But don't get me wrong; I appreciate that you gave me an exclusive." She couldn't help letting a hint of gloating show.

He laughed then. "Not that I gave you much. As I recall it was about five minutes. But you definitely wrote the most correct version of events I've seen yet. And you didn't even misquote me. How would you like to celebrate by having dinner?"

She swallowed hard, her usual poise faltering. Joyce's words came back: *I need your objectivity on this story.*

But his voice squelched the imaginary one. "Say 'yes.' I'm sure you don't ordinarily date your sources, but I haven't asked a woman out for almost a year. So make an exception for me."

Low blow! Her mind whirled. "How about this? I never got the chance to ask you my additional questions about your research. What if we have an interview dinner?"

"No way. I don't want your work spoiling my meal. What if we have an interview and then dinner? Tuesday night at six?"

She let out a breath. "All right. Should I come to the Carver Center?"

"No, I'll meet you at the *Times* building. I'll be downtown anyway for another meeting at DPH. And we can borrow an office there if we want."

She knew this was a bad idea. What if Joyce saw him meeting her? She would only tell Joyce about the interview, not the dinner. "Great," she sounded a little breathless and paused to control her voice. "I'll meet you in the lobby at six." The newspaper's main lobby was a relatively safe meeting place because Joyce never used that door, preferring to slip in and out the back of the building.

"I'm looking forward to it." He said in a voice that sent blood rushing to her face. "Oh, and I have something to celebrate. The article on the success of my mouse trials just came out in *Science*."

"Wow!" She did not know every scientific journal, but she knew *Science* was the big time. "Congratulations! I would love to look at it."

"I'm sure you would," he said drily. "Bye."

She hung up and stared at her hands. How had this man just persuaded her to violate her journalistic principles? To be fair he hadn't even tried very hard. She grabbed the phone again and dialed Nina's number.

"Oh, Nina, you're home!"

"Ari! Yes, I'm home all day. What's the matter, sweetie?"

"How's Ruby?"

"Well, she's got strep throat. That's why I'm not at work. But she's all right. I'm dosing her up with amoxicillin and reading her *Little House in the Big Woods*."

"Sounds like fun. Give her a kiss for me, and tell her Aunt Ari orders her to get well soon. Nina, I've got a problem."

"What else is new?"

"I'm interviewing this scientist for a story, and he invited me out to dinner."

"So, what's the problem? Ugly? Poor hygiene? Smokes a cigar?"

Ariella laughed. "No, you idiot, he's extremely attractive, smart, intuitive, well-mannered if somewhat stubborn, but I'm not allowed to date my sources."

"Ohhh..." Nina's voice fell into the low registers. After a moment she asked, "What do you mean, not allowed? Is it in your employment contract?"

"No, no. It's just journalism school ethics, and I promised Joyce an objective story."

"If you ask me, there is no such thing as an objective story. Well, if I were your editor I probably wouldn't want you dating the guy either. But I'm not. I'm your idiot big sister, and I say, date the paragon. Only he may not turn out to be such a paragon after all."

"Oh, Nina, I know that! But what about the ethics of it?"

"Well, not being a rabbi, I really don't see what the big ethical question is. If you want to write a fair news story, write one and don't let the date get in the way. And if you find you absolutely can't do it, then tell Joyce. But I'm sure you can do it. After all, if he's a slime-ball, you won't be dating him for long, and you'll be glad to tar and feather him in print. Joyce just doesn't want you going soft on her, right?"

"Yeah, that's true. I don't know, though. In journalism school..."

"Don't tell me what you learned in school. N.Y.U. gave you an excellent education and a one-track mind. How are you ever going to get married if you never go on a date? A beautiful girl like you..."

"Oh, Nina, don't start on that again. I don't know why you think I'm beautiful. A shrimp is what I am."

"Petite, Ari, petite. But we won't get into that. So did you say 'yes' to the date?"

"Um hm."

"You did? Good for you. So what's his name?"

"Sam."

"Sam what?"

"Becker."

"Samuel Becker. I like that name. It has a nice ring to it. And what kind of scientist is he?"

"An immunologist."

"Oh, a doctor. Well, I'll stop dragging information out of you and let you go."

"He's working on a cure for cervical cancer, Nina. Isn't that wonderful?" Ariella laughed at her own dreamy tone, then said quickly, "I'd better get to work. Give Ruby a kiss for me. And say hi to Lenny."

"Will do. Good-bye Ari, and remember, I'll expect a full report." With a click her sister evaporated, and Ariella moved to the computer to initiate a search.

7

Friday dawn struggled with the gloom outside her apartment window. Curled into a pretzel in her pajamas on the couch she reread the brief, three-year-old *Detroit Free Press* article her computer had produced. It said that a Dr. Kurt Schaus of the University of Michigan had developed a wonder drug for kids with a strong family history of diabetes which would prevent them from getting the disease. At the end of the article Sam received mention as Dr. Schaus' "lab partner" and was quoted as saying, "I wish him luck."

Ariella puzzled over that sentence. As Schaus' lab partner, Sam must have been doing diabetes research at Michigan. Why had no one mentioned this to her? But a partner in the research would not say, "I wish him luck." That statement showed a remarkable lack of enthusiasm for a colleague who had just made a break-through. Of course, Sam was not a man who wore his heart on his sleeve. He had offered only measured praise of her piece on the storm. Yet even his words to her, a new acquaintance, had been stronger: "I liked your article.... You write well." Perhaps the *Free Press* had misquoted him or edited his comments to the reporter. She would not be surprised if the editor had imposed a strict word limit on such a piece, and Sam was hardly its focus. Still something troubled her about this article. She resolved to find out more about Kurt Schaus, his diabetes research and his connection to Sam.

Ariella spent the whole day in Dorchester in the *Boston Times* building shivering through meetings and finishing a piece of her own and two articles for her colleague, David, who was stricken with pneumonia. Each time she approached the windows, she could feel the late November chill seeping through and see the soft, ceaseless rain. By the time she reached her late afternoon meeting with Joyce, Ariella's brain and fingers felt equally rigid with cold. Joyce waved her into her sanctum with a frown.

"Fine time for David to get pneumonia! Did you finish his articles?" It was a slow news day, which always made Joyce restless.

"Yup." She handed Joyce some sheets of paper, and changed the subject. "You know, it's freezing in here. My hands are really sore. I hope I'm not getting a repetitive stress injury or anything. Do you think you could call Systems Management and ask for a bit more heat?"

"Oh, get a grip, Ariella. It's not that cold. And can't you call them yourself?"

Ariella stifled her irritation. Joyce's bark was worse than her bite, but her abrasiveness could almost make Ariella forget that her boss had steadily boosted her career, giving her choice assignments and defending her stories' importance in the daily editorial meeting. Sweet Joyce was not, but she was an ally. "I did call them several times today to no avail."

Joyce narrowed her eyes, picked up the phone and dialed. "Yes, this is Joyce Aldrich in the newsroom. I want some more heat up here right now. I already have one writer out with pneumonia, and I can't afford to lose any others." She stabbed a memo pad with her pen. "That is not what I want to hear. What's your name? All right, Al, let me speak to your supervisor. Ten minutes? Fine, but don't make me call you again, Al. All right. Thanks." She gave Ariella a stare and hung up.

"You're so good at that, Joyce." Ariella shook her head. "I just don't seem to be able to...."

"It's backbone," Joyce snapped. "Yours needs stiffening. Speaking of which, where's my Sam Becker cancer research story? I want it for this week, and I don't want a eulogy."

"Actually I'm interviewing him again tonight. I'm meeting him in the lobby at six." She absently caressed the arm of the brown leather chair.

"Good. Now look, Ariella, if there's a lot of material there, I'm willing to let you do several articles. But only if you get me something juicy. I want that women's health angle, and remember: people get that virus by having sex, and sex sells papers."

Ariella nodded.

"Now I'm going to give David's stuff a quick edit and bring the changes out to you, and then I want you to fax them home to him. I want his okay, but he is not to quibble over every word. Only glaring errors. Please make that clear to him." She ran over a few other ideas for future articles and dismissed Ariella with: "And if it isn't warmer by the time I bring you those edits, just say the word, and I'll give Al a taste of my displeasure." Her eyes narrowed in amusement.

"Better him than me," Ariella threw over her shoulder as she scurried back to her desk to wrap up her work. It was already five o'clock.

❧

Jogging past the windows of the classified ad room, she emerged into the empty *Times* lobby, searching. A chill mist slipped through the revolving doors as several workers left for the evening, but most did not use the formal front entrance, preferring to take the back stairs right to the parking lot. Pulling the belt of her raincoat tighter, she tried to swallow the lump in her throat and made her way to the security guard's desk below an eighteen-foot high, turn-of-the-century map of New England. The gray-haired guard assured her that no one of Sam's description had recently appeared, and no one had asked for her. So she positioned herself on the edge of the vast room on a wooden bench, partially hidden behind a potted palm, where she could catch her breath and watch for him. A sigh escaped as she shifted the strap of her briefcase, which had been cutting into her shoulder, so that it rested on the bench beside her. She hated meeting people in public places; the waiting always made her anxious.

Suddenly a hand tapped her shoulder from behind, and she jumped. Her head snapped sideways. "Oh, it's you! Where did you come from?"

"Hello, Ariella. You seem so pleased to see me!" Sam looked down at her from his full six feet, draped in a gray trench coat, face ruddy from the weather, his magnetism definitely intact.

"Sorry," she said. "You gave me a shock. I'm kind of jumpy tonight, and I didn't expect you to come in the back entrance. Have you been here before?"

"No, but it seemed like the most efficient way. Hard day?"

"Yeah. I've been cold since I came in this morning, and I've been trying to do both my own work and some stuff for a sick colleague."

"Well, then my job is to warm you up with some delicious food and help you wind down. How does La Cantina sound? Do you know about it? It's fairly new—some southwestern food, some Brazilian dishes, wonderful grilled steaks and fish...."

"Oh, I've heard great things about it, and I've never been there. But Sam—we should really do the interview first, don't you think?"

"No. Let's go straight to the restaurant. I've had a long afternoon of cantankerous DPH meetings, and I'm hungry."

"I don't know, Sam. I think it's better to work first and play later."

He laughed, and she colored at the unintended implication. "Listen," he said, "you'll get your interview. But you look freezing, and I'm starving. Both of us need some hot food. It's common sense."

"Well, I just wanted to congratulate you on getting your research into *Science*—impressive. I got the article from our in-house library, and I had one question for you..."

"Later." He picked up her briefcase and slipped it under one arm. "There'll plenty of time for that later."

She gave in gracefully but not without a vein of uneasiness as he threaded her arm through his, pushed through the swinging "staff only" doors to the public relations department, and led her confidently through twists and turns of halls to the parking lot exit as if he had been wandering the bowels of the *Times* building for years. Pausing to open a giant black umbrella he drew her underneath and walked them across the slick asphalt to his car, a peppy blue sedan that smelled brand new.

❧

He swung the glass door of the restaurant wide, and she slipped through, gently shaking the sodden hem of her coat before venturing from the stone foyer onto the rich rust-colored carpeting where the hostess waited. After giving his umbrella a few shakes out the door, Sam strode forward and gave his name in a peremptory tone. Ariella blanched at his high-handed manner, then shrugged it off, gazing around the room at the warm southwest desert colors, woven tapestries on the walls, polished oak tables, flickering candles everywhere. An indefinable spiciness greeted her nostrils beginning to quiet her shivers and excite her palate. On the way to her table she passed a waiter laden with platters of fragrant paella and sizzling fried plantains, and she felt sudden hunger pangs. The hostess seated them with careful attention.

"So what ever happened to that school smoking bill you were covering?" asked Sam as he took a big swig of water.

"Well, it passed in the House, but the State Senate has been sitting on it. There's a senator from the Melrose area who is trying everything in his power to squelch the bill. He must be getting big tobacco industry money. Last time he ran for office tobacco lobbying money was the biggest single source of funding for his campaign."

"Really? How do you know?"

"Oh, it's a matter of public record. You just have to know how to look it up at the State House."

"So are you saying he's totally in their pocket?"

"Well, it sure looks that way. Maybe he really believes what he says about the anti-smoking zealots threatening teachers' freedom to smoke. But even if that's his personal belief, he's still supposed to represent his constituency. So we ran a poll in his district. We found that seventy percent of the people supported a total smoking ban on school property."

"That's pretty strong data."

"Um hm. Look for the article in tomorrow's paper."

"I will, especially if it's yours."

"Well, the one out tomorrow will actually have David Ellman's byline—although I put a lot of research into the story and did the re-write. But he's been out sick, so..."

"Can't they credit you as co-author?"

"That would be nice, but no. David's been around a lot longer than I have. He has a name, and I don't."

"So that's an excuse to give you no credit?"

"It's the news business. You pay your dues."

"I guess I know about that. Science isn't so different. Grad students do an awful lot of research for their professors, some of which never gets credited. But I think it's wrong. I always give acknowledgment and co-authorship to colleagues who work with me, even if they're students just starting out in the field. Look at the article in *Science*, and you'll see that."

She pursed her lips and shrugged. "It's out of my hands."

Leaning back, he studied her face for a moment, a smile playing across his lips. "I just want to see you get the recognition you deserve," he said more mildly, his look hard to read. She allowed herself to gaze into those eyes a little too long until trickles of warmth stole through her body, and she returned the smile ruefully. "Would you like a glass of wine while we look at the menu?" he asked.

"I would love one."

He called the waiter and within moments she was sipping from a fluted glass and savoring a large plate of the plantain hors d'oeuvres she had seen passing by. She asked him a few questions about his day and was rewarded with a discourse on the grant proposals he had been reviewing and his successful fight to get one funded. Usually she loved to talk, but tonight she welcomed the respite, content to listen and watch emotions play across the planes of his face as he told his story.

Sam insisted on a bottle of wine and although she rarely drank that much, they somehow finished it. By the end of the meal she could hardly remember how cold she had been. A trip to the lady's room showed her a flushed face and shining if slightly pink eyes.

"Am I am fool?" she asked her reflection. An elderly woman came out of the stall and gave her a strange look; so she shut her mouth, though she could not quite stifle a giggle.

Back at the table, Sam asked her, "Would it be excessive to order dessert?"

"Excessive?"

"Well, we've eaten a lot." He cocked an eyebrow at her, and she could not tell whether he was serious.

She broke into giggles, thinking of his trim torso. "Oh, let's! I saw chocolate mousse on the menu, and I can't resist. You can work it off tomorrow. What kind of exercise do you like?" She gestured to the waiter who approached with alacrity and took their order.

"Well, I swim and I run." Sam answered her after the

pause. "I play a lot of tennis in spring and summer, but not this time of year—and I ski."

"Really? Down-hill or cross-country?"

"Both. But lately a lot of cross-country." The waiter presented them with two glass dishes of chocolate mousse sculpted into the shape of rose blossoms, and Ariella gave an appreciative sigh.

"Wow, I love cross-country skiing," she said between bites. "Of course, I'm not very good. But I used to ski with my relatives in Vermont when I was younger." She shook off the pang of memory and gave him an encouraging smile, willing him to offer. It would be wonderful to ski again. It had been several years.

"We should go some time." He nodded. "Do you have skis?"

"No, unfortunately. I actually haven't skied for a few years. It was hard to get away while I was living in New York City, and last winter I never went because I didn't know any skiers."

"Well, you do now. Shall we leave?" He summoned the waiter, took the check, and put up a forefinger to forestall any objection.

"Thank you, Sam. It was a wonderful meal."

He rewarded her with that sweet smile that transformed his usually stern countenance. With a flicker of nerves, she reminded herself that she still had a long list of interview questions for him, some of them confrontational. She was reluctant to change the atmosphere of the evening, but she had a job to do.

"So where to?" he asked, following close in her wake as she wound her way towards the door.

She stopped in the foyer and spun on her heel. "Well,

I really need to ask you some questions, Sam."

"I know. Don't look apologetic. I want to help you."

"So can we still use that office at the DPH building?"

"Oh, I hate to go back there at this hour. Those hulking file cabinets and green vinyl chairs." He shuddered. "I was there most of the day, Ariella. Anyway, I'm afraid the building may be locked. It's 8:30."

"Oh." She looked at her watch. "Well, what about your office at the medical center?"

"No. I share it with Roland—it's really his office—and he's there late tonight writing a paper. Don't take this the wrong way, but what about your place?"

She started. "My apartment?" Actually, it was a practical idea, much closer than the medical center, and it was getting colder by the minute outside. Still, she rarely had men in her apartment, and she didn't know this one very well.

"Don't you live on Clarendon in the Back Bay?"

She gave him a hard look. "How do you know that?"

"You must have mentioned it that day in the Public Garden."

She let it drop, but she did not think she had. She tried never to reveal her home address to strangers, especially after the incident with Carl in college, but perhaps her neighborhood had come up in the conversation in the park. How else could he know? "Well, I do live fairly nearby, although you'll have a terrible time parking...." *Oh, what the hell.* "But I guess we can go there. I'll make us some tea or cocoa or something."

8

As she wrestled with her key in the narrow hallway of her building with Sam Becker looming over her, she felt like a cornered mouse. Maybe this had been a bad idea, but she wanted the story. She managed to get the door open and was greeted with a feline harangue.

"Come in. This is Miranda, and as you see, she can be very chatty." The cat continued her series of yowls, glaring at Sam to Ariella's amusement. Perhaps Miranda had read her mind and meant to protect her from this mountain lion invading their turf.

He started forward, hand outstretched to pet her, but she darted to the kitchen and in two leaps reached the top of the refrigerator. "She doesn't seem to like me."

Ariella bolted the door, slung her coat over a wooden coat rack and followed Miranda, calmly pouring out some dry food and holding the dish up towards her perch. "Come on, pussycat. Come have some dinner and be polite to my guest." The woman and the cat engaged in a brief staring contest, and then Miranda leapt gracefully to the counter and stalked to a corner, where Ariella placed the dish. Sam watched in amused silence from the living room. He had followed her lead with his trench coat, tossing it on the rack with his umbrella. Ariella straightened a few couch cushions and urged him to sit, chatting with him while she put a kettle on the stove for tea. She hoped he could not see the tremor in her hands as she arranged cookies on a china platter and slid her interview materials from her briefcase. Placing the teapot, some cups, and the platter on the coffee table before him, she perched at the other end of the couch looking down at her page of questions while observing him through the corner of her eye.

He bit into a cookie and delight spread across his face. "Are these molasses and spice?" She nodded. "Amazing! I love these cookies. You didn't make them yourself?"

"Yup. My grandmother's recipe." She preened.

He gave her a dazzling smile and offered, "Well, you've softened me up like a lamb to the slaughter. Ask away."

Never one to miss an opportunity she jumped in. "First, what stage have you reached in the development of your vaccine?"

"As my article says, I have a version for mice. When it's injected into them they no longer show any signs of the human papilloma virus."

"Okay." She was scribbling. "Who would use the vaccine—and where and at what age would it be administered?"

"Are you going to sit six feet away on the other end of that couch all night and miss out on these great cookies?" He stretched out his long arm to offer her one.

She blushed, slid closer, accepted the cookie, and responded, "Hey, I'm supposed to ask the questions."

"The vaccine could be used for both males and

females. It could be given in school, maybe middle school age."

"Why?"

"Best to get them before most become sexually active."

She schooled her features not to respond to that. "And is it just one shot?"

"We don't know how many times would be needed because we haven't completed any human trials yet. That's why I didn't want a lot of publicity. It might not work in people."

"Are there other vaccinations in use today that don't require a booster shot?"

"Most require at least two shots: one original and one booster." She opened her mouth, and he quickly added, "I haven't made a comprehensive study of the question, though."

"So yours will most likely require a booster?"

"Yes."

"And this shot would not help people who already have cervical cancer?"

"Unfortunately, no. It offers no hope to those people. So it's important to stress that it's not a cure. It's preventative."

"What about side effects?"

"Well, I don't know yet." He tugged absently at his earlobe. "But when you activate the immune system with any vaccine you have to anticipate possible muscle aches, fever and rashes. All of these could be side effects of our vaccine."

"Does your discovery have implications for other cancers?"

"Not that I know of." He chuckled. "But it might

help stop warts!"

"Warts?"

"Yes—because they're caused by a similar strain of the same virus."

"Now, how does your work relate to Dr. Chan's research?"

"He's working on viral protein expression in general; that is, why some viral proteins induce an immune response, and some don't."

"Okay." That went over her head, but it wasn't really important to the story. "Now, how are you funded?"

"Well, Roland is very well funded. The lab gets grants from a variety of sources. My work is funded by NIH grant number 5233AQR59610."

Ariella raised her eyebrows and stifled a smile. "What a mouthful. I'm surprised you can remember it."

His eyes twinkled. "I have a good head for numbers, and I have to put this one on every progress report; so it helps to have it memorized. NIH is a huge bureaucracy, but they do make some key scientific advancements possible."

"Have drug companies expressed any interest in this vaccine?"

"Not yet, but they're sure to be interested. I try not to use drug company money to fund my research, though— to avoid conflict of interest."

She nodded and scribbled. "How long will it take the vaccine to get to the public?"

"I'm finished with the mouse trials; I've isolated the human protein I need, and I'm in the middle of Phase II human trials. Are you aware of the FDA phases?" She cocked her head. "To prove a new drug is safe and effective. Phase I is animal testing. Phase II checks whether the vaccine is toxic to humans. Until I finish Phase III, which will show whether the vaccine works and what dosage to use, it's premature to give the public any great hope...."

She would not allow him to evade the question. "But assuming it's successful, how long before the vaccine hits the pharmacies?"

"Several years, probably."

"Really? That long? So where are the human trials taking place?"

"In the women's health clinic at Beth Israel Hospital."

"How do they pick the women?"

"Oh, they're volunteers—women in good general health who have the virus but no cervical dysplasia." At her raised eyebrows he added, "Normal cervix."

"May I see your lab and visit the clinic?"

"You may see the lab, although there's not much there to look at, but I can't allow you to bother anyone at the clinic." She stiffened at the word, "bother," and he continued, "We have to protect patient confidentiality, after all."

Ariella moved on to the next question. "Why do women get the human papilloma virus? Does everyone have it?"

"No, not everyone. It's passed through intimate contact and is extremely common among those who are sexually active. But studies of nuns have found virtually no incidence of the virus or the cancer."

"Nuns! Oh, I guess that makes sense. So how does a woman know she has the virus?"

"A Pap test will usually show it, and there's also a more sensitive test for it called PCR."

"Is it found in men?"

"Yes, but it's fairly benign in men."

She grimaced. "It figures. Now let's talk about experimental subjects for the human trials. Who are they?"

"You mean demographics?" He asked, and she nodded. "Well, I don't have those stats on hand yet because we haven't finished enrolling subjects in the study. Basically they are women from the area surrounding the hospital—from Mission Hill and Roxbury."

"Meaning you have a lot of poor black and Latina women—why?"

"Well, first of all, this population has a lot of human papilloma virus."

"Wouldn't it be better to use a more diverse group?"

"Actually, diversity doesn't matter at this phase of the study because we're not trying to prove that the vaccine would work in every segment of the population—that's Phase IV of the trials. Right now we're just trying to prove that it works at all, in *some* population! Also, diversity doesn't matter at this point because we're just studying the vaccine's general safety in *any* population."

"Why subject poor women to potential danger, though?"

"Oh, that's just academic in this case because we're only injecting women with a small amount of a benign protein, and the other ingredients have been shown to be safe when used in other vaccines."

"Well, if it's so safe, why do safety tests?"

"FDA requires them, and anyway, we do want to see the extent of any side effects. But, keep in mind, Ariella, that we're only doing this research because we believe the benefits of the vaccine greatly outweigh the risks."

"Well, I would really like to interview some of your experimental subjects—with their consent, of course."

"I'll think about it." His tone had cooled, and she did not press him.

"Are there any women researchers working on this project?"

He frowned. "Not in the lab. But I'm working primarily with two gynecologists at Beth Israel, and one is a woman."

"How would you feel about my talking to her?"

"If she has the time, it's all right with me."

"And her name?"

"Natalie Ward. So does that about wrap up the interview? Are we getting done?" He slid closer to her on the couch.

"Not quite. I have one more question. Who is Kurt Schaus?"

"What?" His eyes bored into her.

"Kurt Schaus—didn't you work with him on diabetes research at the University of Michigan?"

"Who on earth told you that?"

"Nobody, I just did a little digging for background."

"Digging! Yeah, that's the word for it. Excavating all the ugliness of the past, and getting it wrong to boot. You *are* just like all the others, aren't you?" He stood up, snarling. "That's it. We're done here."

"You know, Sam, why don't you cool off a second. I told you when I first met you, if I make a mistake just set me straight. I'm not trying to manipulate you."

"I'm asking myself what good reason you could possibly have to dredge up that old history at Michigan except to harass me—since it has absolutely no bearing on

my current research. Sorry, Ariella, but I can't think of one."
He headed for the door, grabbing his coat from the rack.

"When you won't even answer a simple question, it sure does make it look like you're hiding something." She had risen to her feet.

He swore. "Kurt is an M.D./PhD. who did a study of childhood diabetes at Michigan when I was there. He shared lab space with me. I never worked with him. Satisfied?" His tone was grim, and she stood rooted to the spot while he threw her door open and slammed it behind him. As her trembling subsided, she suddenly noticed his umbrella still dangling from her coat rack, swinging gently from side to side.

9

Late the next morning Ariella approached the white desk with a swallow and stood behind an extremely pregnant black woman who was speaking to the nurse—or was it the receptionist? City doctors' offices made her uneasy, and these days she rarely understood the roles of all the staff, who seemed to have proliferated. When she was little, there had been only Dr. Bellamy, with his chipmunk face, and his nurse, Erma, in her starched uniform. Now nurses often wore green or pink surgical scrubs, or street clothes that did nothing to distinguish them from the receptionists, clerks and bookkeepers doctors needed to keep tabs on their patients' insurance companies. So she was forever finding that the woman in front of her could not answer her question.

Of course, the previous night's debacle was not helping her mood, but she tried to repress that thought. Sam had given her permission to talk to his gynecologist colleague, and she was going to get it over with, write the story and clear the decks for Thanksgiving weekend in New York. She could not wait to see Ruby's little face and bask in her uncomplicated adoration.

The pregnant patient was complaining of shortness

of breath, and a male doctor (his stethoscope gave him away) quickly appeared to usher her through a half-glass door. The woman behind the desk turned away and wrote something on a form.

Ariella waited a few minutes, then said, "Hi, I'm Ariella Richardson, and I have an appointment to talk to Dr. Ward."

"Is this your first visit?" asked the woman, who did not look up, although her tone was pleasant.

"Yes, but..."

"Fill out the yellow form on the clipboard to your left, and don't forget to answer the questions on the back side, and when you're done I'll take that and your insurance card, if you have one." The canned speech marked her as a clerk.

"No, no. I'm only here to talk with the doctor. She isn't going to examine me."

The woman looked up from her paper work into Ariella's eyes. "Some sort of consultation?"

Feeling the eyes of the four women in the waiting room on her back and remembering Sam's words about confidentiality, Ariella said, "Uh—yes, that's it."

"Well, I suppose if she wants you to fill out forms you can do it after you see her. Go ahead and sit down. We'll call you when she's ready."

Snagging a *People* magazine from the pile on an end table, Ariella sank into a plump sofa. At the other end sat a thin, dark woman chewing gum. Ariella opened the magazine and began reading a silly article with large photo illustrations of America's best and worst dressed stars. The bad taste inherent in some of the costumes made her smile. The woman at the end of the couch was tapping her nails on an end table. Finally she jumped up.

"You're Nancy, right?" she demanded of the clerk, who nodded. "I need to see the doctor right now, okay?"

"Just sit down and take it easy, Ms. Moreno. The doctor is finishing up with another patient."

"That's what you said fifteen minutes ago." The thin body was taut.

"That's right."

"If I don't get in there in five minutes, I'm going to walk right on in and find her."

Nancy had reddened. "Did it ever strike you that you're not the only patient Dr. Ward has? We have patients here with some very serious problems—like cancer," she said pointedly. The thin woman flushed and sat down again, muttering.

A few minutes later, a figure in pink scrubs appeared in the half-glass door, pushing it open and calling, "Moreno, Angelica Moreno."

The thin woman sprang up, the large pocketbook dangling from her shoulder slapping legs incased in airtight black leggings. The pink figure, probably a nurse, opened the door wide to let her pass and followed her into the mysterious recesses behind it. Ariella leaned back with a sigh, expecting a long wait while Dr. Ward saw this belligerent patient. She read through an article comparing actors who had played Superman on film and television, noting some grammatical errors in the piece. Maybe she should quit trying to be a reporter and focus on a career in editing; that way people like Sam Becker would not hate her so much. They might find her job boring, but never threatening—but who cared what Sam Becker thought anyway? A man rude enough to walk out of an interview without a word certainly deserved no consideration on her part. Of course, she felt a pang of guilt that she had touched the sore spot of his mother's death by mentioning his time in Michigan. If her parents died, she did not know what she would do. Still she suspected he was hiding something.

"Richardson. Ariella Richardson."

She snapped out of her reverie to see the thin woman emerging with a set expression, and the pink-clad nurse calling her name. Jumping up with her briefcase, she joined the nurse and followed her through the door and down a white corridor to a small office. Standing beside a heavy desk was a six-foot-tall woman with regal bearing and pale eyes, her wheaten hair in a chignon. She wore a white blouse buttoned to the neck, an intricately patterned cardigan sweater in shades of mint green beneath her open white coat, and a pleated skirt. Ariella could imagine her on horseback, trotting through the fields of an ancestral English estate.

"Please come in," said the doctor, gesturing to a chair. "What can I do for you?"

"Well," Ariella began, fumbling for her notebook in her briefcase, "as I told you on the phone I'm a reporter with the *Boston Times*, and I'm doing a story on Dr. Becker's vaccine research. He said that it was all right for me to contact you, and I have a few questions."

"Yes, I know," said the woman patiently but without warmth. "What would you like to know?"

"Well, first of all, how are the women chosen for the study?"

"I have an ongoing practice here, as you see. We advertised the study with signs here at our clinic, on bulletin boards around the medical center and at local community centers. We asked for sexually active women, and when they came into the clinic we screened them with PCR—that's a test for the virus that causes cervical cancer. Those who tested positive, which was most of them, were asked to join the study."

"Any danger in having a PCR test?"

"Nooo." Her eyes widened with sincerity, and her tone took on a pedagogical tinge. "It's simply a more accurate version of the Pap test. In fact, it benefits the patients to get this test for free as it can predict pre-cancerous states. And unfortunately most of these women do not get regular Pap's."

"Why not?"

The doctor leaned back in her chair, clasping her hands together on the edge of the desk. "Miss Richardson, is it? My patients come here with all kinds of psycho-social problems. They are hardly model patients: they miss appointments and rarely follow my recommendations. These are poor, struggling women, transient, without transportation to the hospital or insurance to pay for the treatment, and they often do not value medical care. Usually I can only get a Pap test during pregnancy because that's when they come in, and after the birth many are lost to follow-up. I do my best to explain the value of the Pap and of preventive care generally, but it usually doesn't work."

"Maybe they don't have the luxury to worry about prevention when they have so many immediate problems."

"Perhaps, but it's a shame when they come in some years after their pregnancies with a cancer I could have detected with a regular Pap. I would *love* to have a shot to give them in their teens so that I could prevent such tragedies." Her voice rose slightly, colored with passion, and Ariella found this break in the regal facade reassuring.

"I'm sure," she offered. "So how often do you see the women in the study?"

"Every six months they come in for a check-up to see if they have developed cervical dysplasia, which would be a sign that they were developing cancer. And it's a ten-year study."

"After ten years free of cancer, you'll feel certain that the vaccine is working?"

"It would be very good evidence."

"Do you pay the women?"

"Yes, twenty dollars per visit."

"Why pay them?"

The doctor gave her a look of mild reproof. "We're asking them to spend their time to come in, and these are often women who cannot afford to take time off from work without pay. It isn't much money, but at least it's cab fare. It helps us to keep track of them in that it's an incentive to keep in touch with us. Ten years is a long time, especially for most of my patients."

"I assume that most of them are blacks and Latinas, at least that's what I saw in the waiting room. Why concentrate on them for the study?"

She shrugged. "These are my patients," she said, "women who come to the clinic because they live nearby. We do have a few white college students, and I'd be happy to enroll any others who want to participate. But I want to give my patients the advantage of participating in this study—they have so few advantages—and this vaccine could save one of their lives."

"So what would you say to someone who called this patronizing racial bias?"

The doctor drew herself ramrod straight; even seated

she could tower over Ariella. "I would say that those are strong words and that she doesn't know what she's talking about."

"Well, I think it's an important question to raise. I didn't mean to insult you. Now are any women ruled out? Women who smoke, for instance?—I've read that they are at higher risk of cervical cancer."

"They are, but we do not exclude women with risk factors like smoking because even if they have a heightened risk of developing cancer, the vaccine should suppress it. We do want to *know* whether our subjects smoke."

"Why is that?"

"Well, although she should not get cancer after vaccination, a smoker may show more dysplasia than a non-smoker, which would make the vaccine look less effective. So we need to know so that we can record the results for smokers and non-smokers separately."

"So you'll take anybody?"

"Not exactly. We can't accept women with HIV, and we'll be doing an AIDS test at every six-month visit to verify that the women remain negative."

"Hmm. That could be seen as another benefit of participation."

"I think so. I think it gives them a subtle incentive to stay safe, and in the worst case, if one gets sick, at least we'll have an early diagnosis." The telephone rang. "Excuse me for a moment." She picked up the receiver and cradled it so that it did not quite touch her hair. "Yes. Yes, certainly. I'm on my way." She hung up. "That was the maternity floor. They want me upstairs for a C-section. Are we finished?"

"One last question: do you happen to know a Dr. Kurt Schaus who did some important diabetes research at the University of Michigan several years ago?"

Her eyes unfocused for a moment as she seemed to search her memory. "Sorry, the name's not even familiar."

"All right. Well, that's it, but I hope that I may call you if anything further comes to mind, and I wonder whether I might interview one of your subjects?" As she said the word, 'subjects,' she stifled a smile as she imagined Dr. Ward on the British throne.

"You may call me at the office any time, but patient care must of course take priority, and I don't think interviewing the patients is such a good idea."

"Why not?"

She just shook her head, adding dismissively, "I really must get to the operating room. It's a high risk pregnancy—I'm sure you understand."

Thoughts of Ruby gave Ariella instant pangs of guilt. "Oh yes," she agreed. "I do appreciate your time, Dr. Ward. I didn't mean to be pushy. It's just my job to ask certain questions that the public has."

"I understand," the doctor replied, shaking hands, and she swept out, leaving Ariella to pack up her notebook and meander back to the waiting room lost in thought.

❧

Trudging up the concrete stairs to the third level of the Beth Israel parking garage, Ariella's thoughts whirled round and round like a gerbil on a wheel. She wondered whether she should try to contact this Kurt Schaus. She was leaning against it—it seemed like a blind alley—but Joyce's demand for thoroughness and a juicy story reverberated in her mind. She emerged on the windy roof of the garage and started toward her Mazda. A few spaces from hers a woman was standing beside a dirty, white station wagon smoking a cigarette. As Ariella approached she instinctively held her breath.

"Hey, weren't you just in Dr. Ward's office?" It was the thin woman, looking at her with a mixture of hostility and eagerness. "Would you happen to have a coat hanger in your car? I locked my keys in—can you believe it?"

"I don't think so."

"Well, would you mind looking?"

Despite her angry tone, the woman's drawn face inspired pity, and Ariella hurried to search her car. In the trunk she immediately saw two forgotten blouses she had picked up from the dry cleaner, both on wire hangers. Gently removing one from the collar of a blouse, she carried it over to the station wagon.

"How about that?" she said in a forced tone, but the woman did not seem to notice.

"Thanks. You know, I've been trying to get some help here for twenty minutes, freezing my butt off, but nobody has a coat hanger. Or nobody wants to get involved. What do they think I'm going to do, knife them? I'm Angelica, by the way." She was wrenching the hanger into a long straight wire. "How come you wanted to talk to the Amazon? You having sex problems or something?"

Ariella laughed, and her tension evaporated. "I don't have enough sex to have problems."

"Oh. Oops. I've got a big mouth. Well, I know how that can be. Of course, most men are dogs, anyway—you're better off keeping your pants on. So what's your trouble? The old biological clock is ticking too fast?"

"Well, to be honest, I'm not really a patient of Dr.

Ward's at all. I'm a reporter."

The black eyes lit up. "Really? Where do you work? What's your name? Do you ever write about the movies or interview soap stars or anything?"

"I'm Ariella Richardson, and I work for the *Boston Times*, but no, no movie reviews or celebrity interviews. I'm on general assignment—parades, conferences, weather disasters, and this time a science story."

"Huh. So were you interviewing the doc about that study she's doing with the shots?" She had formed a hook at the end of the hanger and had slipped it through the crack at the top of the driver's window toward the depressed lock button. The dirty station wagon was too old to have embedded door locks.

Ariella hesitated, unsure how to respond. She had not intended to question experimental subjects, had in fact resolved not to speak to them at all.

"You are, aren't you?" The woman gave her a shrewd look. "You know, I'm in that study. How about a little interview with me? I wouldn't mind seeing my name in the paper!"

"Oh, I don't know," said Ariella with a grimace. "Anyway, I probably couldn't ever put your name in the paper. I think the names of people in the study have to be kept strictly confidential."

"Why? Do they think somebody's going to come find me and bribe me to mess it up?"

"I don't know—but sabotage is always possible, I guess. Speaking of which, do they know you smoke?" It was just a guess.

Angelica looked defensive. "Okay, I told them I don't smoke, but I really don't smoke much, and I needed the money."

Ariella couldn't resist: "It's only twenty dollars, isn't it?"

"Yeah, but it'll buy a lot of diapers this month. And I like getting those blood tests, you know what I mean? At least if Renaldo's cheating on me, I'll know fast, and I can make plans for my baby before I get real sick." She hooked the lock button, gave it a tug, and it snapped upward. "Muy bien. Got this baby open! You know, I don't care about getting my name in the paper. I still want to be interviewed. How come the Amazon gets all the action? She doesn't know everything. Don't you want the patient's perspective, the ordinary person?"

Pressing her lips together as if to stifle words, Ariella nodded slowly. She was startled at this woman's passive acceptance that her husband or boyfriend might give her a fatal disease.

"So how about we go get a cup of coffee or something?" Angelica opened the car door and stale tobacco smoke poured out.

"You sure you smoke only a little?"

"It's my Cousin Bobby's car. He smokes in it all the time."

"Dr. Ward said she did accept smokers in the study. Why not just tell her?" Angelica gave her a look of disbelief. "Well, anyway, why don't you follow me? I know a nice, little diner about two blocks from here where we can talk."

Angelica nodded knowingly. "Clanahan's?"

"That's the one."

&

"I came here from the island when I was twelve," Angelica was saying, deep-set eyes staring over her coffee cup at Ariella. "Puerto Rico. My father was pretty abusive, and when Mami couldn't take it any more she just up and left him cold one day and moved us to her brother's in Boston." They were seated in a booth with red vinyl seats, and Ariella toyed with a French fry. "I hated it here, though. People treated me like I was stupid because I didn't speak good English, and baby, it was freezing. That was the year of the big blizzard, remember? I had asthma, and the cold just did me in. Oh, did I miss home."

"I bet." Ariella could remember the wrench when she moved north from Florida. "Did you get any medical care here?"

"Medical care? Not much. Mami was pretty suspicious of white doctors and hospitals, and with good reason. My abuela—that's my grandmother—got caught up in that famous experiment on the island where they went in for an ingrown toenail and came out sterilized."

"What?"

"You never heard about that? Figures. But an educated woman like you ought to know. Good old FDR was President, and they were using women on the island as guinea pigs for this sterilization experiment."

"Did the president know about it?"

"Probably. I don't know. Look it up—you'll find out some nasty stuff. Anyway, that didn't give Mami much confidence in the medical system. My abuela wanted to have six kids, but all she ever got was Mami and Tio Luis, and then boom, those doctors tied her tubes. After that, she prayed to the Holy Virgin for fertility every day till she turned fifty, and she would drag Mami to church too so that she would be spared this fate. Mami never forgot all that, and she hated hospitals. Even when I was born she wouldn't go to the hospital; she had me right in her own bed with no complications. But poor Mami, her fear got her in the end."

"What do you mean?"

"Well, Mami got cancer, cervical cancer, only we didn't know it because she refused to see a doctor. We just knew she was sick as a dog and getting sicker: weak, dizzy, bleeding. I tried so hard to get her to a clinic, but nothing worked until finally she just collapsed. She was a stubborn woman, my Mami, suspicious to the end—even when we got her some pain medication she never believed it was helping her—said it was the Holy Virgin answering her prayers."

"How long ago did she die?" asked Ariella gently.

"Four years."

"I'm sorry." A heavy-set waitress in a dingy checked apron approached with a water pitcher, but Ariella waved her away.

"Yeah, thanks. It was really tough at first, the emptiness, but now I feel her spirit around me all the time...." Her voice tapered off, and she gestured in the air around her head.

"And what about you? Are you suspicious of doctors too? You're clearly not too scared to see one."

"Well, I have to admit I'm suspicious, but I learned long ago you've got to try to take what you can get in this country, and so I'll take any free medical care I can. But I speak up for myself, ask questions till they're sick of me. I don't forget my abuela, but I don't forget Mami either. I've got to take a middle path."

"So you joined this study because..."

"I joined it for Mami—because one shot to prevent all that terrible suffering would be incredible."

"Yes, it would." Ariella nodded, paused, then spoke hesitantly. "You know, I want to say something personal to you, although it seems unprofessional to do it, and I don't want to offend you...."

"It's all right. I've probably heard it before, and anyway I like you." She gave a crooked smile. "Go ahead."

"Well," Ariella searched for the right words, "it seems to me that someone so aware of the preventive benefits of this cancer vaccine would also not smoke—especially since you have asthma—or ever risk HIV."

Angelica rolled her eyes. "How old are you, girl? You've got a lot to learn about this world. Yes, I know smoking's bad for me and causes cancer and all that, but I need my cigarettes to get through the day. Without them I'd probably beat my witch of a boss within an inch of her life or abuse my screaming kid. And sex, well, you can't force a man to use protection, especially not some of these Latino men. It cuts right to the heart of their machismo, which is *sacred*." She crossed herself with a wry grin. "Don't you get it? That's why shots against cancer are such a good idea; they're practical!"

"Maybe," said Ariella, "but you're an intelligent woman, too smart to be smoking and having unprotected sex. I know that if you put your mind to it, you could join a quit-smoking program and make some demands on your man."

Her eyes had hardened. "Well, I appreciate your concern and all, but it's my life, and you don't walk in my shoes."

"Okay, I'll drop it. It was very presumptuous of me. But I meant what I said: you're a smart cookie."

The gaze softened. "Yeah, well, you know what they say: flattery will get you everywhere." She laughed, and Ariella smiled.

"So what do you think of Dr. Ward?"

"The Amazon? Oh, she's all right. Pretty stiff and a bit out of touch with reality if you ask me, but a good doctor. She'll give you a straight answer without all that medical mumbo jumbo, I'll give her that."

"Yeah, she's clear and to the point."

"Um hm. She definitely wants to improve my health, but she's got a touch of missionary zeal that makes me nervous. She's thinks she knows all about poor people because she's published some papers about us—even though she has a trust fund, lives in Concord and drives a Jag."

Ariella nodded. "Did she discuss the possible risks of the study with you?"

"Oh, yeah, rashes, fevers.... She covered it very thoroughly. But she also said they were pretty minimal risks compared to the chance of preventing cancer, and I can *certainly* agree with that."

"Have you ever met a Dr. Sam Becker?"

"No, just Dr. Ward. She's the only doctor I've got."

"Well, this has been really interesting, Angelica. I appreciate your talking to me. The doctors weren't crazy about the idea of my bothering patients...."

Angelica raised one black eyebrow and nodded. "Don't need to spell it out. I won't tell the Amazon I spoke with you. It's been fun. As you can tell, I like giving my opinion."

Ariella dug through her purse and pulled out a card.

"Here, if you want to contact me to add anything, this is my phone number. Do you mind giving me yours?"

"No problem." She scrawled it on a napkin. "Only don't call after nine at night or you'll wake the baby."

"What's your baby's name?"

"Yolanda—she's eighteen months old. Want to see a picture?" She flipped open her wallet to display a photograph of a dark-eyed curly-haired child propped in an armchair with the most winning smile Ariella had ever seen."

"Oh, is she adorable!"

"Yeah," Angelica's eyes were soft with pride, "when she's not whining. Actually, Tio Luis says I should try to get her into commercials, says they're looking for little ethnic kids now. She already has the personality of an actress. Look at how she plays up to the camera. But do you think she's pretty enough? Her forehead's kind of big."

"Her forehead? Nonsense. She's darling, beautiful! I'm sure she could be in commercials if that's what you want for her. I would be careful, though. I'm sure there are some pretty sleazy agents in that business who'll take your money and run."

"True. Thanks."

"I could ask my editor whether she knows any reputable people in advertising. She might. She's been in the news business a long time."

Angelica's eyes lit up. "That would be great!"

Then Ariella's eye wandered to the round wall clock over the lunch counter, and she realized that she was late for a meeting with Joyce. "Speak of the devil," she said.

10

In black as usual, Joyce beckoned her into the office with impatience. "You're late, Ariella. Not that that's unusual. I have a stack of phone messages to deal with before 5:00; so let's get through this efficiently. Now first of all, there's an annual meeting of the National Urban League at the Weston Hotel Monday; this year's theme is violence in the community. I want you there to cover the story."

Ariella took a long look at the swirling primary colors in the Sam Francis print over her editor's head, then shut her eyes a moment before answering. "Fine," she said, "but you know last time you sent me to one of those conferences it was quite a sleeper. No story."

"We've got to have someone there, and you're elected. General assignment, you know the drill. The *Boston Times* has to cover more on the black community than just murders." Joyce shuffled some papers in front of her. "Now I also have a guy named Jerry Lesniak I want you to talk to. He's an anti-smoking lobbyist at the State House, thinks he has a story for us, and Cecile Chan's secretary asked me to give him a chance. Here's his number."

"Oh, I know Jerry—from that school smoking ban law I was covering. I call him 'Jerry the Giraffe.'" Adding quickly, "Not to his face, of course. If you saw him you'd understand."

"I'm sure. Now where's my cancer piece?"

"Late today or tomorrow. I have a couple more sources to reach. Also, I managed to get an interview with one of the study subjects. It would make a good side-by-side or a follow-up human interest piece."

"Can we use her name? I don't like pseudonyms. They weaken the credibility of a story."

"Becker and his colleagues won't like it if we print her name." Not that she should care about Sam's opinion after his rude behavior to her yesterday.

Joyce snorted. "They don't have to like it. What about the source? Will she agree?"

"She won't mind, I don't think. I can call her and ask."

"Yes, do that, and write it up, and I'll see if I want one or two pieces. So do these colleagues of Becker's include any women? Or are women just the guinea pigs?"

"One of the gynecologists is a woman, and I interviewed her. She seems very much behind the research."

"Hmmm. Bully for her. Anything else?"

"I don't know. I'm looking into something about Becker's past work. It seems as if there may have been some scandal at his previous lab in Michigan.... But I'm clutching at straws."

Joyce's half-smile came out for the first time since Ariella entered the room. "Interesting. So the diamond may be flawed. Well, I want to see something in writing as soon as possible. I'll be here till 8:00 tonight, and I'd like to see something by then—with or without this old scandal, all right?"

"I'll try...."

"You look glum. You can continue to investigate the thing if you want. Maybe there's another story there. Just get your other work done on time. Oh, and speaking of Becker, I got an invitation from Cecile and Roland Chan today." She waved an ivory card with gold lettering in the air. "Their annual Christmas open house in Lexington. Saturday, December 19th. I have a prior commitment that day. Will you go for me?" Ariella pulled out her daily calendar and began leafing through it. "I'd really appreciate it if you made an appearance. I'm trying to cultivate Cecile for her connections, and she wants an ear on the *Boston Times*. The old 'you scratch my back, I'll scratch yours....' I'd be glad to call and ask to send you in my place."

"I don't know. I'm not you." She sounded foolish, but she had been hoping to escape to New York again that weekend. Although she had not even begun the four-day Thanksgiving trip to her sister's she already yearned to plan the next visit. Joyce would never understand this, though; she never mentioned family, seemed to focus all her energy on her career.

"They don't want me, they want the *Times*. I would really appreciate it," Joyce repeated, adding with narrowed eyes: "You might see Becker there."

Ariella willed away a creeping blush; she hated to admit it to herself, but she wanted to see him again. Thank goodness Joyce did not know Sam had been in her apartment—and had stormed out. "Okay, okay. I'll go."

"Thanks. You'll enjoy it. Cecile is famous for her house parties, and her Chinese cooking is legendary."

"Why do I have the feeling I'm being railroaded?"

Only the eyebrows responded. After a moment's silent standoff, Joyce said, "All right, Ariella, unless you have something else to discuss let's get back to work. I have calls to make."

Later Ariella was hanging up the phone when her eye fell on a yellow post-it note peeking out from a white stack. She dragged it out, knowing what it said: just the two words, Kurt Schaus, and his Texas telephone number. She had spoken to three prominent immunologists that afternoon, one at Sloan Kettering, one at Johns Hopkins, and one at Tufts, and all had confirmed that Sam was pursuing promising research and using exemplary techniques. The Tufts man, a Dr. Yarrow, had offered some clipped criticisms but in the end dubbed them "minor issues unrelated to the soundness of Becker's experiment." So she would refer to them for balance, but briefly.

Schaus was the only remaining problem. She could not forget the vehemence of Sam's reaction to the name. It seemed so out of character that she had to get to the bottom of it before she could turn in her article to Joyce. Perhaps she was straying into tabloid muck, but for her own peace of mind she had to know what kind of man was dominating her thoughts.

Her fingers skittered over the telephone key pad, tapping in the numbers fast before she could reconsider. It had been easy to find Schaus's number on the internet; he now worked at Baylor and his publications revealed a continuing interest in diabetes.

A sugary drawl came on the line. "Dr. Schaus' office. How may I help you?"

She hoped the woman could not hear her heart hammering; it sounded deafening in her own ears. "This is Ariella Richardson. I'm a reporter for the *Boston Times*. Is Dr. Schaus available?"

"What is this regarding?"

"Well, I'm writing a story on some cancer research here in Boston, and I would like to get his opinion on the researcher. I would just like a minute of his time."

"He doesn't usually mind talking to the press." The drawl seemed to hold a hint of amusement. "If you would please hold, ma'am, I'll check for you." For several endless minutes Ariella listened to a muzak version of an old Patsy Cline tune. Too nervous to sort the mail in front of her she tapped on the desktop with her pen in time with the muzak until David gave her a laughing look and dragged a finger across his throat. She ripped open a piece of mail, then heard, "Hold for Dr. Schaus, ma'am."

"Hello, Kurt Schaus here." A bass voice, neutral.

"Yes, Dr. Schaus, I'm Ariella Richardson of the *Boston Times*." She heard herself stammering and bit her lip. It had been years since her voice had wavered like this on a business call. She cleared her throat and pushed out a more confident tone. "I'm writing a story on some cervical cancer research at the Carver Cancer Center and wanted a quick comment from you. The principal investigator is Dr. Samuel Becker. I believe you worked with him in Michigan?"

"Becker. Well, this is a surprise. Surely he didn't give you my name as a reference." He gave a strange little laugh.

"Why wouldn't he?"

There was a pause. "I'm not doing that sort of work, for one."

"Any other reasons?"

"Let's just say we're not close."

"How did you come to know him?"

"We shared laboratory space in Michigan. Different research, though. Mine was my ground-breaking diabetes work; his was on liver transplant rejection—at least until the accident."

"What was the accident?"

He snorted. "This doesn't seem too relevant. Yesterday's news."

"Maybe I should be the judge of that."

"I suppose. Well, far be it from me.... Becker's research at Michigan fizzled due to a lab accident. An undergraduate research assistant didn't shut a refrigerator properly or something like that—I don't remember all the details—but his experimental cells were ruined."

"Was your research affected?"

"Not at all. I was too careful to allow undergraduates to work on my research, only upper level graduate students." He sounded self-congratulatory, but then he had been right to be protective.

"What happened after that?"

"Well, Becker lost some grants, had to regroup, moved into another lab."

"How did his research progress after that?"

"I really can't say. After he left my lab I lost touch with him. My own diabetes work was taking off—grants, papers, speaking engagements, collaborators coming out of the woodwork. It was a busy time."

"Do you have any idea what happened?"

"I don't believe it went well."

"Dr. Schaus, would you say that Dr. Becker envied your success, coming as it did at the time of his failure? Is that why you're not close?"

"I wouldn't know."

"Is it possible?"

"Possible."

"So how would you explain your, uh, lack of closeness?"

"We always had very different styles."

"Are you aware of his current research into a possible cervical cancer vaccine?"

"I saw that the animal study was published."

"What was your opinion of it?"

"Looked all right. It's not quite my area, though, as I told you. Say, you're not the *Times'* main health reporter, are you?"

"No, that's David Ellman."

"Yes, I've spoken to him in the past. He's run several stories on my childhood diabetes work. What's your angle? Do you mainly cover health?"

"Somewhat. I'm on general assignment, but I've been focusing on health lately, women's health in particular."

"Well, I would be glad to fax you something on our new work here. Childhood diabetes is a widespread problem, and we're making tremendous strides. It certainly affects numerous little girls, if you want to take the female angle...."

Ariella stumbled over her tongue, still processing the notion that Sam's anger had come from jealousy. It perplexed her. "Ah, well, I..."

He cut in smoothly. "May I use the same fax number I have for David?" He rattled off a number.

"Sure." Why not look at his material? She could always use a story. "Do you have any further comment on Becker's study? Do you have any reason to believe human trials will be unsuccessful?"

"No. I assume by now he's learned not to leave his refrigerators open." The joke fell flat.

She could not resist pushing just a little more. "How

would you rate his competency?"

Now his tone sounded strained. "He's quite competent. Are we about finished?"

"Yes. I appreciate your time, doctor. Thank you."

"No problem. I'll have Lila send you that fax right away. Must go. I have another call. Good-bye."

Left cradling the telephone receiver, Ariella tried to fit the pieces together in her mind. She still saw gaping holes in the puzzle, or maybe it was just that she found the picture ugly.

∽

Early Thanksgiving morning in her bathrobe she scanned the paper for her article, then read it over several times. It was a familiar ritual, and although she had only two hours to reach Logan Airport she would not forego the pleasure. No matter how many articles she published she always got a little thrill seeing her words in print. She also always found a fault in her work, and this time was no exception. The second paragraph flowed awkwardly from the first, and a phrase that would have fixed the dissonance sprang to mind. Joyce had put Angelica's story in a side-by-side box. Reading the two pieces from start to finish once more she decided that they were good: competently written with engaging subject matter, solid journalism. She wondered what Sam would think, especially about the use of Angelica's name; she could imagine him choking over his coffee as he turned the page of his newspaper and his eye fell on that box. Would he call—like last time? Suddenly she felt the need to flee to the shower, where the rushing water would drown out the ringing of the phone—just in case.

When she emerged from the shower she wrapped a towel around her torso and dripped her way through the apartment to the kitchen phone. Sure enough the answering machine light was blinking red. She hit the "play" button.

"This is Sam Becker calling." His tone was grim, and she winced. "I can't believe you would really interview my subjects. I should have expected it, I guess. But you could have told me, at least. You know, you really piss me off...." Crack, the phone had slammed into its cradle and cut off the message. She bit her lip. He could have said *something* complimentary. Then she snorted at her own temerity— actually she should be grateful that he hadn't sworn at her or resorted to personal insults. Another recorded voice began speaking, accented and animated.

"Ariella, uh, Ms. Richardson, it's Angelica. I just saw your article in the morning paper and had to call you. You are a great writer! And I couldn't believe it: my name in the paper. My cousin Bobby called me—gets up early for his watchman job—and he says, 'Angelica, get your big butt out of bed, run out to the corner and buy yourself a newspaper.' Out I went in my housecoat and boom, there it was! You made my day." Ariella grinned as the machine beeped and fell silent. To hell with men, she thought. Her wet feet were chilling on the cold linoleum floor, and so she retreated to the bedroom to dress and throw something into a suitcase for her flight to New York.

11

Three weeks later on a Saturday afternoon she found herself sliding along icy Lexington back streets trying to follow Joyce's lousy driving directions. Over an hour late she pulled into a long driveway searching among parked cars and snowdrifts for an empty space. Halfway down the lane there seemed to be a spot between two minivans. Edging the Mazda forward she reached the first one only to realize that her car would not fit. She glanced around and seeing nothing better, drove into the space on a diagonal, the nose of her car plunging onto the snow-covered lawn. A poor parking job, but she did not want to spend fifteen more minutes looking for street parking among the snow banks and plowed-in cars. Glancing at the rearview mirror, she ran her fingers through her curls, smiled encouragingly at herself, and opened the car door.

Cecile Chan stood in the entry, the picture of calm elegance: black hair in a sleek pageboy cut, lips bright red, slender body swathed in an aquamarine silk shift with a square neckline that showed off a set of gold beads the size of marbles. Unwrapping her black wool coat from her body, Ariella was glad that she had chosen red rather than a more docile print: a sleeveless rayon dress with wide straps that contrasted with her white shoulders, a shirred bodice that emphasized her figure and a skirt just short of the knee.

"So nice of you to come." Cecile gave her an appraising look. "Lovely dress. Red certainly becomes you." Ariella nodded her thanks; she loved red and knew it gave her confidence. "You know, we believe red brings good luck," Cecile continued. "Chinese brides wear red, and it's often a color used for special occasions."

"Yes, I had heard that." Ariella smiled, remembering the one Chinese wedding she had attended. Tempting and exotic smells were wafting into the foyer, and she noticed that on the staircase behind Cecile glossy gold ribbon twined around the mahogany banister.

Cecile ushered her into the crowded living room and led her toward a Christmas tree covered with handmade ornaments. There was no sign of Sam, and Ariella's shoulders relaxed a little. As she drew nearer she could see hanging in the branches dozens of delicate Chinese figures carved of wood and brightly painted: peasant men, women holding babies, oxen, cats, donkeys.

"This is exquisite, Cecile," she burst out. "Who made all these decorations?"

"My father and I have made them over the years—with a little help from my daughter, Margaret, this year, but she's only six." With an indulgent smile Cecile pointed out a rough-hewn purple animal hanging near the bottom of the tree, and the two women exchanged a conspiratorial glance.

"She hung it there herself?"

Cecile nodded, adding rhetorically, "How did you guess?"

"I'm assuming she's not very tall," answered Ariella, and they laughed a little.

"Let me introduce you to some people. I want you to meet some of my American Lung Association colleagues, and our new friend, Dr. Victor Janofsky, a psychiatrist and expert on substance abuse. He's running some cancer survivors' support groups at Carver."

Introduced as a *Boston Times* reporter, Ariella had no difficulty getting attention. Cecile's three women friends from the Lung Association were only too glad to provide a chorus of explanations of the group's programs. Dr. Janofksy proved to be a dapper man with a receding hairline, shaggy black brows and a loud laugh; his forest green jacket, mustard silk shirt and color-splashed tie marking him as a foreigner to Boston. When the three women ran out of steam she asked him his origin.

"Russian. Russian, of course. Can't you tell from my accent?" He took Ariella's arm and led her into the dining room insisting that she try the food. "They tell me Cecile is famous for these marvelous Chinese delicacies. The fish! You must have some of the fish. And the dumplings! You haven't lived until you've tried those dumplings." Ariella smiled at his enthusiasm. Then she shivered and glanced to the left with premonition. His back turned to her, Sam was listening to a gray-bearded man with glasses and an air of authority, no doubt an eminent Harvard physician.

"Come, come," said Janofsky making her realize that she had stopped in her tracks. With a determined smile she began her progress again and tried to focus on the Russian's remarks. "It is thus a great pleasure for me to know an American reporter," he was saying. "I salute you and your First Amendment. In the Soviet Union scientists had great need of such a law so that the atrocious misuses of the medical profession could be exposed. Psychiatry! Why, it was a travesty. My own father was confined to a mental institution for over twenty years for his political views. But perhaps you do not know of these things?"

"I know something about it because of a course I took in college," she said, wondering whether she should approach Sam. She decided to let him make the first move if any move were made at all. She did not need to make up with him to enjoy the party.

"Ah! And how did you like this class?" Janofsky was asking.

"It was compelling and disturbing."

He nodded approvingly. "Yes, that is Russia. Well, here we are. Have a drink." He offered her a cut crystal glass of red wine. "And allow me to fill a plate for you." Wide-eyed at the array of colorful platters she drank in the beauty of Cecile's holiday table, particularly the centerpiece of red roses, white lilies and holly leaves which she strongly suspected Cecile had arranged herself.

"Cecile is amazing."

"The perfect hostess," he agreed. "Look at her circulating among the guests introducing people, making them feel welcome and included. And watch this table. The platters are never less than half full when Cecile appears to replenish them."

"I could never run a party like this."

"Perhaps not. It is instinctual with a woman like Cecile. But no doubt you have other talents. She is not a writer."

"Yes, but she gives such clear pleasure to others in a party like this. Newspaper reporting is so controversial—and people seem to only call the paper with complaints, never with praise."

"Of course. People love to complain. It is human nature. But your job is not to please people; it is to expose truths that lie hidden." He was warming to his subject, his shaggy brows rising and falling to emphasize his heavily accented words. "Your job is to preserve the free press by telling stories of controversy, giving them the attention they deserve. There are always those who would keep scandals hidden, and they will complain. It is irrelevant!"

"I guess so. Maybe I don't have the guts for it." She was rapidly demolishing the heaping plate of hors d'oeuvres he had handed her.

His gaze bored into her eyes for a long moment. "You have the guts. I can see it there in your eyes. But do not care so much what others think of you. People are filled with darkness; don't let their darkness affect you. Just remember Russia and what happened to her with no free press—then you will cherish your own."

Despite an urge to giggle at his mix of passion and psycho-babble, his words lifted her spirits, or maybe it was the delicious wine, the food, the Chans' beautiful home. Just then Roland came into view wending his way toward them with two bottles in his hands, greeting guests and refilling glasses.

"Ariella, what a pleasure. Red?" He poured some wine into her goblet. "And Victor. Delighted to see you. Glad you two have met. Victor, if you don't mind I would like to introduce you to Roger Walters, that statistician I told you about. He'd be a great help in shaping up your data for publication. Ariella, have you seen Sam? He's right over there."

"I don't know that he's dying to see me."

"No reason why not. Good pieces you wrote in the

paper." He gave one of his characteristic nods, and she smiled in surprised appreciation. "Why don't you just wish him a Merry Christmas and get past whatever unpleasantness there might be? In the holiday spirit." He winked at her so fast that she almost thought she had imagined it and bore Victor off without another word.

She swallowed the new glass of wine in one gulp and threaded her way through the crowd to Sam's side. The bearded man had just moved on, leaving her a clear field.

"Hi!" she said cheerfully with no noticeable tremor in her voice. "So. Still holding a grudge or can we wave the white flag?"

He looked down at her without a smile, his height creating even more distance than usual. "I don't know," he said shortly.

She had come this far, and she would not retreat. "Have you tried the steamed dumplings?" she asked. "They're scrumptious. Come on, I'll get some for us."

"That's all right. I can feed myself."

Ariella stiffened. "I'm doing my best to make up with you, but you certainly are stubborn. What can I do to get you to crack a smile?"

"I'm not feeling all that jolly tonight. In fact, I wouldn't have come at all except that Roland insisted. If you're looking for holiday cheer, I'm sure you can find someone else who'll be glad to oblige." He gestured with his chin towards Janofsky's back.

His snide tone unleashed her temper. "Look, I'm sorry that my articles upset you. And I'm sorry that you're having a rotten time." She took a breath and looked straight into his vivid blue eyes. "But you know, most of all I'm sorry I ever got up the gumption to walk over here and prostrate myself before such a rude, arrogant, unbending...."

"I can't imagine why you bothered," he interrupted icily.

"Can't you?" she flung at him and fled through the living room and into the dining room, where she poured another glass of red wine with a shaky hand and began loading up a plate from a corner dessert table.

Sam stared after her, regretting his sharp tone. He did not entirely trust her motives—after all, she seemed to be using this party as a networking opportunity—but what did he care? Baffled by his own strong reactions he tried to subdue his feelings and reassert logic. Perhaps she had simply wanted to make peace with him. He disliked polite cocktail party lies, but he also held to European standards of politeness handed down by his mother.

Ariella was staring determinedly out the window at the blowing snow and toying with a pastry when a finger touched her shoulder. He had followed her.

"I don't understand you," he said. "I feel like you want to use me."

"I don't need anything you have to offer," she spat out, wishing he would just leave her alone to gorge herself in humiliation. "I was enjoying myself till I ran into you."

"Maybe I've misjudged you."

"Maybe you have."

"You know," he said, a ghost of a smile on his lips, "my sister used to call me rude and arrogant sometimes."

"You have a sister?"

"Um hm. Listen, I apologize for my bad manners." He paused for a moment as if making a decision, then said in a gentler tone, "Will you share some of those pastries with me if I promise to behave better? Come into the other room

with me for a minute. I think I ought to tell you something."
He looked stern, with little of the charm he had possessed
that day in the Public Garden, and she hesitated. She found
it hard to sustain her anger now that he had taken the blame,
but she was wary. If only this man did not fascinate her. A
simple, jovial guy like David wouldn't put her on this roller
coaster ride, but David could never have this man's effect on
her pulse. So she followed him into a smaller room at the
back of the house, a study with floor-to-ceiling bookshelves.
He led her to a plush sofa, taking the plate from her hand,
placing it on the mahogany coffee table, and gesturing for
her to sit down.

She began to speak, but he put a finger across her
lips, and the intimacy of the gesture sent ripples through her.
Much too much wine, she thought.

"I really don't like playing games," he said. "So I want
to be honest with you. Something about you makes me
behave irrationally." A twinkle seemed to light his eye for a
moment. "At first I thought it was just my dislike of
reporters, but I can't kid myself; I'm attracted to you. The
problem is that even though I don't trust you I keep thinking
about you." His eyes burned into hers. "You're beautiful."

Ariella blushed crimson and looked at his knees.
Rarely had anyone but her mother or sister ever called her
beautiful—Carl certainly never had—and she brushed it
aside as flattery. Yet she could not resist the lure of the word
despite Sam's distrust. At least he had not brought her in here
to pick her articles to pieces. She wondered what he would
do next and whether she dared touch him—but his harsh
streak gave her pause, and she jerked her gaze from his lap
to the pastries.

"My goodness," he mocked, taking one of her hands

in his and playing with her fingers, "I think I've reduced you to silence."

She turned her face upward and looked into his eyes warily, but she saw no vestige of anger, only warmth, humor and a profound attention that threatened to envelop her. It was far more intoxicating than the wine, and she leaned toward him. Immediately, as if he had been waiting for the slightest sign, he slipped his free hand into her hair and captured her mouth with his. He kissed her surprisingly gently for a moment, then wrapped his arms around her, drawing her to his chest, chin on her head. She could feel his heart hammering, and she let herself go—sliding her hands up his forearms and shoulders to twist her fingers in his thick hair. His arms tightened convulsively, his head snapped down to eye-level, and his mouth suddenly devoured hers, driving away any thought of their fight or the party, throwing her into a whirlpool of sensation that overwhelmed her. His hands roamed her back, glided under her and pulled her closer, and she strained to feel every inch of him, reveling in his solid mass. His kiss seemed to send lava flowing through her veins, and she abandoned herself to it, hungrily exploring every corner of his mouth.

Suddenly loud voices began approaching in the corridor, and she started. He sprang up, shut the door, and turned the skeleton key dangling in the lock, giving her an intense look. She said nothing, trying not to think. Sliding back onto the couch he pulled gently on her hands until, frustrated, she threw herself against him and slid full-length along his body, letting his heat brand her. She didn't care what he thought of her. All she could think was that no man's body had ever sparked such a wildfire in her, and she would not let it end yet. She claimed his mouth, and his response made her shiver. His hands wandered everywhere, making her rayon dress seem only a whispery veil. Then he broke away from her mouth and before she realized what was happening, gripped her, rolling her beneath him in one swift stroke, and pinned her, letting her feel how much he wanted her. Braced on his elbows, his eyes gloated at her.

"You have no idea how much I've wanted to touch you," he almost growled. "For a long time, I thought I was dead inside, but ever since I met you I've wanted you like this. Just out of the blue. I had to see if this is what I needed to stop me snapping at you." A hint of irony crept into his voice. "And you don't even seem to mind."

To her body the weight of his felt glorious, but now that he had stopped kissing her, her ambivalence surged. "Oh, Sam," she whispered, searching for words to describe the frisson of fear in her. The wildfire in her had made her forget that he was her source, infusing her with a heady mix of confidence and power that she could make him feel this way. "I've been dreaming about you," she admitted. "And I don't understand you at all most of the time. No one has ever questioned my integrity as fiercely as you, and I wish you'd just give me the benefit of the doubt. But trusting someone new, I guess that takes time."

"True." He gave her a long kiss. "You'd better watch out, or I'll keep you here all night and have my way with you. I don't know how I'd explain to Roland why I had to take over his study, but I'd think of something." He lowered his head to nestle it on her shoulder, his body pressed along the length of her side, one leg flung across her.

Just then the knob turned against the lock, and there was a sharp knock. "Is that you, Sam?" asked a voice unmistakably Roland's.

"Yes," Sam called, in an artificially crisp tone. Ariella giggled, trying to squirm away, and his eyes widened warningly at her, but Roland had heard.

"So long as you're not in there killing each other...." he said with a smirk in his tone.

"No chief, no killing," called Sam.

"Well, if you wouldn't mind rejoining us soon, there's a potential funding source I'd like you to meet." They could hear his footsteps retreating down the corridor.

"I'll teach you to laugh at me," said Sam with intensity and began tickling up her sides and along the edges of her breasts; she gasped and jerked away, but he rolled atop her again and pinned her like a wriggling worm.

"Please, stop!" Grabbing his wrists she tried to force them away. He acquiesced suddenly, lowering his face to hers and kissing her lips longingly; then he broke contact and stared at her.

"You said out there you don't need anything I have to offer," he said. "Maybe it's me that needs something. Before you leave this room, tell me you'll see me again."

She sighed, a touch of ambivalence creeping back. "I doubt I can keep away from you," she said. "Especially if you kiss me every time you want to snap at me."

"Much more fun that way." He smiled, then lifted himself from her and stood, stretching his long limbs and reaching for her hands to pull her up. As she stood, she realized she was trembling. Not surprising, considering that she had actually considered making love to a man in a virtual stranger's study in the middle of a party. She was glad she hadn't. It had all happened much too fast as it was. She moved to a dark wooden door and into a lavender bathroom, where she silently combed her hair with her fingers and tried to straighten her dress. Coming up from behind he wrapped his arms around her and massaged her stomach, playing havoc with her efforts to smooth the wrinkles.

"You know, you're magnetic in that red dress," he said, with no idea how often that word had come to her mind to describe him. "Every man at the party noticed you, and I wanted to strangle that guy in green."

She was sure he was wrong about the other men, but said only, "Did you? You sound a little possessive."

"I am," he said intensely, and although she pursed her lips at him, the mirror reflected an answering glow in her cinnamon eyes.

12

Ariella emerged from the study slightly dazed, pulse still running high, with Sam behind her. Not three steps into the hallway she almost slammed into an auburn-haired woman in black.

"Joyce!"

"Well, hello Ariella. Fancy meeting you here. And the infamous Dr. Becker, isn't it?" She inclined her head and stretched out a hand. "I don't believe we've had the pleasure. I'm Joyce Aldrich of the *Boston Times*, Ariella's assignment editor."

"Good to meet you," he murmured, moving into the breach and taking her hand. "So you're the dragon in the newsroom."

"You might say that. I can breathe fire when I need to." She turned her eyes on Ariella. "So I was looking for the bathroom. Is that where you were?"

"Uh, well, yes," she stammered. "It's through the study door and to the left—but Joyce, I thought you couldn't make it today!" She knew her voice was registering too much shock but could not seem to contain it.

"Last minute change of plans; so I thought I'd drop by, press the flesh and sniff around. And maybe it's a good thing I did." With that parting shot she headed for the bathroom leaving Ariella feeling as red as her dress.

"Interesting woman, your boss. I don't know that I'd like her much if I got to know her." Sam started down the corridor for the dining room, and Ariella trailed behind him without comment, disciplining her features for the crowd.

Roland spotted them the moment they crossed the threshold, and he led three men and a woman in their direction. Immediately Ariella recognized Dr. Natalie Ward in an ankle-length dress of dusty blue dotted with tiny white stars. She wore pearls around her neck and in her ears, her wheat-colored hair in the chignon Ariella remembered, her bearing erect as ever. Beside her slouched the slender, narrow-faced Rich Carruthers of television fame, the man whose research Sam's acrobatics had saved. After learning about his Michigan refrigerator disaster, she began to see the storm incident in a new light.

Rich's face lit when he noticed her. "Why, Miss Richardson, how are you?" he asked, offering a hand to shake. "I didn't expect to see you here. You're looking very nice tonight."

"Sam," Roland interposed, "you know Natalie and Rich, and these two gentlemen are from the Donald Benson Foundation." He gave their names and pedigrees. "Natalie and I have been telling them about your research, and they have a few questions for you." Sam shook hands while Ariella hung back with Rich, uncertain of her role and reluctant to draw attention.

"Merry Christmas, Sam," Natalie almost cooed, her eyes displaying a watery warmth that Ariella had not thought possible. "I was just describing my end of the human trials, but I explained that the theoretical basis and study design are really your province." She linked her arm with his and turned him away from Ariella and toward the foundation men, leaving Ariella and Rich to their own devices. Ariella felt her hackles rising but bit her tongue.

"I'm not really necessary to that conversation," Rich explained. "Don't have a project to pitch, and even if I did Roland has bigger fish to fry tonight."

Ariella suspected that the rudeness had been directed at her, but she did not say so to Rich. Instead she said, "They're an important foundation, aren't they?" She needed a moment to collect herself and hoped he would entertain her for a little while.

"Oh, yes. Among the biggest supporters of medical research. Of the non-corporate sponsors, that is. They're a charitable trust based in New Jersey, and they support all sorts of basic research and public health initiatives. May I offer you some champagne and a Christmas cookie? They're delicious."

"All the men at this party want to feed me tonight," she found herself babbling. "How do you expect me to fit into my dress?"

He glanced down at the dress, colored and ran a hand through his thinning hair as he replied, "Well, I didn't mean to cause any trouble. If you'd rather not... But I don't think one cookie would hurt."

Knowing she had taken the wrong tack, she smiled gently at him; Sam was now deep in conversation surrounded by Natalie, Roland and the foundation people; so she squeezed Rich's forearm in a friendly way. "I was only kidding. I would love some champagne—and several cookies."

She spent a pleasant quarter of an hour with Rich,

who made up for his nervousness with a sharp wit and a prodigious memory. If her mind wandered occasionally he did not notice. Something at the party reminded him of the poet, Wallace Stevens, and after a second glass of champagne he began reciting Stevens' poetry, much to her amusement. After the tension of her encounter with Sam and the shock of meeting Joyce she found it soothing to sip and nibble and listen to poems. Whenever she looked in Sam's direction he did not meet her eye, and Natalie's head remained cocked toward him like a bird's, her fingers frequently straying to his arm.

Just as Rich launched into the poet's life story, Joyce barged into their tête-a-tête. "Ariella, I'm very sorry to disturb you, but the paper just paged me. We've got a big story breaking on that Griffin murder case." She gave Rich a hard look. "You're not a reporter, are you?" At his vehement shake of the head, she continued, "The Griffin baby just died, making the case a double homicide, and that ratchets up the pressure on the Boston police. Commissioner Coughlin is holding a press conference in half an hour, and I need to get down to the newsroom fast. Would you take me?" Among Joyce's eccentricities she had never learned to drive. "I think I could get you a piece of the story, Ariella, if you want it."

Ariella was flustered; the Griffin murder depressed her more than most crime stories, and so far she had avoided it. Although she did not want to leave without speaking to Sam again, she knew that Joyce's request was a command. She wanted to at least say goodbye to him, but without further arousing Joyce's suspicions. "I'll just find Cecile and thank her," she temporized, stalling for time. She turned and spotted Cecile across the room. With her back to Joyce,

Ariella tried desperately to catch Sam's eye, but he seemed oblivious. Natalie noticed, though, and gave Ariella an appraising look that made her feel like one of the steamed dumplings she had earlier eaten. She thanked Cecile warmly for her hospitality and her story ideas. "If you come up with any others feel free to call me."

"Don't worry," said Cecile. "I will. By the way, which direction are you heading?"

"Well, actually, right now I'm heading for Dorchester. I have to drop Joyce at the *Times* building."

"Really? Would you do me a favor and take Fiona Boyle with you? She lives in Dorchester, not far from the *Times,* I believe. You've met her, haven't you? Roland's administrator?" Ariella nodded as Cecile began easing her from the room toward the foyer. Casting a final desperate glance in Sam's direction she followed, and allowing Cecile to introduce Joyce to Mrs. Boyle, shrugged into her black wool coat and led her small party into the bitter cold.

∽

A couple of hours later, the sound of good-byes floated into the kitchen through the open door; then Cecile appeared in it and moved rapidly to the sink.

"It's all right," said Roland, placing a hand on her shoulder. "I'll start the dishes. You go change."

She hesitated. "All right, but don't wash the good china. I'll do that myself. And remember not to put real silver in the dishwasher." She fixed him with a severe look.

"I know." His eyes mocked her.

"Last year you broke that crystal candy dish."

Roland turned to Sam, who was sitting in a kitchen

chair polishing off leftover shrimp rolls from a silver platter. "Women have memories like elephants," he said. "It's amazing. At Carver I'm known for my Midas touch, but here at home I'm just a clumsy oaf who broke the candy dish."

"Roland!" Cecile reached up to kiss his cheek. "Stop it. You know I think the world of you. It's just that..."

"Someone has to keep you in line, or your head might swell to Humpty Dumpty size," Sam finished dryly.

"He said it, not me." Cecile disappeared around the kitchen door; both Roland's and Sam's eyes fixed on the empty space she had vacated for a moment before they turned to each other.

"You know you're very lucky."

Roland nodded and gave a smile broad enough to show his dimple. "So did you enjoy the party?"

"It got better as the afternoon wore on."

"After Ariella turned up, you mean."

"Not at all."

Roland cocked an eyebrow. "So what happened with you two in my study?"

"Nothing much."

"It sounded like something to me. I thought her *Times* articles were excellent, by the way, not to mention great publicity for you and Carver. Did you apologize for storming out of her apartment, complement her on her talent, and then kiss and make up?"

"Oh, lay off, Roland." His tone sounded bitterer than he intended. "She has no genuine interest in me, just men. When she wasn't with me she was busy cozying up to that guy in green. And then Carruthers."

"Victor and Rich!" Roland laughed. "They're no competition for you—unless they're nicer to her. You're still angry at her, aren't you?" Although Sam refused to dignify that with a response, Roland pressed on. "Don't tell me you disliked the articles? Her explanation of the science was crystal clear."

"Come on, Roland; she went behind my back and interviewed my study subjects, even printed one's *name* in the paper—it's outrageous! She wants to dredge up that mess with Schaus. And she waltzed out of this party without so much as a good-bye." Sam realized he was almost shouting, and worse, had allowed himself to be drawn into this conversation.

Roland gave him a bemused look. "She does keep you guessing—a far cry from that insipid woman in Michigan you almost married. Any good reporter for the popular press would want to talk to a patient in your study—makes the story human. Will it really do the study any harm?"

"Probably not. Why don't we drop it?"

"She's really gotten under your skin, hasn't she? Why don't you just pursue her? Don't answer that. I know. She's a reporter, the lowest form of life." Sam would not give him the satisfaction of a reply. "You know what, Sam? That's bullshit. Don't punish her for what a pack of Michigan reporters did to twist Schaus' diabetes findings. It's time to move on. And I'll bet she left the party because you spent so long with Natalie and the Benson funders—which was really my fault."

"That's enough, Roland. I don't need you to defend her. I have work to do." He rose to leave, pulling his jacket from the back of the chair.

"Work." Roland snorted. "You know, you used to give people more of a chance."

The parting shot rankled all the way home in the car,

and the feel of Ariella's body haunted him. Lying in his arms looking at him she had seemed so sweet that he could not bear to let her go, but now his distrust consumed him. It rankled more than it should that she had not taken the trouble to say "goodbye." At the very least, it proved that she still required chasing, and he was not in the habit of chasing women. He had never needed a woman before, and he was not about to need one now. As he slid into his parking place he used his formidable force of will to push the whole topic of Ariella from his mind. He did not want his emotions veering recklessly back and forth as they had this afternoon. He had a major grant proposal to write for the Benson Foundation, and he would not let her interfere.

13

Christmas week had passed, and he had not called. Sitting in the newsroom Monday morning she felt a rush of energy and decided to take a chance. Joyce had just given her a New Year's Eve assignment, but perhaps Sam could help her put the sparkle back into another working holiday. It annoyed her to see her fingers tremble as she dialed his number. She had placed business calls to many eminent people without a qualm—well, at least without physical tremors—but this time a few deep breaths would not still her hands. The phone rang, and disappointment and relief flooded her as an answering machine clicked into action.

"You've reached Sam Becker," said a recording of the familiar gruff voice. "Leave a message, and I'll call you back. Thanks." No excess baggage for him. She frequently changed her own message on a whim and always included cheerful pop music in the background.

The tape was running. "Uh, hi Sam," she said belatedly. "This is Ariella Richardson. I was wondering whether you have plans for New Year's Eve. That is, are you going down to the First Night celebrations? Because I've been assigned to cover them for the newspaper, and I thought you might like to join me—if it's convenient. Let me know what you think...." She gave her number and hung up, cursing her lapse into babbling.

Her awkward words of invitation repeated in her head as she tried to edit a story she had written on last night's fire at Filene's. Realizing she had read the word, "blaze," four times in a row she pushed the copy aside and sprang up from her desk. Time to get out of the newsroom. Perhaps she ought to go down to Filene's and check on any appreciable effects on business today. She jumped up, and coat over her arm, she threaded her way to the corner stairwell, jogging down the three flights of white concrete stairs to the parking lot. Pushing through the heavy doors she met bracing cold and drifts of graying snow on the sidewalk. Sunshine sprinkled the crowded lot, where she paused to put on her long coat, gloves and scarf. When she reached the car, the door opened sulkily, its hinges frozen. The engine started like a charm, though, and she turned cautiously out of the lot into the slippery boulevard.

When she reached Government Center, the effects of the previous day's blizzard surrounded her. People were still digging out cars and picking their way along slippery streets. Ariella dropped off her car at an indoor lot—no chance for street parking on a day like this—and fought her way through pedestrians and snow banks around a corner until she reached a path the merchants had more effectively shoveled and sanded. She marched along drawing her scarf upward to cover her ears and squinting at the sunshine reflected on the snow. At Filene's she stopped to look at a black evening gown in the window. The fire seemed not to have hurt business—customers were flocking in and out. In a rare moment of self-indulgence, she decided to take a coffee break. Feet crunching on the pavement she made her way to a coffee shop a block away where she could buy her favorite morning boost, a cafe mocha.

Sipping from a tall cup and perched on a high stool inside she thought of her parents in Italy. She had not spoken to them for several weeks. Last time Dad called he had sounded very happy with his sabbatical. He had finished five chapters of his new philosophy of law text, and he was confident that he could complete it within the year if he continued to work hard. She was a little worried about Mom, though. How was she occupying herself, torn from her round of bridge, baking, gardening, gossip and volunteering at her beloved Palmdale Home for the Aged? Mom so hated to travel that she had never visited either of her daughters in New York, refusing to come even when Ruby was born.

Ariella had always been impatient with her mother's timidity. Ever the good girl, Nina had gone to the family school, the University of Florida, as expected, and when the time came, held her wedding at home despite the inconvenience to her husband's New York family. Not Ariella—she graduated from high school a year early and shot north to the University of Pennsylvania, ignoring her parents' protests. Like Nina, Dad had always indulged Mom's desire to sleep in her own bed—until now.

After twenty years at the university he had requested a sabbatical, and his department chairman had arranged the opportunity in Padua. All last spring Ariella had expected to hear that the trip had been canceled, that Mom simply could not go through with it, but now there they were, six months into the sabbatical. Her refrigerator was plastered with postcards to prove it. Of course, Mom's idiosyncrasies had not disappeared with her trip across the Atlantic. She was afraid to place international calls, some combination of her fear of Italian-speaking operators and her fear of the cost. So only Dad called, and absent-minded as he was while writing a book, the calls came infrequently. Mom *had* mastered the postal system and sent each of her girls a weekly postcard full of questions and vague, cheerful remarks (hence the refrigerator build-up).

Ariella supposed her mother could be drinking cafe mocha every day, but she had no idea. She had no idea at all what her mother was doing, and it troubled her. What was worse, it rankled that her mother had never once visited her in college or journalism school or seen any of her apartments. Every curse had its blessing though, and her mother's absence from her adult life had brought her closer to Nina. Sometime in freshman year she had ceased to resent her older sister's tractable nature and begun to appreciate her as a person. It was Nina who visited her every year at Penn and stood at Dad's side beaming on graduation day, Nina who met her roommates and friends and the boys she dated. Nina had helped her find an apartment and a job in New York, and then after Ruby was born her sister had begged her to move in. The years together had cemented their bond, and even after she had left for New Haven and Boston the closeness remained. Nina continued to visit, knowing how much the dreary train rides with a fidgeting little girl would mean to her sister when they arrived, but Ariella made the more frequent trips.

"Ariella!" A voice broke through her reverie, and she looked up startled to see Joyce in front of her in a tawny fur collar. The woman had an uncanny way of turning up at the wrong moment.

"You look as if you're seeing a ghost," said her editor, settling on a stool across the table and unbuttoning her heavy coat. "How's the cappuccino today?"

"I don't know. I always have mocha."

"Their quality seems to vary. I think it depends on who's working. But I suppose I'll have to chance it. I need my caffeine fix. So are you pondering a new story?"

"No." She drew out the syllable. "The coffee made me think of Italy, and Italy of my parents...."

"They must be having an incredible time. It's just about now when the blizzards start that I get very jealous of people on the Mediterranean."

"Well, they're not really on the Mediterranean."

"No snow there, though. Actually, I shouldn't complain. I think I'm going to take a week off in February and go to the Greek isles. My travel agent found me a great deal on airfare, and I'm craving a vacation. How about you? Any plans to visit your folks?"

Ariella stifled irritation. Joyce took exotic vacations every six months, but she not only had a higher salary to pillage, she also had some sort of inheritance. "I would like to go, maybe in April, but I doubt that I'll be able to afford it."

"You only live once," said Joyce. "Isn't that what credit cards are for?"

I can't just call my stockbroker and sell some shares when the bills come, thought Ariella. But she said nothing. Joyce meant well.

"So what's going on with Jerry Lesniak?" her editor asked in one of her usual lightning changes of topic.

"Well, I spoke to him on the telephone, and I'm actually scheduled to meet with him tomorrow. He wants me to do a story on how the tobacco industry funds medical research that helps cast doubt on whether smoking causes cancer. They've been at it for years, he says, and he has evidence."

"Is he a lunatic?"

"No, I don't think so. He's a man with a mission, probably eats, sleeps and breathes the cause, but he seems bright and sane enough. A late sleeper maybe, but sane."

"Hmm?"

"Oh, he didn't want to meet at nine, pushed it to ten thirty."

"Well, you can sympathize. You're not exactly the early bird yourself. Sounds good. Now is that Filene's fire story ready to go?"

"Just about."

The eyebrow lifted. "Well, I'll grab that cappuccino and head back with you—if you're going."

14

When she reached her desk the light on her phone was blinking. Hope surging she snapped up the receiver and punched in the code for her messages. She heard a series of beeps, then Jerry the Giraffe's nasal voice asking to move their meeting to eleven o'clock. The telephone beeped again, and a thickly accented voice materialized, Victor Janofsky asking her out to see a revival of the Russian film, *Alexander Nevsky* on New Year's Day. After another beep she heard the voice of a source for the Filene's story confirming the final detail she had requested. It was sweet of the woman to leave a detailed message. No need to play telephone tag any longer. She waited for another beep, but instead heard the long tone indicating the end of her messages.

"Shoot!" She hung up.

"What's the matter, Ariella?" David had crept up behind her, and as always she gave an involuntary shudder. It was a frustrating reflex. "Didn't mean to startle you," he said. "Or maybe it's just that I make your skin crawl." He grinned.

"Need some ego-stroking? No, David, you don't make my skin crawl."

"Boy, that's some faint praise if I ever heard it. I don't know whether I should even continue after that, but what the hell, I've never been called shy. A fool, maybe, but not shy. So are you free tonight for dinner?"

She was surprised. "What's the matter? Kelly's busy tonight?"

"No, suspicious woman; actually we broke up." He raised a finger as she opened her mouth. "Again. Don't say anything. Just nod if you'll have dinner with me tonight, and you can give me all the advice you want then."

She smiled and nodded, and he bounded off, forestalling further conversation. As she watched him go, the smile turning rueful. David Ellman was a compact man with black curls like her own and an awkward loping gait that reminded her of a puppy although she would never tell him so. Ten years her senior he was the *Times'* respected health reporter with an impressive file of stories to his credit and a dogged instinct for the news beneath the science. She looked up to him professionally, but it was difficult to take him seriously on a personal level. He was a born prankster and delighted in telling her of his roller-coaster relationship with Kelly, a temperamental surgical nurse who kept trying to convert him to Catholicism. When Ariella started at the *Times* David had made his interest in her plain, but she had fended off his advances. She thought it unwise to date a co-worker and in any case was unsure whether such a clown would be serious about her. So when she heard about his off-again-on-again girlfriend, Kelly, she was glad that she had refused him. They became buddies, and although David was a physical man and gave her more than a few hugs he held the relationship within comfortable limits.

৯৯

Ariella stood shivering on David's veranda in the ethnically diverse Jamaica Plain section of Boston, pushed the buzzer a second time and rapped on the door with her free hand. A bottle of Chianti in the other did nothing to warm her through her glove. Wondering whether she had chosen the right wine, she idly glanced around. David lived in a white-shingled Victorian house, the faded sea green columns holding up the porch making it unmistakable. At one time it must have held an old Boston Irish family with ten children, or so Ariella thought, for it certainly seemed spacious enough. Now David lived on the first floor, rented the second-floor apartment to a young Latino couple, and used the renovated attic on the third floor for his office and a guest suite. Icicles hung from the eaves, and a white crust covered the front walk and several steps. David had all the lights on, the windows unshaded and the blues blasting so loudly that she could hear the lyrics through the double doors. At last he appeared wearing an apron decorated with fist-sized cartoon lobsters.

"Come in, come in. Welcome." He seized the wine and swept her into the foyer closing the heavy oak door with a thump. Shrugging out of her coat she stepped tentatively past the stained glass second door into the front hall, where a six-foot square oil painting of Ella Fitzgerald dominated.

"Hi Ella," she said smiling. "So what are we listening to?"

"Mr. Keb Mo." He flourished a hand in the air. "Blues. Do you like it?"

"Well, I've never heard of it till this second, but I do."

"Got a rock 'n' roll heart, haven't you Ari? Well,

come on into the kitchen and taste my sauce." He led her through the familiar living room lined with floor-to-ceiling shelves teaming with books, records, cassettes and CD's. As often as she saw the collection it always dazzled her.

"Can't I stop and browse?"

"Nope, not yet. I want to toss the tortellini with this sauce, and you have to use that sensitive tongue of yours to tell me whether I need more salt or basil or something." She crossed her arms, grimaced and stuck out the appendage, but he only laughed and pulled her to the connecting door and into the spacious old-fashioned kitchen. "It's good to have you here. It's been a while." He lifted a giant wooden spoon from a blackened cast iron kettle and held it to her mouth while she blew gently, then sipped the red sauce.

"Oh, David, you've outdone yourself."

"Doesn't it need basil?" For once he did not seem to be joking, but you never knew with him.

"No. It's marvelous. You're going to make somebody a very happy wife some day."

"If you're offering I might just take you up on that," he said, kissing her cheek lightly. She blushed and gave his forearm a shove.

"Not me, idiot. Now don't tease me with that sauce and leave me here salivating. I'm hungry and cold; let's eat please." She extricated the wine bottle from the fingers of his left hand, turned her back on him and crossed to a drawer where she knew she could find a corkscrew. Behind her she could hear him ladling pasta onto plates or bowls. She was wondering what possessed her to use that hackneyed phrase about wives; that was hot water she needed to stay out of. With a moment of concentration she extracted the cork and began to pour wine into blueberry-colored glass goblets he had waiting.

"Do you mind if we eat in the living room on the coffee table? I've been painting, and I've got drop cloths spread all over the dining room."

"Sure. Japanese style."

"I should have thought of that and made tempura." He hit his head in mock despair. "Have I ever made you my tempura?"

"No, David, and I'm very offended. In fact, I'm coming back tomorrow night for some."

"Okay," he said straight-faced. "Now that Kelly's out of the picture I've got lots of time to cook for you."

Ariella made a rude noise and carried the bottle and glasses back into the living room to the square glass coffee table, clearing scattered magazines and science journals into a pile and setting down the wine. She slid to the floor, pulling off her boots, wiggling her black-stockinged toes under the glass, and spreading her arms wide against the couch in an arching stretch. He had followed with a bamboo tray laden with bowls of pasta, salad plates, and a bread basket, and stood taking in her posture with laughter and a question in his eyes.

"So," she said, grabbing a bright pillow from the couch and easing it behind the small of her back. "Tell me all about it. Why did you break up this time? Same old stuff or something new?"

"No sympathy." He opened his eyes wide and pulled his mouth into a pout. With that round face the expression made him look like Harpo Marx. He laid the bowls and plates on the table, and she watched, sipping wine and waiting for an answer. "Well, she really pissed me off this time because she not only made another appointment for me with that priest last night—without even discussing it with me—but then she tricked me into coming over, said she was desperate to talk to me and then unleashed the priest when I got there."

"Oh boy." She was trying not to laugh.

"I know it sounds funny, but I'm getting kind of sick of it. Why can't she take me for who I am?" The light had faded from his eyes, and he downed a big gulp of wine.

"I don't know, David," she said. "But we've been around this block before. Part of Kelly's way of loving is to want to save your soul, and I'm not sure she can be satisfied any other way. That's the way she was brought up."

He sighed. "I know, but can't she bend a little? And the dishonesty. How can she think that trapping me with a priest would actually make me see the light? It's crazy."

"It is odd to think you would respond well to a ploy like that, but David, you're so easy-going. You've made her think anything goes; so no wonder she pulls stunts. You're what my sister calls a pushover." Ariella was making a sizable dent in the heap of tortellini.

"I care about her." He looked away and poured himself another full glass of wine.

"Yeah. She cares about you too. She also pushes you around."

"Not any more. It's over, Ari. It really is. I'm not going to convert to Catholicism, and I'm not going to stay with a woman who doesn't love me for who I am."

"Oh, David...."

"What? Do you think I'm wrong?"

"No, I just think you're not serious."

"You think I'm a real fence-sitter, don't you?"

She took a swig of the wine. "This meal is amazing, really. No, well, I think that when it comes to work you're incredibly assertive, and when decisions need to be made, you make them. But with Kelly you're different. It's not just the religion thing. It's all the stories you've told me about her controlling every date, never going to blues concerts, always making you stay at her place, asking for endless loans and favors. You asked her to marry you, and she said "no"—what does that tell you?" She ran her hand through her hair and looked him in the eye.

"You're right," he said, "but is it so terrible to be flexible, to try to please the woman you love?" He seemed to want an answer; so she shook her head and said "no," stretching a hand across the glass to clasp his.

For a moment they were silent. Then he blurted out. "You're a good friend, Ariella. So how's that wacky mother of yours? Still sending you those 'wish you were here' postcards?" He grinned, and she let him change the subject.

"Yeah. I've never seen anybody convey less in writing than my mom. But hey, why talk about her?"

"Well, if Mom's out, how about men? Anyone new in your life?"

At that she broke hand contact. "None of your business."

David pouted deeply again, and although she struggled to keep her lips pinched together she knew her eyes were laughing. He refilled her wine glass, and she took another sip.

"What a clown you are! You really ought to join the circus. Okay, so I kind of met somebody, but it won't go anywhere."

"Why not?"

"Oh, I don't think he's that interested, and anyway he hates reporters."

"Well, but doesn't everybody? What makes you think he's not interested?" His eyes were alight with curiosity.

"Oh, I don't know. He said he would call and he didn't. He made it seem like he was eager to... to start something... and then he didn't." She rearranged the tortellini in her bowl.

"I'll bet he wanted to start something. You're a hot ta.... Oh, but I can't say that to a co-worker, right? It might be sexual harassment." His eyes twinkled.

"David!"

"Maybe you need to give this guy a little time. Men don't always like to be rushed. Of course, sounds like you thought he *was* in a rush, but he'll have cooled off some now that you're out of sight. So what's he like?"

"Oh, he's a cancer researcher, tall."

He shook his head. "So you don't feel like talking about him either? Why is it that I tell you everything about Kelly, and you never tell me anything?"

"There's nothing to tell."

"Um hm. Sure. Have you fooled around?"

"David!" She sipped more wine, and he waited. "Well, a little. Nothing major. Not that it's any of your business."

"Of course not." He sat and looked at her for a while with an unreadable expression on his face, and when she could no longer meet his eye she swirled the wine in her glass and slowly drained it. When she dropped her gaze, he slid along the floor around the corner of the table until he reached her side. "Ari," he said softly, "how about a hug?" She felt a tangle of mixed emotions, but she opened her arms, and they held each other for a long while, hearts beating an erratic rhythm, eyes never meeting. At last he pulled away, lifted her chin with a finger, gave her a quick kiss and moved away a foot. "I wonder..." he mused. "How many glasses of wine would it take to get you to go to bed with me?"

"Oh, David, you know I think that's a bad idea. We've..."

"Been over that ground before. Do you truly think it's a *bad* idea or does it just scare you?"

She sighed and crossed her arms on her stomach. "We work together. And I don't do this. And it would change everything.... Oh, I sound like an idiot."

"I could argue all of that, but I won't except to say that you're no idiot, a little wacky sometimes and refusing me shows a touch of bad judgment, but otherwise a brilliant and ravishing creature." She bit back several retorts. "You can't blame a guy for asking," he added. "One of these days you'll say 'yes' and find out what you were missing." He puffed out his chest and preened outrageously until she had to laugh.

"You must love all those old silent comedians like Charlie Chaplin and Buster Keaton," she said, glad to have seized a safe topic.

"Yup. Those guys were incredible. Buster Keaton especially. I used to try out his minor stunts when I was a kid. Hey, I've got a great biography of Keaton if you'd like to borrow it." He jumped up and began running his eye over the bookshelves, knelt down, pulled out a book from the bottom shelf and handed it to her.

"Hey, since you're Mr. Connections, I have a question for you. Do you know anyone in advertising?"

"Sure, I have a college buddy at Sarcosi and Brand downtown."

"Do they handle commercials?"

He gave her a bemused look. "Definitely. They're the biggest ad agency in Boston; haven't you heard of them?"

She did not rise to the bait. "No. Listen, do you think he'd do you a favor? It sounds cheesy, but I know a little girl who would be wonderful in commercials. She's adorable. 'Personality plus,' as my sister says." She widened her eyes. "Is there any chance...?"

"Well, my friend, Bart, would have some ideas, that's for sure, but it would help if I had seen the kid and could vouch for her. I've never done this kind of thing before, and I don't want to tick Bart off." A vague unease flitted across his features.

"If you're willing to meet her I would be glad to set it up." She could feel the possibilities opening for Angelica, and it excited her. "I'd be very grateful, David."

"I want to ask how grateful," he said with a twinkle in his eye, "but don't worry, I won't."

Ariella looked down at the Buster Keaton book, flipped through it for a moment, placed it on the couch and stood. "Maybe I should think about heading home," she said, picking up her dishes and carrying them off to the kitchen.

"Do you have to?" He followed.

"I probably should," she told the kitchen sink as she rinsed her plate. "I have a big day tomorrow."

"Well, I hope my invitation isn't driving you away."

At that she turned, rubbing her wet hands on her black pants. "It's okay, David. It's really okay. I'm kind of tempted, that's all, and I'm not going to give in; so we might as well call it a lovely evening and, well...." She faltered, and he handed her a dish towel, and she absently rubbed her hands in it for a moment trapped between the sink and the warmth in his eyes. Then he gently removed the towel and walked out of the kitchen, leaving her to trail behind, collecting her bag and the biography on the way to the front door. He held her coat for her with straight arms stretched away from his body, but she slipped her arms around the sides of the coat, crushing it as she clasped him around the waist and lay her head on his shoulder. "Please don't be hurt. I'm here for you. This just isn't the right time for either of us." She could feel the laughter shaking his chest.

"While we're on the clichés, I'll just have to remind you of that old Stones tune, 'Time is on my Side,'" he said. "Although maybe "You Can't Always Get What You Want' is more apt."

She giggled, released herself from the hug and opened the glass door. "You're impossible. Just so long as you don't start singing 'Under my Thumb....'" She threw the coat over her shoulders and let herself out into the frigid night air.

15

The following morning Ariella found herself in the dirt-streaked foyer of a turn-of-the-century brick building on the Fenway facing a sign board in a glass case that listed the Massage Therapy Institute, Healthy Women Inc., Holistic Health Group, Massachusetts Asthma Association, and Jerry the Giraffe's group, The End Smoking Project. Pushing her way through the heavy swinging door she made her way along narrow corridors, up a creaky staircase and past a host of closed, unmarked doors to the back of the building, where she found TESP, its door decorated with an enormous poster of a cowboy-hatted skeleton dangling a cigarette from its bony fingers.

With a limp handshake Jerry Lesniak ushered her inside, his own gaunt frame a humorous counterpoint to the poster. He was a tall, long-necked, rumpled man whose appearance matched the cramped office, which, he explained, Sisters of Providence Hospital grudgingly leased to him. Across the desk he greeted her with kind eyes framed in black squares, glasses that reminded her of old Woody Allen movies. On the desk was a crumpled paper bag, its aroma of stale onion rings wafting into the close atmosphere.

"I like your tie," she said, admiring the dubious charm of a polyester, mud-colored appendage dotted with red international no-smoking symbols.

"We sell them, you know." He rummaged around and pulled a handful from a drawer, waving them gleefully. Around him lay chaos. Half his file drawers stood open with papers sticking out in every direction. On the floor, the windowsills, the chairs, on every surface papers vied for attention. She longed to take a broom and sweep half of it out one of the smudged little windows.

"So, Mr. Lesniak, what have you got for me? What's this big story you're pitching?" Her nostrils flared as she stifled a yawn and tried to look alert. She felt sluggish, perhaps from the previous night's drinking, or was she getting sick? Outside a cold rain fell on slushy streets, and the temperature hovered around 35 degrees, perfect weather to promote a chill. Or was she just moping because Sam had not called her? Nina always told her that half her minor ailments were psychosomatic. With effort she dragged her mind to the man in front of her.

"The Tobacco Research Association—you know, TRA, the industry's trade group that lobbies in Washington, D.C.? Well, they've always claimed to be studying smoking and disease—though they never seem to find that it actually causes any diseases. All their research has to conclude that smoking is safe, and it's some other factor causing all that lung cancer, emphysema, heart disease. Our organization got interested in who is doing the industry's dirty research, especially today when the evidence linking smoking with, say, cancer, is staggering. It seemed like it had to be some pretty sleazy medical researchers who would even consent to try to prove otherwise."

"Why does the industry actually want to do any research if it's so likely to prove their product is lethal?"

He leaned forward across the desk, resting on his elbows. "To keep up the fiction of an ongoing controversy. They need to keep saying there's not enough proof yet that smoking is dangerous. And for another thing, they promised and then kind of set themselves up in the research business. Ever heard of the 'Frank Statement to Cigarette Smokers?'" When she shook her head he hurtled on. "In 1963, the TRA published this full-page ad in all the major newspapers. They said they were concerned about the claims that smoking might be harmful and that they were committed to producing the safest, healthiest possible cigarettes. So as of that day they were setting up a research fund. They promised to 'get to the bottom' of the issue and to keep the public informed of their conclusions."

"Wow!" She could hardly believe they had been stupid enough and arrogant enough to make such a promise in print.

"Never heard of the 'Frank Statement,' huh? Well, you probably weren't even born then." He stood, turned his back and began digging in a file drawer. "Of course, it also helps them with litigation to be doing pseudo-research. They can get on the witness stand and defy all the medical data against them and say, '*Our* scientists haven't found a shred of evidence proving cigarettes cause cancer.'"

"So do they run their own labs?"

"They do, but those scientists are mostly cooking up tobacco products, adding extra nicotine, etc. They don't do much cancer research. No, the TRA gives out grants to money-hungry researchers all over the country. They give it to anybody with a hypothesis that something other than cigarettes causes cancer—milk, Martian invaders, anything!"

"So what's the local angle?"

"We think that our very own world-famous Carver Cancer Center is taking tobacco money. The TRA, whose products cause 440,000 American deaths per year, is funding Carver researchers. Now don't you find that a little sickening? Not to mention the conflict of interest. Nobody takes tobacco money and then comes out with anti-tobacco findings...."

"Are you saying that Carver isn't rigorously pursuing research on tobacco and lung cancer?" She thought of Sam and could not imagine him falsifying data or holding back results, but of course, there were many researchers at Carver.

Jerry shook his head. "No, lung cancer research is over and done with. The hot research now is on how smoking increases the risk of breast, cervical, bladder and other cancers. Of course, the industry says these claims are totally false, a conspiracy by a bunch of health nuts to deny adults their God-given right to smoke."

"And Carver?" she prompted.

He echoed her own thoughts. "Oh, Carver is big and diverse. I'm sure some folks are doing good research there. But how can a medical center devoted to the eradication of cancer take money from the nation's biggest cancer-causer? If the story got out I doubt all those wealthy donors whose loved ones died of cancer would keep quietly giving. People in this town would be up in arms."

Ariella nodded. "Even foundation grants might dry up. Foundations are big on purity these days. After the much-publicized problems at United Way, they're all leery of scandal."

"And I wonder whether Carver researchers are cynically pursuing dubious hypotheses on TRA money, especially if they know Carver is producing other contradictory studies."

"Well, wondering isn't enough for a *Times* story," said Ariella with asperity. "My editor won't touch this until you can get me facts. Which researchers at Carver take TRA grants, what are they studying with that money, and does their research ignore the findings of other Carver researchers?"

"It's really tough to find out exactly what studies TRA is funding. I thought you might find it easier, being a reporter." He was whining, and it annoyed her.

"Look, I'm sure you can get the facts if you want to," she said more sharply than she intended. She did not want to take out her frustration with Sam on Jerry Lesniak; so she softened her tone, explaining, "I have to be convinced that there's a story here before I'll work on it. Once you give me names I'll be glad to go over to Carver and ask some hard questions." She was surprised at herself for taking such a hard line with Lesniak. A few months ago she would probably have agreed to do all the story research herself, but somehow today she heard Joyce's voice warning her to think of her career and not to let people walk all over her. If she could not control Sam she would at least control her work.

"All right. I'll work on getting you names and some documentation." He looked glum.

Her next question would not improve his mood, but she had to ask: "And by the way, can you give me the name of a local tobacco industry rep so that I can get both sides?"

To her shock, he brightened instantly. "Hey, great idea. Hit up old Brendan Dornan for the info. If you can convince him you're doing a pro-industry piece he might even tell you all about TRA's generous support of medical research!"

"And, uh, who is Brendan Dornan and how do I reach him?"

"Oh, he's TRA's Massachusetts lobbyist, their main one anyway. He's always up at the State House opposing me on pro-health bills. Dornan, Grubb and Withers, Associates: 691-0422. By all means give Brendan a call. But be careful—he's not as nice as he looks."

16

Sunday dawned clear, dry and slightly warmer than the previous week. Angelica arrived at Ariella's apartment first, shoulders taut as wire, in a long-sleeved, lime-green dress with a square neckline and enough Lycra in the fabric to display all the contours of her slim curves, a slash of red lipstick brightening her face. She had arranged her hair in a complex style, some atop her head, some tendrils curling down to her shoulders, the effect infinitely more sophisticated than Ariella remembered her. Clinging to her mother's leg, Yolanda eyed her hostess with suspicion. She wore a dress too, high-waisted in white cotton patterned with brightly colored tropical fruit, a red ribbon tied like a headband in her wind-tossed curls. It was the first weekend after her dinner with David, and Ariella flushed with hope that his good nature would propel her protégé into the spotlight. She could not quite understand the extent of her nervous anticipation, but there was no time to analyze it with Angelica bursting into chatter.

"So how's it going? Nice place you got. This is Yolanda. She's doing her shy act at the moment, but she'll get over it. Is the editor here?" Angelica was swiveling her head in every direction as if expecting David to pop out from behind the draperies.

"No, not yet. Hi, Yolanda!" Ariella tried to mimic Angelica's pronunciation of the name, which sounded like 'Jolanda,' and squatted on the floor about three feet from the child to look into her eyes. "You're a beautiful little girl," she said sincerely, struck by the huge, dark eyes, the perfectly rounded nose and cheeks and the strawberry mouth. "How would you like a cookie? I bake some very special cookies my grandma taught me to make."

Suddenly light dawned on the little face, lips twitched, then broadened to a smile. "Gookie," said Yolanda softly.

"You are definitely the cutest thing I've seen in a long time," said Ariella, shaking her head in mock despair.

"Don't swell her head," Angelica growled, but when Ariella glanced up at her she looked pleased. They drifted to the couch where a plate of molasses and spice cookies waited on the coffee table and Yolanda snatched one with a sidelong look at her mother. Angelica said "si, si" and launched into some rapid-fire Spanish that Ariella did not understand.

"I've got bagels and coffee, grapefruit or orange juice...."

"Coffee! I could definitely use some coffee. D'you make it strong? I can't drink that watery Boston stuff."

"Oh, I'll make you a strong pot right now. It'll only take a second." She crossed the living room to the kitchen and took the coffee from her freezer. "I know what you mean because my mom is that way. I used to say she'd sleep through life without strong coffee." Ariella could hear the acid tone in her voice and regretted it. She should not be criticizing her mother to a virtual stranger.

But Angelica responded with surprising acuteness, "Yeah, my Mami was like that, afraid of her own shadow, liked nothing better than to be napping or watching the soaps. Not me, man. I'm impatient. I gotta be out there making a stand, beating the bushes for what I want. And you're like that too, aren't you?"

Ariella nodded slowly. "I'm active," she replied, "and curious; so I always poke my nose into things, even when maybe I should leave well enough alone."

"Nah, I don't believe in that. 'Leave it be' is just an excuse for spineless weasels. Renaldo is always telling me to "let it alone," and he's got less backbone than God gave a slug."

Ariella laughed, and the phone rang. "That must be David," she said, reaching for the telephone. "He's not really an editor, by the way; he's the *Times* health reporter." Then she was speaking to David and pressing the buzzer to let him into the building lobby. A moment later he was knocking.

"Oooh, muy bonita!" David winked at Ariella and eyed Angelica with admiration. After a lightning once-over, he addressed her directly. "Buenos dias, senora. Me llamo David Ellmann. Como se llama usted? Que bonitos ojos tienes!" he rattled off, bending in an exaggerated bow. Angelica's eyes lit with challenge as she told him in a disparaging tone that he must have gotten C's in Spanish class and then launched into Spanish herself.

"What did he say?" asked Ariella rhetorically, as neither one was paying any attention to her. She had rarely seen David flirt so obviously with a complete stranger—it perplexed her.

"Pitty eyes," said a small voice.

Ariella looked down at Yolanda who was clutching a glass elephant lifted from a low shelf. "What sweetie?"

"Pitty eyes."

Angelica stopped speaking Spanish long enough to explain, pointing to her daughter. "Big ears down here is telling you he said 'pretty eyes.'" Ariella couldn't believe David had come out with that—and that one-year-old Yolanda had actually translated it.

"Hey, no fair," protested David while Ariella broke in, "Amazing! Thank you, Yolanda sweetie. You're amazing. Some day you'll be working for the U.N.!" She knelt to gently extract the figurine from the girl's hand and substitute a smooth brass hippo that her niece had always loved. "David, you've been holding out on me. I had no idea you could speak that much Spanish."

"Four years in high school, three years in college, a semester in Spain; it's a wonder I'm still so bad at it."

"You're really not that bad," countered Angelica. "Only I'll never understand why American schools insist on teaching the kids to speak Spanish like some Castilian prince's snotty grandmother when not one of the Latinos they're gonna meet in real life will ever talk that way." She screwed up her face and gave a high-pitched, simpering imitation of David's accent. David barked laughter, and Ariella grinned, then intervened.

"Let's get down to business—in English if you don't mind since the only Spanish I know is an insult my college roommate taught me."

"What insult?" Angelica's eyes fixed on her.

"Come on, spill it, Richardson." David had crossed the room and sprawled in her rose-patterned armchair.

Ariella hesitated for a moment. "Two no tennis pinga."

"Ugh, you butchered it. Tu no tienes pinga!" The words rolled from Angelica's tongue like melting chocolate.

"Pinga? What's pinga?" asked David.

Ariella looked embarrassed, and Angelica looked smug.

"It's slang. I'm not sure I should say more in front of a toddler," Ariella said, and Angelica added, "You know, Mr. Happy," gesturing vaguely toward her crotch.

David's eyes opened wide, and he laughed. "Ahhh. Okay, this talk of missing private parts is making me nervous. Let's get down to talking about this charming young lady." He gestured to Yolanda who was offering him one of her half-eaten cookies. "So I have a friend in advertising, Bart Wexler," he began, gesturing for them to sit down. Angelica perched on the sofa end closest to him, and Ariella pulled in a kitchen chair, taking the moment to bring some glasses, a pitcher of orange juice and the coffee pot to the table. Her mind wandered while David described his first meeting with Bart years ago and some of Bart's accomplishments in the ad business, something about a "wacky" beer commercial with a chimp in a clown costume. Angelica was laughing far more in David's presence than Ariella would have thought possible, and her whole body had softened from its usual rigid lines into a slim roll of dough. Just when Ariella could no longer stand Angelica's silent absorption in this meandering tale, she interrupted with her usual fire:

"So do I have to sleep with this guy to get my baby in pictures or what?"

David raised his eyebrows but to Ariella's relief did not take the bait. "What you really need to do is get this guy that Bart recommended to shoot a quick portfolio and some video of Yolanda to see how she does in front of a pro camera, and then meet with this woman agent he suggested who handles toddlers. I've got the names right here." He pulled out his wallet and extricated a yellow scrap of paper.

With a crumpled face Angelica let slip a Spanish curse and then clapped a hand over her mouth and glanced guiltily from her daughter's face to David's, but David just laughed. "Who said that?" He formed a spyglass with his hand, circled an eye with it and peered into the high corners of the room.

"Listen, King Clown, how do we know these are reputable people who won't take Yolanda for a ride?—" put in Ariella, "and how much do they cost?" Angelica gave her a grateful look.

"Oh, they're not going to charge. It's been arranged." David nodded for emphasis when met with two skeptical pairs of eyes. "They're friends of Bart's, and he'll make sure they get their cut when Yolanda becomes the next Shirley Temple."

"Are you sure?" Angelica stared into his face with a fierceness akin to anger.

"Absolutely."

With a little cry Angelica launched herself at him, threw her arms around his neck and kissed him soundly on the cheek. Ariella could not suppress a grimace, which luckily neither of them noticed. He had reddened, and Angelica drew back slightly, squatting about a foot from his knee, but continued spouting gratitude in Spanish.

"We're in hot water, Yolanda." Ariella was about to kneel to the child's level when a knock on the door distracted her. Who on earth could it be? It had to be the 'super'—only he ever appeared at the door without ringing from the lobby. This did not seem like a particularly good time for him to appear, but she did not want to irritate a man who kept her plumbing running. Without even checking the peephole, she flung the door open and gazed dumb-founded at Sam Becker.

"Hi Ariella." His eyes crinkled with amusement at her surprise. "May I come in?"

"Uh, sure." Grudgingly she stepped aside to let him into the scene, wondering whether his presence would spoil the fledgling business and personal relationship within. Adding to her surprise, he kissed her lightly on the check on his way past, and as she turned she met David's bemused expression.

"I'm David Ellman," he said, rising and stretching out his hand, ever eager for a story.

"Sam Becker." The men shook hands, but Sam quickly turned to Angelica and Yolanda, who was hugging her mother's leg, her enormous eyes trained on this imposing newcomer. Snapping back into hostess mode, Ariella introduced "my friend, Angelica" to "Sam, a scientist I know." She did not mention the vaccine trials, breathlessly explaining that they were looking into Yolanda's future in commercials, although a minute later she wondered why she had blurted out what was none of his business.

"Sorry to interrupt," he said, "but I'm here gambling that you're the kind of woman who can't resist the ballet."

"The ballet?" Her mind whirled, taking in his pressed white shirt and a red tie with tiny acrobats tumbling across the silk, the gray slacks and tweed jacket, and trying to avoid the trap of his deep eyes.

"Roland just gave me two tickets to the matinee, Boston Ballet's new *Cinderella*. Cecile was going to take Margaret, but she's got the flu. Would you like to go?" He ignored the appraisal of her guests and focused on her face as she struggled to respond.

"Sure," she said finally, attempting a light touch. "What time is the curtain?"

"Two o'clock." His eyes reflected glee and perhaps a hint of surprise that he had succeeded so easily.

"Oh, Sam, I love dance," she gushed suddenly, "And the reviews of that production have been fantastic. It's supposed to be sublime—the new choreography, the costumes, the sets...."

"Wait till you see it before you get excited."

Her eyes glowed. "No way." She turned back to David, who was eyeing her with a mixture of humor and speculation, and Angelica, whose face was set with suspicion. "So what do we have to do to wrap up this meeting so I can get dressed up? Or better yet, why don't you two continue without me? You don't really need me, do you?"

"I don't know," said Angelica. "Maybe we do." She was giving Ariella a hard stare.

"No." David put in quickly. "We don't. Let these two have their fun." He gave the phrase a sexual tinge. "I can lock up here, Ari. I've done it before." He let that remark hang.

17

Light snow dusted Sam's jacket as he walked Ariella from the parking garage to the Wang Center, the newly renovated theater where Boston Ballet made its home. After a moment's hesitation he grasped her forearm with a light squeeze. If she protested he would chide her about wearing high heels on an icy day, but she did not object. He could hardly believe that they were together with no work agenda. It felt good to be out with a beautiful woman on a Sunday afternoon instead of caged in the lab like a rat. If he were honest with himself he would admit that only this woman would draw him out, that although he was determined to keep his emotions in check this time, he had given in to his craving to see her.

He had Roland to thank for the excuse. Roland thought he was subtle, but he was obviously working to throw the two together. Sam was not sure why, but then that was Roland: he formed snap judgments, moved heaven and earth to get his way, usually got it, and often turned out to be right.

Ariella walked quickly for a woman, particularly a petite one. She matched his stride, which pleased him. In fact she was gliding along beside him with so much repressed excitement that he had ask, "Did you ever dance yourself?"

"Oh, yes. I danced for years. From age four to age sixteen. My mom has yards of pink tutus to prove it. That was one thing my mom and I really had in common, our love of dance. She took me to dozens of ballets, and she never missed one of my performances, even if she had to drive hours across Florida to get there."

Sam smiled at the image of her in a pink tutu and at her contagious enthusiasm. It seemed to seep into him through the fingers he had laced around her arm. "My mother loved ballet too. She told me many times about her very first time—when Aunt Helen and Uncle Charles took her to *Coppélia* at the Royal Ballet in London. She was only seven years old, but she remembered it for a lifetime."

"The Royal Ballet—how marvelous! Why was she in London?"

"Oh, she grew up there, from '34 to '48. She saw *Coppélia* before the war broke out." Perhaps the memory of that magical night at the ballet had helped sustain his mother through all the privations, bombings and losses of her London childhood, but he did not want to share all that with Ariella.

"So did she take you to the ballet?"

"Yes, she dragged me along with my sister, Debbie. I must say that at first I didn't think much of it, but after a while I became enamored of ballet music, and then when I hit those randy preteen years I just loved the chance to see scantily clad women." He grinned at her. "Actually I developed quite an affection for ballet, and even a little knowledge."

Ariella's eyebrows had risen. "That's rare in a man."

"I know—gives me an edge over the competition."

"Tell me about it. My boyfriends found dance

performances horribly boring."

Sam stifled his desire to inquire about the boyfriends. If he wanted to remain detached he had better not think about other men in her life. He was not surprised to hear that she was a dancer, though; he had suspected it from the first, something in the way she carried herself. It also helped to explain his attraction—ballerinas had always fascinated him.

When they reached the massive doors of the Wang Center the crowd embraced them—like a bacterium swallowed by a macrophage cell, he thought, and then let out a little laugh at his whimsy. She looked at him inquiringly, he explained, and she shook her head in amusement, black curls tossing in a way that made him suddenly yearn to run his fingers through them. She was gazing around, absorbing every detail of the restored grand entrance hall, ornately carved pillars sparkling with gold leaf and ruby-colored carpeting up the broad stairway, although little of that was visible beneath so many feet.

After disengaging his hand from her arm to show their tickets to an usher, he found his fingers reaching for her again as soon as they took to the stairs. When their fingers met and hers curled warmly around his he felt a current shoot through his body. It unnerved him a little, but he did not let go. A bedroom image floated into his mind, and he banished it fast.

"I hope the seats are good."

"I'm sure they'll be fine. I'm so grateful to you for inviting me. I hadn't seen the new Wang Center, and I actually haven't been to the ballet since I moved to Boston. I've really missed it."

"Expensive, isn't it?"

"Yes. It's hard on my salary. I didn't pick a very

lucrative profession." She squeezed his hand for no apparent reason, sending heat coursing up his arm. He hadn't felt so sensitive to a woman's touch for years. It must be the effect of his long drought, he thought—only he did not remember ever feeling this way about Sarah's tiniest touch, not once in their five-year relationship. He swallowed and resolutely thrust his hands into his pockets.

Then they reached the doorway usher and followed her to their seats, perfectly placed in the center of the orchestra level. Ariella shrugged out of her long wool coat, arranged it carefully on the back of her chair and sank into it. Seated, her dress fell only to mid-thigh, exposing most of her crossed black-stockinged legs. He dragged his gaze to the program and thumbed through to an article on the history of the *Cinderella* ballet. Ariella stowed her purse beneath the seat and opened her own program. In moments the house lights dimmed, the conductor's head appeared to a polite round of applause, and the first strains of the overture filled the hall with anticipation.

When the curtain fell on the first act, he slid his arm around Ariella's shoulders. "So are you enjoying it?"

She leaned her head against his arm and gave him a breath-taking smile. "Oh, Sam. It's absolutely wonderful. Cinderella is exquisite, and the Ugly Sisters—they're so funny!"

"They're male dancers, aren't they?" It was more a statement than a question.

"Yes, well, men often dance those roles, at least in Sir Frederick Ashton's choreography."

"Umm. The program said Ashton himself used to dance one of the sister roles at the Royal Ballet, the downtrodden one."

"Yes." She sighed. "It would be incredible to see the Royal Ballet."

Her face was so close to his and so filled with joy that he had an insane desire to squeeze her cheeks between his two hands, kiss her soundly and promise to take her to London immediately. He settled for tracing her jaw line with his forefinger. Trapped in the center of the aisle, he made no move to seek the lobby during the intermission, content to revel in the forced closeness of their seats, and she did not object. All too soon for him the bell sounded, the lights dimmed, and the music began again as the curtain rose on the second act, Cinderella's Ball. His hand twitched, and then he let it slide across the arm rest, take hers in his own, and idly caress her fingers for the remainder of the performance.

When the ballet ended, Ariella was on her feet in seconds to give the principal dancers a standing ovation. As he moved to follow her she turned, leaned down to his face and kissed him lingeringly.

"Thank you *so* much for this, Sam." She was blushing but did not stop talking. "You have no idea how much it meant to me!" Pulling him up she clapped furiously and rose to her tiptoes to catch last glimpses of the ballerina who played Cinderella. He clapped too, still savoring the kiss, determined to bring her home with him. He glanced at his watch—five o'clock. The applause was finally dying down and the audience beginning to filter out.

"What are you doing for dinner?" he asked.

"Not much."

"Would you come over to my place? It's right on Commonwealth Ave., very close to your apartment, actually. I can show you my etchings."

Her eyes responded with a hint of laughter, but her

lips pressed together as if to hold back assent. In her long pause before responding he twined his fingers in hers. "Yes," she said finally. "I would like that."

They slid down the aisle and glided to the door, holding hands, Ariella still floating on a cloud of music and movement, Sam aware that his cloud was more of lust than Prokoviev, yet illuminated by her enthusiasm. As they stepped into the street she stopped to put on her slim leather gloves.

"Ariella," said a familiar voice, and he groaned inaudibly when he recognized her boss with the same half-sneer on her face as at the Chan's party. "And Dr. Becker— what a coincidence. Were you two at the ballet together?"

"Yes." Ariella had dropped his hand like a hot coal and stiffened. "We just saw the matinee—marvelous performance. Were you in there too?"

"No, just walking past. I have an appointment around the corner. So you decided to take my reporter to the ballet, did you Becker? Softening her up, eh?"

"Happened to have an extra ticket."

"A good line; old, but plausible. Have you heard the latest on the Griffin story, Ariella? They held a secret funeral today for the baby. To keep us press vultures away. But the *News* somehow found out and got the scoop."

"How sad!" Sam muttered.

"Yeah, we should have had that story. But a bigger one's on the way, mark my words. The Boston Police are still mostly Irish and Catholic, and they get upset about the death of a baby named Mary Christine Griffin. Someone's going to pay for that baby's death. Well, on that cheery note I'll leave you two to your evening. I'm glad we got your cancer research story in print, Ari," she said pointedly. "Don't do anything I wouldn't do."

As soon as she was out of earshot he asked, "Why does that woman wear so much black? She looks like a crow."

"I don't know." Ariella looked withdrawn, and he cursed his luck. He knew those last two comments were intended to make Ariella feel guilty about dating him and to keep her out of his bed.

"Still game?"

As she examined her gloved hands he found himself captivated by her incredibly long eyelashes; then she lifted her chin, hesitated, studied his face for a moment. "Sam, I forgot to ask you something. You told me one time you knew I lived on Clarendon Street in the Back Bay. How did you know?"

He tugged on his earlobe, then looked her straight in the eye. "I looked you up on the internet, kind of checked you out. I was very curious about you, couldn't get you off my mind, and I found my fingers initiating a little search one day. In fact, I invited myself over to your place that first time for the same reason. We could easily have gone to mine, but I really wanted to see your home. I didn't mean to be devious."

Squaring her shoulders she nodded, took his hand again and marched them toward the garage. "It's okay. I understand about insatiable curiosity." She cocked her head upward, eyes glinting at him. "And any good reporter would do the same."

His spirits began to rise.

18

The foyer of Sam's building, although in the same neighborhood, was grander than hers. The gilt-edged mirror reflected the crystal chandelier overhead and the vase of lilies on the mahogany occasional table below. As they waited in front of spotless mirrored doors for the elevator to arrive, Ariella noted that the flutter of nerves inside did not show in her reflection. Following him to his apartment meant nothing, she told herself; she could leave at any time. But even as she reassured herself she knew that accompanying him home had given him a message. She wished that she had firmly decided how far she wanted this relationship to go, but she hadn't.

The old elevator lifted them at an unhurried pace, releasing them to a floor with only two doors at either ends of a corridor. Sam led her to the left, opening a black door into a spacious square foyer with creamy walls, an emerald oriental carpet and hand-carved moldings. He took her coat and hung it in an enormous, empty front closet. To the left a doorway opened into the dining room, although Sam clearly used the room for work rather than dining. Papers and journals scattered the dining room table covering its entire surface, and along the back wall of the room below two picture windows lay a computer table and desktop heavy with machines.

"This is my lair," he was saying. "I've got the complete communications set-up: fax, modem, copier...."

She noticed no pictures on the dining room walls. A door from the dining room gave a partial view of the kitchen. Glancing right from the foyer beyond the closet she could see through another doorway into a sunken living room, and beyond the dining room to the left lay a hallway, presumably to the bedroom and bath. She had no time to investigate because he brought her straight to the kitchen.

"So what shall we do? I can cook something for you or order out. Maybe Indian. There's a fantastic place around the corner, India Palace, that delivers. I have to admit I don't cook as much as I might. Work takes precedence."

"Either way," she said. "Indian would be lovely."

In the kitchen corner polished wooden benches built into the wall around a square table formed a breakfast nook, an elegant version of a cozy diner booth. Ariella slipped into one of the seats and ran her palm against the Mexican tiles set into the tabletop. Fishing a paper menu from a drawer Sam slid in beside her. His side pressed against her, and she leaned into it, the heat of him branding her from shoulder to ankle, and to prolong the contact she dallied over what to eat. She had never experienced such magnetism in a man, and she laughed inwardly at her own reaction.

"Why are you smiling?" He turned her chin toward him with his index finger. When she did not respond he searched her eyes for a moment then bent to kiss her. Torrents of heat rose in her, and she reached for him almost without thought, her fingers twining in his hair to keep him with her. At length he broke away, eyes glittering. He brushed a lock of hair from her face. "So what was it we wanted to order?"

They chose a curry and a spinach dish, rice, nan bread and several chutneys. Sam disentangled himself from her and from the bench, called in the order and rustled up a bottle of wine, which he uncorked and poured into heavy glass goblets that he told her had belonged to his mother.

"If I'm not going to cook, then let's go into the living room," he said, taking her hand to pull her to her feet again. Ariella dropped his hand when she reached the door and trailed after him with her wine glass dangling, taking a peek down the dark hallway beyond the dining room in a vain effort to see his bedroom. Three shallow steps led down to the living room, oversize windows on two walls providing views across Commonwealth Avenue and on across the rooftops of Boston's Back Bay. Like the rest of the place, the living room was sparsely furnished but with elegant old pieces, a mahogany and glass keepsake cabinet in a corner, a flowered antique wing chair beneath a window, and a long navy sofa with carved feet dominating the far wall.

"Your furniture is beautiful." Crossing the room she peered into the shelves of the glass cabinet.

"It was all my mother's, except for the coffee table and the bookcases. My sister insisted that I take these pieces after Mom died. Deb already had a lot of antiques that belonged to my Uncle Charles and Aunt Helen; so she wanted me to have these. This cabinet in particular meant the world to my mother because it was the only thing of her parents' she ever had."

"Why?"

"Oh, it's a long story. She was sent to England from Vienna when she was four years old—with her older sister—

and she never saw her parents again."

"World War II?"

"Yes."

Ariella sighed and touched his arm in a comforting gesture. He was surprised and relieved that she did not pry further—so she was actually capable of stifling her questioning nature. He pointed out several Royal Doulton figurines that he had loved since childhood, particularly the Court Jester standing on his head. Suddenly she darted to the other side of the room and curled up on one corner of the sofa, kicking off her shoes and tucking her feet under her. She needed to sit to calm her nerves and decide whether she really wanted to seduce or escape.

"I love old things," she said. "Your mother had wonderful taste." She did not mention that her family too had suffered wartime loss.

"European taste," he amended. "The Viennese artist tradition ran strong in her, along with Germanic strong-mindedness and a touch of English restraint. She never was the slightest bit Americanized despite living here for forty years."

"Funny how that happens. Well, I could never call my mom strong-minded."

"What's she like?"

"Like a mouse. Oh, she's quite the American. Born in New York to poor, immigrant parents. Her dad was a traveling salesman, quickly took up a southern route and moved his eight kids to Florida. She spent most of her life there and never wanted to set foot outside her garden. Only she's in Italy now...." Ariella broke off, feeling foolish. Why was she discussing her mother with a man she hardly knew when she made it a policy not to discuss her with anybody?

This was not the proper prelude to seduction.

"Italy?"

"My dad's on sabbatical in Padua this year, writing a book, and Mom got dragged along. But we don't have to talk about her."

"Why not?" He had settled beside her on the couch and was regarding her with intensity. "I'm curious. You don't get along too well, do you?"

"Well, we're very different," she temporized, as usual amazed at how astutely he read her. "My mom is exceedingly timid, and I never was. When I was little I climbed trees and got stuck, chased raccoons till one bit me, hitched a ride on the back of the postal truck. I was always doing something that frightened my mother; I couldn't seem to help it, and she never approved of me. It's the old story: Nina was the good girl, and I was the bad girl. So when I turned sixteen I left home, and Mom and I have never been the same since."

"You ran away?"

"Well, it wasn't all that dramatic. I just moved in with a friend and her family for a year, and then I went to college early." He waited until she added, "U. Penn. Far, far from Florida. That was the last straw for Mom, I think. She wanted me to follow my sister to the University of Florida, which is where my dad teaches. I don't think she ever even considered another possibility."

"She loved you enough to want you nearby."

"It was stifling, though. I have this fiery curiosity in me, and she was never proud of it; she just tried to keep it down." Ariella did not know why she had told him this much, but she was somehow glad she had. "But it's water under the bridge now. I only wish that Mom would try to understand my life."

"Maybe she's trying."

"Maybe." She knew she suddenly sounded peevish, but she did not want his advice. "You wouldn't understand. It sounds like your mom was more of the sainted variety."

"Oh, she was no saint, and we had our disagreements. But you know something, Ariella. You've only got one mother, and she won't be around forever. So maybe it's worth giving her the benefit of the doubt."

His voice held an uncompromising quality that made her think for a moment about how the world would feel without her mother. She had rarely ever entertained such a notion, and an image sprang to mind of the bowl of brittle beach-tossed shells in her mother's sewing room. "I don't understand her very well," she said at last, dismissing the image. "I could try to talk to her again...."

The telephone rang, and he rose and disappeared to the kitchen, leaving her to gaze pensively out the window. It was almost impossible to believe that her parents would one day no longer be a phone call away; yet this year she had already met two people not much older than herself who had lost parents: Angelica and Sam.

When he called her into the dining room he had cleared most of the table of papers and set it with blue-rimmed white stoneware plates, clearly his own not his mother's. In fact she felt she had left parents behind in the living room. The food arrived moments later, he produced and lit a blue octagonal candle, and they settled down to eat.

"It was so sweet of Roland to give us those tickets," she said between bites of spinach that melted in her mouth. The room had grown dark in early winter twilight, and aside from the flame Sam made no move to light it, although some light from the kitchen stole in behind her back.

"He hoped I would ask you. He likes you."

She looked him in the eye. "He thinks you're alone too much."

"Yeah. He's a good friend. What else did he tell you?"

"That you've known each other since college. That you weren't so serious back then…"

"Nope." He grinned suddenly. "He was my roommate for a couple years. We pulled a lot of stunts. You want me to tell you a story?" She nodded. He was irresistible when he was happy. "Freshman year there were some grouchy juniors at the end of the hall. One of them complained that our loud music kept him up so he couldn't get to class on time. Then there was a courtyard party, and the custodian put up an outdoor stage for the band—just some plywood on a lot of concrete blocks. I went to the party, did some drinking, and got inspired. So when the party was well over at 4 a.m., Roland and I and some friends from our floor stole those concrete blocks and bricked up the hallway. When the juniors woke up they not only couldn't get to class, they couldn't get to the stairs, not even the bathroom.

"Out the windows?"

"Well, we were on the third floor. They were pretty mad. Took them hours to break down that wall, but that's not the best part of the story. Two days later all of us at the other end of the hall got official letters in our mailboxes on the dean's stationery. They said we were accused of serious conduct violations punishable by expulsion. We were asked to meet with the dean the next morning to discuss the matter. Well, Roland hit the roof. He spent hours ranting about how he would be kicked out of Princeton, and then his parents would never speak to him again."

"What about you?"

"I wasn't as worried, but I was a little nervous. It wasn't a fun night. Then we woke up, went to brush our teeth before our morning interview with the dean, and found the full text of his letter in lipstick on the bathroom mirror."

"The juniors?"

"They just lifted some of the dean's stationery from his office, and presto, revenge."

She giggled. "I can almost see your faces in that bathroom. But why weren't you as worried as Roland?"

"I don't know. Guess I thought we could talk the dean out of it. Roland cares more than I do about what people think of him."

She studied his face in the flickering candlelight. His mouth beckoned. "You were pretty cocky."

He grinned. "Maybe." Then he pushed away from the table. "Let's clean up." In the silence that fell as they cleared the table she realized that she had been in his apartment for over two hours, and he had hardly touched her. They had talked and talked. He had been a perfect gentleman. And she was tired of it. She wanted to feel his lips on hers again; she wanted to know what he could do to her senses. As she stood in the kitchen doorway holding a plate, Joyce's disapproving face floated through her mind, but it only roused the rebel in her.

Still she stood motionless for several minutes admiring him from behind as he washed dishes and gathering her courage. Then she stole up behind him, pressed against his back and encircled him with her arms, feeling his heartbeat in her ear and against her palm, her hands still at first, then tugging his shirt free of his waistband to steal over his chest and stomach, tracing his nipples as she buried her mind in the simple sensation of skin she had yearned to touch. He made no sound, but she could feel a tremor go through him as he carefully rinsed the last plate, placed it in the dish drainer, wiped his hands on a towel hanging above the sink, and then turned swiftly. He bent to her, his kiss unyielding, his hands everywhere. She danced backwards drunkenly on tiptoe pulling out of reach then reaching for him, then backing away again with him guiding her all the while, kissing her, touching her.

"You damned elf." At his bedroom door he caught her face in his hands. "Little and magical and irresistible. Are you sure about this?"

"Yes."

With that he swept her from the carpet and carried her to a hulking bed covered in navy blue that dominated the empty room. Then he silenced her giggles with his mouth, and she was sliding from her clothes and he from his, and soon they were so tangled that she could hardly tell where her arm ended and his leg began. Every inch of his smooth strength touched some part of her until she felt so high and hazy she might have been flying. Wherever he touched her, her body sang. Then she drew him into her until for that one moment he was utterly hers, and she let thought go and submerged herself in his urgent rhythm, buried in an impenetrable dark cloud of sensation. She spun crazily in a black hole that had no end—till it shattered into stars.

When she emerged from it trembling she could hardly believe she was in one piece, but the bulk of him against her, pinning her to the mattress, reassured her. She smoothed her hands on his back, and when he moved to free her, she held tight, not letting him go. He raised his head to look into her eyes, and a flush of power spread through her that she had never felt before. Carl had never looked at her this way, as if memorizing her face, as if the world lay in her eyes. For this moment at least, the rope of desire that bound her to Sam bound him just as tightly.

"You're so sweet," he murmured, "so sweet."

19

That same Sunday morning that Angelica visited Ariella, her cousin Bobby's station wagon skidded on the icy Huntington Avenue trolley tracks as he careened past the Veteran's Hospital into Jamaica Plain, turned at the first traffic light and pulled into a familiar street, jumping the curb to rest on the edge of Papi's snow-dusted lawn. It wasn't much of a front yard, the size of a postage stamp, and Papi wouldn't care about tire tracks; he was no gardener. Papi was a faithful Catholic, though; so Bobby hoped his father had gone to the early mass and come home already. He leaned on the buzzer and then rubbed his bare hands together in the cold, his muffled curses hanging in white froth before his face. At length the creaking of footsteps on the old floors reassured him. The sound grew louder and then halted. Bobby knew Papi was peering at him through the peephole. He banged on the door.

"Papi? It's me, Bobby." The door swung open and the thin grizzled face of his father peered suspiciously around it.

"Cuál es el problema?"

"No problem, Papi. Come on, let me in. It's freezing out here."

"Pasa." Luis Rodriguez grudgingly stepped aside to let his son across the threshold and snapped the three bolts back into place. "You could at least wear a warm coat instead of that leather jacket. Maybe you wouldn't be so cold—and you wouldn't look like a thug."

Bobby crossed his arms over his narrow chest, hands gripping the black sleeves of the offending garment. His eyes simmered, but he did not take the bait, turning instead and leading his father along the mustard-carpeted hall to the back of the house. He felt the habitual airlessness of home seeping into his throat, the walls pressing inward, and when he reached the kitchen the blessed Virgin glowered down at him from her place of honor, so high over the table it seemed as if she rose closer to the stained ceiling every year.

"So, how are you, Papi?" Go to mass this morning?"

"Of course I went to mass. Prayed for your soul and your cousin's too—living in sin like she is. Bobby, qué pasó? Are you in trouble?"

Bobby slammed a hand down on the counter. "Why, Papi? Why you always assume I'm in trouble?"

"Maybe those drug dealer friends of yours have something to do with it. And the fact you never stick with a job...."

"I'm working security now. It's a good job; you know that. Papi, I didn't come here to fight with you. I need to talk to you. I need your advice. For once I try to do right by you, and what do you do?"

"Okay. Talk."

Bobby squeezed the back of a chair until his knuckles whitened, waiting while his father rounded the corner of the Formica-covered table and lowered himself into his usual place below the Virgin. "You see, I was over Angelica's place yesterday. She took the baby out someplace. It was just Renaldo and me, and we got to talking, and I ask him about that job that got him seven years at Walpole. So he tells me all about it—armed robbery, shot a guy in the leg. He pulls out a shoe box full of news clippings, shows me some from back then about the crime, even his arrest." Eyes riveted to his son, Luis grunted.

"Then I ask what else is in the box, and he says it's other jobs he done. Starts pulling out dozens of clippings, unsolved robberies, telling me about 'em. Even that liquor store job a couple months ago, Halloween night—you remember that one, Papi. It was all over the news." Bobby had started pacing.

"Madre de Dios! Por su puesto. In Allston." Luis swallowed hard, his Adam's apple bobbing beside the veins standing in relief against the tight skin of his rooster neck, as Bobby rushed on, intent on spilling out his whole story.

"Si, that one. I don't know why, but it was on my mind, and I ask him, 'Renaldo, how 'bout that Griffin job? Did you shoot them too? And Papi, he just looks at me real strange for a while, and then he says, 'Yeah,' and he laughs. I try to laugh too, but suddenly I'm feeling like a drowning man. Can't get my air and he's making me real nervous, drumming on the table and drinking out of a..." Bobby swore and looked at the ground.

"Scotch bottle? Or was it rum?" His father spit out.

"You knew. Tu sabias." Bobby swore again. "That part I wasn't going to say; I know how you feel about drinking, Papi. A thousand times I told Angelica he's a hard drinker—es un borrachon—but she don't listen. Well, that's what happened. I got out of there quick as I could. Been thinking about it all night. That poor Griffin woman..."

"Dios mio! What were you thinking? Trying to remember how to dial 911?"

Bobby looked him in the eye for the first time since he began his story. "I don't know what to do. What do I do?"

"What do you do? You call the police; that's what you do. Did you hear the morning news? Family had a private funeral for that poor little baby yesterday; Mary Christine, they called her; one month she lived. Never had no chance against a bullet wound. Our priest prayed for her in mass today. All the women were lighting candles, crying. Bobby, a man tells you he shot a pregnant woman to death for her jewelry, and you do nothing all night long? He's a double murderer! Think what he can do to Yoli and Angelica. Do you have any brain in your head?"

"I thought of that, Papi. I thought of that. But I wasn't sure. Maybe he was kidding about the Griffin shooting. Angelica knows he did time, and she's with him anyway. I told her to leave him before, but she never listened. So why would she now? And even if he shoots rich, white people, it don't mean he'd shoot Angelica. She's one of us."

"One of us? Are you crazy? He's Dominican trash. You know I can't stand Dominicans. They're messed up," lifting a palm to forestall argument, "and don't give me that Latino solidarity crap. I got good reason for my prejudice. I know what you think. You think the police are out to get you because they arrested you a few times. But that's your fault— driving around with drug dealers! Be a man. I know you're scared, but the Blessed Virgin will watch over you."

He stood, grabbed the receiver of the wall phone and held it toward Bobby, who glanced at the picture of the Madonna. "So, you gonna call?" The dial tone bleated in the stillness.

"I don't like cops. You know that. And what's Renaldo gonna do to me when he finds out?"

"Maybe he won't."

Bobby rolled his eyes.

"What's the matter with you, Bobby? I raised you right. A man shoots a pregnant woman dead like that, over and over in the stomach—and the husband in the hospital six weeks. It's sick, Bobby. Evil. You gonna let it go? Let scum like that walk the street? Listen, I have an idea. I know a vice squad detective at church, Fernando Diaz—why don't we call him, explain it all, and he'll pass it along. He won't do anything to you, Bobby; he's from San Juan, knew your Tia Mirza...."

"What about Angelica?" Bobby broke in. "Shouldn't we talk to her first? Tell her to get out of there? I think we owe her a call before we bring in the cops. What if they drag her off for questioning?"

"Serves her right for living with a man like that. Does she have any sense? You know she'll tell you back off, defend that piece of crap, maybe even tell him. No. The police come first. We're the men in the family. We take care of it. And then we take care of Angelica."

He punched some numbers into the telephone, pinning Bobby with his gaze. "Hola Fernando. Te necesito..."

20

Bobby stood hunched in a phone booth on a windy corner of Harrison Avenue outside the District D-4 police station, heart beating unpleasantly loudly as he listened to the phone ringing. On the fourth ring, Angelica picked up.

"Ana, it's Bobby. Is Renaldo there?"

"No, he'll be out till late; what's up?"

"Good. That's good. Now listen. You gotta pack up some clothes for you and Yoli and come to my place tonight."

"What?"

"Don't argue with me. Just do it!"

"Don't you yell at me, Bobby. You sound terrible— what's wrong with you?"

"Look, Renaldo told me something last night, okay? Something real bad he did."

"Oh, Bobby, if you're getting into that again, I know he did time for armed robbery. But things are different for him now. Why don't you just butt out for a change...?"

"No! Ana, it's not about that. He told me he did the Griffins—that pregnant woman and her husband."

"What?"

"You heard me. Listen, I can't stand here chitchatting with you. We haven't got time. Papi and I want you to pack up the baby and come home with me till this thing gets straightened out. The cops might be on their way to your place this minute. You don't want them busting in on the baby, do you?"

"No—But my God! What have you done? Tio Luis too? Are you kidding me? The police are coming for Renaldo?"

"It's no joke. Now I'm on my way. I'll be there to get you in fifteen minutes; so be ready."

Angelica looked around her in a daze. Then she sprang from her chair and ran into her room. Yoli was sitting in the middle of the double bed, toys scattered around her, rocking a naked doll with wildly tangled black hair and a bald spot on the crown of her head. When her mother appeared she put a finger to her lips, crawled to the head of the bed and slipped the doll under the covers.

Despite her racing pulse Angelica smiled. "Putting Rosa down for her nap?" she asked.

The little girl nodded sagely. "Nap," she said.

Angelica dragged a battered suitcase from the closet to her bureau and began dumping out clothes, her nerves taut as she listened for feet on the stairs outside their door. The building had paper walls; so she knew she would have at least a minute warning if Renaldo or the cops arrived. "Sweetheart, we're going to visit Tio Bobby. He's coming to pick us up in a minute; so Mami's in a big rush."

Yolanda watched with wide eyes as her mother dumped the meager contents of her jewelry box into the suitcase and then stuck her head into the closet, riffling through the hangers pulling out handfuls and grabbing shoes from the floor. She kicked off the sneakers she had on and slammed on her boots; the sneakers joined the pile in the suitcase. Leaving Yolanda in peace in her nest atop the bed, she gave the room a final glance and headed out of it. In ten minutes Angelica hurtled through the apartment, stuffing Yolanda's wicker toy box with her tiny clothes, baby blanket and teddy bear. Into a couple of oversized Filene's Basement shopping bags went old photographs, a few paperbacks, tubes of make-up, a toothbrush, her floral address book, her mother's glass bowl, wrapped in a towel, and a shoebox full of cassettes.

The intercom buzzed, and she swallowed a foul burst of bile as she crossed to answer it. "Hello," she said cautiously, imagining a blue blur of police on the stoop.

"Angelica? It's me, Bobby." She let out a huge sigh, pressed the buzzer, opened the door, and listened to his feet echoing in the stairwell as he ran up the two flights. "No one been here since I called?" he bit out, panting.

"No. You know I'm going to kill you for this."

"Yeah," he said without rancor, "and if you don't get out of here Renaldo's going to kill *you*." Across the room Yolanda was standing in the bedroom doorway holding the doorframe with one hand, the opposite thumb stuck in her mouth. Angelica ran her fingers through her hair; she was shaking, but her voice didn't show it as she pointed out the suitcase, shopping bags and toy box to Bobby. As he grabbed the suitcase and bags and ran out the door again, tears began dripping down Yolanda's face.

Angelica picked her up, kissed the top of her head, and carried her into the bedroom, rescuing the doll from the bed and tucking it between her body and her daughter's. She shook a pillow out of its case and stuffed the toys scattered across blanket into the pillowcase. "Look," she said. "I'm bringing all your toys to Tio Bobby's house. You can show him every one as soon as we get there. Now don't cry. It's going to be all right."

Bobby returned for the toy box faster that Angelica imagined he could descend the stairs. "You taking your mami's Virgin?" he asked.

"Oh!" Angelica slapped her forehead and shifting Yolanda to her hip, crossed the room to an alcove where a dusty, notebook-sized painting of a black-haired Madonna and Child on horseback hung askew. "Thanks, Bobby, I almost forgot her." She lifted the Madonna gently from her hook and slid her under one arm. Bobby had already started down the stairs as she took a final glance and holding Yolanda close, pulled the front door shut behind them.

Yolanda rode in the back seat, thumb in mouth, the seatbelt buckle covering half her belly, the pillowcase stuffed with toys looming beside her. Angry words swirled in the smoky station wagon, Angelica sucking on a cigarette, Bobby driving hell for leather out of the neighborhood. Angelica made him repeat exactly what words Renaldo had said that made him go to the police, and when she heard the story she called him every kind of fool, refusing to believe her boyfriend had shot the Griffins. Stung by the insults, Bobby began to swear, and Angelica snapped at him for using foul language in front of her baby.

"You know I'm going to call Renaldo as soon as we get there, find out if he's okay."

"No you're not, not from my phone; what if he figures out where you are? You won't reach him, anyway. Cops'll get him by then."

"How's he going to figure out where I am, genius? I won't tell him. You think I'm that stupid? I don't want him to hurt you, though maybe I should."

"Jesus, Angelica, it's not like you love him do you?"

"I don't know," she said soberly. "I guess I don't. He's good in bed, pretty decent to me and Yoli, but lately I know he has other women."

"He's no good trash—and dangerous. Good riddance."

"You're really one to talk with the useless crew you hang out with." She lapsed into silence and glanced into the back seat, arm snaking back to grab one of Yolanda's pudgy legs for a friendly squeeze. The corners of the little girl's mouth rose in the slightest of smiles, but her thumb remained planted in her mouth.

As soon as they reached Bobby's Roxbury apartment Angelica began having second thoughts about spending the night. She had forgotten how run-down his neighborhood looked: the dilapidated buildings, boys hanging out on the corners, mud-brown bundles in doorways that turned out to be homeless men, some sleeping, some clutching bottles in paper bags. She almost hated to take Yolanda out of the car. Following Bobby up the cold concrete stairwell to his door, she wondered how long she would have to stay there; maybe Tio would take them in, but he was probably afraid of Renaldo.

When Bobby had lugged all her things upstairs he grabbed the telephone to report to Papi.

"Si. I did what you said, Papi. I talked to the police, an Officer Hanlon. Told him everything. I told him Renaldo might have been joking or bragging or something, only that made him mad. He said didn't I know what a serious crime this was, and why would someone joke about it? Then he left me alone a little while in a locked room, which made me very nervous.

When he got back he said he knew all about me, called me a drug courier. He said no matter what your friend, Fernando, told me he could put me in jail in a split second if he wanted to. And did I know what kind of a beating some people got on the way to jail? I was sweating big time. But then he got nice again, said I just had to put my story in a written statement, only what happened, not how I thought it might be a joke. I knew he was jerking me around, and it pissed me off some, but I didn't want jail, sure didn't want no beating. And you know what, Papi? When I wrote up that statement he thanked me, real pleasant, gave me a $20 bill and told me to go celebrate!

No, I didn't tell anybody but you about the twenty. But it must be legal, Papi; he's a cop. Give me a break, Papi; it's my money, and I'm going to spend it. Now listen, there's more. I called Angelica from the station house, and I brought her and the baby here. How could I wait? The cops are probably busting in there searching for Renaldo this minute. I wasn't going to leave her and the baby to be arrested!"

Angela was listening to all of this, fuming. She hated to hear Bobby admit that he knew Renaldo might have been kidding. She hated the image of the Irish cop browbeating her idiot cousin into making a statement, and then, with a big grin plastered on his face, paying him off. The reality of the police combing the city to find Renaldo hit her in the gut; although she had mixed feelings about him she hoped they would not shoot him. A lump of fear slid up her throat until she felt she might choke on it; she knew they would want to talk to her too. And if he remembered yesterday's conversation with Bobby and figured out who turned him in, Renaldo would be planning revenge. She had to get out of here if she was going to protect her baby. She needed some advice from someone other than her screwed-up cousin and her sanctimonious uncle—but who?

When Bobby got off the phone Yolanda was complaining of hunger. Bobby's kitchen contained little food, but Angelica found a few hot dogs in the back corner of the freezer and put them on the stove to boil. Further forays into the cabinets revealed a bag of rice, canned kidney beans, garlic salt, even a chipped white casserole large enough for a big mess of rice and beans. Doing something with her hands helped to calm her nerves a little, but she still felt like a tightrope walker, lump still lodged in her throat. Tio Luis had hung up the phone without even asking to speak to her, which infuriated her so much that she could not turn to him.

As she was slicing a hot dog for Yolanda she replayed Bobby's evening with Renaldo in her head. Renaldo loved to play the big man; after a few drinks he always bragged about his jail time. She was sure he hadn't shot the Griffins. How could he have done that without showing any sign of it? Renaldo just could not be cold-blooded enough to shoot those people for their jewelry, fence the stuff, and then come home, throw Yolanda in the air till she squealed and go right on living with them for two months as if nothing happened—with the hunt for the killer on the news every night. He would have cracked somehow. She was sure of it. But the cops would hang him out to dry. She was sure of that too. He had a record, and they needed a killer more than they needed the truth.

Only one person might be able to help her: that reporter, Ariella Richardson.

21

Monday morning Ariella was putting the finishing touches on a piece on that morning's youth talent contest at the Roxbury Community Center's Martin Luther King celebration when her desk phone rang. Grimacing at her computer in the afternoon glare she grabbed the receiver and answered curtly. As Angelica began explaining her plight, Ariella's face whitened. David, who had looked up from his desk at the ring, found himself distracted enough from the medical insurance article he was struggling to write to keep his eyes trained on her. Ariella was gripping her telephone and biting her lip, not at all her normal behavior. Clearly some far greater drama than insurance was unfolding in front of him, and David could not resist it. He rose, wound his way around the few empty desks that separated them, and leaned on hers with an expectant look. Swatting the air as if at a fly, she refused to meet his gaze, but he stayed.

"Well, the first thing has to be safety, doesn't it?" Ariella was saying. There was a long pause until she seemed to cut in, "I can't think about him or any story until I know you and Yolanda are in a safe place."

"Hey." David's palm came down on the free hand Ariella was using to nervously twirl the telephone cord. "Is it Angelica? What's wrong?"

"David, leave me alone. This is a private conversation. Confidential. Now get off my desk and do some work." She listened to the phone again. "Are you sure, Angelica? I don't think.... Okay, okay." Glancing around to make sure that no one in the semi-deserted newsroom could hear, she turned her face back to David's. "Angelica wants me to tell you what's going on, though God knows why. She may be in a lot of danger from her boyfriend. She's at her cousin's place right now, but the boyfriend could come looking for her there." She covered the base of the receiver with her hand and whispered, "Should I offer to take her in, David?"

"No," he said. "I'll do it."

"You! I'm not telling you this to get you involved, you moron; I need your advice. There's more to this than I told you, but I can't explain it here. Believe me, you don't want to get mixed up in it."

"Ariella, I do want to get mixed up in it." He winked at her. "It's my chance to play Prince Charming, how can I resist? No one would ever connect me with her; so she should be fine at my house for a while—not to mention that I have a house, while you have only a little apartment. The boyfriend may have heard your name from Angelica, but he's sure as shootin' never heard mine. Come on, give me the phone."

"David, this could be extremely dangerous."

"You're forgetting I've been in Boston a long time. I know a lot of people, and I can get protection if I need it. Come on, Ari." His eyebrows lifted pleadingly, and his palm moved from her free hand to press the one holding the receiver.

"I'll never forgive myself if something happens to

you," she said, and his eyes lit because he knew he had won. She shook his hand from hers and grudgingly told the receiver, "If you want to hear it, David has an idea for you." As soon as she handed him the phone, he launched into a rush of Spanish. Ariella cupped her hands over her nose and mouth, shut her eyes, and pressed her jawbone with her thumbs. Was she grabbing the chance to keep Angelica out of her apartment just in case she could get Sam into it? Dumping her problems on David, even endangering his life so that she could sleep with some guy who had no respect for her chosen career? "David?" she began, but he was already writing down directions to a Roxbury address and did not respond.

When he hung up, she asked again, "Are you sure you want to do this?"

"Ari," he said with laughter in his eyes, "you have no idea how badly I want that woman to come home with me. Now stop worrying."

"Not until I tell you the whole story. I'm coming down to your car, and we're going to sit in there until you hear what I have to say, and then if you still want to go I'll butt out."

Huddled in his Toyota without her coat a few minutes later, she rubbed at her arms while she explained to him that Angelica and her daughter might be next on the hit list of the Griffins' murderer. David's eyes widened, but he shrewdly asked whether Angelica had turned her boyfriend in and whether she thought he had committed the double murder. When he heard that she believed the man innocent, he brightened.

"You'll just have to run a story on it."

"For crying out loud. That's what she said."

"Great minds think alike. See, we're perfect for each other."

Ariella made a rude noise.

"Come over to my place tonight about eight to interview her, okay? Unless I leave you a message not to." When Ariella did not answer, he added, "It's an incredible story, Ari. I mean, if for any reason she's right and the Boston Police have the wrong man, you owe it to him to interview her. The police are dying to pin this murder on somebody, and they might be overzealous."

She nodded slowly, for the first time since the call came pushing her fear aside and allowing her reporter's mind to assess the situation. "God, I hate crime stories. But I'll be there at eight. Give her my best, okay? And buy the little girl some brownies or something." She allowed herself only a moment of regret that she would not be able to see Sam tonight.

David saluted, and she pushed the car door open, climbed out and ran through the biting wind back to the *Times* building, then turned in the doorway to watch his car shrink into nothing as it sped away down the boulevard.

৵

When Ariella reached David's house it looked like a turtle tucked into its shell: blinds tightly drawn, a curtain blocking the view through the glass-paned outer door, no music.

David came quickly at the sound of the doorbell and ushered her into the living room where Yolanda sat cross-legged in the corner of the couch clutching a baby blanket and chatting to her doll in what sounded like Spanish-accented nonsense syllables. She stopped briefly to give

Ariella a stare, glanced at her mother, who made no move to leave her side, and then continued to play. Shedding her coat Ariella pulled up a chair to face Angelica on the couch.

"Are you doing okay?" she asked when the other woman sat in uncharacteristic silence.

"Yeah." Angelica rolled her eyes. "I've had better days." David was hovering in the doorway and offered tea. "Pleeease! No self-respecting Puerto Rican woman wants tea when she can have coffee," she snapped at him, but rather than taking the bait he just looked amused and left the room. "Can he be here while you ask your questions?" she asked Ariella in a defensive tone.

"Sure. And look, Angelica, we don't have to do this if you think it might endanger you."

"No, no. We do have to. Renaldo didn't kill anybody, and I need to say so. David thinks so too."

"Yes, well, David's a reporter. He thinks it's a great story, but he might not be thinking about what's best for you and your child—speaking of which, do you want her to hear all this?"

Angelica leaned forward and gripped one hand in the other. "She needs to be with me. She's had a scary day. And most of it will go over her head anyway. What's the matter, Ariella, are you afraid of this story? 'Cause if you're not you better start asking questions before I have to put this little girl to bed."

"I am anxious about it, getting both of us mixed up in such a dangerous situation without thinking it through, but it's not going to stop me from interviewing you. So..." she let out a sigh and slid a note pad from her coat pocket, "do you think your boyfriend, Renaldo Colon, committed the Griffin murder?

"No. *Madre de Dios*—no! He's not perfect—he drinks—but he's been good to me and my baby, and like I told you, he's a spineless weasel. He wouldn't have the *cojones* to shoot somebody."

"Do you have any proof that he didn't do it?"

"Well, it doesn't make sense. I know him, and it's been two months since that Griffin woman got shot, and Renaldo, he just keeps coming home, laughing with Yolanda, showing no sign of being the killer in the biggest murder case to hit Boston maybe ever. He hasn't seemed tense about being caught, nothing. I *know* when he's in big trouble—and he's not. Before the Griffin murder I thought he might be in some kind of trouble, but after it he seemed fine again."

"You mean you thought he had committed a crime earlier this fall?"

"No, no. I don't want to talk about that. Just let's say that I notice when he's tense about the cops. He's served time in the past; so he gets tense easily. That's why I don't see how he could cold-bloodedly murder Laurie Griffin and then go calmly about his business when cops are crawling all over the city looking for the killer."

"Okay. So he doesn't act like the killer. But what about the night of Sunday, November 14th? Do you remember what he was doing that night?"

"He was home with me and the baby."

Ariella stopped scribbling and looked her in the eye. "When did he get home?"

"Around eight o'clock."

"How do you know?"

"I was just starting to watch the CBS Sunday night movie, and it comes on at eight after '60 Minutes.'" Angelica was holding herself taut, hands still clenched together, and meeting Ariella's gaze. Out of the corner of her eye she could see David lounging in the doorway.

"You're sure that happened on the 14th and not some other Sunday?"

"Well, I think so, yes, because it was when I had the flu, and I had it two weeks before Thanksgiving. I was feeling miserable and watching T.V. all the time."

"Do you remember what Sunday movie it was?"

"Yeah, that Tom Hanks movie, 'Big.' Renaldo was disgusted with it because he thinks Tom Hanks is a fool, and he only likes action pictures anyway."

"But he stayed in the rest of the night?"

"Yeah. He was concerned about me, believe it or not." Her gaze swept to David, then back to Ariella. "I had a fever and chills and a cough, and he stayed awake with me to cheer me up."

"Are you certain he never went out? Maybe you were so feverish you forgot or dozed off on the sofa."

"No. I get testy when I'm sick—not sleepy or stupid. I remember him sitting around with me complaining about the movie and eating pizza and talking on the phone, and then we went to bed at eleven or so, after the movie ended."

"Do you know who was on the phone with him?"

"It's so long ago, no. That I can't remember. I wasn't paying much attention because I was watching the movie."

"And no one else came over that night?"

Angelica rolled her eyes. "Why would I invite anyone over when I was sick as a dog?"

"Okay. Now would you describe Renaldo as a black man?"

"No, he's Latino—Dominican."

"But is he dark-skinned?"

"Well, he has darker skin than you or me, but he doesn't look like an African American, not to me—not at all."

"Why not?"

"His face, his hair, his build...." Angelica looked annoyed.

"I don't mean to sound ignorant, but Brian Griffin said the killer was black; so I need to ask. Now does Renaldo have a beard?"

"Yes, if you can call it that. A little scrubby, wha-d'you-call-it—goatee."

"How would you describe his voice?"

"It's low, and he sounds like a smoker, like his throat might be sore."

"Now you said Renaldo had served prison time before. Why?"

"It was for an armed robbery of an Apple Mart about ten years ago, I think, but I don't know much else about it. Just ask the cops—I'm sure they've looked up every detail of it by now!"

"Apple Mart, the convenience store?" When Angelica nodded Ariella continued, "So how long was he in jail? And when did he get out?"

"Seven years. He got out about two years ago."

"To your knowledge has he committed any crimes since?"

"No. He told me he's cleaned up his act, and he really has—got some work driving a truck, came home to me and Yoli at night...."

"But you did once tell me you thought he might be, uh, unfaithful...."

Angelica sighed. "That doesn't mean he shot

anybody. Men are dogs. Can't keep their pants on sometimes. And he likes to hang out at El Lagarto Bar, where a lot of slutty women go."

"That where you met him?"

Angelica gave a bark of humorless laughter, and her eyes slid to David, who winked at her. "Yes, and don't you dare say what that makes me!"

"All right." Ariella gave a half-hearted smile and pressed on. "And how long have you been living together?"

"Maybe a little over a year?"

"So, in that time has he ever been arrested or jailed?"

"No."

"Does Renaldo use cocaine or hard drugs?" She looked Angelica in the eye. "Please be honest with me."

"No, no. Only drinks. He doesn't like that other stuff. He saw some guy O.D. and die on the street one time when he was sixteen, and it made an impression."

"Well, is he impulsive?"

"Impulsive? No, not really. Renaldo gets dead-set on something and then he's pig-headed. But not impulsive. He tends to have a plan, sometimes a dumb-ass plan, but a plan."

"Okay, last questions. Did Renaldo know the Griffins?" Angelica shook her head. "Did he ever mention them either before or after the murder?"

"Not before. Of course, afterward he heard about the murder like everybody else. You would have to have your head up your butt to live in Boston and not hear about it. One time he said it was a good thing the cops had the Griffin case to keep them busy."

"So they would be too preoccupied to investigate any other crimes?"

"So they would be too busy to harass ex-cons like

him."

"That's all he said?"

"That's all I remember. He never seemed overly interested in that murder, one way or another. He thought the cops were making too much of it because a rich white woman got shot instead of the usual poor black woman."

"A philosopher, no less," David piped up from the doorway. Ariella gave him a quelling look, and a distracted Angelica turned to her daughter at her side. Yolanda was asleep in the corner of the couch slumped over its arm with her doll and blanket hugged to her chest.

"Okay, that's enough. She needs to go to bed. You going to write the story?"

Ariella nodded. "Definitely. And you're going to have to go to the police. It would be best to go early tomorrow morning before my story can get into print. They don't like it when you give a story to the paper before going to them. But let me give you some advice: don't show up with David, and no matter what don't say where you're staying or give his phone number. Tell them you're scared of the real killer, and tell them you can be reached through me at the paper or through your cousin or something. Keep David out of it, okay?"

Angelica was hugging herself. "I don't like cops." Ariella opened her mouth to argue with her, but Angelica cut her off. "Can't stand them, in fact, but I'll go. Tomorrow morning. David already said he would watch Yoli for me. And I won't say where I'm staying. I'm not stupid, you know. I'll let them think I'm at Bobby's. But take your own advice and don't say where you interviewed me—cause they'll be talking to you just about as soon as they get through with me, you know." She stood shakily, knocking a book from the coffee table by mistake, swearing softly at it and looking back up at Ariella. "I been meaning to ask you. Are you sleeping with that guy who took you to the ballet?"

Ariella blushed, knowing David was all ears, but after all the probing questions she had asked she could not refuse one. She settled on a simple "yes."

"I know who he is, you know. I've seen him a couple times with Dr. Ward, and he's a hardass. At least he's not the kind to run around behind your back, though. Just don't let him push you around." Then, with a nervous dignity, she scooped up her sleeping child and headed past Ariella toward David.

The two reporters' eyes met around her side, but David said only, "Do you mind letting yourself out, Ari? And slam the outer door shut."

22

Victor pounced on Mrs. Boyle first thing Tuesday morning when she had just settled her not inconsiderable bulk into her desk chair and turned to the phone to listen to the answering machine messages. Surprised to find a wiry man in a shiny tomato-colored shirt bounding through her door, she snapped, "Who are you?"

Undeterred he smiled, offered a hand, and began in his Russian-accented English. "Victor Janofsky. I met you at Roland's Christmas party...." He waited for some sign of recognition and when none came continued, "I have a favor to ask. Roland said that if I ever needed any assistance in understanding Carver Center policy and bureaucracy, you were the expert." He paused again.

"Well, I suppose that after fifteen years I ought to know something."

"Yes. Well, I'm trying to find out more about funding at the Center. I am a group therapist, you see. I run support groups for cancer survivors. And I wondered: how are these things funded? In the Soviet Union money came from the government or not at all. But in America I do not know." He looked at her inquiringly.

"Out of the general budget, maybe. Or perhaps

there's a specific grant from a group like the Donald Benson Foundation; they support a lot of direct services like support groups."

"Is there an annual list of grants received by the Center?"

"Well, the annual report lists some grants individually and amalgamates others. But they must have a comprehensive list at the budget office." She gave him a sharp look. "You just want to know how your groups are funded, or something more?"

He suddenly dropped the disingenuous look. "More. I have recently been told that the Cancer Center may be taking grant money from the tobacco industry."

"What?" She dropped the pen she had been chewing.

"I can hardly believe it myself. Not in America, I thought. So I ask your expert help in discovering the truth."

"Well, in fifteen years I've never heard of such a thing. Who told you this? It's a disgraceful rumor, I'm sure." Mrs. Boyle's face had turned from pink to red. "I can tell you that our department has never taken a cent from any cigarette company. Camel cigarettes ruined my sister Noreen's life, poor soul. She died right here at the Carver Center eight years ago."

"I'm so sorry," Victor said, and eyes very bright, added, "but I'm glad that you agree it would be a disgrace if it were true."

"It certainly would. But its hogwash. I'll call Jeanie Upshaw in the budget office right now and ask her." She reached for the phone.

"Ask about TRA, the Tobacco Research Association. They're the ones who fund grants for the tobacco companies."

She nodded and dialed while Victor paced and grinned like the Cheshire Cat at the Ansel Adams photograph across the room. She was too focused on the telephone call to notice. "Jeanie, this is Fiona Boyle. How are you? Oh, that's good. Jeanie, I have a question for you. Does the Center take any grants from TRA? Oh, really? Would you mind if I took a look at it? I can stop by after lunch. Thanks Jeanie—and we should have coffee one day this week. Sure, Friday is fine. Bye." She hung up looking thoughtful.

"What did she say?" Victor was pressing his hands on the edge of her desk, eagerly leaning towards her.

Mrs. Boyle looked grim. "She thinks she's seen that name on some grants. But in any case they just produced a ten-year compendium of funding sources for the president's office. It's still in draft, but she said that I can take a look later today."

"Unbelievable. This story may be true!"

"I certainly hope not."

∽

That evening Victor arrived half an hour late to pick up Ariella for dinner, but she hardly noticed; she was too deeply engrossed in a book on domestic violence she had grabbed at the library. When she emerged from the elevator in her long, black coat he was pacing in her building's tiny lobby.

"Ariella, you look beautiful. What do you say in English—a sight for sick eyes?"

"Sore eyes. Thanks." She smiled distractedly.

"Nu..." He took both of her hands in his black-gloved ones and looked at her face for a long moment, while she subdued the urge to back away. "I don't know about my eyes, but I certainly have a sore brain tonight, and I hope you will be the cure."

"Funny." She gave an unconscious little sigh as he released her. "I feel that way too. I've been obsessing about one thing all day."

"A newspaper story?"

"Sort of. Only a friend of mine is involved; so it's gotten personal."

"Interesting. I think my headache will give you yet another newspaper story. But let's go to dinner, and we'll talk. Shall we?" He ushered her out the door to his red sports car, which was double-parked right out front, then sped through yellow lights to the fashionable Newbury Street district.

Ariella found herself in a booth at a dark, cozy restaurant called Blini, tucked into a side street that she had never explored. Since her host was Russian she allowed him to order for them, and then he launched into his story, waving his hands as he spoke.

"When you told me you were investigating tobacco company funding at the Carver Center, I did not believe you would find anything. I did not think such blatant corruption was happening here in the United States, but I was wrong."

"Really?" Ariella pushed Angelica's story from her mind for the first time in almost twenty four hours and listened while sipping borscht.

"As you suggested I spoke to Mrs. Boyle today, and my support groups, *my* groups for cancer survivors, are being funded with TRA money! Even my lung cancer group. The irony of it! It's too much."

"Directly or indirectly?"

"Indirectly. TRA gives money to the Carver Center

which goes into a general fund, and that fund pays for my groups. But TRA money amounts to 65 percent of the fund. And the TRA money is meant for research, but most of it goes to administrative expenses and office products. Although there are also a few cancer researchers profiting from tobacco money as we speak—can you believe it?"

"Now how did Mrs. Boyle discover all this?"

"She has a friend in the budget office. But Ariella, aren't you shocked? I mean, survivors of lung cancer, people who smoked for years and have had multiple surgeries, radiation, chemotherapy, they are sitting in a support group funded by the tobacco industry. It's disgraceful."

"Some might say it's poetic justice. But Victor, what kind of proof did Mrs. Boyle's friend have? And who is she? What's her job?"

"Her name is Shaw. No, Upshaw. Americans have such peculiar names. She's a secretary, and she let Mrs. Boyle borrow a new comprehensive list of funding sources the budget office is making for the President of Carver. Mrs. Boyle copied the pages relating to the tobacco funds."

"What for? I mean, what's Mrs. Boyle's take on all of this?"

"She's angry. It turns out her department just got a new copy machine bought with money from that same general fund. So she got out her feelings by using it to copy the incriminating documents from the president's office. She lost a sister who smoked and hates cigarettes. In fact, she's planning to accost Roland as soon as she sees him to find out whether he knew who really paid for their copy machine."

"Hmm. Good. Thanks, Victor. I do think we have a story."

"Think so? Of course you do. This is a big scandal. What's the matter with you, Ariella? I thought you would be excited." His accent became more pronounced as he grew more emotional.

"Oh, Victor, you're right. It's a great health/science story and a great break for me. I'm just preoccupied. I'm afraid two friends of mine are in danger, and if I write about it for the newspaper I might somehow make it worse."

"Write the story." Victor tapped the table with a forefinger. "I doubt it will increase the danger, and probably it will diminish it."

Ariella was mildly surprised by the force of his opinion on a subject he knew nothing about, but then, he was Russian. "Okay, well, I don't really want to discuss it.... But as for your tobacco story, I'll have to tell Jerry the Giraffe. He'll be thrilled."

"A giraffe?"

"Oh, I just call him that on account of his looks. I'm thinking of a guy named Jerry Lesniak who got me into this tobacco funding story in the first place. He's an activist and lawyer who sues tobacco companies for fun."

"A lawyer!" Victor's face lit up. "Would you give me his telephone number? I have an idea!"

"Well, he works at TESP. You can look it up in the phone book. But what are you up to, Victor? Planning a lawsuit?"

"I promise you'll get the story, my dear, but I have to talk to your Mr. Giraffe first and see what he thinks."

By the time Victor returned her to the lobby of her building her head was spinning with the possibility that she finally had her big break. It had taken a little while to dawn on her, but when she finally pushed the Griffin murder from her mind, she realized that Joyce would love this tobacco scandal. Sitting in her briefcase lay documentary evidence that the Carver Center was taking tobacco company money to research cancer—bad enough—and then using it for administrative expenses. If she could just get a balancing quote from the tobacco industry, she thought Joyce would push this story for the front page of *Metro*. She tried not to wonder what Sam would think of her slamming his institution in print.

As Victor swept the door open for her, out of the corner of her eye she spotted a man in the single beige armchair in her lobby. A lump swelled in her throat. It was Sam, long legs stretched out in front of him, reading the New England Journal of Medicine.

"Sam!" Victor's tone held not only greeting but an inquiry. "A pleasant surprise!"

"Janofsky," he acknowledged with a cold nod.

"My dear." Victor turned her toward him, took her hands and squeezed them as if to emphasize his words. "It was lovely, and I appreciate all of your enthusiasm and help. If you need more from me for your story—nu, you know you can telephone me at any time. And I will see if this Mr. Giraffe you spoke of can help me to get a little revenge." He dropped her hands and kissed her four times in the European fashion, alternating between cheeks. "Goodnight. I will speak to you later in the week."

She thanked him and watched as with a wave to Sam he sauntered out into the icy Boston night. Expelling a breath she turned and approached the chair. "So what are you doing here?" she asked. He was already on his feet and pulling her into his arms, his hands and mouth hard and possessive. Unprepared for the onslaught she clung to him at first, then struggled away. He held her to his mouth for a moment as if to demonstrate his new physical and emotional power over her, but then released her partially so that she remained in the circle of his arms yet far enough away to see into his eyes.

"You never called me last night."

She sighed, still shivering from the kiss, mind jumbled with the Griffin murder, the brewing scandal at the Carver Center—torn between her passions. "I'm sorry. As you see I had a dinner date with Victor tonight, and I would have called you as soon as I got in. Something very important came up yesterday, and I wasn't sure whether I should tell you about it. So I was taking today to think it over before I called you."

"What happened with us on Sunday seemed pretty important to me. Of course, I don't have your rip-roaring social life. But I thought it was important to you too."

"Of course it was, Sam. Look, I've had a very emotional couple of days..."

"Were you out with Victor last night too?" He looked fierce.

"No. No, I..." she faltered and looked over his shoulder at the wrought iron lantern attached to the hallway wall. "I was at David's."

"Good God, Ariella. How many men do you need in your life?"

Her lips tightened, and she broke out of his embrace. "Maybe none! Look, Sam, you big idiot, it isn't like that. It's work. I suddenly have the two biggest stories of my career, and David's involved with one of them and Victor with the other, okay?"

Tension drained from his face and fighting her resistance he pulled her slowly back to his chest. "Sorry." He kissed the top of her head. "I really missed you. I shouldn't be so suspicious, but I really don't know you very well yet, and I don't trust those other men buzzing around you. So will you take me upstairs and tell me about your big stories?"

"Are you truly interested? Because I have a lot to do tonight, and I probably shouldn't let you distract me." It intrigued and pleased her that he believed her and that although he had a hot temper, it cooled quickly. So different from Carl.

"Please." He had that boyish entreaty in his eyes that she had seen once before on the Boston Common, and she could not rebuff him.

Upstairs in her apartment he immediately noticed the domestic violence books scattered on the coffee table. "Doing a piece on battered women?"

"Sort of." She was heating the kettle for tea while he wandered restlessly around the living room. "Why don't you sit? You're making me nervous."

"I like to walk. What I really want is to get my hands on you again, but I don't want you to think I'm not interested in your work." His voice held an ironic tinge suggesting he knew that was just what she thought. "So what's the big story on battered women?"

"Well," she said, bringing in two steaming mugs, "that's still speculative. But I'm considering the possibility that Brian Griffin murdered his pregnant wife."

"What?" He stopped pacing and stared at her. "But the police just arrested an ex-con named Renaldo Colon for that murder."

"I know. My big story is an exclusive interview with his girlfriend."

"Don't tell me. The girlfriend says he's innocent." He

looked at her as if she had sand for brains.

She placed the mugs on the coffee table, sat on the sofa and patted the spot beside her in invitation. His sarcastic tone did not disturb her as she knew she would face the same attitude from the police. "She provides him with an alibi, and she's persuasive."

"But, honey, I heard the story on NPR today. This Colon guy spent years in jail for an armed robbery where he shot someone. He's a perfect match for Brian Griffin's description of his wife's murderer—raspy voice, scruffy beard—and he's also being held for that Allston liquor store robbery on Halloween. He's a very bad egg. I mean, his girlfriend may not think so, but look at the evidence." When he dropped beside her his big body seemed to dominate the couch and radiate conviction.

The word, "honey," distracted her a little, but she was determined to explain her position. "He may not be a very nice guy, but that doesn't mean he shot Laurie Griffin. There are plenty of nasty guys in Boston who didn't shoot her. And if Brian Griffin wanted to turn suspicion away from himself, why not give the police the description he had read in the paper of the Allston liquor store robber? It strikes me as odd that he used the very same words to describe the murderer that we printed in the *Times* about that robber."

"Don't you think you're going a bit far out on a limb here, Ariella? I mean, in science we generally assume that the likeliest hypothesis is the best one. The evidence points to Colon. Why come up with a convoluted theory to exonerate him?" He took her hand and began absently tracing designs on the palm.

"It's a hunch. I listened to what the girlfriend said about Colon's personality and his behavior lately, and I believe he probably robbed the liquor store, but I just don't think he forced the Griffins at gunpoint to drive to a deserted area and then shot them so that he could steal a little jewelry. That doesn't sound like the same kind of guy who occasionally holds up stores. The kind of guy who would force his way into a car like the Griffin murderer supposedly did, that sounds like a guy strung out on cocaine, impulsive, anti-social and desperate for money. This Colon doesn't fit the profile at all."

"Why? Was he a Boy Scout? A choir boy?"

It was becoming harder to ignore his caressing fingers, but she would not succumb to their subtle persuasion. "No, wise guy. It's that he's a drinker not a drug addict, a guy who sounds as if he plans out his hold-ups and targets stores not individuals. He just goes for the cash register, and his gun is mostly a prop, which he uses when necessary but not for thrills. He doesn't sound like a sociopath—he's capable of a year-long relationship with a woman and a one-year-old child. Supposedly he's good with the kid, and it's not even his own."

"Nice to children and dogs, huh? Ariella, don't you think you're a little naive? Or at least inexperienced? I mean, you're not exactly trained in criminal psychology, and I thought you rarely dabbled in crime stories." At that she dropped his hand.

"I don't like crime stories, but I've done my share. And I'll bet I know a lot more about it than you do."

"Okay, okay, don't get huffy on me."

She gave him a hard look. "I'm not crazy about the word, 'huffy.' You raise an interesting point, though; maybe I should talk to a criminal psychologist about the Griffin murderer—maybe someone from the Northeastern School of Criminal Justice."

"I'll banish the word, 'huffy,' from my vocabulary." He smiled, and she struggled not to respond. "In any case, I'm sure your interview with Colon's girlfriend will make a provocative article, and it will definitely get you some attention. So what's your other big story?"

She stifled the urge to tell him that she was not seeking attention, just a career boost from general assignment to the health care beat. "This one is going to be closer to home for you. The Carver Center is taking tobacco company funding to do cancer research and using most of the money for administrative overhead."

"What? Are you sure?" His eyes widened, and his jaw tightened.

She was never gladder to have hard evidence. "Roland's administrator apparently got accounting documents showing funding sources and where the money went, and I have some of the data. It's true, Sam."

"Unbelievable! And what's your angle? Hypocrite cancer purveyors fund cancer research? Morally bankrupt cancer center takes their tainted money? Or, tricky cancer center bookkeepers take corporate money for one thing and spend it on another?"

"All of the above, but especially the first. Apparently the tobacco companies have had a campaign to fund cancer research since the 1950's to try to generate studies that they can use in court to say that smokers might be getting cancer from something other than smoking. It's a sleazy tale. But those who take the money are also at fault."

"You bet they are." His tone had turned serious. "I can't stand the way corporate money twists researchers and research institutions. It's terrible for science."

She was grateful that he did not blame the messenger for the bad news. "Why?"

"Instead of pursuing the truth people start trying to prove what companies want to hear—mainly that their drugs are harmless and effective. And if an important hypothesis has no corporate support it doesn't get investigated."

"Well, this story could use your help—if you're willing."

"I'm willing. It's outrageous that with all of its other support the Carver Center would take tobacco money. I mean, they're the best funded cancer center in the country, probably in the world. What do you need?"

She took a deep breath and expelled it. "Would you help me persuade Roland to show me all the documents?"

"You know how I love exposing myself to the press...."

She giggled with relief at his flippant tone. "Is that what you did Sunday night?"

"You bet your butt. And that reminds me..." His eyes wandered for a moment, then settled back on her face as he shook his head like a puppy shaking off water. "Okay, we can put that on hold for half an hour. This is a story that seriously needs to come out. Carver shouldn't be allowed to take tobacco money in the shadows. Stay right there, and I'll call Roland." He stood, and she bounced up and kissed him impulsively, then dropped back into her corner of the sofa and grabbed a pillow to hug.

"One other thing. I'd like to look at the list of projects funded by tobacco money to understand what kind of research got company funding and why. I mean, are these researchers trying to discredit the conclusion that smoking causes cancer? And if Roland knows them, can he arrange for me to speak to them?"

Sam had a faraway look. "Roland will know them all. I don't know whether he'll help you to interview them, though, unless it's in his best interest to do so. But I'll ask."

He headed for the kitchen telephone, and she pulled a notebook off the occasional table at her elbow. As soon as he began talking, she started to scrawl some story outlines and make a list of calls to make tomorrow. She could hear the indignation in Sam's voice, but she disciplined herself not to listen, as if she were in the newsroom surrounded by other reporters on the phone. Sooner or later Sam was going to coax her toward the bedroom, and since she knew she would not object she needed to be ready to work hard first thing the next morning.

23

Sitting at her desk in the newsroom late Wednesday morning Ariella suddenly buried her face in her hands just to block out external stimulation and think. She had spoken to a Northeastern University criminologist whose comments on the Griffin murderer's psychological profile gave her enough material to make the case for Renaldo's innocence. With a controversial story like this one, she might even make the front page of the Metro section. She had finished the story; now she had only to perfect the lead and headline and meet with Joyce at five o'clock for editing.

As for the tobacco money story, several calls to the Tobacco Research Association headquarters in Washington, D.C. had yielded only "no comment" and a refusal to confirm that the association had donated funds to Carver. To write a balanced story Ariella needed an industry response, and she was curious what defense it would offer. Suddenly she remembered the local tobacco industry lobbyist who worked at the State House. Jerry the Giraffe had given her his name, Brendan Dornan of Dornan, Grubb and Withers—she would give him a call.

ⴰ

Meanwhile at the Beth Israel Hospital cafeteria, Victor was standing in line waiting to buy a cup of tea. A true Russian, he liked his tea strong and laced with sugar. The woman in front of him looked familiar, a tall, statuesque blond.

"Did I not meet you at Roland Chan's Christmas party?" he asked her.

Natalie Ward started at the accent and the unusual locution and turned to him with a glazed look in her eye. "Uh, yes, probably."

"Victor Janofsky." He stuck out his hand, and she took it awkwardly. "I remember now. You are a gynecologist. You do research with Sam Becker, yes?"

"Yes. And you are?"

"A psychiatrist. I run cancer support groups at Carver, although I am thinking of leaving. I feel dirty working here."

He made no effort to modulate his voice, and Natalie's lips pursed in annoyance. The last thing she needed today was an overwrought psychiatrist making a scene in a public place. She did not want to get involved, but perhaps the best way to quiet him was to do just that.

She sighed and said gently but without warmth, "Natalie Ward is my name, and if you don't mind my saying so, you seem a bit agitated."

"Not agitated. Angry. This institution is up to its ears in dirty money. It's a disgrace!"

She had reached the cashier and was paying for a bran muffin and a cup of decaffeinated lemon tea, and although she cursed herself for offering she found herself asking, "Do you want to sit for a minute and tell me about it?"

Naturally he jumped at the opportunity, and she soon found herself in a corner of the cafeteria imprisoned in a booth while he leaned his elbows on the table and spouted invective at her about the Carver Center accepting tobacco industry grants. She was surprised that the center would take tobacco money but was unable to work up a head of steam about it. Finally she stifled a yawn; she thought he had missed it but he hadn't.

"You seem overtired," he said, switching into therapist mode. "Is everything all right in your life?"

"Fine. I haven't been sleeping all that well, but otherwise fine."

"Is something on your mind?"

"You're very perceptive," she said, mouth twisting with irony. "Yes, but I don't want to talk about it."

"A personal problem?"

"More a professional problem."

"I will not pry." He crossed his arms in front of his chest and then jerked them apart. "But I'll tell you who helped me solve *my* professional problem—Ariella Richardson. She was also at the Chan's Christmas party. Do you recall?"

Natalie's eyes widened in disquiet at hearing the reporter's name, both at Victor's eagerness to talk to the press and in uneasy recognition that her own problem too was newsworthy. "I know her. How exactly did she help you?"

"She provided me with a very useful connection—a lawyer who sues tobacco companies. I may just help him to find a few new clients tonight. And Ariella is going to report this funding scandal in the newspaper." He finished his tea in a gulp.

"Are you sure that's wise? The Carver Center is not going to be pleased with you for publicizing its failings."

"Of course they won't. That's the point. This is an injustice, and it must be made public. I grew up under communism in the Soviet Union, a world of injustices hidden from the people beneath a fabric of lies. Now I believe in speaking—speaking *up*, as you say—and I will not remain silent. Too many evils have been perpetuated because of silence."

Natalie said nothing for a moment, then gave a thin laugh. "I was brought up to believe in keeping silent—a combination of good breeding and the old stiff upper lip. But you may be right that silence is sometimes the wrong answer." Her pager began to beep, and she pulled it from her monogrammed leather pocketbook and read the telephone number with some relief. "Oh, you'll have to excuse me. That's the labor and delivery floor. I need to call back right away."

"Certainly. A pleasure to see you again, Dr. Ward. I hope that you resolve your professional problem soon and get some more sleep." They both rose, and she hurried to the house phone on the far wall while he watched her flight with a thoughtful expression on his face.

❦

Back in the newsroom Ariella was considering running down to the first floor coffee shop to grab a tuna sandwich for lunch. She had too much to do to attend the stress seminar the personnel people were sponsoring that day, but a quick jog down the stairs might clear her mind for the tobacco story. The lobbyist's secretary had taken a message, but he had not yet called, and she was beginning to think that she would have to write without an industry response. Just as she rose to leave her desk the telephone rang, and it was Sam.

"Hi," he said softly without identifying himself—after a pregnant pause continuing, "I keep thinking about last night, and I'm not going to get anything done till I ask you whether you'll come over tonight. Will you?"

She blushed and smiled to herself, fascinated, baffled and flattered by his intensity. "If I had a moment's time I'd be mooning over last night too. I've got so much going on, and some of it I'll have to do at home later. But I do want to see you. I don't know."

"Maybe I should come over there and persuade you."

He sounded just serious enough to make her shiver and babble, "Okay, I'll make it all work out somehow. But can you come to my apartment? I'll be there by eight. And would you be able to feed me? I'll probably be ravenous by then."

"No comment."

She could tell that he was smirking and rolled her eyes; she had no time to trade double entendres today. "Goodbye Sam," she said firmly, hung up the phone, and looked up to find a short dapper man gliding across the newsroom toward her desk.

As he neared she could see that he had the chiseled features of a Greek statue, a pointy chin, black hair perfectly combed, and wore a dove-gray suit with a red vest peeking from beneath, probably cashmere. He looked far too polished to be a reporter or an editor, more like a top New York advertising executive astray in the *Boston Times* building. When he noted her regard his mouth widened to an arresting smile. Perhaps it was the calculated elegance of the man, but Ariella immediately felt wary. She acknowledged his smile with her eyes and let her face settle into a bland mask. Minutes later he had reached her desk.

"Are you Ariella Richardson?" he asked, although he clearly knew it was she. When she nodded he gave her a firm handshake. "I'm Brendan Dornan. You called me earlier. I had to meet with someone here in the ad department anyway; so I thought I'd come speak to you face-to-face. I always like to meet in person." He favored her with another of his electric smiles, rows of small perfectly-formed teeth gleaming at her. She would bet that he didn't smoke. When she said nothing he continued, "Have you had lunch? I would be happy to take you out."

Rarely did a source ever appear at the office, probably just because of the *Times'* out-of-the-way Dorchester location, but Ariella felt cornered and flustered. Still a nuanced tobacco industry perspective might move her story toward the front of the Metro section. This was her chance to make an impression on the Managing Editor, Lester Hardman, and get one of his coveted congratulatory e-mail messages. She had better eat lunch with this tobacco lobbyist and find out what he was so eager to say that he had made a special trip to do it.

She took control of her face and smiled at him. "I would be delighted to get out of here for a while and have lunch with you. It's been a crazy morning—new developments in the Griffin murder case—" she waved vaguely, "and I'm a bit frazzled."

He murmured sympathetically while she gathered her bag, gloves and coat. "I know just the place. It's a French restaurant near the State House called Le Bistro, a quiet place to soothe your nerves and chat."

Despite a frisson of uneasiness at his velvety control, she agreed. Ten minutes later, after a ride in a shining black BMW sedan, she found herself at a table in the back of a crowded dining room so quiet that the mauve and white striped wallpaper must have had sound-proofing panels beneath it. She tugged absently at a corner of the spotless white tablecloth, then rearranged the carnations in the centerpiece. For some reason instinct told her not to pull out her notebook, at least not yet, so she was listening without her accustomed scribbling to keep her hands busy.

"I was surprised to learn that the *Times* wanted to report on our donations to the Carver Cancer Center," Dornan told her, "because the press rarely shows an interest in my industry's good deeds. We're like the little kid who's often kicked, never praised. So I'm very pleased that you want to report on our concern about cancer and our research grants to help battle it."

"Do you have figures on how much the tobacco industry has given to Carver, for what purposes, and in what years?"

"Well, you asked me that in your phone message, and I have some figures," he passed her a sheet of paper. "This is information on how much the Tobacco Research Association has given to the Carver Center annually since 1980, but it does not list individual studies that received support."

She glanced at the paper. "Is it just TRA that has given money, or individual companies as well?"

"As far as I know just TRA. My industry is very efficient and well-organized; we pool our resources for certain purposes. Since TRA is our research arm, that would be the entity to give research grants to outside institutions."

She decided to get tough. "Wasn't TRA established as a public relations ploy to make the public believe the tobacco companies cared about preventing cancer when in fact they just wanted to prolong controversy over whether smoking causes cancer at all?"

He did not flinch. "Well, Ms. Richardson, I wouldn't call TRA a public relations ploy. The industry was concerned about some initial studies suggesting a link between smoking and cancer, and we needed to look into the matter. The tobacco companies joined forces to do it because it made financial sense; we all needed to research the same questions. As for whether we care about the public, the millions of dollars we've spent on medical research should count for something. Our money has supported some important break-throughs on how cancer cells operate."

"But not on how cigarettes cause lung cancer?"

"No, our studies have never shown that to be true."

"Do you think cigarettes cause lung cancer?"

"I'm not a scientist, but no, I don't think so, and there are certainly scientists who agree with me."

"You don't think cigarettes cause lung cancer?"

"No. I think there are anti-smoking zealots out there who want to stop all smoking, and they're willing to use scare tactics to do it. But adults have a right to make the decision for themselves. Prohibition of alcohol didn't work in the beginning of our century, and it won't work for cigarettes now."

"Do you believe smoking has *any* health consequences?"

"I think there may be some health risks, but smokers have plenty of information in the public domain with which to make the decision to smoke."

She was amazed at how guileless he looked and how persuasive he sounded despite her disagreement with him. "Do you see any problem with Carver accepting your industry's money?"

"Problem? No."

"Most doctors believe that smoking causes lung cancer and a number of other diseases too. Some will say that your industry knows this, and that it cynically gives grants only to scientists who try to prove otherwise. Then it can use the studies in court to show that there still is no medical consensus on whether smoking causes cancer."

He gazed straight into her eyes. "We have supported a lot of general research on how cancer works precisely because our products have been blamed for causing cancer. Naturally we would like to show otherwise, but we also want to advance medical research on the understanding of cancer and the immune system. Our industry is made up of people just like you, people who get sick and whose relatives get sick, and we want some of our profits to go to finding cures for their problems."

Ariella was having trouble maintaining a poker face. "But your cigarettes make people sick, don't they? Some say they're a killer product."

"Ms. Richardson, forgive me but you're not a doctor, and neither am I, although I understand you want to specialize in health care reporting."

That startled her. "Yes, actually." *How did he know?*

"Well, I happened to hear of something that might interest you. You know, Reddington Tobacco owns the Hearst newspaper chain, including the Chicago Tribune, and they're looking for a new health reporter in Chicago. I know the editor, and if you're interested I could put in a good word for you. I looked at some of your articles this morning, and you're an excellent writer."

Ariella stared at him. He had a solicitous expression on his perfectly symmetrical face, and she could almost believe that he just wanted to provide her with an opportunity. But however angelic the face, this was bribery. "I don't think so."

"I could call my friend at the *Tribune* right now if you say the word." He pulled a cellular phone from his pocket and snapped it open with an inviting look. "Come on, isn't this the chance you've been waiting for—a medical reporter job at a top newspaper? I'm very serious about this."

Ariella could not help contemplating it for a minute, but how could she trust him? The so-called job might not exist, or it might go up in smoke as soon as her tobacco story hit the presses. She smiled inwardly at her unintended pun.

"Why are you smiling?"

"Oh, I was thinking about things that go up in smoke."

"If you want you can talk to the *Tribune* yourself right now or go back to the office and verify that they do have an opening for a health reporter."

"No, no. It's all right. I just don't think this is the right time for me to leave Boston." If she were Joyce she would call him on his manipulative tactics, but she did not want to alienate him just yet. It interested her that he cared enough about this story to have prepared the perfect bait. She wanted to go back to the newsroom and think about that, and she might need to speak to him again. "I appreciate your offer, though. It's not every day I hear of an opportunity like that."

"I'll tell you what," he said, "the job offer stands open till the end of the day. Don't say 'no' now. Just call me before five if you decide you want it." His eyes pulled at her, almost mesmerizing her.

She smiled at him. "You could sell cheese in a cheese factory," she said. "And I mean that in the nicest possible way. Now I had better get back to the office."

As he rose to leave she realized that the check had never arrived; he must have made some arrangement with the management. "I'd like to pay for my lunch."

"There's no need. It's all taken care of, and I'm happy to do it."

"My story..."

"Don't say it." He flashed his glittering teeth at her once more. "You'll write the best, fairest story you can write. Now let's go."

❧

As soon as he disappeared from the *Times* parking lot she darted to a chair in the lobby and began scribbling notes as fast as she could. She had always had a talent for verbatim recall of conversations. Even as a child her telephone messages were legendary in the family; she could tell Mom precisely what words one of her bridge friends had used on the telephone. Now she knew she remembered several juicy quotes from Dornan for her article, one of them not as positive for the tobacco industry as he had thought.

Back at her desk a short while later Ariella batted out a draft of the tobacco story on her computer and tried not to think about Dornan's offer. She could not take it, of course, as it was clearly meant to buy a positive story for the tobacco industry, but it tempted her. Dreams of the health beat had motivated her since journalism school, and here at the *Times* there would always be David Ellmann to overshadow her. Chicago winters would make her miserable, she told herself, and again tried to push thoughts of the job offer aside while she struggled to achieve a balanced tone in what was a fairly damning article. She changed a few sentences to let the facts speak for themselves, and she moved Dornan's defense of the industry to a more prominent position in the piece.

At four thirty Ariella sat waiting for Joyce beneath her Sam Francis print and the hanging ferns, which, she noticed, looked a little unhealthy with some grayish fronds. Joyce breezed in, wearing a mahogany-colored pants suit and a wide black belt and spouting complaints about her busy schedule and the other editors' crazy priorities.

"You know, you could end up with two stories on the front page of the Metro section tomorrow." She sank into her leather chair and focused her full attention on Ariella. "Anything connected with the Griffin murder is hot, and this scandal at Carver really had editors talking. Every reader in Boston knows the Carver Center; more people than you'd think have had a relative treated there, and the public hears about Care for Kids at every movie theater in Boston."

"Care for Kids?"

"Ariella, you need to get out more. Haven't you noticed that all the movie theaters run a short film about Carver and collect donations for the Care for Kids fund for children with cancer?" Ariella shook her head. "Anyway, I was advocating for you in the editors' meeting just now, but there are some strong national news stories for the front page tomorrow, and that may push big local stories into Metro.

The big question is whether Congress passes tax reform today because if not there'll be a lot more flexibility in tomorrow's paper."

Ariella said a quick prayer that Congressional bickering would last one more day, and then the two women launched into the editing process. Taking the interview with Angelica first, Joyce read it, thought for a moment and then suggested rearranging the paragraphs to make it more dramatic. She also asked Ariella to add some description. Ariella did not want to reveal where the interview had occurred, and Joyce suggested describing Angelica herself to add to the human interest of the piece. Together they rewrote the lead several times to emphasize that Renaldo Colon's alibi meant that in their furor to find a murderer, the Boston police may have arrested the wrong man.

When they moved on to consider the tobacco story, Joyce pointed out that the writing had to be crystal clear so that the reader would quickly grasp the main point: that tobacco money was supporting a world-famous cancer center. Ariella posed the question Sam had asked her: whether the lead should stress the tobacco industry's or the cancer center's cynical behavior, and how important to make the bookkeeping shenanigans. They debated briefly, but Joyce insisted that the story should emphasize the cancer center's conduct over the tobacco industry's since Carver was the local institution. Nevertheless the story did not flatter the TRA, and it would not win favor with or further job offers from Brendan Dornan.

At her desk again making final changes, Ariella sighed over the loss of the Chicago position but felt relieved to have passed the point of no return, her story untainted by outside influence and the time to call Dornan now past. All around her reporters and editors were discussing leads. Studiously ignoring them she tapped at her keyboard for a few more minutes and then sent the finished articles off to Joyce through the computer network. Joyce would have a last chance to edit and then would send the computer files on to the copy editors' desk. Just out of the final daily news meeting, chief copy editor Harry O'Neal gave her a wink and a smile. As she straightened papers on her desk and rooted out some notes on an article for tomorrow, she wondered about which stories editors had pushed for the front page during the meeting. Out of the corner of her eye she could see managing editor Lester Hardman, who had the final say, sitting silently at his computer in the middle of the newsroom, sipping from a mug and considering possible front page stories. She dared not even hope for one.

At six o'clock the newsroom buzzed with activity, editorial assistants bringing photos from the composing room, the switchboard clamoring for people not at their desks, copy editors calling to one another. With the evening rush to print the paper in full swing Ariella knew it was time for her to head home, time for writers to let the editors take the field. She grabbed up her black wool coat and with a last wistful glance at the managing editor's back, left the newsroom.

24

When the twenty-odd members of the Wednesday evening lung cancer support group gathered in the hospital's second floor lounge and began filling their usual places on sofas and in armchairs, they immediately noticed a newcomer. He was a tall, long-necked man in an ill-fitting suit. Sitting beside him drumming his fingers on his knee and eagerly watching them enter sat Victor, their facilitator. Generally they began the group sessions by going around the circle reporting on the past week and its struggles, but this time Victor did not give them the opportunity.

"Friends," Victor announced with a flourish and continued in his usual stilted English, "we are fortunate to have with us a special guest tonight. He is Jerry Lesniak of the End Smoking Project, a lawyer who specializes in fighting the cigarette companies.

Now, all of you are here because cigarettes gave you lung cancer. Each week we talk about your sufferings and struggles, your defeats and victories, and some of you have been depressed; others angry at your fate. Together we try to stay away from cigarettes, rebuild hope and improve our lives, and Jerry is here because he wants to help you in that effort. I do not know that Jerry's approach will be right for everyone here, but I think he is worth hearing if you are willing to listen. Will you agree to hear his presentation? There will be much time for questions after."

As a chorus of agreement met his question, Jerry disentangled his crossed long legs, one from another, leaned forward in his chair, and looked around the circle at each of the group members. "You," he said, "are the reason for all the work I do. Every one of you is a victim of the tobacco industry." A burly gray-haired man began to protest, but Jerry held up his palm to stop him. "Some of you may not know or accept this fact because you blame yourselves for smoking, but legally speaking the tobacco companies are at fault and should be made to pay. They have violated the public trust, lied to consumers for over forty years, and sold a deadly product as if it were candy."

He paused to let that remark sink in, and the group leaned toward him to catch his words, his passion and sincerity overcoming his awkwardness.

"I am putting together a Massachusetts class action lawsuit against the cigarette companies, and I would like you to join me as plaintiffs, as complainants in the suit, because you have been seriously injured by smoking. I think we can win this fight, and in winning gain not only money to pay your medical bills, but publicity about the evils of cigarettes and stiff fines called punitive damages, which will make it hard for the cigarette companies to survive. Let me pause for questions, and then I'll go into some specifics."

The burly gray-haired man spoke first, and then the questions came fast and furious. Victor sat back in his chair, crossed his arms over his chest and allowed a grin to spread across his face for a moment. Instead of the usual glum faces around the circle, the cancer survivors had animated expressions, some eager, others hostile, but none flat. The hour fled fast, and at its end several people asked whether Jerry could join them again the following week to continue the discussion. A few were willing to join the lawsuit right then and there, and they lingered as Jerry retrieved the necessary papers from a battered briefcase. And Victor wallowed in the glory of his small revenge—that the tobacco industry was paying for this night's group session.

∾

Later, as it neared eight thirty at night, the *Times* copy editors were hard at work hunting down errors in computerized story files. As soon as they completed copy-editing one story, Harry O'Neal would immediately assign another. The night owls of the newspaper, copy editors rarely dealt with daily reporters personally, but if they wished to make a major change in the content of an article they had to clear it with the assignment editor for that story. If they could reach neither the editor nor the writer, Harry O'Neal made the decision.

At eight thirty Harry had just reviewed a story on a possible transit workers' strike and pressed the "send" button in the newsroom to transmit the article to the photographic typesetter in the composing room. The telephone rang on his desk.

"Harry," said a silky voice, "it's Brendan."

"Brendan! Listen, it's crunch time here, but how are the wife and kids?"

"Oh, Deirdre is becoming a star gymnast, and Sean loves that basketball hoop you gave him, but Harry, I'd like to ask a favor. I hear there's a story for tomorrow on cigarette company contributions to the Carver Center. Can you confirm that?"

Harry glanced around and lowered his voice. "Yup, there is."

"Would you mind telling me how it reads?"

"Well, I have it right here. I can't read it to you, Brendan, but I can tell you that you won't love it."

"That bad?"

"Don't get me wrong. It could be a lot harder on the industry, but it's tough enough to make certain people squirm. Worse than the last tobacco story we printed."

"Can you tone it down at all?"

"Well, Brendan..." Harry scratched the back of his neck and tugged on his collar. "I can soften a few sentences, but you still won't be thrilled."

"Would you do what you can? I'd be grateful."

"Sure, sure. Only don't expect miracles."

"I'd appreciate whatever you can do, and Patty and I would love to take you and the family sailing on Saturday if you want."

"That would be great. Listen, I have to go."

"Okay. Thanks, Harry. See you Saturday."

❦

Half an hour later in a penthouse apartment overlooking Boston harbor the telephone rang beside Leland Chambers' overstuffed armchair, where he lounged, sipping scotch and making notes for the new United Way campaign he was running. Grandson of the original publisher of the *Boston Times*, Leland had strong feelings about *his* paper, but he generally left the nitty gritty to the Editor-in-Chief and focused on finances and highly visible charity work.

Annoyed at the interruption he answered curtly, "Yes."

"It's Brendan Dornan. I'm sorry to disturb you at night, but I have something rather urgent to discuss with you."

"I'm listening."

"There's a major anti-tobacco story coming out in tomorrow's paper. You're aware of that?"

"Actually, I heard that the story hits Harvard harder than it does you."

"Well, it's a pretty tough story, from what I hear. We would rather you not publish it."

Leland rapped his knuckles on the mahogany occasional table beside him. "I'm the Publisher, Brendan, not the Editor-in-Chief. I don't get mixed up in editorial business."

"We both know you can kill that story if you want to."

"Maybe so, but it'll make my troops furious."

"I'm asking you to kill it." Brendan used his smoothest tone. "My bosses are pretty upset about the negative publicity they've been getting lately. Just last month you ran several stories on the legislative fight to ban smoking in schools. Isn't there any real news out there?"

"Some people think this is real news," Leland said mildly.

"I'm sorry about this because we go way back, you and I, but I've been asked to convey to you that if this story runs the tobacco companies will be forced to pull all of our advertising from the *Times*. That includes our subsidiaries: Hearst Media, Desktop office products, Barnes movie theaters, First Foods, and the Panda Beverage Company."

"You're serious about this one."

"The big boys are dead serious. They do not want to read the word 'tobacco' in tomorrow's paper."

"Let me ask you something, Brendan. Since our days at Boston College, have you ever known me to cave in to pressure?"

"Don't think of it as pressure, just a smart business decision. We offer a lot of ad revenue, and we don't ask for much. In ten years it's been a handful of times I've called you."

"That's true. And last time I accommodated you, but there was no talk of pulling advertising permanently."

"Talk about pressure—the industry is under intense pressure these days. We just want to keep things quieter for a little while."

"I won't do it, Brendan. I won't muck around in the Editor-in-Chief's job, and I don't see you calling him. Because you know he won't listen. He doesn't give two hoots about ad revenue."

"You do, though. You're a businessman, Lee. You know a newspaper can't live without its advertisers. We have a good working relationship; I'm bringing in a lot of money for you; don't let me down. Don't let me go."

Leland stared hard at the ruby tones in his oriental rug. "That's your decision. I'd like to keep your ads, but if you go, you go."

"At least think it over for an hour. I'm asking you as an old college buddy. I'll call back in an hour to see what you say then."

"No, don't."

"All right, you call me at home in an hour if you

change your mind. Think about all that revenue."

"There's not a snowball's chance in hell I'll change my mind, Brendan, but I'll be sure to call you if I do."

"All right, Lee. Think it over." Brendan hung up and swore.

25

The phone rang at 6:45 a.m. Thursday morning. Ariella groaned and let it ring twice more before she answered it.

"Have you see the paper?" David asked her.

"No, and since when do you get up at this hour?"

"Since a one-year-old moved into the guest room. Yolanda's up at six every day, and she's off and running around the house. I've got to be up to supervise."

"What about her mother?"

"Okay, you got me. I actually like watching the kid. Anyway, when she comes in my room at six and climbs into my bed and tells me it's morning, it's hard to argue with her."

She wondered whether Angelica ever climbed in too. "You always let women push you around."

"Story of my life." He chuckled. "But Ari, there's an article in the *Daily* that you've got to get out of bed and read."

"The *Daily*?—I don't get the *Daily*, just the *Times*. And I'm not in bed." It was a transparent lie, but she wasn't thinking straight. She just did not want him to know that Sam had spent the night. Staring at the rumpled pillow beside her, she wondered whether he had gone to the bathroom.

"Don't wreck my illusions. I was having such fun fantasizing. But Ariella, you should get the *Daily*; it's important to know what the competition is doing, especially today. They have a jailhouse interview with Renaldo Colon on the front page, saying he was with his sister at a bar the night of the Griffin murders, not home with Angelica."

"What?"

"That's what he said. And his sister backed him up."

She was sitting up straight now, gripping the phone. "Is he at M.C.I. Walpole?"

"Yes, but I doubt you'll be able to reach him."

"The *Daily* reporter talked to him."

"That was before his alibis became big news. The police department is going to think there's far too much interest in Colon's possible innocence, and they'll clamp down on the press. They want this Griffin murder case tied up neat and tidy."

"Did Angelica tell me the truth?"

"She swears she did. She says he does go to that bar a lot, though."

"El Lagarto?"

"That's the one."

"Oh, God. Joyce will be furious. I look like a fool, and the paper looks pretty silly too. Who could have imagined there'd be two conflicting alibis for Colon on the same morning in the city's big rival newspapers? And mine definitely looks weaker. What do I tell Joyce?"

"Tell her you need a little time to back up your story. She won't be happy, but she'll support you."

Just then Sam emerged from her bathroom, naked.

"I'd better go, David." She put a finger over her lips hoping Sam would not betray his presence.

"Wait, I also have to congratulate you. Your tobacco story is terrific."

"So it got in after all? I got a late night call from Joyce that they might hold it for another day."

"Got in? Ari, it's on the front page."

"What?!" She felt blood rushing to her head. "Oh my God, I've got to go see it. Goodbye, David."

"You're in the big leagues now. Bye!"

She jumped out of bed and hurtled into Sam's chest, squeezing him with all her might, then bouncing on the balls of her feet. "I did it. The front page, Sam! I can't believe it."

"A front page story? Oh, honey, that's fantastic!" He gave her a sloppy, enthusiastic kiss.

She batted him away. "Hold on a minute and let me grab my newspaper from the front door."

As she jogged into the living room, he called after her, "Does David call you every morning?"

"What's wrong with you? Are you terminally jealous? You're not going to spoil my big moment, are you?" She returned to the bedroom with a smile, clutching the paper. "For your information he has a woman living with him right now."

"That doesn't mean he doesn't have the hots for you."

"That's very flattering. I've always wanted to be part of a harem. Now be quiet so I can read this."

He complied, settling back onto the bed, limbs splayed, watching her. After a few minutes she resurfaced from her thoughts.

"They toned it down a bit, rearranged some things, but it reads well. The folks at Carver sure won't like it, though."

"It's the tobacco piece? I assumed it was the murder."

"Are you upset?"

"No, not at all. Just surprised at the paper's courage in standing up to the tobacco industry. So what happened to the other story?"

"Well, that's the bad news David told me. The *Daily* has a different alibi story—Colon says he was with his sister at a bar when the murders happened."

"Ugh. That looks pretty bad for you. Colon's girlfriend must have lied."

"Not necessarily. Colon himself might be lying."

"Oh come on, Ariella. Why?"

"Because he didn't know whether she would back him up, whether she was still loyal to him. She left him only a couple of days ago. His sister might have seemed a safer bet."

"Did the reporter talk to her?"

"Yeah. The sister corroborated his story."

"The girlfriend must be lying."

Ariella felt her temper rising. "How do you know? I'm the one who interviewed this woman at length, and I feel she's credible. Now I just have to get some support for her story—or discredit the bar alibi."

"You're nuts."

"So nuts that I have a front page story in the *Times*." She hugged the newspaper to her chest in a protective gesture.

"Oh honey, I know this means a lot to you. What a crazy day. A front page story and a serious professional headache all before seven in the morning." He reached for her hand. "You're a great reporter. I still think Colon probably did it, but you have a right to think otherwise. I only wish these stories hadn't broken just as I was getting to know you."

She sighed and stifled her urge to apologize, thinking of Angelica's advice about standing up to him. "It's true the timing hasn't been the greatest. But this is who I am. I'll always have stories popping up out of the blue. If you want to hang around me you'd better get used to it." The second the words left her mouth she regretted them, and fear surged within her that he would simply gather up his clothes and walk out. Instead he pulled her against his warm body and held her close. Then his fingers began to explore.

Back at her newsroom desk late that morning Ariella shoved a stack of papers aside, jostling a red pen into slow motion. She took a deep breath, let it out, and deliberately ignored the pen as it rolled off the desktop, bounced, and came to rest beside her boot heel. Just as David had predicted, the police department and prison authorities at M.C.I. Walpole had refused to let her talk to Renaldo Colon. The assistant superintendent of the prison had treated her with suspicion, lecturing her on prison discipline and saying that Colon would receive no special privileges. He would not allow a media circus at Walpole, he said, and would do everything in his power to keep Colon from becoming a celebrity. Despite her urging, he would make no appointment for her to interview Colon and would not even consider scheduling one for at least a week. To a reporter, a week is an eternity, but Ariella tried to contain her frustration and remain pleasant.

As for the police department spokesman, he was downright hostile, clearly viewing her as an enemy because of her alibi article. He emphasized that Colon remained the prime suspect in the Griffin murders and that his two conflicting alibis canceled each other out. Furthermore, his sister and his girlfriend were just the kind of witnesses likely to lie for him. He reminded her of the horrible nature of the crime and the suffering of the victim's family and stressed the department's determination to bring the perpetrator to justice, all the while casting aspersions on her own motives in covering the case.

After several futile phone calls, a quick trip to El Lagarto Bar had also borne little fruit. The regular evening bartender had no recollection of the night in question and could only concur that Renaldo frequented the bar with his sister and might have been there the night of the murders. One of the waitresses claimed that Renaldo had not come to the bar as often as usual in the week before Thanksgiving. She had worked there the night of the Griffin murders but could not remember for certain whether Renaldo had stopped in. Although Ariella suspected the waitress might remember more than she admitted, no magic words had yet jogged her memory.

Ariella knew that she should pay the bar another visit that night and try to find a useful witness among the regular customers, but she was feeling frustrated. It would be difficult to establish for certain that a frequent patron like Renaldo had not visited the bar on a certain night, especially when his sister claimed he had. Ariella needed several witnesses with ironclad stories, not a bunch of drinkers at a bar who could easily be accused of poor memory, inattention, or even hallucinations.

So here she sat trying to think of another line of attack to support her story. An early meeting with Joyce had yielded less scolding but also fewer suggestions than she had expected. Several reporters had given her pitying looks, and a couple had stopped at her desk to commiserate, but none had offered a good solution to her problem.

The police commissioner was holding a press conference on Colon at noon, but the *Times* city editor had assigned a police beat reporter, not Ariella, to cover the story. Although this assignment was standard practice, not a punishment, she felt ignored, and now that it was too late to arrive on time, wondered whether she might have gotten some hint of a lead at the press conference.

She picked up the phone and twirled the cord. Perhaps she should ask Sam to accompany her to El Lagarto that night. Usually she worked alone, but it had seemed a risky place for a lone woman to visit. She had never before needed a man to protect her during an investigation, but she had also never investigated a murder. It galled her to admit it, but she probably ought to bring a companion. Just then the telephone receiver barked, "If you'd like to make a call, please hang up and try again; if you need help, dial the operator." She hung up with a bang. She wished she could ask David to come to El Lagarto; he believed in her story, and as a reporter he might actually help her turn up a lead, but she did not want anyone who knew Renaldo Colon to meet David. His and Angelica's safety might depend on it. In any case, if all she needed was protection, Sam's height and his scowl made him far more intimidating a figure than pudgy David. She smiled a little at the notion of using Sam as a beefy security guard, picked up the phone again and dialed his number.

"Why are you doing this?" he asked her.

"Because I want to know the truth."

"What if your story was wrong? What if Angelica is lying?"

"Then I'll have to write about that."

"Okay," he said. "I'll go. But on one condition."

She snorted. "Of course—a condition. What?"

"If I say it's time to leave, you don't argue with me."

"Well, I need time to poke around and talk to people. How will you know I've gotten enough material? Don't you think I should be the one to decide when we're done?"

"Ariella, you want me along because you're nervous about this bar, right?"

She offered, "Actually, I thought it would be a fun date," but he didn't laugh.

"All I'm asking is that if something goes wrong, or someone seems threatening to me and I want to get you out of there, you'll listen to me." He paused. "Look, I'm glad you called me because I've been worried about your working on this murder case. I have to admit I care about your safety more than I do about the integrity of the story or your reputation at the paper. I really don't want you to get hurt, Ariella."

She could have found his choice of words offensive, but overriding any annoyance was a wave of pleasure that he was worried about her, that he cared about her.

He was continuing. "I definitely want to come tonight, and I want you to know I respect you for pursuing the truth."

"Yeah, well, I don't have high hopes that some drunks are going to straighten out this mess."

"Well, if they have nothing to offer I'll buy you a drink and then carry you off to my apartment to distract you from your troubles."

"It's a deal." She smiled, wondering for the thousandth time how he could find her so attractive. But he did. It struck her then that she had finally accepted this as fact and no longer harbored the belief that he was sleeping with her for convenience until Natalie Ward offered her long legs. Although she knew she ought to further analyze how she felt about him, she had too much work to do.

26

Boston's South End neighborhood, little known to tourists, packed an explosive mix of gays, blacks, Latinos, yuppies and students from nearby Northeastern University. Flanked by downtown on one side and Roxbury on the other, it was a place of contrast, a rare meeting ground in a city famous for segregation. Ariella and Sam found a parking space on a dingy side street where gentrification had not yet swept through. Grime caked the old brownstone walk-up buildings, and rubbish danced along the sidewalk in the stiff January wind. Turning the corner onto Columbus Avenue, they found far more light, not only from the streetlamps but from headlights of cars zooming past. Halfway down the block between a check-cashing establishment and a grocery mart studded with cigarette ads lay the solid black door and tinted windows of the bar they sought.

When Ariella swung the heavy door of El Lagarto open at ten thirty that night, Sam trailing in her wake and trying to keep a low profile, she found the joint packed with smoke and people. She had told him to dress in unobtrusive clothes, and he was wearing faded jeans and a pale nubby sweater, but clothes could not diminish his height or his powerful physical presence. She glanced around, taking in the scene, and moved to the end of the bar, where two swarthy men slid aside a little to let her stand close. Whether to demonstrate possession or simply to be heard, she did not know, but Sam bent to her ear and asked, "Do you want a beer?"

"Sure." She twisted her head to smile at him. "A Sam Adams, if they have it."

He continued to whisper in her ear. "Whoever decorated the place must have loved dark green."

"Maybe the original owner was an Irishman."

He nodded and ordered for them while she examined the crowd.

When the thin, bearded bartender arrived with their order, he recognized Ariella. "Hey, the newspaper lady. You know, you ought to talk to Fermin and Kenny. Maybe they can help you out. They're regulars, already set up in their favorite spot." He pointed. "See the two guys at the other end of the bar? One's in a black turtleneck, the other in a blue shirt." Ariella did not show her surprise at his help, just thanked him with a big smile.

She had asked him that morning, but since he seemed in an expansive mood she tried again: "So what do you think of Renaldo Colon?" Several people heard the question and looked up.

"He's okay. Never started a fight in here. Paid for his drinks."

"Do you think he killed Mrs. Griffin?"

The bartender drummed on the bar with the flat of his hand. "I got people waiting to be served here. Like I told you this morning, I couldn't say. I wouldn't think so. Why would he? But I don't know nothing about his personal business."

"Did he seem like a killer to you?"

"No, but I don't like to think anybody in here is dangerous. Might give me high blood pressure. Maybe I'm kidding myself."

"The world is a dangerous place," Sam put in, glaring at a man who had leaned close to Ariella to hear their conversation over the din.

She raised her eyebrows at him. "Uh, Sam, I'm going down to the end of the bar to talk to Kenny and Fermin, but I think you should stay here."

He looked disapproving but said only, "If you want me, just wave."

She slipped through the crowd to the other end of the bar where a man in his forties wearing blue, a dark and stocky figure with protruding eyeballs, sat with both hands wrapped around his glass, sipping amber liquid. His gaunt companion in black looked closer to fifty and had a receding hairline and a lumpy nose that might have gotten its shape from a well-placed fist.

When she introduced herself and her purpose, Kenny, the stocky one, proved far more voluble. "Renaldo," he told Ariella, "Known him for years. Knew him since he was sixteen or something. Ain't that right, Fermin?"

The other man nodded sourly. Kenny then launched into several colorful stories about Renaldo's career as a teenage shoplifter, and his string of girlfriends, whom he impressed with tall tales of his criminal adventures. "He's a schemer. Now and then he'll get some idea in his head, and then no one can talk him out of it. Like when he got revenge on Luis Amarillo."

The right corner of Fermin's mouth tilted upward and the eye above it narrowed in amusement at the memory.

Kenny went on, "Luis had been going out with Renaldo's sister, and it came out Luis gave her a black eye, and Renaldo was mad. But he didn't just go beat the hell out of him. He arranged for Luis' boss at the warehouse to find out Luis was sneaking money from the office, and the boss smashed him so bad he ended up in the hospital. Then Renaldo told everybody it was him masterminded it. Nobody ever knew how he figured out Luis was stealing on the job, but I guess it takes one to know one."

"Did he ever hit his own girlfriends?"

"Not Renaldo. For one, he's not hot-tempered like some. He don't fight much and never with a woman. Mostly he just likes to brag, and you know, get lucky. If he don't like what a woman does, he don't bother to hit her, he just disappear for a while." Kenny's hands trembled as he brought his glass to his lips.

"Disappears?"

"Well, finds another woman for a while. You know...."

It did not take a specialist to diagnose Kenny as an alcoholic, not the world's greatest witness, but he had given her some worthwhile background. So she asked: "Do you think he killed Laurie Griffin?"

"No. Not him. It's not like him. They say he jumped into the car, held a gun to the guy's head and forced him to drive all over Roxbury, then shot them both just to steal a little jewelry. The guy's wallet wasn't even taken. I can't see Renaldo carjacking like that—too random—or shooting some pregnant woman straight in the stomach either. That would make him sick. He never worked alone, and he never went for jewelry before, that I know of, only cash in the register or something out of a store he could use."

"Fermin?"

"Wasn't Renaldo. Doesn't have the balls." Fermin sneered. "Cops can tell, but they'll hang him high anyway." He took a big swallow from a beer bottle.

"Were you guys here the night of the murders?"

"Yeah. Must have been," said Kenny. "It's our home away from home." He grinned at her showing uneven front teeth.

"Was Renaldo in here with his sister?"

"That's what she says. He probably was. He's here with her once a week or more."

"You don't know for sure?" When he shook his head she did not even press him, just turned to Fermin.

"You asking me to go back months and tell one night from another?"

She sighed. Then she glanced up at Sam and saw him raise his eyebrows and nod her over. He had an intense look as if he had been trying for some time to get her attention. "Well, I appreciate your talking to me. Do you mind giving me your last names?" They did mind, especially Fermin, and in fact she had to promise to disguise their first names in the newspaper. Since they had not given her any key facts, she agreed.

Threading her way back to Sam she felt a pinch and a murmur of "Nice ass, lady," but when she whipped around she could not tell who had done it. It was a relief to reach Sam, and to feel his arm draped around her again.

His head bent to her ear. "Why weren't you looking at me? I was trying to get you away from those two drunks the last fifteen minutes. A waitress came by and asked me if I was with you. When I said I was, she told me she wanted to talk to you, had something to tell you. She said to meet her in the hallway out to the kitchen by the door to the ladies' room. Just wait till she comes." Ariella was pulling out of his arm to head for the bathroom when he snapped, "Wait." He tightened his grasp and whispered, "I want to come as far as she'll let me. I don't like you following her into some dark corner at the back of the building. What if she's up to something?"

"Like what?"

"I don't know, but I'm following you."

She gave in gracefully—in light of the pincher, grateful not to run the gamut of that crowd alone again—and led the way through the room, through a swinging door and into a dingy corridor illuminated by light spilling around the half-open kitchen door at the hallway's end. Near the kitchen she spotted a fiberboard door marked in black and gold decal letters, "Damas." She stood there and waited, Sam lingering several feet away trying not to cramp her. Just as she was beginning to get impatient, the waitress appeared from the kitchen and approached with a blank face. She was a woman with ample curves, heavy thighs, skin the color of milk chocolate, and short-cropped hair atop a face the shape of an upside-down egg.

"It's nice of you to talk with me," Ariella offered, to relax her.

"Yeah." She grabbed the door knob of the ladies' room door. "Come in here a minute."

"I'll come with you." Sam spoke softly but with determination.

"No." The waitress kept her back to him. "I'm talking only to her. You can stand right outside the door, Mr. Machismo. It'll only take a minute."

"It's okay, Sam." Ariella gave him a long look, hoping

he knew that she was perfectly capable of screaming for his help if she needed it.

The waitress snorted. "Let's get this over with." She swung the door open to reveal a one-stall bathroom the size of a closet and ushered Ariella inside, where graying white surrounded her, except for the ceiling, which someone had once painted with fat green shamrocks and pink roses, now peeling away. Sliding the rusty bolt lock shut behind her the waitress turned to Ariella, only inches away in the cramped space, the cloying smell of vanilla deodorizer filling the air. Ariella coughed and folded her arms across her chest.

"This is against my better judgment," the woman grumbled, "only he won't listen to me. You want to know if Renaldo Colon killed Laurie Griffin, right? Well, my boyfriend—he knows something about that."

Ariella chose her words carefully. "Something good for Renaldo or bad for Renaldo?"

"That's for him to say. None of my business. I don't want to be any more mixed up in this than I am. Renaldo's an ex-con, you know, and he may be locked up, but he's got some rough friends walking around the streets right now."

"You're afraid of him?"

"Shit, yeah. If you had any sense you would be too."

"Um." Ariella decided polite subtlety was of no use in this situation. "So how can I see your boyfriend? I assume he gave you this message for me."

The waitress gave her a peevish look. "Unfortunately, yeah. He works across the street at the pizza parlor, Torchia's."

"What's his name?"

"E.R."

"E.R. what?"

"I don't know if I should give you that. You have to have his full name in the paper?"

Ariella decided to be honest with her. "If I think his information is important, then yes, I need his name to show he believes in his story. It'll be up to him, though, whether I use it."

"Well," the waitress drew out the syllable and seemed to shrink a little as she gave up the name, "it's Johnson."

"E.R. Johnson?"

"Yeah. Ernest 'E.R.' Johnson. Fool that he is. He's over there at Torchia's tonight, but he might be out delivering. You'll have to wait till he has a break or finishes his shift in about an hour."

"That's all right. I can wait. So he knows I'm coming?"

"Well, after I told him I'd seen you this morning nosing around asking questions about Colon, he told me if you ever came back to say he wanted to talk to you. I called him ten minutes ago to say you were here, and he told me to send you over there. He's set on telling you what he knows, though God knows why. You just be careful what you print 'cause if he gets hurt these next two weeks I'll personally kick your... butt."

"It'll be okay."

"Sure. Like you know anything about ex-cons."

Ariella smiled. "More than I used to. You know who understands just how you feel, that guy outside the door. He wants me to get my nose out of this case, pack up, go home, and sit quietly in my rocking chair where it's safe."

The waitress nodded. "In his lap. Yeah, he's no fool. Stay out of trouble when you can, that's what I say. But you won't listen. All right, let's get out of here." She slid the bolt open, and pushed on the door, practically smacking into Sam, who had to step back in a hurry. "She's yours," the waitress told him with a smirk and hurried down the corridor, through the swinging door into the crowd of customers before Ariella could even thank her.

"We have to leave," Ariella told him. "Let's get our coats."

"Are we going home?" he asked, as he grasped her hand and led her toward the bar.

"No."

27

They crossed the broad, dark expanse of Columbus Avenue, still busy with speeding cars at eleven thirty at night. A horn blared, and a black woman on the corner screamed at someone in a car stopped at the traffic light in front of her. Ariella shrank back into her coat at the desperate edge to the scream, suddenly wishing she were home in bed. Impatient with herself, she focused on the question at hand: would Johnson have a story for her? Sam took her hand as they walked down the sidewalk among the long shadows of telephone poles and past a ragged man asleep in a doorway.

Torchia's lay in the converted basement of an old brownstone house, and they had to walk down half a flight of steps to its glass door, lit by a glaring scarlet neon sign. Pushing the door open they found a surprising number of people sitting at rickety tables eating pizza. Leading Sam to the counter in the back Ariella ordered two slices and two Cokes from a bored-looking girl with a long ponytail and asked whether E.R. was around. Informed that he would return from a delivery in a few minutes she asked the girl to give him the message that his friend, Ariella, wanted to say "hello."

Sam gave her a curious look as they slid into folding

chairs at a table for two in the corner, but rather than say anything bit into his pizza. When she did nothing to illuminate their situation he finally said, "Not bad."

"The pizza?"

"No, your self-control. Although the pizza's pretty good too."

She gave him a deadpan stare. "Well, if you think that's going to provoke any information, you have another thought coming."

"Is there anything for me to be worried about?"

"I don't think so."

"Well that's a definitive statement. Okay, let's talk about the weather. Cold, blustery day, isn't it?"

She smiled. "That sounds like Winnie the Pooh. I used to read it to Ruby all the time, and I had to explain to her what a blustery day was."

"Charming."

"You're laughing at me."

"No, actually, you really are charming. If I sounded edgy it's because I'm nervous, and I want to get out of here and take you home."

"Shouldn't be long." She polished off her pizza slice. Just then she spotted an erect young black man behind the counter talking to the woman with the ponytail. He moved around the counter's corner and headed toward her with unhurried directness. "That's him," she murmured to Sam.

"Who?"

But before she could answer, the man had reached their table and was stretching out his hand to Ariella. "E.R. Johnson," he said. "You want to hear what I know about Renaldo?"

"Yes, and I'm Ariella Richardson. But maybe we

should talk in a more private place."

"I don't know where."

"I've got a car," Sam offered.

"Who are you?" E.R. asked mildly but with a hint of challenge, looking Sam over.

"Sam Becker." Sam offered neither a hand nor a smile.

"He's my boyfriend," Ariella put in quickly. "Not a reporter. Just hanging out with me tonight."

"Protecting your woman." Ariella pursed her lips at that but said nothing. A flash of bright teeth crossed E.R.'s face, and his erect bearing relaxed slightly. He had the muscular but slight frame of a runner and stood only a few inches taller than Ariella. Unlike his girlfriend he seemed to keep emotions in check. "Okay, we can talk in your car, Sam. I'm still on delivery, but there aren't any orders right now, and I can take my beeper."

She led the way out of the pizza parlor and then walked along beside E.R., Sam following a few paces behind them. Within moments her toes began to ice over beneath her thin leather boots, and she wished she had worn lined work boots instead, but image had been important tonight. No self-respecting Latino woman would wear frayed men's work boots to a bar in the evening.

When they reached Sam's car he ushered her into the driver's seat, unlocked the front passenger door for E.R. and got into the back seat behind her. His silent looming presence both unnerved and comforted her, creating a tangle of emotions that she shoved aside as she pulled out a small notebook and turned to the young man beside her.

Without preamble she asked, "So what do you know about Renaldo Colon?"

"I know he's innocent, you know what I'm saying?"

"How do you know?"

"Well, they say the killer car-jacked the Griffins just after nine over on Longwood Avenue, right?" He had a wide-eyed, earnest look as if urging her to come along on his mental journey.

"Yes. The police say they came out of a childbirth class at Brigham and Women's Hospital at nine and were probably in their car turning onto Longwood by five after."

"That's it, then. I delivered a pizza to Renaldo and his woman at their place here in the South End just after nine that night. No way he could have been running the Griffins all over Mission Hill and Roxbury at the same time."

Ariella's eyes widened, but she tried to control herself. "You're sure it was that night?"

"Um hm. I had just taken this delivery job that week. It was my first Sunday on the job and my first call over to Taylor Street, which is a damn little alley off Dwight, and I had to ask the boss where it was at, and he said I better learn the South End quick if I want to keep this job. The order was for Renaldo. First time I been over there, but I been there a lot of times since." He seemed pleased that she was listening so hard.

"How many times?"

"Five or six. He likes our pizza."

"It's true that Renaldo was living with his girlfriend on Taylor Street. But which Sunday was it? What was the date?" She didn't want to irritate him, but she had to push him on the details.

"Had to be November 14th. I started the job Monday the 8th."

"What time did you get to Renaldo's?"

"Maybe ten after nine."

"How can you be sure?"

"Well, I start my shift at nine. I work every night— nine to midnight. And that was my first call that night. Got into work and had to go right out to Taylor Street, and like I told you I had to ask where that was at, and it pissed off the boss real bad. Takes about five-ten minutes to get over there. It's not far."

"When you got there what was going on?"

"Not much. His woman was lying around bitching and moaning 'bout not feeling well. She was watching T.V., and the little kid was running around in her diaper."

"And Renaldo?"

"He came to the door."

"Do you remember what he said?"

"You know, I hadn't remembered it. But then I read what you wrote in yesterday's paper about Renaldo's woman, what she said about that night and watching that movie, 'Big.' I think that was the time he asked me what women see in Tom Hanks. Must have been that night. I said I thought Tom Hanks was ugly as a cockroach, and damn, he liked that one. Told it to his woman: 'You hear what this guy's saying, that Tom Hanks is a cockroach?' And he started laughing, and she started swearing at him for drowning out the T.V."

"Could you see what she was watching?"

"Nope. I didn't go in or nothing, just stood in the door. It's not my business to be busting into people's homes. I just get paid and get going."

"Had you ever seen Renaldo before Sunday, November 14th?"

"Nope."

"And when have you seen him since?"

"Outside of those five-six pizza deliveries, never."

"Ever met the Griffins?"

"Me?" E.R. laughed. "Shit, no. Let me tell ya, people like that don't come around my neighborhood. They just stay holed up in their little suburbs."

"Do you know anybody connected to this case?"

He gave her a hard look. "Nope. Otherwise why would I be talking to you? You the only one I know. I read what you wrote about Renaldo in the paper, that his woman says he was home with her. And it's the truth. The cops are something else. They don't care who did it, just want to lock somebody up."

"Why do you care?"

"Don't like to see another brother go to jail who didn't do nothing."

"You know much about that?"

"You grow up black in Boston, and you know plenty. So, look. You believe me or what?"

"I do." She nodded her head slowly, taking it all in.

He flashed her a smile, and some current of understanding passed between them.

"How old are you, if you don't mind my asking?"

"Nineteen."

"Why do they call you E.R.?"

"'Cause I like life fast and hectic, you know what I'm saying?"

Ariella nodded and her lips curled upward in a slight smile. "Well, E.R. I'm really glad you found me. You've got an important story here, and it's going to help a lot backing up what I wrote in yesterday's paper. If I find I need to ask you a few more questions how can I contact you?" He scribbled a phone number in her notebook. "And may I use your name in the paper?"

"Sure, sure. My woman'll kill me, but sure."

"She's afraid for you."

"That's 'cause she don't believe me, and she thinks somehow Renaldo's going to come after me. That's crazy, and I can take care of myself. But you know what? You should watch your back. You pointing the finger away from Renaldo's gonna make the real killer mad, you know what I'm saying?"

"I know what you're saying," came Sam's voice from the back seat, the first words he had uttered since they entered the car.

E.R. twisted around. "Yeah, well you better look out for her, man. Something deep's going on, and the cops don't know shit about it. There's some crazy scum out there that don't care what he does—shot one pregnant woman in the stomach, who knows what's next?"

"You're right," Sam said.

She tried to lighten the mood. "Maybe he doesn't read the papers." Neither man laughed. "It's cold. I'll drive you back over to Torchia's. Would you pass me the car keys, Sam?"

He did.

⤚

When Ariella and Sam finally reached her apartment well after midnight, her mind was racing, and her fingers shook as she tried to get her key into the lock. Once inside she dropped her bags inches from the door and ever the reporter, jogged straight to the kitchen to check her messages. The machine showed four phone calls, but oddly all four times the caller had hung up. Sam was stripping off his sweater illuminated only by the streetlamp outside the window, neither of them having bothered to flip the light switch. As he dropped the sweater on her sofa she noticed how the shadow he cast rose over him, its head spreading to the ceiling.

The phone rang.

"What the hell?"

"I hope it's not Nina. She's the only one who ever calls at this hour, and it's always that Ruby's been hospitalized." She grabbed the phone. "Hello."

"Ariella Richardson?" a man's voice grated out.

"Yes."

"I read your articles, and I'm warning you. You better quit writing about my business in the paper, or I'll get somebody to break your arms. Your arms, your fingers, maybe your head. Don't think I can't do it." She stood there in shock, gripping the receiver as his voice rose, "Are you listening to me, you slut? Don't you dare hang up. I'm not a violent man, but fuck all, you're provoking me. Stay out of my business, you hear?" With a slam the connection was cut.

"Oh my God," she whispered. In an instant Sam had his arms around her, and she hugged him hard, burying her face in his chest.

"What is it? Is it Ruby?"

She didn't answer for a minute, giving in to the shaking that possessed her body. When she spoke his chest muffled her words. "It was a man. He threatened to hurt me if I keep writing about his business."

"Renaldo. I'm going to call the police right now and tell them to..."

"Sam," she spoke sharply and looked up into his face,

"How could Renaldo phone me at this hour from prison? They get locked in for the night at like nine o'clock, and it's after one in the morning now."

"He found a way. Or he had someone call for him."

"I don't think so. This guy was mad. He was taking my articles personally. And he had a little of that flat Southie accent. I don't think a Dominican guy would sound like that."

"Have you ever heard Renaldo speak?"

"No. He told me to stay out of his 'business,' though. He said that twice. Good God, do you think it could be...?" She balled up a fist and bit down on her forefinger joint.

"Who?"

She sighed. "I met a guy for lunch. A tobacco industry lobbyist. Irish, a very smooth talker, but with a hint of something... I don't know. I just didn't trust him. He was incredibly controlling, used to winning, the kind who might turn nasty if he snapped. I can usually recognize that kind of guy because I almost married one."

His eyes were wide. "Almost married one? No, don't tell me now. What exactly did the caller say to frighten you?"

"He said he'd break my arms, my fingers and maybe my head." By force of will she stilled the shaking.

"Holy shit. You think some lobbyist would threaten you like that?"

"He said, 'Don't think I can't do it.'"

"Colon might say that, meaning he had a long reach from prison."

"He said, 'I'm not a violent man, but you're provoking me.'" She began trembling again.

"Well, you always tell me Colon's not violent, or thinks he isn't, though he spent ten years in jail for armed robbery and shooting a man in the leg...."

"I don't know who it was. I'm just scared."

"Of course you are, honey." His tone gentled, and he stroked her back. "I can't believe you can recall every word and analyze it after being threatened like that."

She smiled into his chest. "I'll take that as a compliment."

"It is one. Look, we need to call the police, but before we do, I want to get something straight. I don't want you to be alone until this gets resolved. I'm going to stay with you tonight, but I have to go away tomorrow night for the long weekend—up to northern New Hampshire. I'm presenting at a conference at a cross-country ski resort in Jackson. Would you come with me? It'll get you away from this guy, whoever he is, give us time to think, and I won't have to worry about you."

"Would you worry?"

"Damn right, I would. Come on, Ariella. It'll give us some time together."

"Yes." She didn't even stop to think about work. "It would be a relief to go."

28

The next morning Ariella was in Joyce's office early, sparring.

"E.R.? His name is E.R.?"

"E.R. Johnson. He's a totally neutral witness and backs every word of Angelica's story."

"That's true. But his name had to be E.R.? And what about the sister? Why did she come up with a different alibi?"

"I don't know, Joyce. Should I find out? I thought I should focus on supporting my own story."

Joyce sighed and rubbed the bridge of her misshapen nose. "Yes, I suppose that's right. We don't really want to spill any ink over that sister. She made us look bad enough as it is, didn't she? But what about Colon? Have you put it to him that his girlfriend's alibi looks better for him now than his sister's?"

"No. I've had a rough time with the warden. The prison people don't want any more reporters interviewing Colon. But I'm going to try again today. I'm driving out to Walpole to see whether I can persuade them to give me just two minutes with Renaldo."

"Okay. Be persuasive. It's a good story, Ariella, very good. You'll be back on the front page. The big boys are dying to clear our name and show up the *Daily*. Plus

Saturday's a slow news day; so they'll love this. Then over the weekend I want you to start a follow-up on Carver. How are they reacting to our tobacco funding story?"

"Joyce, I'll start that as best I can, but I'm going away this weekend."

"Going away? Ariella, this may be the pivotal moment of your career. You've just had two major stories, and you may have another tomorrow. The big boys are fickle. You need to keep their attention. Can't you cancel your plans?"

"I can't."

"Is it your niece? Is she sick again?"

"No, she's okay. It's me. I was threatened, Joyce."

"Threatened?"

"Last night I got home very late, and a man called up and threatened me if I keep writing these stories."

"Which stories? Murder or tobacco?"

"I don't know."

"Did you call the police?"

"Yeah. They weren't too interested. They said Renaldo Colon is safe in jail, and anyway he ought to love me for suggesting he didn't do it. They said it was probably some lunatic newspaper reader and that one threat usually doesn't translate into real violence."

"Probably true. Look, I can see that you're scared, but there's no need to leave town. You're not the first reporter on this paper to be threatened. Would you like to stay with me in Beverly for a few days?"

"No, Joyce. That's sweet of you, but.... This guy threatened to break my arms, and I'm really upset. I need to get away. You'll have this story by the end of the day, and I'll contact my sources at the Carver Center by phone over the weekend, okay? But I'm going to New Hampshire."

"Alone?"

"No." Ariella paused, then spilled the beans. "With Sam Becker."

"Well, I hope you don't expect me to print any more of your stories about him. And he'd better not turn up as a quoted source at Carver."

"He won't, he won't. The tobacco story had nothing to do with him, Joyce. You know that. I got the tip from that activist, Jerry Lesniak, and then this Russian guy I met at the Chan's Christmas party got in the act."

Joyce grimaced, then let out a long breath. "I can see that Sam's an attractive man, and I'm not opposed to your having fun. Your private life is none of my business. But I thought you were still working on an investigative piece on this guy. You told me you had information from a doctor in Texas."

"I do, but I wasn't planning to write about it. Not any more. Don't you think I have enough to cover between the murder case and the tobacco funding scandal?"

"For the moment, yes, although you'll need more medical stories for your clips file. I'm just trying to advise you. If you want to move up and be a health reporter, as you've always told me—and you're poised to do it right now—then you need to keep a distance from your sources. To put it bluntly, sleeping with them isn't good for your career."

Eyes broiling, she spoke softly but with chiseled clarity. "I know that, Joyce."

"All right. We'll drop it. But I need all your contact information at the hotel where you're staying, and I hope they have a fax."

"They should. It's a big place: the Silver Cascade Resort Hotel. I'll give you the number, Joyce, but I don't want you giving it out. Not even to David, not to anyone. You're the only person I want to hear from up there, all right?"

"My lips are sealed. Now, do you want me to send an intern with you to the prison today? There's that big oafish guy, Christian Miller. Maybe he'd make you feel safer."

"Football jock from Northeastern? About six four?"

"That's the one. Want him as your shadow?"

Some of the tension in her shoulders dissolved although her tone remained chilly. "I would love it."

✦

An hour later Ariella was listening to a guard through a bullet-proof window at the visitor's entrance of M.C.I. Walpole as he instructed her and Christian to put their jewelry, watches, wallets and valuables into a locker behind her. Although he had never been to a prison before, Christian stood stolidly by, showing no anxiety and expressing little interest in the place. She had already decided that such an uncurious person would never succeed as a reporter, but she did not breathe a word of that to him. She was grateful to have him as escort.

Having given her message for the warden to the guard, she waited on a hard chair, scribbling on a print-out of her pizza story, as she had dubbed it. Christian sat staring into space until she gave him a copy of today's paper, and then he turned immediately to the sports section. She considered giving him an assignment of some sort, then let it go. The two of them sat for almost an hour waiting, Ariella wondering whether she would have time enough to write up this interview with Renaldo Colon, even if she got it. Finally, she saw the guard behind the window answer a phone and then glance at her.

Moments later another guard appeared to shepherd them into the prison. At the metal detector, Christian had to remove his belt and his shoes before the guard would allow him past. Then the two of them passed through a chain of locked rooms that looked like boxcars on a train, two doors to lock them into each boxcar, then another to let them out, then two more to lock them in again. In this halting fashion they made their way into the interior of the prison, at last finding themselves in a narrow corridor where the guard silently took the lead. Glancing anxiously at her watch Ariella worried that they would end up in another waiting room, but she did not want to ask the guard. She had demanded to speak to the warden himself, and she needed to preserve an aura of self-importance.

When they finally reached their destination, a small room where yet another guard sat at a desk, she found her fears groundless. The warden appeared in the doorway only a minute after they had.

"Your note said you're Ariella Richardson of the *Times*. The one who wrote that Renaldo Colon's girlfriend has an alibi for him?"

"Yes." She was surprised that he had remembered her name from the paper. The prison authorities must have been pretty upset by the story.

"I assume you want to talk to Colon."

"Yes. I just want to talk to him for three minutes. I've heard more details about what happened the night of the murder, and I want to ask him what he thinks of the story I heard."

"I'd be glad to tell you what I think of the story you heard."

Ariella almost smiled but thought the better of it. She could not quite tell whether he was joking, and she did not want to alienate him. "Three minutes?"

"Why bother? An ex-con with too many alibis? Unless you're very naive you know this guy's guilty. It's just a matter of time before he's convicted."

"Then why are you afraid to let me talk to him for a few minutes? It won't make any difference."

"You're right." He looked her in the eye. "It won't. You can talk to him by phone for five minutes."

"I can't see him?"

"You'll see him. We'll clear the visitors' room. You'll see him through the glass wall. But you'll both be under video surveillance with guards at both your doors."

"Fine." She gave him a bland smile.

"And this guy, who is he?" He gestured at Christian.

"A student intern from the paper."

"Yeah, well he stays out."

She thought about challenging him but did not like Christian enough to fight for him. She just wanted to get her quote from Renaldo, get this story written and get out of town. As a guard led her down another corridor, she wondered whether seeing Renaldo would give her any hint of whether he or a friend of his had threatened her, and she shivered a little, then tried to squelch her fear. Meanwhile the prison staff showed that they could move fast when they wished. In a matter of minutes she was sitting, looking through glass at a dark, bearded man of medium build with a stony face.

"What do you want?" he asked over the phone. His voice did have the rasp of a smoker, just as Angelica and Griffin had described, and he had a strong Spanish accent, definitely not the voice she had heard threatening her the previous night. She felt inexplicably relieved, even though she now had to assume that her harasser was not safely behind bars.

"I'm Ariella Richardson, a *Boston Times* reporter. I would like to talk to you for a minute about the night Laurie Griffin was shot," she told him, striving for a mild, pleasant tone. Her voice did not betray the dryness of her throat.

He nodded. "You the one talked to Ana."

"Ana?"

"Yeah. Angelica. I call her Ana. She's saying I was with her that night."

"She did say that, yes, and I put it in the newspaper."

"I heard."

"Now I've heard another story, Mr. Colon, and I'm going to put that in the newspaper too. But I wanted your take on it. I talked to a man from a pizza parlor who says he delivered pizza to you and Angelica that night, just at the time the Griffins were being forced to drive into Roxbury. He says you were standing around asking him what he thought of some movie star just when the police say you were threatening the Griffins with a gun."

"He does?"

"Yes. You've said you were at El Lagarto Bar that night with your sister, right? Are you sure about that?"

"Ana left me, you know." He sounded angry.

"She did, but she also told the whole world she thinks you're innocent."

"By telling the newspaper?"

"Yes."

"True. She stood by me in the paper. You know how the baby's doing?"

"Baby's just fine. Did you worry that Angelica would turn against you?"

"I knew she had. She left me. Didn't even say why. Then the cops came and arrested me—same day."

"Are you sure you were at El Lagarto Bar with your sister at nine o'clock the night Laurie Griffin was shot?"

"No."

"Were you at home with Angelica?"

He looked at her and said nothing.

"Do you remember ordering pizza or talking to a delivery man?"

A belligerent look crossed his face. "I don't know."

"Did you shoot Mrs. Griffin?"

"No."

"Have you ever met Mrs. Griffin?"

"No. I never even heard of Ms. Griffin till the same day everybody did—when that murder hit the papers."

"Is it possible that you were home with Angelica that night?"

"Yeah. It's possible. My sister and I go to El Lagarto a lot, but maybe that night we didn't. Hard to know."

"You know, I don't believe you shot anybody that night. But I might be the only one in Boston right now; so if I were you, I'd get my story straight fast. Do you have a lawyer?"

"Yeah."

"Well, I suggest you talk all this over with your lawyer as soon as you can."

"You gonna talk to Ana?"

"Maybe."

"Can you get a message to her?"

"Yes."

"Tell her thanks. And my sister's got the stroller for her." He paused and gave her a hard look. "So her family told her to leave me, didn't they?"

"I couldn't say."

"They did. Wanted to protect the baby. She ain't mine, and they don't know I'd never hurt her."

A buzzer pierced the tomblike silence of the room, and Ariella saw a guard enter a door directly behind Renaldo.

"My time is up, but I want to ask you one more time, were you at home with Angelica at nine o'clock the night of November 14th, the night Laurie Griffin was shot?"

He shrugged, eyebrows rising, palms thrust upwards, fingers spread, his mouth carved in stone above his thatch of beard.

"If your lawyer wants to talk to me, remember my name is Ariella Richardson."

A guard had appeared behind her and was saying, "All right, lady. That's it. They're going to cut the line now." She replaced the receiver and waved at the most wanted man in Boston. It seemed a ridiculous and ambiguous gesture, but she did not know how else to end the interview. He gave her a nod and was led away.

29

At six o'clock, her story safely filed, she reclined low in the passenger seat of Sam's car and closed her eyes to shut out Boston as he wended his way through congested city streets to Route 95 north. She had a small overnight bag at her feet, blue jeans, turtlenecks and a heavy sweater jumbled inside. Letting a deep breath escape she imagined pines heavy with snow. Tears prickled behind her eyelids until she had to lift an arm to dab at them with her sleeve.

"You're not usually this quiet. Are you okay?" Sam asked.

"Maybe it was being at that prison today, but I feel like an escaped convict. I had no idea I wanted to get out of town so badly."

"Well, after that call last night..."

"No, not just that. It's everything. Being drawn into this murder case—the ugliness of it. The thought that this Griffin may really have shot his pregnant wife to death. It sickens me. Nobody's going to want to believe that. They so much want it to be Renaldo Colon, the convicted felon. Even I would rather have it be him. But he didn't do it. I saw him today, and I know."

"I don't want to get into that with you, Ariella. Let's

try to talk about other things."

"He talked about a stroller, Sam. The last thing he said was to tell Angelica that her daughter's stroller was at his sister's house. And with all that I had to do today, I made sure I called and gave her that message."

"I don't see what that has to do with his guilt or innocence."

"No, you wouldn't."

"Please, let's drop it. I want you to relax and get away from it all, not argue about the case."

"You're right. But I do have to do some work on the tobacco story while I'm in New Hampshire."

"That's okay. There'll be time when I'm preparing and giving my lecture, for one thing. But I'm determined to take you skiing. You need to get outdoors with just me and the trees."

She took a shaky breath and said hopefully, "Sounds great."

"Listen, why don't you take your mind off the Griffin case by looking at the hotel brochures? Reach into the outside pocket of my briefcase—they should be right on top. We've got free run of this resort. Might as well tell me what you want to do."

Ariella pulled them out and gave a little sigh at the cover photograph of a long, three-story, red clapboard inn, snow dotting its roof. Turning the page she began to read. "It looks beautiful. Says: 'Secluded, tranquil mountain setting. Built in 1911. Sample creative gourmet cuisine by candlelight in our Cascades restaurant or giant muffins in our bakery cafe.' Health club, pool, saunas and Jacuzzi. Ski equipment and instruction offered. Trails begin at the back door. And Sam, they have ice skating too. Oh, I want to go ice skating on the pond."

He grinned. "I would be honored to take you ice skating."

❧

They reached Jackson at nightfall and wound their way up a treacherous, icy, mountain road for several miles through the snowy woods until they reached a red, hand-painted sign for the Silver Cascade Resort Hotel. With relief Sam turned into its meticulously plowed and sanded access road and long circular driveway. The main house twinkled with welcoming lights, three feet drifts of snow heaped on its roof and eaves and piled high to the first floor windows. As they pulled up to the front door, Ariella heard tinkling and spotted a romping Alsatian with bells on his collar, his coat the color of the snow.

She let Sam go into the office to check in and reclined in the car seat, feasting her eyes on the snow-clad pines. But when he did not return for many minutes her curiosity got the better of her, and she buttoned her coat and ventured into the crisp air, and then into the wood-paneled foyer of the hotel, where she found herself facing a red-carpeted staircase, its bannister carved with Swiss cut-outs of hearts and flowers. Beside the stairs a door led to an office where she found Sam with a disgruntled look on his face, leaning an arm on a polished wooden counter. A middle-aged woman had her brows drawn together, her hands clasped tightly in front of her, and was apologizing in a wavering voice.

"I'm so sorry. If you say you were promised the Nathaniel Hawthorne suite, then I'm sure you were. But

Susie must have made a mistake because it's already taken."
The telephone began ringing.

"The room you just described doesn't sound as nice.
Does it have a view?"

"No, sir. Just one minute, please. I have to answer
this." She picked up the telephone.

"It's okay, Sam. It doesn't matter," said Ariella, hating
to make a scene.

"I wanted a very special room for us." He had that
implacable look in his eye, and Ariella did not know how to
sway him.

The woman was speaking in monosyllables, but she
mentioned something about a refund and got off the phone
visibly relaxing. "Well, we're in luck. We just had a
cancellation. How would you like to have one of our private
cabins? It's just charming, spacious, has an office alcove with
a fax/modem line for your computer, and there's a private
Jacuzzi in back, secluded by stone walls and woods. Usually
cabins cost a little more than suites, but I'll give it to you for
the same price since we misled you."

"Oh, that sounds great!" Ariella burst out.

Sam smiled at her and nodded at the woman.

"You won't regret it. The cottages are darling. I'm
putting you in Emily Dickinson cottage. You pull your car
down to the lower lot and take the path on the south side of
the parking area. The third cottage is yours, and you'll know
it by the red cardinal on the door. Here are your keys."

Sam took them and signed the papers on the counter
in front of him. "Thanks," he said.

Ariella grabbed his hand on the way out the door.
"I'm glad you thanked her. She was trying her best."

"Well, they had told me I was reserving a particular

room. It seemed like a bait and switch."

"Sam, you're so suspicious sometimes."

"I'm not suspicious. I just stick up for my rights," he said without rancor.

"Demanding, then."

"I suppose I am that. As long as you're fair with people it's okay to be demanding. If you don't look out for yourself no one else is going to do it for you."

"I just feel sorry for low-paid waiters and clerks who deal with pushy customers all day. But I suppose I sometimes think too much of the other guy and too little of myself. After all, your complaint got us this fabulous cabin, much better than being in the main hotel where every time you step into the hall you see a million other doctors."

"Yeah, there's only one you need to see."

"That's right." She smiled at him and squeezed his hand. "He's got the cure for my raw nerves."

"A long soak in that hot tub, for one thing."

Not long afterward they were submerged to their chins in hot water, their legs intertwined, and watching clouds of steam rise from the surface and waft away into the darkness. The soft strains of classical guitar trickled from a portable radio Sam had found in the cabin. Conversation had lapsed, and Ariella closed her eyes while Sam studied the stars, numerous and bright in the sky so far from the big city lights that obscured them. The music ended and a buttery-voiced announcer told them that they had just heard Rodrigo's Espanoleta performed by Julian Bream. The announcer then began reading the news, and reflexively Ariella opened her eyes and listened.

"Our top story at eleven o'clock this evening: New Hampshire has a new lieutenant governor, Thomas Kean, appointed today by Governor Flint. Former Lieutenant Governor Randy Luce resigned Wednesday after admitting to an affair with his secretary's sixteen-year-old daughter, a scandal that rocked his core constituency of conservative Christians. The new lieutenant governor, Kean, a three-term state senator from Concord, is known as a moderate Republican with a strong interest in education. At the age of 63 he is almost twenty years older than Luce. In other news a group of private businessmen are challenging state-owned liquor stores, suing the state for restraint of trade. And in Washington today Congress remained deadlocked on the budget. In medical news, FDA today announced a major recall of the drug, Dibexin, used to treat juvenile diabetes. Parents of diabetic children who take this drug are urged to call their doctors immediately. And the weather will remain clear and cold..."

"Oh, my God." Sam sat up straight, his upper torso thrust into the frigid air above the hot tub.

"What?"

"Did you hear that? The FDA is recalling Dibexin."

Ariella widened her eyes and looked at him expectantly.

"How ironic. That bastard Schaus is going to get what he deserves."

She did not miss the name but did not want to force the issue. "I don't know what you're talking about."

He glared at her. "Ariella, Dibexin is Kurt Schaus's wonder drug, and the world is finally about to find out what a wonder it is." He paused and his eyes softened, but he continued to gaze at her intensely. "You've always wanted to know what happened to me in Michigan, and I guess it's time I told you."

Brushing a wet curl away from her eye he began. "Kurt Schaus shared lab space with me while developing this new drug to treat childhood diabetes, which can be life-threatening. Early on he accepted funding from a drug company that wanted to sell the drug. There are lots of kids with diabetes, a big market. Anyway, I watched Schaus systematically ignore and bury evidence that the drug had serious side effects, that it kills bone marrow.

As soon as he had preliminary results he courted the university media, then the Ann Arbor and Detroit papers. He arranged press conferences, got photographed with the university president, got on local T.V. news. For a while he spent far more time talking to reporters than doing research. Soon more grant money was flooding in from the drug company, and students who heard about him in the news were flocking to the lab to work for him. No reporter ever asked him the hard questions that would have revealed the flaws in his data. Not one.

Eventually his lab grew so much that the university reclaimed my half and gave it to him. They gave me a small space in the basement. Since then Schaus' personal propaganda machine has earned him a prominent position at Baylor. He also got rich buying stock in Phix Pharmaceuticals, which sells Dibexin; he bragged to me about his perfect market timing. Naturally he had insider information.

The whole thing made me sick. I wonder how many children have been disabled or needed major surgery or hospitalization so that Schaus could feed his insatiable need for fame and money."

He took a breath.

She had many questions, but she floated backward

toward the opposite wall of the hot tub and said only, "Wow."

"Of course, my mom's health was deteriorating then. It got bad enough that she needed to have the liver transplant she'd been dreading for years. She never believed that she could live with someone else's liver in her body. In fact she had moral scruples about it too. She felt it might be wrong to violate the integrity of the body God gave her. Debbie and I persuaded her to try it because it was the only hope, and we didn't want to lose her. She was only 56.

"I began thinking my liver transplant rejection research was a race against time. If only I could get to the human subject stage I might be able to enroll Mom in the trials. But, of course, I had to be sure it was safe. Maybe that was what upset me the most. My mother died before I ever had a chance to help her because I was so careful about studying the risks. Meanwhile Schaus blithely subjected children in his initial trials and later across the whole country to massive risks—and for what? I could have rushed my study into human trials and figured that the benefits to my mom outweighed the risks. But I couldn't stomach it."

"Well, and you would never have forgiven yourself if you thought something in your treatment regimen ended up killing her."

"Yeah. Roland says that too. Anyway, there was this lab accident. I lost experimental cells and would have had to start all over again, and my funding ran out. Mom had died, and I was devastated. Roland had come out to Michigan for the funeral—he's an old friend. And afterward he stayed in touch and prodded me a bit. He reminded me of an old research interest of mine that grew into my cancer study, and he arranged a position for me here. I owe him a great deal for that because he gave me the fresh start I needed so badly.

And Schaus... Well, Schaus thinks I hate him because he kicked me out of his lab space, because I failed and he succeeded, because he got the glory and I didn't."

She nodded.

"That's what he told you, isn't it? That's what he would feel in my shoes. But I was glad to leave his lab. Living with his sleazy behavior on a daily basis, hearing him brag about his plans with no regard for who he might hurt—I couldn't stand it."

"And you couldn't stop him?"

"Well, that was just it. Maybe I could have. Maybe I hated the reporters because I kept hoping that they would reveal what Schaus was up to so that I wouldn't have to. I didn't want to get involved. I had only one goal back then— saving Mom—and I begrudged every minute spent on anything else. That's one reason my relationship with my girlfriend, Sarah, failed. But I felt guilty too. That children might die because I hadn't stepped forward. Then I told myself that peer review would take care of it, but until now it didn't."

"Well, it has at last." Ariella lowered herself even further into the water and wrapped her arms around her torso. For a moment she just watched the ripples flow in concentric circles across the tub towards him. "Thank you for telling me."

"I needed to tell you. If I'm going to be with you, you had to know."

"Well, it helps me to understand you better. And I would never write about any of it."

"I know."

"But I think you have to stop blaming yourself. You

did everything you could for your mother. And it wasn't your job to bring out Schaus' misconduct. Maybe in the future you would be more active. Maybe you can learn something from the experience, but let the feelings go."

"It's amazing, but I feel much better already. Maybe it's just the telling of it, the admitting my faults, or maybe it's knowing that the medical community has finally rooted out Kurt Schaus and taken that problem off my plate." He stretched his arms high in the air, fingers splayed to the stars; then he turned his eyes to hers. "How about coming a little closer?"

She launched her body straight at him, grabbed his shoulders as his arms closed around her, and sought his lips.

30

At seven o'clock in the morning Sam woke her with a stroke of his finger across her cheek. He was standing over her, dressed in sweatpants and a ski jacket and holding a newspaper. She lunged for it, but he held it out of reach while he leaned toward her for a lingering kiss, then presented it with a flourish.

"Oh, thank you! You went out in the cold for this? What a sweetheart." She sat up, shoved a pillow behind her back and feasted her eyes on the front page of the *Boston Times*. "Pizza Man Supports Alibi in Griffin Murders," she read. Then she scanned the article quietly, reading it twice as was her custom. "Oh, Sam, this really is a good article. I'm really proud of it. It reads well; it's important. I'm glad it's finally in print." She looked up at him. "And I want to thank you for all your help and your forbearance."

"You're welcome. I think. Forbearance?"

"Well, you think Colon is guilty. You can't even take seriously the notion that Griffin might have done it. But you supported me nonetheless."

Amusement flickered across his face, and he sank onto the bed. "I can believe in you without agreeing with every thought in your head."

"Yes, I guess you can." She gave him a long look. "I think I haven't allowed for that until now. In my family it was so cut and dried: my dad and sister supported my aspirations, my mom didn't. So you were either for me or against me. I put up with a lot of crap from Carl, my fiancé in New York, because he supported my plans in journalism school; only when he tried to change the plans did I leave."

"Well, all I can tell you is that I think you're a terrific writer, precise and thoughtful about your work and dedicated to it, and I'm proud to be associated with you." He took one of her hands and squeezed it. "You know, with my life experience I'll never think highly of the press as a whole, but I think very highly of you."

She threw her arms around him, and he gave her a bear hug.

Then his hands began to roam, and he groaned. "It's amazing. I just can't control myself with you. I want to be touching you all the time."

"I know." She smiled into his shoulder. "I love it. I'm not used to it—Carl was never like that. He didn't like to cuddle, and he always seemed in charge of sex. I mean, he decided when and where and how, what nightie I should wear. He wanted me to lose weight, to grow my hair longer... I worked so hard to please him, always worried that some other woman was doing a better job."

"What an ass. Was he actually cheating on you?" She nodded, and his arms tightened around her. "Well, I have two things to say. I think cheating is despicable, and you don't ever have to work hard with me." He dipped his head to catch her lips with his and laughing into them, said, "Just sit back and enjoy the ride."

❦

At breakfast later that morning she was feeling thoroughly relaxed and pampered as the waitress poured her a third cup of hot chocolate and brought her an extra basket of cinnamon rolls. She had already shared a heap of blueberry pancakes and fresh fruit with Sam, and she was enjoying sitting back and studying the details of his face: the sureness of his jaw, his small neat ears, and the cowlick stubbornly popping up in his dark, slightly damp hair. Now and then she shifted her gaze to the snowy woods through the plate glass window. Sam too kept glancing out the window, and he drummed absently on the table with a spoon.

"Almost done?"

She laughed. "You're as eager to get outside as a little boy."

"You bet I am. As pleasant as it is to eat breakfast with you, I came up here to take you skiing."

She screwed up her mouth. "I'm a little nervous, Sam. I haven't done this in ages. I'm not going to be any good."

"I'm sure you'll be great."

"I don't know..."

"Look, if you're almost finished I'll go sign for the check and get some trail information, okay?" He opened his eyes wide in his pleading look, and she waved him off. As she watched him go, she thought about his revelations the previous night, about the bind he had been in. Some people would say that he should never have studied liver transplantation, that it was a subject too close to home and bound to bring him grief. But she respected his passion, his struggle to use his talents for this very personal goal. Kurt

Schaus had no doubt absorbed some of the anger Sam felt about his failure to save his mother. But from what Sam said, Kurt was reprehensible in his own right.

She could hardly believe that Sam had finally told her the story, and she hadn't even asked. Perhaps there was a lesson there about giving him the time to make the right decision on his own. She giggled at her temerity. He had shown he trusted her, and that was a heady feeling. Now the least she could do in return was to go skiing with him, even if they ended up stranded in the mountains. She pushed her chair from the breakfast table and headed for the lobby and her fate.

∽

Her first embarrassing moment came when he dropped his skis on the snowy lawn behind the main hotel and snapped his feet into them. She dropped hers beside his and began wiggling one ski-booted foot over the pins, her foot vertical, her toes straining to remain horizontal. She thought the boot in place, pressed with her pole on the catch and yelled, "Yowch!" Blood rushing to her face, she removed her foot, positioned it again, leaned down over the ski and tried again. This time she felt no pain, but her boot slipped and did not catch on the ski pins. She tried six times. The seventh time she swore and switched feet. She could just imagine the tables full of guests watching her through the dining room windows. Sam had taken off and was skiing round the lawn with broad gleeful strokes, but after she had failed four more times to put on her skis he skidded to a halt beside her.

"May I help?"

She turned her flushed face toward him, rolled her

eyes and jammed a pole into the snow. "I don't know what's the matter with me."

"You're out of practice. Here." Plunging his poles into the snow he sidled up to her on his skis, crouched and guided her calf into the right position. She used the pole she still held to press on the catch, and miraculously the ski clicked into place. "Now you do the other one."

Feeling foolish she slowly lowered her other foot into the ski and slipped into the pins without a hitch. "I'm an idiot. I want to go back to the fireplace in our cabin and read the Emily Dickinson collection."

"No chance." He gave her a quick kiss. "You'll be great. Now follow me."

She slid awkwardly across the snow, her feet dragging until her body suddenly seemed to remember the proper stride. She let out a pent-up breath, and gave herself up to it, sliding smoothly after Sam toward an opening in the woods. In a few strides she found herself reassuringly surrounded by tree bark; she could no longer see even one hotel window. Moments later Sam seemed to drop from view. She slowed and found herself facing a short but precipitous drop. The trail took a sharp turn around a tree on the way down, and small pines dotted the slope.

"I don't think I'm up to this," she called to Sam.

"Sure you are. It's not bad. Just snowplow."

"I know how to do that, but how do I handle the curve while I'm doing it?"

Shrugging at what he must have viewed as a rhetorical question, he pulled a trail map out of his belly pouch and began looking at it. Ariella stood at the top of the rise, paralyzed. She felt sure that she would break a leg; she was so stiff and out of practice. Why couldn't they have skied around on a flat surface for a while first? She opened her mouth to say that she was going back to the hotel, but she couldn't disappoint Sam after only five minutes. Where was her spirit of adventure? Chastened by too intimate contact with a murder, she imagined. In her heart she wanted nothing more than a plush armchair, a good book and a happy ending. Instead she crouched low, pushed off and tried to direct herself around the bend. She made it around the tree, but then her ski tips crossed; she shrieked and went flying head-first into a snow bank, legs, skis and poles painfully tangled.

Sam was laughing so hard that tears ran from his eyes. She decided that she would never speak to him again.

"Are you okay?" He was beside her offering a hand.

She abandoned her resolution. "No, I'm not okay. My foot hurts right here." She pointed to it and snapped off the ski. "You didn't have to laugh at me."

"I wasn't laughing at you. It's just that it was such a funny sight—you made it around the bend fine, and then you relaxed and stopped steering and just flopped."

She gave him a sour look. "My skis crossed. Look, maybe I'm just too incompetent for this today."

"It could happen to anybody. I wobbled a lot too on the way down that slope. I almost hugged the tree over there." He gestured to his right. "Let me help you up and see how you feel. There's a very easy trail we can take for about an hour or two, and it passes a frozen stream. I'll bet it's very pretty."

Once she was on her feet she felt less pain, but her mood remained gloomy. He must think her the most uncoordinated woman in New England and a bad sport at that. She wanted so badly for him to respect her. Moments later they set off again, and the trail remained level, although it twisted and turned. Taking deep breaths she tried to focus her mind on her ski stride as her father had taught her years ago. Although she had never succeeded at emptying her mind in meditation, with effort she could achieve a similar result while skiing. It required too much concentration to be entirely relaxing, and eventually she always slipped and began thinking, but just now it seemed important to try.

At first she shuffled along behind Sam, conservative after her fall and puffing a little from using so many short strokes to keep up with him. In time the pain in her foot subsided, quiet descended on them like rainfall, washing away her embarrassment, and she relaxed into longer, surer strokes. She began to glide through the woods with almost no exertion and soon found herself overtaking Sam, her ski tips almost touching the backs of his skis.

"Want to lead for a while?"

"No thanks," she said. "It's more fun when I don't have to think about where I'm going."

"That's the part I like," he said.

She adjusted her pace a little and glided along behind him no longer needing to think about her stroke, just savoring crisp air as a slight breeze stirred the pines all around her. The snow lay like lumps of oatmeal on wisps of tree branches that looked too frail to hold it. Only it was oatmeal gone mad as in her childhood story book about the magic porridge pot that produced so much porridge it covered every surface in the cottage, filled the sidewalks, the streets, the flowerpots. The pines grew slim and straight, casting shadow stripes on the snowy ground. They skied steadily onward through the woods, whether for minutes or hours she did not know. Her muscles had warmed to their task and tingled with a long-forgotten pleasure; her hands grew so warm that she removed her gloves and stowed them in her belly pouch. As she followed Sam around a curve in the trail, she thought she caught a glimpse of a deer's ear but didn't mention it. If a deer had really passed by, it would be a secret she and the woods kept. For once she had no desire to speak. She let the whiteness and the silence envelop her, cleanse her of some of the grime and degradation of the city. Just for an hour she allowed the city to seep away. Just for an hour she put aside her prejudices and understood the people who fled from urban life.

Beside a fallen tree the trail forked. A hand-lettered sign with a red arrow pointing left said, "Enchanted Forest Trail." Sam, who had increased his lead, had passed it without comment and taken the left fork, and Ariella stabbed her poles into the snow, pushing forward to catch him.

"Sam!" she called, "did you see that?"

He did not answer, only seemed to speed up. She lengthened her stride and slid along determined to catch up. His only answer seemed to be greater speed. She found herself racing along, struggling to narrow his lead, when suddenly she realized that his figure was descending. All at once his head dropped from sight. She flew along the trail, knees bent, preparing for a downward slope, and in a split second she saw it, a lovely little hill with Sam waiting at the bottom, right in the middle of the trail, facing her. Lacking the skill to stop she prayed he would get out of the way and dropped into a snowplow, slowing herself a bit but not enough to steal the exhilaration of slipping down a hill with the wind whistling in her ears. She was heading right for him, and he did not flinch, simply opened his arms wide, set his feet apart, and let her fly into his arms, absorbing the shock as if he were a tree not a man.

She dropped her poles, held onto his back, and lifted her face to look at him.

"Kiss me on the Enchanted Forest Trail," he said with laughing eyes, "and you will be my snow nymph forever." And she did.

When at last they returned to the hotel, Sam disappeared into his medical meetings, and Ariella to the cabin where she spent hours on the telephone with high-ranking officials in the cancer center hierarchy. She took a mountain of notes, and sifting through the comments given to her began to suspect that within a week or two heads would roll. Perhaps the woods had done her mind some good, but for whatever reason she found her follow-up story spilling out of her onto the page. She faxed it to Joyce from the hotel office without a single revision, and then allowed herself a precious hour of reading in front of the fire before she had to meet Sam for dinner. Curled in an overstuffed armchair she found herself ignoring her book, staring into the fire and thinking about Sam. His face danced before her in the flames. She could still feel his arms as they felt around her on the wooded ski trail at the bottom of the little hill: how strong he was. His kind of inner strength had not turned up often in her life, and she realized that she did not want him to walk out of her life now that he was in it.

❧

Earlier that morning in the silver gray master bedroom of her historic colonial house outside Boston, Natalie Ward had dressed carefully, then fed Ginger, her Irish setter, and driven to the Concord Congregational Church. Although she belonged to it, she had not attended a Sunday service in six months. She recognized only a few people and greeted them perfunctorily before sliding into a pew near the front. As the service began she took a deep breath. Familiar hymns came and went, and although she sang along she paid scant attention to their words. She felt like a bird perched on a high and slender branch and waited for a spiritual peace to descend on her which did not come. The minister's sermon concerned the congregation's duty to do public service, and his words washed over her as she thought about the hundreds of Medicaid patients she had treated in her career.

Then the phrase, "guard against complacency" penetrated her fog. She sat straighter, listened more carefully and became decidedly uneasy.

After church she hesitated on the steps wondering what to do. She had a lunch date with Emily Linsley, an old friend from boarding school who had gone into finance and wanted to advise her on mutual funds. Emily said that doctors were notoriously bad about financial planning—so busy that they always put it off and then made snap decisions. Since she had little interest in investments Natalie was usually all too glad to take Emily's advice. Today Natalie had far more on her mind than her own distant retirement, but the thought of confiding in Emily did not please her. Emily had always insulated herself from the grit of life, preferring numbers to human problems. She would have no wish to hear about Natalie's troubles, and Natalie did not want to admit a possible failing to her in any case.

Natalie's drive to the Wellesley Club took her right through the center of town, where heavy traffic stopped her briefly right in front of the Wellesley Town Hall and Police Headquarters. She could not seem to take her eyes off the building and even considered pulling into its parking lot, but did not. Emily would be waiting for her. Although she had difficulty keeping her end of the conversation going over the filet of sole, Emily did not seem to notice. At last the lunch ended, and Natalie found herself in the car again with a pile of financial brochures and not much memory of what Emily had said. Instead of heading straight home she began to drive aimlessly through the countryside, taking back roads she knew from a lifetime in that county but had not driven in years. She could not seem to resolve what to do, but the minister's word, "complacency" reverberated in her mind. Self-disgust welled up in her. She was a surgeon, accustomed to making snap decisions even when life hung in the balance; why was she so paralyzed now?

At four thirty she made her way back to Concord and headed straight to the police station, parking right in front of it. As she pulled up, a police officer stepped out the front door and turned to walk along the sidewalk. Following him with her eyes she saw him pass another man approaching from the opposite direction, an elderly gentleman in a gray wool coat, an old friend of her father's. He did not notice her in the car but stopped in front of the police station, opened its door and entered. Natalie gripped the steering wheel. She did not want to meet anyone she knew, especially someone who knew her father. He would be horrified at her telling a sordid tale to the police for any reason and had warned her, when taking action, to always consider the effect on the family name. As soon as her father's friend emerged and passed out of sight she would go in. She waited ten minutes for him to come out, and when she could no longer stand the constricted feeling in her throat, she turned the key in the ignition and shifted the gears into reverse. She did not seem to have the courage to take this route, but perhaps there was another.

31

Back in Ariella's apartment Monday night, Sam set her luggage down in the middle of the floor. Reflexively Ariella moved to the kitchen to check her machine. Its clock read 8:12 p.m., and the call light was blinking red; so she pressed the button and heard:

"Hello, sweetheart. How ya doing? This is Lenny just calling to check up on ya. I heard you were kinda broken up a few days ago, and I wanted to tell ya what a super special gal you are, and find out if you need me to come kick some Boston butt for ya. 'Cause you just say the word, sweetheart, and I'll create a little business meeting up there. Anyway, you give me a call at work, y'hear? We need to talk about something. Love ya."

She smiled as she always did at her brother-in-law's pronounced Brooklyn accent; he probably wanted to plan for her sister's upcoming birthday. Then she turned to smile at Sam. "It was a wonderful weekend. I can't thank you enough."

Sam looked serious and a little withdrawn. "Are you feeling safe?"

"Oh, yes. I'm totally over that silliness. After all, I have double locks and a police bolt on the door of this apartment; so no one's going to waltz in here unannounced. I don't want to let that guy's threats control me. And if I get nervous I can always call you."

"Would you feel better if I stayed the night?"

She sighed. His clipped tones did not suggest that he wanted to stay. He had spent so much time on her already; perhaps he wanted some time alone to think and work. "I'm really fine alone. I have a lot of catch-up work to do."

"Okay then." He gave her a quick kiss and disappeared so fast that she wondered whether she had misread his signals.

At nine o'clock the telephone rang. Ariella rose to pick it up, then shivered and let the machine answer. After her own message, she heard a female voice and immediately let out a breath.

"Hello, this is Natalie Ward. I'm the obstetrician you interviewed about my cancer research. I, well, I would like to talk to you if you have the time. I may have some information that would interest you. I'm not certain that I should go public with it, but I would like to at least discuss it."

Ariella picked up the phone. "Hi, Natalie. I just got in. How can I help you?"

Natalie's tone was stiff with tension. "Well, I feel that I may have information related to a story of yours, but I'm not sure whom to tell and what to tell. It's a sensitive matter. Ethics—and quite frankly my reputation—may be at stake."

"Is this about Sam Becker's research?"

"Oh no, nothing about that."

"Is it about the cancer center taking tobacco funding?"

"No, no. It, well..." Her voice dropped almost to a whisper. "It touches on the Griffin murder."

"Oh!" Ariella could not contain her shock. "Well, that's ... very serious. Would you rather discuss it in person?"

"Yes. Yes, I think so. Thanks." She sounded relieved and added, "When can we meet?"

Ariella did not like the sound of this new, uncertain Dr. Ward. "If it's urgent you can come to my apartment right now. I mean, do you think you're in any danger?"

"No, I don't think so, although if I tell you my story I may be."

Ariella felt her heartbeat gathering speed, and she wanted to hang up and dive under the bed covers. Instead she retreated into her most detached business voice. "Would you like to come over here now, or would you prefer tomorrow? I have a busy day, but I could come by your office at about ten thirty."

"I have appointments all morning, unfortunately. But it's late now, and I wouldn't want to intrude."

A hint of steel crept into Ariella's voice. "Listen, Natalie, this murder case has already intruded on my life in ways you can't even imagine. If it's doing the same to you, then it might be better to get it over with and talk tonight."

Instead of running from her candor, Natalie seemed grateful. "You're serious, aren't you? Why are you doing this? You can't be used to interviewing people in your home on a Sunday night."

"No, but I know you, and you're a friend of Sam's. I live at 216 Clarendon Street in the Back Bay, apartment 34. How long will it take you to get here?"

"Forty minutes. Thank you so much for seeing me, Ariella. I'm scared, but I'm already beginning to feel better— that I'm doing the right thing."

She had visions of Dr. Ward crashing her Mercedes

and quickly gentled her tone. "Well, I'll do my best to help. And please drive carefully. There's no need to rush. Your drive time will give me a chance to prepare for work tomorrow."

At exactly nine forty-five the buzzer sounded: Natalie had arrived. A few minutes later she was seated on Ariella's couch, her face taut, her pale blond hair slipping from bobby pins. She wore a white turtleneck under a pearl-buttoned, sky blue sweater and kept her long legs tightly crossed beneath loose, gray wool trousers. To Ariella she looked the epitome of a Concord matron, a Daughter of the American Revolution, the kind of Old Bostonian Ariella had never learned to like. It astonished her that the Griffin murder had shaken not only Boston's black and Latino communities, its Irish Catholics, its police force and politicians, but someone of Boston's privileged class who lived above the fray. She still did not like Natalie, but she could see the anxiety breaking through her guest's usually impassive facade, and emotion she could understand.

"Would you like some tea?" she asked.

"Yes, please." Natalie attempted a smile. "I apologize again for breaking in on your Monday evening."

Ariella made reassuring noises while she busied herself with the kettle in the kitchen, giving Natalie time to compose herself. When she returned she placed a tray with the teapot, cups and saucers, and her trademark molasses cookies on the coffee table. This would be a tricky interview, and perhaps the cookies would help ease the situation; she half thought that they had magic in them. "So," she said. "Why did you call me?"

"I read your article Saturday about that pizza delivery man who claimed Renaldo Colon could not be the murderer." Natalie broke off for a minute. "I don't think I could ever have called a reporter out of the blue, even after you interviewed me. But we met socially at the Chans. And you're Sam's friend. I would like to speak to you in confidence, hear your view of what I tell you, and then decide whether to go public. I'm relying on your discretion."

Ariella met Natalie's unblinking gaze. "I understand. If you don't want me to publish this interview I won't. But I may follow leads that you reveal to me, without mentioning you, of course."

"That's fair." She said nothing more for a minute, and Ariella did not press her, nor pick up her notebook from among the papers on the coffee table. She sensed that Natalie needed to preserve the illusion of privately seeking advice from an acquaintance at the country club, a place where a raised eyebrow or a handshake spoke volumes, where words were often left unsaid and never put on paper.

"I called you," Natalie said, "because I could no longer sit back and read about the Griffin murder. Even before your alibi articles I doubted that Renaldo Colon had killed Laurie Griffin." She took a breath. "You see, I knew Laurie Griffin. She was my patient."

Ariella's breath caught in her throat. For a moment she could not think. Then she inwardly berated herself. How could she have failed to remember that a pregnant woman like Laurie Griffin would have an obstetrician and that the doctor might know something?

"Did anyone ever question you?"

"No. When it first happened I thought the police would come, but they never did. They talked to the people who saw Laurie that last day: the nurse who ran her childbirth class, some pregnant women in the class. But I hadn't seen her for a week. They didn't bother me, and I was relieved. I did not want to get involved. I was horrified at the murder, and I attended the funeral, but I did not want to think about who had done it. When the police commissioner announced Colon's arrest I buried my suspicions. But your stories..."

"What do you suspect?" Ariella almost whispered.

A feverish look replaced Natalie's natural pallor, and words rushed out. "I suspect Brian Griffin. Brian Griffin is a volatile and highly irrational man. He was one of the worst husbands of a patient I have ever had to deal with. He physically and verbally intimidated his wife in my presence and tried to intimidate me." She paused, let out a breath, then spoke more slowly. "He never wanted Laurie out of his sight, whether during physical exams, ultrasounds or chats in the office. He was fanatical about protecting Laurie's modesty, as he put it, and wanted her to expose as little bare skin to me as possible. I tried to probe Laurie's wishes, but she would never oppose him to his face.

I could see they had a bad marriage and wondered whether he had ever hit her, but I had no evidence of it. I've never had any training in domestic violence, and I questioned my judgment. Then at 24 weeks—at the six month visit—Laurie arrived alone. She spent ten minutes with me before he burst into the examining room, late and cursing the traffic. He was very angry that I had begun without him." She took a sip of tea, and Ariella sat riveted, burning with questions but ruthlessly silencing herself.

"In those ten minutes before he came, Laurie showed me her back. It was covered with contusions, welts, burn marks. She also had classic cigarette burns on her upper arms. It was bad. I never imagined anything like that was happening. In routine prenatal visits a women lies on her back and reveals only her belly. We measure her girth and listen to the fetal heartbeat. We don't examine the rest of her. I have asked myself what else I might have missed or should have done.

Anyway, I tried to call the hospital social worker right away to find out about battered women's shelters. But Laurie became agitated and begged me not to call. She said that this was a private matter, and that she only wanted to know whether the beatings could have hurt the baby. She claimed that she had brought this on herself by becoming pregnant, that Brian had figured out she was worried she might love the baby more than him. She said that a week ago she had admitted this to him and promised that from now on she would always put him first. They had both confessed their sins to the priest and done penance, and Brian had promised never to hit her again.

It was true that she had no fresh contusions. Her injuries were probably at least a week old. But I was disturbed that she excused the abuse as she did. At the same time I was uneasy about interfering in a religious solution. Yet I knew enough about abuse to worry that Brian would hit her again. I did not know what my obligation was. I told her that as I had just assured her on physical exam, the fetus appeared healthy, but she had been lucky and further beatings could certainly jeopardize it. If Brian hit her again I asked her to please call the social work department, and I gave her their business card. She secreted it in her purse, said she did not think she would need it, and asked for my silence.

I told her that communications between patient and doctor are always confidential."

She stopped and bit her lip.

"I don't see how I could have said anything else. Then Brian burst in, followed by one of my nurses who had tried to keep him out. I asked her to remain with us. It was all very unpleasant, but I said nothing to indicate to him what I had seen. I re-examined Laurie's belly in his presence and then did the only other thing I could think of. As I completed the billing form for the receptionist I checked the box for a 26-week appointment. Laurie was at 24 weeks, and usually we don't see patients again until Week 28, but Brian would not know that. After they left I checked at the desk to make sure Laurie had made an appointment for two weeks from that day."

She stopped again to sip her tea for a long moment, but when Ariella opened her mouth to ask a question, Natalie waved her hand as if swatting away a mosquito. "Laurie and Brian arrived together for the 26-week appointment, and as usual he refused to leave her side. After examining her belly and listening to the fetal heartbeat, both of which were normal, I said that at this visit I usually had a private talk with the woman about the labor and delivery experience.

But Brian absolutely refused to leave us alone. He spoke with a condescending politeness that did not quite mask his hostility to me. I tried to assert that this talk was my ironclad policy, but Laurie intervened. She said that she and Brian were a particularly close couple, especially at this moment in their relationship and asked that I make an exception. I did not know what to do. So I gave a short speech about labor and recommended pain medication or an epidural. Brian responded that she would not need any of that.

I could not think of how to keep her there. Then, as they were leaving, she turned and took my hand and squeezed it. "I'm so glad the baby is doing well. I'm doing well too, and I appreciate your taking such good care of us."

That was the last time I saw her. The following week I was in the office one morning seeing patients when I got a call from a colleague at Brigham and Women's Hospital; he said that my patient, Laurie Griffin, had just died of bullet wounds."

She stopped speaking, but Ariella just sat there looking at her. When she finally spoke she did not ask a question. "What an awful burden."

Natalie began trembling, and her voice broke. "Thanks."

Ariella gave her a questioning look.

"For not condemning me."

Ariella sighed. "I've been reading about domestic violence, and this sounds like a classic case. I can't believe they don't teach you about it in medical school."

Natalie shook her head. "And even if he had beaten her, I didn't want to believe that he could kill her."

"You're not alone. Nobody in Boston wants to believe that a middle class, suburban Irish Catholic fur salesman could have killed his pregnant wife. Much easier to blame a Dominican immigrant with a criminal record. And you could never have predicted she would be dead a week after that visit."

"I visited the baby in intensive care. The neonatologists did everything they could for her." She gripped one hand with the other and gazed down at them. "It was so awful." Then she looked up. "But don't patronize me. I've been reading up on domestic violence too. There are a lot of things I might have done if I had thought of them beforehand. I'm changing my office policies, and I'm going to train my whole staff."

Ariella nodded. "Are you ready for my opinion?"

"Yes."

"Well, what you told me doesn't prove Brian Griffin killed his wife, but it ought to be investigated. Others who knew Laurie might reveal a pattern of abuse, threats on her life, etc. Did she ever mention any threats on her life?"

"No."

"And you have never spoken to the police?"

"No."

"You know they're going to be very unhappy about that if you allow me to publish this interview."

"Yes. I'm weakening their case against Colon, and I've kept it from them all this time."

"Why?"

"I don't know. I felt I had promised Laurie Griffin to keep it all confidential. I didn't know for sure whether he killed her, didn't want to believe him capable of it. He stood in my office month after month not three feet from me."

"You must be afraid of him."

"That wasn't why I kept quiet, but I am, a little. I kept quiet because I do believe in confidentiality and privacy and resolving personal matters at home. The people I respect most behave that way. They don't turn to social workers, police and courts. And I have always felt that patient confidentiality is one of my most serious obligations. If you recall, I rejected out of hand your idea about interviewing patients in the cancer trials."

"The one I interviewed came to me voluntarily."

Natalie gave her a penetrating look. "I know. I asked her. Anyway, I didn't know how and when to break that confidentiality. Even describing my dilemma to a colleague might have violated my obligations. So I didn't. Then the police and the press seemed so sure that Colon had murdered her. I believed it for a while. But your stories in the paper have made me realize that I may be helping to convict an innocent man. And my reading tells me that Brian Griffin might very well abuse another woman."

"He probably will."

"If I break confidentiality I fear that some of my colleagues will turn on me and my patients no longer trust me."

"If you come forward, I think most of your patients will understand. But there's no doubt that you'll be put under a microscope, probably both by the hospital and the police. I would expect a lot of interrogation. And Natalie, you might need protection."

"I know."

"I can see this might turn your life upside down, but as a reporter I feel that the world ought to know. And if Brian Griffin did commit this horrible crime, he should not get away with it."

"I know. I knew her."

"I have to say, you were very brave to come here tonight. Naturally I want to print the story, but I can see what a big decision it is for you."

"What if no one believes me? What if they say I must be exaggerating?"

"If I write this story, the way I write it will make many people believe you. My editor will push the story too, and Sam will support you at the hospital, I'm sure. But you might need to stay with a friend, even pay for a security guard." She looked Natalie in the eye. "I've believed for weeks that Brian Griffin killed his wife, and after my first alibi story I got a threatening phone call from a man with a Southie accent."

"It might have been him. He does have that accent."

"He killed her, Natalie."

"That's why I'm here." She put her face in her hands for a long moment, then looked up. "Do it."

"Are you sure?"

She sounded irritated. "In surgery I'm trained to make life decisions for my patients in a split second. What is this compared to that? I can't sit by any more."

"I need to ask you a lot more questions."

"Whatever you need."

Ariella picked up her notebook, then paused with pen in the air to say quietly, "I'll stand by you."

A hint of amusement lit Natalie Ward's eyes for the first time that night. "Thanks," she said. "I know you mean that, and I know I'm not your favorite person."

32

On Tuesday, a few minutes before noon, Sam sat in the most secluded booth in Brookline's Golden Dragon restaurant drumming his fingers on the table. Glancing toward the bar he could see a game show flickering on a television. A bell jingled, the door opened, and Roland strode into the restaurant, taking it in at a glance and moving quickly to the back to Sam's table. A waitress followed and addressed him in Chinese as he seated himself. He replied in kind, then turned to Sam.

"I've just ordered soup, a noodle dish and tea. Do you want an appetizer or are you ready for lunch?"

"Neither. I just want to talk."

Roland raised a brow. "Well, you'd better order something. It's my treat, and I'll be offended if a Chinese place can provide nothing you'll eat."

Sam looked exasperated. "Just order for me then. You always get the better dish anyway."

"Yes, well," Roland's eyes glinted, "you have to know what to say."

Impatiently Sam changed the subject. "Did you read Ariella's article this morning?"

"About Natalie Ward? Are you kidding? The whole

medical center's in an uproar."

"I know. What are you going to do? Natalie's career could go right down the drain."

Roland no longer looked amused. He put up a finger to halt Sam's flow of words, gave the waitress some instructions in rapid Chinese, and waited until she was out of earshot. "Now, what is it you think I can do?"

"I don't know, I don't know. Maybe a lot. The hospital is going to investigate her, right?"

"Well, that's the tip of the iceberg. The police are going to grill her, Laurie Griffin's parents may sue her for negligence, the medical board may bring her in, and yes, the hospital will no doubt look into it."

Sam swore. "I never even thought of a lawsuit. Well, she needs support. You know everyone that matters at Carver and Beth Israel. You can sway them. Tell them what a great clinician she is. Don't let them sacrifice a good doctor when what's at fault here is the system."

"Brian Griffin is at fault here, not the system."

"But the article makes it painfully clear that clinicians need more education on physical abuse, not to mention guidance on the limits of confidentiality."

"We have an ethics board."

"Yeah—it meets three times a year and never advises individual physicians about their patients. Come on, Roland, it's a public relations ploy."

"She should have talked to a colleague."

"Maybe so, but it's water under the bridge now. Will you talk to Peter Helm?

"Is she worth it?"

"She's an excellent clinician and one of the best research collaborators I've ever had. She doesn't deserve to be tossed out of Harvard for this."

"It'll be tough. They'll want a sacrificial lamb to throw to the press; they probably won't want to fire her, just urge her to resign."

"What will they do if she refuses?"

"I don't know. Withdraw some funding. Make her life miserable..."

"Can't they tell the press they're launching a new training program or something?"

"Maybe, but that takes time and costs money. It's quicker to fire someone." The waitress appeared with hot and sour soup for both men, and Roland paused while she served them. "I'll talk to Helm, but the guy who really matters is John Masterson on the Beth Israel board. He's powerful. If he backs her, others will follow his lead."

"Can you talk to him?"

"I'll try. Cecile knows his wife. Maybe I can approach him privately, but I can't promise that I'll succeed."

Sam felt the tension in his shoulders ebbing. "I know. Thanks. So what about the medical board, the cops, the lawsuit?"

"If we can persuade the hospital to stand by her, that will sway the medical board. They won't give her more than a slap on the wrist. But she needs a top-notch lawyer to deal with the police and any possible lawsuits. And it seems to me that she should reach out to Mrs. Griffin's parents as soon as possible so that they focus on the murderer as their real enemy, not her."

"That makes sense. Know any lawyers? I try to avoid them myself."

"I don't." Roland grinned. "It's best to have a couple of smart lawyers in your camp. You can never beat 'em; so you might as well join 'em."

"Did Confucius' say that?"

"You're a barrel of laughs. I must say you owe me for this. I see no good reason why I should get involved in it except for a misguided sense of loyalty to you. And you're angry at Ariella again, aren't you?"

Claws of tension gripped his back. "Angry doesn't even begin to describe it."

"It won't do any good to tell you that I know just why she published that article.

"No."

"Since we're old friends I'll tell you anyway. She published it because she's still idealistic enough to believe in justice."

"What about the injustice of destroying the career of a terrific clinician?"

"Ariella obviously had Natalie Ward's full cooperation."

"Well, Natalie's overwrought, thinks she has some kind of responsibility for that murder. Ariella could have talked her out of going public. She could have called me— she knows Natalie is my friend. Hell, I introduced them. But it would kill her not to run with a story, no matter what the price."

"I think you're being harsh."

"I don't. You don't know what it is to have one mistake you make send your career into the toilet."

"No, I don't. And I see why you sympathize with Natalie. But your career is doing fine now, and hers too will probably survive."

"If we help her it will." The waitress reappeared with steaming silver dishes of noodles, rice, and shrimp.

Roland gave him a quelling look. "I said I will. Let me ask you something, though. Do you really think Natalie should have kept quiet about what she knew?"

"Definitely."

"Even if it meant an innocent man convicted of murder and a guilty one undiscovered?"

"We don't know that Griffin killed his wife."

"No, but answer my question."

Sam sat for a moment drumming his fingers on the table again. "Ideally I think I would have sought a middle path—maybe an anonymous tip to the police about Griffin's history of abuse."

"I think before you blow up at your girlfriend you need to talk to Natalie. Just for a minute stop seeing her as a press victim. She chose to tell her story. I think you should ask her why. Maybe she felt that her honor demanded it."

Sam sat there stuck at the word "girlfriend," which felt like a slap in the face. He cared for Ariella; he could not deny it to himself, but did he want to stay involved with someone who could betray him this way? He wanted to slam his fist into the table and watch the dishes bounce. Instead he stretched his arms high over his head to try to ease his tight shoulders. "Jesus do I need to go for a run. But yes, I'll definitely talk to Natalie. I just haven't been able to reach her."

"She might be at police headquarters."

"Damn. She probably is."

In silence they finished off the last of their shrimp. Then Roland broke into one of his unexpected grins. "I'm glad you ate."

"You're like a Jewish mother about this eating stuff. Ever since I arrived in Boston all you do is push food on me."

"The worst problems usually look better after a good meal. And don't you dare ask me if Confucius said that. There are limits to my tolerance—even with you, Sam."

A ghost of a smile shadowed Sam's eyes. "Always were touchy about old Confucius. Come on, let's go."

Roland picked up the bill as they stood and walked to a cash register at the end of the bar.

As they approached, a heavy-set Chinese cashier in a shiny rayon blouse blurted out, "Did you see that?" She was waving at the television, which was showing shifting scenes of bridge traffic, muddy waters and police officers. Then a shampoo commercial flashed onto the screen. "You know that woman, Laurie Griffin, who was murdered? Her husband just jumped off the Tobin Bridge!"

"What?" Sam bit out.

"He just pulled into the shoulder, climbed up on a railing and jumped—about twenty minutes ago. Sounds like he's dead too, though they won't say."

The two men looked at each other.

"Look, it's coming on again," the cashier rattled on. "Bet you that man killed his wife. Morning paper says he beat her, and by noon he's jumping off a bridge."

"It does look bad," said Roland, handing her his credit card.

Sam stood transfixed by the news broadcast, but it merely showed an ambulance speeding toward Boston City Hospital while a voice-over repeated that numerous witnesses had seen a man now identified as Brian Griffin jump from the bridge railing. The Boston Police were refusing to answer any questions until a promised press conference at five o'clock. As another commercial interrupted the story, Roland dragged Sam out to the sidewalk.

"Looks like Ariella was right." Roland gave him a wide grin.

Sam clenched his jaw. "I've got to get a hold of Natalie."

Roland's eyebrows rose eloquently.

"She'll blame herself."

"She'll manage. We're talking about a man who shot his pregnant wife to death in his own car, then shot himself as part of an elaborate cover-up. And now he decides to end it all. Whose fault is that? Not Natalie's."

"It's hard to take in. I guess he must have killed her."

"For a guy who went to Princeton you can be a little slow. Or is it a little stubborn?" Roland's face grew grim. "He killed her. He's a twisted, despicable excuse for a man. Maybe it's having a wife and child, but he makes me angry, and I can't imagine feeling remorse for exposing him. Not to mention that he's thrown a whole city into turmoil for months. The Hispanic community's going to be up in arms about police racism."

Sam did not want to listen. "I need to go call Natalie. Maybe she'll respond to her pager."

"Fine." Roland turned abruptly and walked away. Suppressing a sense of unease, Sam turned and strode off in the opposite direction toward the post office around the corner. He thought they had a phone booth.

❧

Ariella was hunched over a greasy table in the basement of the *Times* building eating a tuna fish sandwich and reviewing some notes on the newly-appointed director of the Carver Center when a hand grabbed her shoulder. She jumped, then swung around in her chair.

"You picked a great time for lunch," said David, eyes bright with unease. "I've been looking all over for you."

"Scared me half to death."

He offered none of his usual quips or apologies. "Ariella, do you know what just came in on the radio? Brian Griffin jumped off the Tobin Bridge."

The color drained from her face. "When?"

"Fifteen minutes ago."

"How do they know it's him?"

"Well, there was a lot of slow traffic on the bridge. Quite a few witnesses, and several recognized his face. It's been all over the paper and T.V. for months now."

"Yeah." Her head began to pound. "Is he dead?"

"Probably, but they took him to Boston City Hospital. Cops want the E.R. to declare him dead, not the paramedics."

"Cleaner that way." She put her head in her hands.

He slid into a chair next to her and rested an arm across her back, his hand stroking her arm. "Hey, don't go soft on him now."

Her head shot up, and she shook him off. "How dare you? I'll be as soft as I want. I never wanted to cover murders. I hate all this violence and death. I didn't become a reporter to write stories that make men jump off bridges."

"Sorry. I know that. But, Ari, do you think you

should take this on? Griffin made his choices in life, some pretty horrible ones. Think of the good you've done for Renaldo Colon, for Angelica who believed in him, for the whole city."

"What have I done for the city except ruin the credibility of the police?"

"Hey, they made their own choices too. But your story is going to force some soul-searching about racial profiling and domestic violence."

"It's terrible what they've done to Renaldo Colon, but it's easy to see why. From the mayor to the police commissioner to the cop on the street, they couldn't face the prospect that one of their own, a clean-cut, white suburban salesman, could do what he did. No group would want to claim such a man. We all want to believe our clans are free of such disgusting behavior. I guess that's racism."

"I don't know, honey. And I know your head is spinning right now, but there's something else I have to tell you." He pulled a yellow slip of paper from his pocket. "There was a message from your sister sitting on your desk upstairs, and it said important; so I brought it down."

She felt a wave of queasiness rise in her throat, and for once she was glad David never minded his own business, but she said only, "Nina," grabbed her papers from the table and pushed it away, leaving a quarter of a sandwich sitting on its plastic plate. She was already halfway to the cafeteria door, David close behind, before she turned to thank him.

"Ruby," he said.

"That's the only reason my sister would call me at work." She turned a corner and gave a grateful prayer to find the hall pay phone free. As she began to dial the number on the message slip, David leaned against the wall and began reading some papers in his hand. "You don't have to wait," she said, as she listened for a ring.

"It's okay. I'd like to."

She shrugged, then turned toward the phone. "Hi, I got your message. Where are you? Is everything okay?"

"Oh, Ariella, thank God it's you." Nina's words poured out. "I took Ruby in to the doctor today. I thought it was just a cough, but they sent her straight to St. Luke's Hospital. That's where we are. They want to do heart surgery tonight. They think her graft is falling out." Her voice broke. "Is there any way you could come down here? Lenny's out of town on business, and I haven't even been able to reach him, and I'm really scared."

"Of course you are. I'll come as soon as I can." She looked at her watch. "I think there's a train that gets into Penn Station around eight, but I may not make it to the hospital till nine o'clock."

"That's okay. I feel so much better just hearing your voice, knowing you'll come."

"Ruby's very strong. She's been through this three times before, and she's always made a great recovery."

"You're right. She has. But it doesn't make it any easier to think of her being wheeled into the operating room again."

"Where is she now?"

"They just took her for some pre-op test with a needle. She's supposed to be back here in fifteen minutes."

"How's she taking it?"

"She's doing better than I am. For some reason she wanted to take her favorite panda bear to the doctor's office today. I don't usually let it out of the house, but today I gave in. And now she has it here, which is really comforting. The surgeon even told her they would bring Pandy into the operating room, which amazed me. That's a first."

"It's a good omen. Now try to stay calm and confident till I get there."

"Confident I can manage, but calm is another story."

"I know. So what's the room number?"

"Well for now it's 251, but you'd better double-check when you arrive. Sometimes post-op you go somewhere else."

"You think she'll have surgery before I get there?"

"They're talking about six o'clock, but it depends on these tests they're doing."

An airplane flashed through Ariella's mind, but she decided it would be no faster—too much traffic on the roads to the airports, too many airline delays, too much uncertainty getting on standby. "I'd better go now, but I love you, and I promise I'll be there by nine. Just tell Ruby Aunt Ari is winging her way there on her magic carpet." She said goodbye, hung up and turned to find David still leaning against the wall.

"Need a hug?"

Torn between amusement and irritation, she shook her head and started for the stairs. "What I need is to get out of here."

"Joyce will think you belong at Boston City Hospital."

"I'm sure we've got crime reporters there already. Where I belong is St. Luke's in New York. Ruby needs surgery tonight, and her daddy is out of town. Joyce can go hang."

"Well, that's your decision, but I would tell her to her face to go hang if I were you. Don't sneak out of here."

She had been contemplating just that. "You know something, David. You're getting on my nerves. Did I ask you to dog my steps and give me advice?"

"No." His eyes lost none of their good humor. "You can snap at me all you want. You're having a rough day."

She ran up three flights of concrete steps with him on her tail, pushed through the newsroom door and glanced over her shoulder into his boyish face as he mounted the last two steps. Curls bouncing, cheeks pink, he looked even more impish than usual, and his eyes gleamed with challenge. She turned away and headed left, away from her desk and toward Joyce's office. Behind her back he raised two fingers in a vee for victory.

Joyce was standing behind her desk, listening to the phone and wearing a sleek, steel-gray, knitted dress, a black and white scarf decorated with bony fish knotted loosely around her neck. A silver clip pulled the hair up from her forehead, making her look even sterner than usual. Unable to gauge her mood, Ariella sat, then stood again. She wanted to look Joyce straight in the eye, not gaze up at her. After several long minutes of examining the ferns and considering what words to use, Ariella got her chance. Joyce hung up.

"I have to go to New York."

Joyce's eyebrows practically took off for the ceiling. "Didn't you hear about Griffin?"

"I heard, but I have to go to New York immediately. It's a family emergency. I'm leaving on the three o'clock train." She figured that if she sounded definite Joyce would have more trouble saying "no."

"Are you out of your mind? This is your story. Is Griffin going to live? What really happened the night Laurie Griffin died? Who knew about it? Who knew all this time that he had abused her and said nothing? There are so many questions to answer."

"Someone else is going to have to answer them. I'm going to New York."

Joyce narrowed her eyes. "If you go, you'll never get back on this story. I'll hand it completely to the City Desk and let the crime reporters go full throttle."

"You know, that's what you should have done weeks ago," Ariella said bitterly. "Laurie's dead. The baby's dead. Griffin's dying or dead because no one could jump from that height and live. And my story's going to die with him. I have to focus on the living."

They faced each other across the desk as if about to draw swords. "The public has the right to know a lot more about this case."

"No. What Boston needs is to acknowledge we made terrible mistakes and move on. A pregnant woman was murdered. A Harvard hospital failed to recognize domestic violence or do anything about it. The Boston Police failed to investigate a husband because he looked like them and railroaded an innocent man because he didn't. The mayor shamelessly used the case for political gain. The city condemned the Councilmen who spoke out against the warrantless searches in Mission Hill and the flimsy case against Renaldo Colon. But that's all old news. You always say: if there's nothing fresh, time for a new story."

"What about the questions I raised?"

"Brian Griffin killed her, and now he's dead. There's nothing left to investigate. He'll never confess, and he'll never face a trial. Why poke into his relatives' silence? Look what it's brought them. It's our institutions that need to take a hard look at themselves and reform."

"Then that's the story."

"If they do anything to change, I'll cover it, but it won't happen for weeks, months, years maybe. Right now I'm going to New York."

"So you say, but you've been running out of town a little too much lately. You can't drop the ball on big stories and expect it to go unnoticed. If you want a career you need to be here."

"I don't know what I want from my career. But I know this. My niece could die on the operating table tonight, and I'm going to be in that hospital with my sister no matter what."

"Maybe you *should* know what you want from your career."

Ariella felt indignation roiling in her. "I do know some things. I know I'll never write another crime story, and I don't ever want to write another story that makes a man kill himself. I'm not the right person for that job. Let someone do it who can stand violence, and give me the health beat."

A flicker of a smile crossed Joyce's face. "I've already recommended you for it. Of course, David will remain our senior person, but they're offering him a dream of his own— to work part-time with the deep investigative team."

Ariella stared at her, then looked at her feet, the wind knocked from her sails. "My God. Thank you," she almost whispered.

"You're welcome. I don't like you running out on me, but let me ask you this: how soon can you be back?"

"Maybe tomorrow, but I have to see how it goes."

"All right. Call me in the morning with an update."

Ariella found that she was shaking; the anger drained from her, leaving her feeling overwhelmed. She took a deep breath and tried to pull herself together. At least having Joyce's blessing eased her guilt about leaving town. "I promise I'll be in touch. I just have to put family first right now."

"You don't have to explain any further." Joyce sank into her chair, her face suddenly looking old despite her flawless make-up. "I've always admired your principles, even when they inconvenience me. Just get back here as soon as humanly possible. I hope your niece will be all right."

"Me too. I've had enough of tragedy and death."

33

Not five minutes out of Back Bay Station on the train she realized that she had not called Sam. She had almost missed the train rushing home to her apartment to pack a bag, then waiting for a cab she called which never arrived, so typical for Boston. With no time left to think, she had dragged her bag into the street, panted her way to the station on foot, charged down the escalator onto the train, and settled for one of the few remaining seats, beside a window decorated with graying wads of chewing gum. When the conductor arrived to take her ticket he grumbled at having to sell her one on the train, especially when she wanted to pay by credit card. Only when he left her alone did Sam come to mind.

She worried about what he would think of her article on Natalie Ward, wondered whether he had heard about Griffin's jump. At least he would now admit that Griffin was a murderer. But suddenly she realized that his refusal to believe her domestic violence theory no longer rankled. If he had shut out the truth, she too had seen only part of the story. It flashed into her mind that she had desperately wanted to believe Colon innocent, not only to vindicate Angelica but to soothe herself. If a stranger had killed Laurie Griffin, then Ariella and all Boston women had to walk the streets afraid of random violence. If Brian Griffin had killed her, they only needed to choose better husbands than Laurie had.

As for Sam, she thought he had resisted condemning Brian Griffin because he so hated the notion of a man killing his pregnant wife. Just as Ariella did not want to live in a world where strangers randomly kidnapped pregnant women and killed them, Sam did not want to live in one where men could so violently turn on their own families. He felt so strongly about duty to family that he could not envision such violence from a husband. Neither she nor Sam had looked beyond their own navels.

Until now she had adopted Angelica's anger at the shoddy police work and racism that led to Colon's arrest, but today she felt for the police too. Just like Sam, they could far more easily imagine a stranger committing such a shocking crime than one of their own. Because Griffin was a middle class Irish Catholic they just failed to see him as a suspect.

Until last night the Griffin case had been a jigsaw puzzle she struggled to solve so that she could put things right. She had imagined Colon set free and Griffin rotting in Colon's jail cell. She had imagined Griffin family members who knew of the abuse publicly shamed for their deadly silence. In her narrow self-righteousness she had never imagined the pain and personal sacrifice it would take for a witness like Dr. Ward to come forward. And she had never thought she might drive the killer to suicide. As terrible a man as he was, she could not relinquish all responsibility. She had set out to get him, she had succeeded, and now she had to accept the burden of the consequences. Perhaps even without her article he would eventually have killed himself— he was obviously unstable—but she would have had no part in it. Catapulted from observer to actor in the Griffin murder drama, she longed for the simple news stories of her early days in journalism school like the Thanksgiving Day parade.

Queasy, she peered out the dirt-streaked window, past the blobs of chewing gum to the sky darkening over clapboard Connecticut houses, and she willed herself not to cry. She wondered how Natalie Ward felt this evening and hoped she did not regret the story. Probably not, she realized. She had put too much on the line to tolerate any vacillation now, and she was the kind of woman who stuck to her decisions. Ariella knew she needed to do that too.

∽

Swerving angrily around an uncharacteristically timid Boston driver waiting to turn left, Sam swore under his breath. Natalie had not responded to her pager, and he could reach Ariella neither at her newsroom desk nor at home. He could not go back to work right now; he had to do something to clear his mind. By the time he reached his parking space at the medical center, he remembered he had some old running clothes and sneakers in the trunk of the car. Throwing on sweatpants in a hospital bathroom he jogged down the street past the medical student dormitory, tossed the discarded clothes in his car, and headed into the Fens to run.

One benefit of working at the medical center was proximity to the Fens, the long strip of marshy park land along the road that led into Storrow Drive toward downtown. City gardeners had ignored the area for a while, and the coarse grasses grew high, some almost to Sam's chin. He ran fast, unable to pace himself with so much emotion flooding his body. He wanted to shake Ariella. How could she have blithely printed an article that would ruin his friend's life? Far from calming him Roland had only raised new spectres: Laurie Griffin's angry parents filing a lawsuit and the medical board grilling Natalie in endless hearings. Natalie did not deserve this kind of treatment. She hadn't killed anyone.

Try as he might he could not understand why Ariella had printed that article and printed it without telling him. He had thought she felt close to him, thought she cared for him. Why would she skewer his friend and colleague in the newspaper without even warning him? He felt sure that he could have dissuaded her if she had given him the chance. Maybe that was why she had not called. Maybe she felt her reasoning too shaky to contend with an argument, and surely she could predict his opinion. If so, she was a coward. If she wanted to be with him she had to face him with their differences, not hide.

She would never understand how much power she held, how with a few taps on her keyboard she could fuel the career of a fraud like Kurt Schaus or demolish a promising doctor like Natalie. Even after hearing about everything that he had seen in Michigan, Ariella had learned nothing. Or at least, she had not learned enough. Once a reporter, always a reporter. She could not shy away from what was no doubt the biggest story yet in the Griffin case and one which newspapers all over America would cover. All over America Natalie Ward's name would be synonymous with negligent medical care for battered women. It made his blood boil. He had seen Natalie go the extra mile for so many patients, cut vacations and weekends short for complicated deliveries, postpone or cancel research meetings to see patients with emergencies. She had a deep commitment to her patients;

that was what had led her to join his team; she wanted badly to provide her patients with a chance of preventing cervical cancer.

From the facts laid out in Ariella's article, he could not figure out what Natalie could have done to save Laurie Griffin's life. How could she have guessed that a husband, even a belligerent and possessive one, would actually murder his pregnant wife? How could anyone predict or prevent such an unspeakable crime?

If he were honest with himself, he knew that he had felt even angrier since he heard that Griffin had jumped off a bridge. It hit him right between the eyes that the very moment he had finally accepted that Griffin murdered his wife, he also had to accept that the man would never be brought to justice. He would never face a jury of his peers. He would never spend a day in jail. He would never have to confront the public outrage that had simmered in every Boston citizen since November. Now the case would sputter out like a campfire in a drizzle, and no one in Boston would ever be made whole.

Brian Griffin had done more than murder his pregnant wife, he had opened huge gashes in his city that would take years to heal. The fear and resentment flaring against the police among blacks and Latinos would now spread to women, who would blame police for refusing to consider a theory of domestic violence. And the mayor, the police, and all the elected officials who had called for a crackdown on inner city crime would close ranks and retreat, defending their actions all the way.

The whole thing made him sick to his stomach as he ran along the path through the Fens. A bird, dappled with sunlight, squawked from a tree branch, blissfully unaware of the screwed-up state of the world, and Sam gave it a wry salute. He was beginning to calm down, and he felt he had to make some decisions. The question that plagued him the most was how he could continue his relationship with Ariella. He had strong feelings about her, he had to admit, or her behavior would not pain him so much. Hell, maybe he was even in love with her a little. How else could he explain a desire that went beyond the physical to a need to shield her, help her, and sometimes, change her opinions? Maybe he had no right to steer her in any direction. Maybe to have a relationship he had to remain hands-off, to respect her independence in all things, to let her make stupid choices even if they hurt people. He thought he could let her make the choices, but he knew himself well enough to know that he could not to do it silently. As long as he loved her he would always try to sway her.

If she planned to avoid him rather than talking out important decisions she faced, then he did not think they had a future together. His lunch felt like a ball of lead in his stomach, and he slowed his pace almost to a walk. He thought of a long line of nights marching along with no Ariella sleeping curled around him, her hand against his heart. He felt hollow, but he knew he had better break off the relationship. It would be best for both of them. She would do better with a guy like David, who understood and accepted the news business and did not seem troubled by its moral quagmires. But the image of Ariella with David made him want to bash his fist into a passing tree; so he put that line of thinking out of his mind.

Sam stomped back into his office just after two o'clock, disappointed that his run had not lifted his grim mood. Mrs. Boyle looked up from the sheets of budget numbers spread across her desk and assessed him in a look.

"Dr. Natalie Ward just phoned you about five minutes ago," she said, knowing full well the bomb shell she was dropping.

"Damn. Where was she calling from?"

Mrs. Boyle looked as if she had swallowed a quart of vinegar. "From police headquarters, I believe. I see from today's *Times* that she may be mixed up in that murder case. Do you think NIH will want us to replace her in your research project?"

"I hope not! But I can't think about that now. Is she reachable?"

"No, but she said she would try again in about five minutes."

"Thank God. How did she sound?"

"Strained." The telephone rang. "That might be her now."

Sam reached across Mrs. Boyle's desk and snatched the receiver. "Sam Becker."

He could hear voices buzzing indistinctly and a sound like drawers shutting; then a familiar voice said, "Sam, you're there."

"Are you okay, Natalie?"

"Tired," she said in a voice so hoarse it hardly sounded like hers at all. "I'm in Roxbury at police headquarters – off Tremont Street. I didn't sleep last night, and I've been here for questioning since seven thirty this morning."

Sam felt the bile rise in his throat. He said only, "Man," but he wanted to kick the desk.

"Apparently Brian Griffin has just killed himself, though. So the police suddenly believe me, and they say I may go as long as I'm available for further questions tomorrow."

She sounded so awful he had to ask: "You're not blaming yourself for his suicide are you?"

"No. I'm glad he's dead. I don't have much professional objectivity left." She gave a peculiar half-laugh.

"I'll come pick you up."

"That isn't necessary, Sam. I just wanted to ask whether, well, whether you would have dinner with me. I could use the company."

"I'm coming to pick you up. You shouldn't drive if you've had no sleep. We'll go somewhere quiet where you can unwind."

"It's really not..."

"I'll be there in fifteen minutes."

"All right." She sounded defeated. "I'll be outside in front of the building. I need some fresh air."

"I'll bet you do."

34

When Sam pulled up to the curb in front of Boston Police Headquarters he found Natalie in a royal blue wool coat with a high Mandarin color, leaning heavily on a lamppost. He took a moment to recognize her because he had never seen her long, pale hair flying loose in the breeze. It whipped across her face, and she did nothing to stop it. She slid into his car as if her bones were liquid, tipped her chair back and closed her eyes; beneath them lay deep lavender circles. Just before she clasped her hands in her lap, he saw them tremble.

"Can you just get over to Storrow Drive? Then I'll direct you out to Concord." She did not open her eyes and sounded as hoarse as a longtime smoker.

"I think I should take you to my apartment." He knew that she would argue, but he refused to just drop her at home in this condition.

"It's right in the middle of your work day," she whispered.

"It's almost three, and I haven't been getting squat done today."

"Okay." She let her head roll away from him.

He pulled into traffic and took a deep breath, surprised at how little she had protested. She seemed to be in shock, either craving direction or little caring where she went, he could not tell which. Adrenaline coursed through him, although he tried to tell himself to calm down. He ought to feel much better now that he had freed Natalie from the clutches of the police, but he did not. He remembered his own shock at his losses in Michigan and the years it had taken him to recover; he wanted to spare her that, and he couldn't.

As he wound his way into the Back Bay, Natalie reclined beside him saying nothing. He wanted to ask her a dozen questions, but he felt he should respect her exhaustion. With a stroke of luck he found a parking place only a few doors down from his building. Even after he turned off the ignition, got out and rounded the car to the curb, she remained still with her eyes closed and her head tilted toward her door. So he opened it, slung her briefcase under his arm, crouched, and took one of her hands.

"Ready?" he asked gently.

Her eyes opened, she nodded, and he stood, pulling her from the car and into the stiff breeze. The sun had begun to lose its battle with the wind, and it no longer seemed like a good day for a run. Natalie shivered a little and flicked some hair from her face, but the wind blew it back again.

"It's right up here." Sam gestured up the street with one hand and took her arm with the other. "Let's get indoors." He bundled her off to his lobby, all the while struck by her odd behavior. Natalie had always impressed him as completely self-contained, and he would never before have presumed to make decisions for her, much less physically push her in any direction, but today she seemed like a lump of wet clay. She remained silent in the elevator, silent down the hallway and all the way to his sunken living room, where she sank into the couch, her usual ramrod posture gone.

"Do you want some tea?" he asked. Like the adopted Englishwoman she was, his mother had believed firmly in the restorative nature of tea. His mother had been good in a crisis.

"Yes, please." Natalie's voice remained a disinterested whisper.

"All right. Black or herbal?"

"Black. Earl Gray?"

"Yup." He noticed that her hands were still trembling. Of course, his mother had also believed in the restorative nature of food. "I'll bet you could use a good meal. When did you eat last?"

"I had a little toast at six thirty this morning and a candy bar at the police station, but I don't feel very hungry."

"Well, I think I'll order us some take-out from my favorite Indian place. They deliver, and if we don't want it now we can have it later." He thought back to an Indian lunch they had shared months ago. "You like Chicken Tikka, don't you?"

She nodded.

He wished that she would say something. Her silence unnerved him. He was used to women who talked, women like his mother, his sister, and—damn her—Ariella, who talked constantly. Of course, Natalie was capable of professional conversations, but under emotional strain she seemed to have snapped her clam shell shut. He would have preferred a tirade.

Leaving her to her own devices, he began boiling water for tea in the kitchen, telephoned India Palace and placed an order. On a whim he dug out his mother's blue and white china teapot, and brewed the tea in it; coming from Boston aristocracy Natalie might appreciate it. The food arrived more quickly than usual because of the hour, too late for lunch and too early for dinner. He decided to offer the tea first and put the food containers into the oven to keep warm. Having given Natalie fifteen minutes to herself, he brought the teapot into the living room and set it on a side table. Ariella would have offered molasses cookies too, he thought, and he swore under his breath at his preoccupation with her. Heedless of his grumbling, Natalie sat turned away from him on the couch, looking out the window behind it, her hair falling like tangled hay against the back of the wool coat she still wore.

"May I hang up your coat?" he asked in more formal tones than he intended.

"Oh." She turned to look at him with glassy eyes and then focused. "Sure." She shrugged it off and handed it to him. "You must think I'm very rude. I'm sorry. I'm just not myself."

"It's all right. You've been through hell. Pour yourself a cup of that tea, and I'll put this coat away."

He had struck the right note, given her the right task, and she automatically moved to pour tea not only for herself but for him. Although she never took cream and sugar, today she helped herself to a liberal amount of both. She did not know what she needed, but at least cream and sugar were a harmless indulgence. As she sipped the strong, sweet tea she felt her head clear a little, and she sat up straighter. An hour ago she had felt so bone-tired, so beaten, so frightened about the future that she could only withdraw, but here in Sam's elegantly appointed living room, high above the streets and far from furious police detectives, she began to feel flickers of her old self emerging.

When Sam re-entered the room, she attempted a

smile and handed him a teacup. "So how's the analysis going? When do you think we'll be ready for Phase III trials?"

"Soon—maybe June."

"That is soon." She wondered whether she would ever get to participate, or whether she would be asked to leave the hospital. "It'll be great to see whether the vaccine really works. I have a good feeling about it if we can just get the details right." She meant it, but she knew her tone sounded half-hearted.

"We're a good team. If it can be done, we'll do it."

She looked away for a minute, then met his eyes again. "Thanks for picking me up."

"No problem. Damsels in distress are my specialty." He perched in an armchair beside the couch, added a couple of spoons full of sugar and a splash of cream to his tea, then took a gulp. "Natalie, I don't want to harass you, but it might do you good to talk about it."

She nodded, sipped her tea, and gathered her thoughts. Her voice came out a croak, and she stared into the tea. "They really grilled me. I'm used to tough questions when I present cases at the hospital, but this was different. The officer questioning me was angry, very angry. He took it personally that I had not come forward sooner, and he was livid about the newspaper article."

"Well, I wasn't too thrilled with that myself."

She gave him a quizzical look. "Why not?"

His gaze hardened. "Well, I don't need to get into that right now. I just thought that Ariella showed poor judgment printing it."

Natalie sat up straighter. "It was my decision."

"One that has already cost you and will have a lot more ripples before it's done."

"Keeping quiet cost me too, Sam. It was eating me alive. I had to tell someone what I knew about Laurie Griffin."

"Sure you did. But I wish you had told me or some other friend of yours instead of a damn reporter. We could have strategized about what, if anything, to tell the press."

She was startled. "I never thought I'd hear you sound like my parents. And that 'damn reporter' is supposed to be a friend of yours, isn't she? So you think I should have kept it to myself that Griffin severely beat his wife?"

"Well, it's not as if you killed the woman yourself." He passed over the reference to Ariella, pausing as if to choose the right phrase. "And I'm afraid this is going to be hard on your career."

"No need to mince words." Her tone was caustic. "It may wreck my career. But I knew that last night. I had to do this. I haven't slept well for months. Laurie Griffin was my patient, and I failed her because I didn't let myself see the abuse. I did nothing to stop that man when she was alive, and I did nothing after she died. I'm not a big church-goer, but I have a conscience. How could I let that monster go free to batter again?"

"But the point is that he's the monster, not you. You probably couldn't have saved Laurie Griffin, and now that she's gone you don't have to throw away your career out of guilt. And it makes me sick that Ariella would rub her hands at getting another great scoop and encourage you."

She put down her teacup. "If I wanted prudence I would have told my father. I didn't turn to Ariella for that, though I did trust her discretion, and she did warn me of the consequences. I went to her because she would know whether this was important news, and she had the power to publish it. The moral question was mine alone to resolve."

"Maybe there was some middle ground you could have found—a way to safeguard your reputation while helping the police investigate Griffin."

She pushed her hair from her face and looked him in the eye, a flash of arrogance welling in her gaze. "There isn't any middle ground here. This was about justice for a murdered woman that I knew personally. Once I was certain her husband had done it, I couldn't let him get away with it."

"Well, he'll never go to trial now," snapped Sam.

"He'll never kill another woman either," she replied coldly.

"I'm sorry. I shouldn't have said that. You're right that justice demanded that Colon be released and Griffin be arrested. But I care about you as a colleague and a friend, and I just wish you could have been protected from the storm. This is the biggest murder case to hit Boston in years. Why did Ariella have to mix you up in it?"

She lifted her chin. "It's ugly, I know. I wasn't brought up to spend my time in hard, dirty chairs in police interrogation rooms. Believe me, that alone kept me silent for weeks on end. But Ariella didn't mix me up in it, Sam. I did."

"Why?"

"I couldn't live with myself any longer." To her embarrassment, she suddenly lost her fragile composure and felt tears welling up, and she knew he saw them.

He moved to her side on the couch and took her hand. "I'm an ass. I've been coming on much too strong. You've been through hell for months, and I didn't even notice, and now I have the gall to give advice. It's water under the bridge. You did turn to Ariella, and she did write about it in the paper, and now we have to go forward and see this thing through."

"Well, I have to." She did not remove her hand from his.

"I want to help. I already asked Roland to put in a good word for you with the people he knows at Beth Israel."

"Oh, Sam!" She knew just how powerful Roland's friends were.

"Shh." He put a finger to his lips. "I don't want to lose one of the best collaborators I've ever had. The press screws scientists every day, but I hate to see it happen to you." Then he hugged her.

She felt weak to allow it, yet she sank into his embrace. For a year she had fantasized about him, and now, far too weary for caution, she simply relished the feeling. She lay her head on his shoulder and thought about kissing him. That very morning, unasked, he had been rolling out the cannons to protect her job at the hospital. For that alone she wanted to kiss him. Of course, he was probably holding her out of pity, and she suspected that he was involved with Ariella, although perhaps not very seriously. Yet after making one grand gesture for another person's sake in twenty four hours she could not manage another one.

She lifted her head and when he turned to look at her, his full lips only inches away, she leaned in and quickly kissed him. He looked surprised. "You really care," she whispered.

"Of course." He shifted her so that she sat close against his side with one of his arms around her shoulders. "I hate to see you kicked around by the hospital. You're such a devoted clinician. They should just leave you alone to do your work."

"Ummm." She wanted him to kiss her back, but he kept talking.

"I think you should make a pre-emptive strike: go to the administration to admit your faults and offer a plan."

That remark got through to her mind. "Well, I plan to do intensive domestic violence training with my staff as soon as possible. Maybe I should tell the administration I'll plan training sessions for all of Beth Israel. I'll bet there are a lot of people on the hospital staff who know even less about it than I did. I can bring in some speakers from battered women's shelters, and I know an expert, a dynamic woman prosecutor in Cambridge. I almost called her a few weeks ago to tell her about Laurie Griffin, but I couldn't bring myself to talk about it to a stranger."

"That's a great idea. Offer to organize a training conference. They can also use it as a way to deflect negative publicity." He did not kiss her, but neither did he shift away from her.

Some combination of the physical contact and the frank talk was reviving her, and she burst out: "If I can show myself and the Harvard community that we can prevent future Laurie Griffin tragedies it will go a long way toward healing the misery I've felt these last couple months. And I want to meet with Laurie's parents, tell them personally how sorry I am."

He frowned. "Before you do, maybe you should see a lawyer—just to plan how to phrase things. Roland said you should take care not to open yourself up to a lawsuit."

"Maybe, but if the parents will see me, I'm going to meet with them—no matter what the lawyer says. And I'm going to propose something to the Beth Israel board." She felt the words rushing out of her, and stopped to take a breath. "I really think we need somewhere to go with these hard ethical questions like whether it's ever okay to violate doctor-patient confidentiality. We need a hospital ethicist. Things might never have gotten this bad if I had a neutral colleague to advise me, and there must be other doctors who need it too."

"I would think the board would run to hire one—they'd get more good publicity about how they're working to protect patients. But you could have come to me."

"No, I really couldn't. I wanted to talk to someone who didn't know me very well, someone who would help me assess the situation in a dispassionate way."

He squeezed her forearm and smiled. "I guess I haven't been acting dispassionate, but I don't want to give you the wrong idea or anything. I only brought you here to my place because it was close, and you seemed like a basket case, and I wanted to cheer you up before leaving you alone at home to brood. I know how awful it is to brood at home alone; I've done it."

She did not like being described as a basket case. "I can take care of myself."

"Of course you can, but everyone can use a cup of tea and a hug now and then."

She let her fingers trail down his arm, weighing what to say. "The hug was especially nice."

He gave her another, massaging and stroking her back until she ached to kiss him, but his remarks gave her pause. After a brief tussle with herself, she asked the obvious question: "Are you seriously involved with Ariella?"

"I was, but after these last couple of days I don't know that I can continue to be."

Her shoulder blades tightened. "Look, I don't want

to be the cause of a rift between you. I doubt that Ariella fully understood the effect her article could have on my career—if that's what's bothering you."

"Well, she should have, or she should have inquired into it, or given you a day to pave the way, talk to some people at the hospital before going public."

She pulled away, clasped her hands tight, and looked him dead in the eye. "You're not listening to me, Sam. I couldn't have done it that way. I couldn't bear to tell anyone I knew. Telling her was a way to force myself over the cliff. And she *did* warn me that the story could hurt my career—though she focused more on my safety."

He looked puzzled.

"Griffin wasn't dead 24 hours ago, and she was afraid he would hurt me. She told me to sleep at a friend's house, maybe hire a security guard."

Her words washed over Sam like an icy waterfall. He had never even thought of the danger, not only to Natalie but to Ariella, who had already been threatened in his presence, no doubt by Griffin. Ever since he had read the *Times* article that morning he had thought of nothing but the injustice to Natalie, never considering that Griffin might be hunting down Ariella. He swallowed hard, remembering that he had not spoken to her at all that day.

Natalie went on, but he was only half-listening as she said: "Her news story was absolutely fair. In fact, it painted me in a better light than I ever would have expected. I don't know why you're angry at her about it. After all, she was only the messenger."

He was about to excuse himself to go to the telephone, when she added, "Since this seems to be confessional week for me, I might as well tell you something else. Maybe you know it, but I suspect you don't. It's very awkward for me to be in the middle of your dispute with Ariella because I'm attracted to you myself. I have been all year."

"Oh." He felt like a fool. "Been told I'm oblivious to that kind of thing. I guess this is another example."

"And I'm pretty good at hiding things. I hoped we might have a relationship some day, but you didn't seem open to that; so I waited. Today's been rough, and I'm grateful to you for spending time with me, but I can see that you need to work things out with Ariella, and I probably need to work out a lot of things in my own life before I can focus on someone else." She gave a small smile. "If you're free in six months and I'm still in Boston, let me know, okay?"

"Sure." His mind was churning, and he had no idea what to say; so he folded her to him in another embrace. She accepted it for a few moments, then pulled away.

"Would you mind if we had that Indian food now? I'm suddenly hungry."

He jumped up, grateful for something to do. "No problem. I just have to make one quick phone call, and I'll bring it right out."

35

Ariella sat on the edge of an ivory bedspread wearing a fuchsia flannel nightshirt, digging her bare toes into the ivory carpet and staring at the speckled ivory wallpaper of her room in the Inn at Saint Luke's. It was almost one in the morning, and she needed to go to sleep, but in spite of the hotel's attempt at soothing décor her mind was racing over all she had seen. She had rushed from Penn Station to the hospital, where she found Nina anxiously watching Ruby sleep in a little glassed-in area of the intensive care unit. Ruby had survived the operation, but her body was showing some strain, and the doctor kept repeating that they would know more in the morning, his uncertainty disquieting for Nina. She had finally reached Lenny, and he would be flying home on the first morning plane out of Dallas.

Since the nurses allowed no food around intensive care patients, Nina had just been starving herself, and Ariella would not allow it. After much arguing and cajoling, Ariella had persuaded her sister to go to the cafeteria for fifteen minutes for a bite, leaving Ariella as bedside sentinel. Sitting beside an inert Ruby for those fifteen minutes had seemed an eternity to Ariella. She heartily disliked the mechanical world of intensive care where silent nurses made endless rounds checking and re-calibrating rumbling, beeping machines while pallid patients lay sleeping or unconscious, she knew not which. When Nina returned, Ariella felt pathetically glad to see her; she could withstand her sister's raw nerves far better than the lonely watch.

They sat together and whispered over Ruby's bed for hours. At first Nina repeated and analyzed all the events of the day: every symptom Ruby had, every remark the doctors and nurses made. Then she asked Ariella to pray with her, and they whispered a healing prayer together. Nina choked on its final words and sat weeping while Ariella searched her memory and recited a psalm she knew by heart. After that Nina kissed her cheek and held her hands and said that they had better change the subject. So Ariella began to tell her sister about Dr. Ward's revelations, the newspaper article and Brian Griffin's fatal jump. Finally, after midnight the nurses asked her to leave; only a mother had the right to spend the night curled awkwardly in an armchair beside her child's bed. She had planned to stay at Nina's, but she could hardly imagine standing frozen on a dark corner trying to hail a cab back to Nina's empty apartment. When the nurses suggested the hotel next door, she had jumped at the idea, forgetting how poorly she slept in hotel rooms.

Here she sat in her nightshirt, teeth brushed, hair combed, face washed, no further excuses to stay awake. She drew down the coverlet and swung her legs onto the bed, snuggling with one of the four ivory and rose striped pillows. Just as she reached for the chain on the bedside lamp, she glanced at the telephone beside it and picked up the receiver instead. Suddenly she wanted desperately to call Sam. She could not bring herself to dial his number at one o'clock in the morning, but maybe he had left her a message at home.

She dialed her own number and punched in the code to retrieve her messages.

After several clicks and a beep, she heard a breathless voice. "Hi, this is Angelica. I read today's paper, and I just had to call you. I don't know how to thank you for what you've done. The Good Lord brought us together in that parking lot, and you've been my good luck charm ever since. And did I tell you that there's a talent agency going to represent my baby? They say they can get her into department store ads and catalogues. I can't believe it! All because I met you and David. Anyway, you take care." Ariella sighed and smiled a little.

As soon as she heard the first syllable of the next message, she knew it was Sam. "Ariella, I've been trying to reach you at work all morning. I'm not going to repeat myself except to say that I'm really angry, I need to talk to you, and I can't believe you're avoiding me like this. Do you realize you've destroyed Natalie's career?"

Then came another. "This is Sam, wondering where the hell you are. It's five o'clock, and the newsroom just told me you left hours ago. I'm at my apartment with Natalie, who is not coping well with her new-found celebrity. I *wish* you had trusted me with her story before you printed it. Call me when you get this message—will you please?" The machine gave two beeps, indicating no further messages.

She slammed her fist down on the mattress, then looked at her watch: ten after one. She dialed his number. As his phone began to ring she felt a lump leap into her throat. Her heart was pounding, and it was all that she could do not to hang up. After four rings the answering machine began to play his message, and she bit down on a knuckle in frustration mixed with relief. When she heard the tone she spoke coldly, "This is Ariella. I just got your messages at one in the morning. Actually, I wasn't ignoring you; I just had something a little more important to do than call. I'm in a New York hotel next to Saint Luke's Hospital, where my niece is in intensive care. I had very much wanted to talk to you about everything, but I'm not sure that I can handle your anger right now. So I may just wait to call you until I get back to Boston, and I'm not sure when that will be."

She hung up, her hand shaking, shoved the phone away from the edge of the night table, and then burrowed into the bed. Tears began leaking from her eyes, and she wept silently into the pillows until finally she drifted into a restless sleep.

The next morning, at seven o'clock, the blaring ring of the bedside phone startled her awake, her heart stuttering as she grabbed the receiver. It was Nina. "Ariella, you've got to come over here, quick. Ruby opened her eyes and said, 'Mama.'"

"Oh my God." Ariella took a shaky breath. "Is she still awake?" Every muscle in her body ached, her throat felt like the Sahara, and she wondered whether her legs had turned to lead.

"No, she went right back to sleep as soon as she saw my face, but it's a very good sign. The nurses say so." She sounded pitifully hopeful.

"I'll take a quick shower and be right there."

When she arrived Ruby was sleeping peacefully on her side, arm curled around her panda. Ariella thought she detected a little more color in the plump cheek than she had seen yesterday, and Nina's face had gone from the haggard gray-green of midnight to a rosy flush. The sisters settled into two plastic chairs in a little alcove waiting area just outside the intensive care unit. Sipping from a Styrofoam cup of scalding hospital coffee, Ariella tried to find the energy to meet her sister's rush of words.

"Do you think she looks better? I really do. The nurses say all her numbers look good—blood pressure and all those things they check. They gave her a mild sedative and don't think she'll wake up again till one. Do you think she's going to be all right?" Hugging herself, Nina gazed at her sister with wide, anxious eyes.

"I really think she's turned the corner. She does look better, Nina. But let's just take it one step at a time, all right?" Ariella grimaced as she burnt her tongue on the coffee.

"Yes, you're right." Nina paused, ran her hands through her long hair and took a series of breaths, but then she burst into words again. "Lamaze breathing. Supposed to be good in any crisis. I wish Lenny would get here. He should be here already. This is his only daughter lying here—you'd think he'd move a little faster."

"Wasn't he in Dallas? It takes hours to fly in from there, even if he left at five in the morning—and there's a time difference too. Give him a break, Nina."

"Well, I shouldn't have to face this alone. I mean, I know you're here—I just think both parents ought to be with a child at a time like this. What if she gets worse? What if I have to make some big medical decision? I don't know if I can do it. I don't think I'm thinking straight enough." The tears began to flow.

Ariella placed the half-full coffee cup on a table and took her sister's hand. "Oh, Nina," she murmured. "It'll be okay."

Nina clutched her hand and sobbed. "I'm an idiot," she gasped when she could talk again. "Things are getting better, and now I break down. I should be happy."

"No. Be upset. You have a right. You were strong when you had to be: you got her here, you got through surgery. It's okay to cry now." And Ariella realized that she was crying too.

"What if Ruby sees me?" Nina choked out.

"Now you're talking crazy. She's too far away." Ariella peered over her sister's shoulder through the glass. "Anyway, she's sound asleep." They sat there with wet eyes, holding hands. Ariella knew that the lines and shadows on her sister's face reflected her own.

Finally, Nina said in a calmer but still husky tone, "I wish Mom were here."

"Do you? She'd just be fussing at you."

"She'd do some of my worrying for me, and I could reassure her, and I would feel better."

"And she'd be running off to your apartment to make chicken soup." Ariella rolled her eyes.

Nina gave her a reproachful look. "I could use some of that chicken soup right now, and so could Ruby."

Ariella looked away for a minute, then said, "So call her—phone's right there. And I will make you chicken soup as soon as I get to your apartment. I can make a good chicken soup."

Nina looked dubious. "I can't call Mom. I don't have her number."

"I do. I can even charge it to my phone card." She fished a plastic card and an address book from her pocketbook, flipped through to the right page and stepped to the phone on a side table. She lifted the receiver, dialed a long string of numbers and stretching the cord, handed it to her dumbfounded sister.

"Hello?" Nina croaked. "Mom. Oh, Mom, I'm at the hospital with Ruby. She's having more heart trouble. I was really missing you, and Ari made me call you." She paused and twirled the phone cord, and Ariella retrieved her now cooler coffee and sank back into her chair to observe.

"She had to have another surgery last night, and she's sleeping it off now. They tell me she's recovering fine so far." She listened. Ariella stared at the bare unit walls and swore to herself that by one o'clock today she would buy something to cheer Ruby up.

Nina was saying, "No, this was an emergency. Something they put in stopped working. And Lenny is in Texas on business." She paused. "I sure hope so." Her voice began wavering again. "He caught the earliest flight." Then she was silent for a while. "Well, Ari got here in a couple hours, and she'll be with me as long as I need her. All right, Mom. I love you too. Here she is. She's had a rough week herself." She held the receiver out toward Ariella, who took it reluctantly.

"Hi, Mom," she told the phone.

"Oh, darling, I'm so glad you girls are together. It was wonderful of you to come so quickly. How does Ruby look?"

"Better than last night."

"That's good. I know you'll look after Nina. She must be under such strain. I remember how I felt when you girls got chicken pox, which is nothing compared to a heart defect! But darling, why have you had a rough week?"

"Work."

"What happened?"

"Well, do you remember the murder case I was writing about?"

"The pregnant woman. You think the man in jail

didn't do it."

"Yes. Well, a couple days ago her doctor came to my apartment and admitted that she had seen evidence that the pregnant woman's husband was abusive. The doctor wanted me to reveal it in the paper. I had a front-page article yesterday, and at noon the husband jumped off a bridge. He's dead, Mom."

"Oh, my God. How awful for you to be mixed up in all of that. What a horrible man."

Ariella found herself blurting out, "Do you think I did the right thing publishing that article?" She wanted to kick herself for asking.

"Because the man killed himself?" Her mother's voice lowered to a more serious tone than Ariella had heard in years. "Darling, you are not responsible for that man's taking his life. He had a twisted and disturbed mind."

"I didn't want him to die. I just wanted to free an innocent man."

"And you did. The rest isn't your fault."

"But people are saying that Griffin deserved to die, Mom. It's as if my article lynched him."

"Oh, Ariella, you're all mixed up. For once listen to me, darling. That man killed himself because he killed his wife. He committed an unforgivable act, and he was living on borrowed time trying not to face it. Anything could have forced him to confront his guilt, and if you had never written that article something else would have. The bottom line is that when he attacked his own wife and took her life, he ended his own."

Ariella felt as if she were holding up the edge of a heavy manhole cover and peering out into the daylight. "Okay," she said softly. "But I hate it all the same."

"Of course you do. Who would want to be caught up in a horrible case like that?"

"Some reporters love it, Mom, but I don't."

"Of course you don't. You're my daughter."

Ariella snorted. "I am your daughter," she said.

"I know you think I'm timid, darling, and in some ways I am. But it doesn't make you timid to refuse to involve yourself with certain kinds of ugliness."

"That's true." She rubbed her right temple with her free hand. "Thanks, Mom. I'm really glad I talked to you." She could not remember the last time when she had said those words to her mother.

"I'm glad too. Give big kisses to Nina and Ruby for me."

"Wait, Mom. Just tell me a little news—what are you up to over there?"

"This and that. I just started taking Italian cooking lessons. Great fun. I have one more question too: what's going on with that Sam?"

"I don't know whether he's still my boyfriend."

"Well, make sure he's good enough for you."

Ariella almost dropped the phone. "Aren't you the one who always said a nice boyfriend was what I needed to smooth my rough edges?"

"Well, yes. I think a man who makes you happy would complete your life, but it has to be the right one."

"Maybe I'll tell him you said so."

"Your dad and I will be flying home in May via Logan, and he wants us to stay in Boston for a week, get a look at your apartment, maybe take you to Cape Cod for the weekend. He wants Nina and Lenny to bring Ruby up too. So tell Sam that if he sticks around that long I'll meet him in

May."

"Oh, Mom! Really? Will you come?" She sounded like a wistful child, but she didn't care.

"Don't say anything to your sister. I don't want to bother her with all that now."

"Oh, Mom, I hope it works out."

"If you mean about our visit, don't worry; we're coming. But if you mean about my meeting Sam, I hope so too. Goodbye, dear."

"I love you. Bye." Ariella hung up the phone and stared at it.

Nina looked as if she were waiting for an outburst. When it never came, she quipped, "When you're a mother you'll understand her better."

"So you've told me," Ariella answered mildly. "Actually, that's the best talk I've had with her in forever."

"It sounded as if she was a little tough on you about the article."

"She told me it's not my fault. You know, other people told me that too, but what she said made more sense."

"Maybe you needed to hear it from your mother."

"Oh, I don't think that was it," Ariella said brusquely, but she was far from sure.

At ten o'clock Lenny jogged into the room, unshaven, his belly bouncing, his scanty hair uncombed.

"Oh, sweetheart," he said, as Nina rushed into his arms. "How's my little girl?"

"They say she's stable. She won't wake up till at least one o'clock."

He squeezed his wife hard, opened one arm to gesture to Ariella. "You too, sweetheart. Time for a group grope. Looks like we all need it!"

Ariella grinned at him and came to snuggle with them both. She was ridiculously glad to see her brother-in-law, polyester trousers and all.

"Thank you so much for coming down here, Ari," he was saying in his nasal voice. "Means a lot. Really it does. Nina would have been a wreck without you."

Ariella swatted his arm. "Very diplomatic."

"If I wanted diplomacy I wouldn't have married Lenny. He's right. I would have been a mess."

"She managed just fine until I got here. She's tougher than you think," Ariella told Lenny.

Her sister squeezed her forearm to make her look at her. "So is Mom." They locked eyes.

"All right, all right." Lenny raised his eyes to the ceiling. "Let's not get into your mother right now. I've had way too little sleep for that conversation. Shake me loose, girls, so I can kiss my sweet Ruby." He shrugged them off and tiptoed into the unit, trailing them behind him as he approached the bed. Kneeling beside it, he brushed a lock of Ruby's hair from her face. "Looks good to me," he announced, kissing her little cheek with a smack.

Ariella made a face at him. "Well, hopefully that sedative's working. And are we supposed to touch her?" A tall stern nurse with a long nose was marching toward them.

"Aaaah. I won't wake her. I'm always loud, and she's used to it." As the nurse drew closer he announced, "And I scrubbed my hands first thing before I came up here. Not an idiot, am I? You know I've been in hospitals before."

"Excuse me," the nurse interrupted, as she glanced at the machines surrounding Ruby, "but we can't have three visitors at the bedside, and I need to ask you to be more quiet. These patients are very sick."

"It's okay, lady. I'm going. I'm going. I'm just this little girl's daddy, that's all."

"Well, sir." The nurse frowned and picked up the chart to read it. "Ruby is doing much better this morning. Her vital signs are excellent. But what she needs is lots of quiet sleep."

Lenny looked as if he might argue, but he just said, "So can I get us some brunch somewhere, Nina honey?"

"Actually," Ariella put in, "now that you're here, I was thinking I might go out for a bit. I want to go buy a present for Ruby for when she wakes up. It'll give you two some time together."

"Where will you go?" Nina asked nervously.

Ariella knew that she was imagining calling her in an emergency and tried not to be annoyed at being interrogated like a teenager. "I think I'll go to F.A.O. Schwarz."

"Don't spend a lot of money."

"Ya, sweetheart, it's not necessary. Why don't you just take a walk and go buy yourself a Danish?"

"It's okay. I really want to." Ariella felt another wave of irritation, which she tried to repress.

Lenny turned to his wife, who was biting her lip. "Maybe it would do her good to get a break from here, Nina." He put one arm around her again. "Go ahead, Ari. See ya later."

"Back by one." She turned and walked steadily away from Ruby's bed, away from the seating area, out into a long hall, boot heels clicking on the hard corridor floor, passing people in blue scrubs and others in jeans and sweaters, around a corner that led to the main hospital. As soon as she was sure that her sister could no longer see her, she began to jog.

She ran and ran all the way down the twisting halls to the second floor atrium, down the wide marble staircase to the main lobby, teeming with strangers, through the revolving door, and out into the sunshine. She jogged slower now, her face hot, threading along the crowded sidewalk, past uniformed doormen, stooped street people, and a corner fiddler competing with the music of honking horns and squealing taxi tires. She jogged all five blocks to the subway station and down the long black staircase into the earth. Only when she reached the platform did she slow to a walk. Her heart was racing, and it was dark underground, but she stood in a beam of light coming from somewhere, some chink in the wall that she could not spot. The light glinted on the railroad tracks as she waited for the train, and just seeing it soothed her. The light seemed to fill her as she waited there, and the harsh voices and foul smells of the subway faded away. Then the downtown train pulled into the station with the peculiar whiny roar of the New York subway, and she boarded it.

36

She was waiting at the corner across from F.A.O. Schwarz in a crowd of jostling people, traffic rolling past, when she saw a yellow taxi stop in front of the toy store's famous red awning. The light changed, and as a flower delivery truck sped through the red light New Yorkers began to push into the street. As she crossed with them she saw a man alight from the taxi who looked like Sam. He started toward F.A.O. Schwarz, and her heart leapt into her throat. When she reached the curb she slowed and watched him pass the Beefeater doorman and go right through the double glass doors, disappearing into the store where she was heading. She shook her head. It couldn't be Sam.

She loitered outside, pausing a moment at the huge store window to gaze at the elaborate train display, and then the double doors opened to emit a regal-looking grandmother with a shopping bag, four small children chattering about a giant piano and frolicking around her like puppies. Stepping across the threshold of the historic toy store Ariella found herself letting out a long breath. Her gaze roamed the enormous stuffed animals in a myriad of colors vying for her attention and lit on one giraffe over six feet tall. A little smile crept across her face at the sight of a wide-eyed toddler in overalls staring up the wall at hundreds of Sesame

Street puppets hanging above his curly head. Unsure what she wanted for Ruby, she wandered off to the left down an aisle displaying bath toys. She stopped for a minute to admire a miniature ocean liner called H.M.S. Bubbles, complete with a blue-hatted captain and uniformed crew.

Just past the bath toys she found the stuffed animals, dozens and dozens of almost any animal she could name. Some were so realistic they might have come straight from a science book, but many were stylized, some hand puppets, some characters from books like Curious George. On a shelf just out of reach she spotted the perfect thing—the shaggy mane, green suit and friendly smile of Doctor Lion, a character in Ruby's favorite story, where a little girl bunny goes to the hospital for an operation and recovers with a big dish of pink ice cream. The stuffed toy even had a removable stethoscope for Ruby to play with. Ariella tried stepping on the bottom shelf to gain some height, but she still could not reach the lion. So she went in search of a store clerk.

At the end of the aisle she found the doll department. There were baby dolls of every shape, size and color—dolls that talked, dolls that cried, dolls that laughed, even dolls that sneezed. Ariella had not thought about dolls for years, but she suddenly remembered how much she had loved her own talking doll, Chatty Cathy. When you pulled the string on her back she would say, "Hi! How are you? It's a beautiful day, isn't it?" Ariella wondered why she had never gotten tired of hearing those same remarks, why they had always seemed a fresh miracle.

Around the corner of a display case she saw a doll on a dais, the biggest doll she had ever seen in her life, over four feet tall. The doll was standing on a red, velvet carpet, her lustrous black hair framing her face in long ringlets, her green eyes gleaming with tiny gold flecks, with a dozen smaller dolls seated around her feet. She wore a gown the color of pea soup trimmed with dark green ribbon, white petticoats peeping out from beneath. Scarlett O'Hara. She drew Ariella as firmly as a rodeo cowboy with a rope around her waist.

She stood beside the huge doll, fingering the soft gown, admiring the delicacy of the lace on the sleeves and bodice, the carefully sculptured fingers, the tiny fingernails. The doll's exquisitely life-like features told Ariella that it must be a Madame Alexander doll. She lifted its skirt to find two ruffled white petticoats with a hoop sewn into the lower one. Ariella could hardly believe it—an actual hoop-skirt exactly like the pre-war Scarlett. The doll had no tag on her anywhere, but some of the smaller dolls at her feet, smaller replicas of Scarlett in red, green and white gowns, had Madame Alexander tags.

Ariella had not seen a Madame Alexander doll in years either, perhaps since her own Alice in Wonderland, a hunk of its hair chopped off by Nina, had disappeared one day. No doubt her childish cocoon of frills and flounces had left her ill-prepared for the grit of modern life, although never as badly prepared as her mother. And what message did Scarlett O'Hara have to offer little girls today: a simple model of determination in adversity, or a cruel nostalgia for a past when blacks were slaves and women could not survive unmarried. Ariella knew that Joyce would snort at this doll, dismiss it with criticism of its excessive size and its inappropriateness in a city filled with people of color, but she could not walk away. This Scarlett had the guileless painted smile of all the Madame Alexander dolls, and she seemed blissfully remote from any injustice. The doll's sheer beauty touched Ariella, and she felt a little of the tension in her begin to drift away like froth in the bath that leaves you staring at your naked limbs.

Then a hand tapped her shoulder. She spun on her heel, and there was Sam in a red plaid flannel shirt and jeans, his grey wool coat slung over one shoulder. A blue Tartan scarf dangled straight down from the left side of his neck about to slip to the floor, and without a thought she reached around the other side to tug it back into place.

"What on earth are you doing here?" she said.

"You don't seem as surprised as I expected. I thought I'd get at least a little shriek." He was trying to kid her but sounded forced.

"I thought I saw you coming out of a taxi. Couldn't believe it. But I guess I was right." She backed up a step and crossed her arms against her chest.

He jerked a thumb at the Scarlett doll and smiled a little. "Don't you think that's a little much for Ruby?"

"I don't think anything is too much for Ruby right now," she snapped at him. "No little child deserves all this illness and pain. But for your information I'm not buying that for Ruby. I'm just looking at it. I want to get Ruby a lion."

"Not very glad to see me, are you?"

"I'm not too crazy about that smirk on your face. Why would I be glad to see you after listening to your abusive messages on my machine?" She felt blood rushing into her face.

"Not abusive, surely."

"What would you call it? You condemned me for destroying a woman's life." Her words pricked him. She looked exhausted, and he did not know what to say to warm her cold stare. He only knew that he felt he had to break through to her.

"I had no idea Ruby was hospitalized."

Her eyes burned with unshed tears, and her voice dropped. "I know that, Sam. I know you well enough to know that. Ruby's okay. She's going to be okay." She plunged her hands into her coat pockets. "I let you know where I was going as soon as I could. You didn't even give me a chance. Never gave me the benefit of the doubt. Condemned me without hearing anything I had to say." Her lips were a tight line. "Have you even talked to Natalie?"

"I've talked to her endlessly."

"And does she say I pressured her?" She held her breath.

"No, not at all." Ariella sighed silently as he continued. "She says it was absolutely her decision, the only right one she could make. She's standing firm."

"She doesn't feel she caused him to jump?"

"She says she refuses to take responsibility for that, that she made her choice and he made his."

There was a pause. "I admire her. I wish I could see it that way," Ariella said reluctantly.

"Ariella, I came here to say that I'm sorry I yelled at you on your machine. Very sorry. I've been doing a lot of thinking. All I really want to do is hug you and put this behind us." A flash of his boyish charm pulsed between them, and then he schooled his features.

"I appreciate the apology," she said without emotion. He could see the dark circles under her eyes and the haunted look lurking in them.

"Look. I've been an ass. I know that. I've been disrespectful to you, your profession...."

She cut in, her words hard-bitten. "Yes, and totally unsupportive to me at the toughest moment of my professional life. Do you think this has been easy for me? You can't possibly imagine how I felt when I heard that man had killed himself because of an article I wrote. You don't care about that. Just want my attention back. Let's just kiss and make up and go home to bed, right?"

"That is unfair!"

"Keep your voice down," she hissed. "This is a public place. I'm not ready to put this behind me. I'm still right in the middle of it. There will be a dozen more Griffin stories coming out in the paper. And my niece hasn't even made it through the first twenty-four hours after surgery. I have no desire to go back to Boston right now, with or without you. I'm staying right here where someone is still alive who needs me. And even with a promotion, maybe I shouldn't go back at all."

"What? What promotion?"

She gritted her teeth. "Joyce recommended me for the health beat. Right before I ran out on her."

"But isn't that what you always wanted? And I do want to be there for you — though you don't seem to know it. What would you do here in New York anyway?"

"Oh, come on. With my front-page stories and Manhattan connections I could land a New York job in a couple of months. I could be with the people who really love and support me: my sister and Ruby and Lenny." Her eyes flashed with challenge.

"And who the hell is this Lenny?" he said without rancor.

She rolled her eyes. "My brother-in-law."

"Okay. I know. I need to stop questioning every male name you spout. But this is crazy, Ariella. You're just going to run away? Why don't you stand your ground? Joyce has offered you your dream job. Take it. Let's face up to the mess we made together in Boston. Help me fix things with you. Help Natalie save her career. Make something good come of all this misery!" He was almost shouting, and she felt a wave of dizziness and grasped a table edge for balance. Too little sleep. Curious mothers and children were glancing their way.

"I asked you to keep your voice down, and if you don't I'm going to march right out of this store and back to the hospital and refuse to speak to you."

He lowered his tone, but it rang with intensity. "I'll quiet down if you'll *listen* to me."

She let out a breath and looked him right in the eye. "Okay, talk." A group of girls in school uniforms pushed past them, and he waited until they had all moved into the board game aisle.

"Ariella, why do you think I chased all the way down here to New York?" His hands clutched her forearms for a minute, then slid down to her hands, and although she did not respond, she did not resist. "I love you. If I didn't care I would never had gotten so angry. I felt you had personally betrayed me by hurting my friend. And I felt terribly left out of your decision-making. I hated the surprise of reading about Natalie in the paper. I wanted to feel that we were a team, that you would tell me important things happening in your life. Not stupid things like what you ate for lunch. But yes, something as big as this article. And I admit I felt cheated of the chance to influence your decision. I wanted to have my say."

"But, Sam..."

He put a finger on her lips. "Hear me out. I know you had to keep Natalie's confession confidential. She berated me for thinking otherwise. But Ariella, don't you see that even though I went overboard, all this is just my need to be a major player in your life. I feel so uncertain of you, of whether you're just going to disappear. It's not that I want to run your career. I just don't want to have a sick feeling in my gut when I can't reach you by phone for a day. I want to know that you care, that you're coming back. I want something real, permanent." His voice faltered. "Maybe marriage..."

Her mouth dropped open.

"I know I've been very hard on you sometimes. Very suspicious of your values. I've got to stop seeing those Michigan reporters in you. That's nuts, and I know it now. It just took me too long. I can't let Schaus off the hook that way. And it's the same with you. If you hold yourself responsible for Griffin's death you let him wriggle out of some of the blame. You're a loving, generous, principled person; don't let a dead murderer make you doubt that for a minute."

She swallowed hard; then a ghost of a smile touched her lips. "Funny, you sound like my mom."

He looked confused. "And that's a good thing?" She nodded, and he felt that something in her had shifted, that she was listening hard now.

His hands tightened on her fingers, and his eyes bored into hers for a moment before he said, "You're the best thing that's happened to me in ten years. I've never met any woman remotely like you, and I know I never will again. I don't want to lose you."

"I don't want to lose you either," she said, "although sometimes you make me insane."

He broke into a smile. "I'll take that as a compliment. Does that mean you'll come back—that you'll at least consider it? I want a chance to make you insanely happy."

She smiled a little. "You sometimes do that too," she admitted. "I don't know. It's been a hell of a week. I haven't slept. I can't possibly decide something like this right now." She tapered off, and embarrassed at herself for spouting clichés looked down at his fingers still clutching her hands, and shivered. Some loud boys were passing them now, pushing and joking and talking about light sabers. She tried to pull her scattered thoughts together.

"You've been very honest, and you deserve the same. For a while now I've been thinking that I might be in love with you." She looked up. "Look, you're pushy, but that's all right. I can stand up to you. I just don't like your jumping to conclusions all the time, and I don't like your bad temper. I don't know if I can live with that. What you said just now about my being a good person—that's what I need. Someone who believes in me, respects my judgment. You're so confident that you don't need that. But wherever I go, I carry my mother's disapproving voice, and I don't need more of that from you. She loves me too, but I ran away from her when I left high school, and I still don't want to live anywhere near her."

"I hadn't thought about it that way."

"No, how could you?" she said tartly.

"But I do believe in you." He was squeezing her hands gently, rhythmically. "I'm really sorry I haven't shown it better. You've challenged me to open my mind, my heart." He took a breath. "Can't we try again? When you're ready. How long do you need to stay here in New York?"

"At least until Ruby goes home."

"Does that mean you'll come back to Boston?"

She sighed, pulled her hands free at last, ran them

through her hair. "I suppose. Yes, I can't leave Joyce in the lurch. And I have to put an end to this whole sordid chapter. Though I wish I'd never heard of the Griffins."

"God, me too." He reached out a hand and stroked her cheek.

Tears threatened in her eyes. "What about…?" She stopped awkwardly, hands clasped tightly below her waist, and raised her chin. The words she wanted to say struggled to burst into the toy store as she stood hesitating on the edge of the precipice. But she wanted to try. She wanted it badly. She counted to ten, face flushed, then blurted out, "What if we… What if we try living together for six months?"

A flash of humor crossed his face as he grabbed her and pulled her into his arms. "Yes, yes. Let's do it. A scientific experiment. I'm good at those. And I promise I won't get mad or make snap judgments or…"

"Don't." She looked pained for a moment. "Don't promise me anything you can't keep. You can't promise you'll never get angry." Then her lips curved up at him, and she shook her forefinger. "You just need to control yourself, and I need to figure out how to handle you."

"Shush," he said, silencing her with a long kiss that reverberated with victory. She clutched fistfuls of his coat, swayed on her feet, and met him with all her pent-up fury, fear and love. A threesome of teenage girls gawked, unnoticed.

A little above the fray, her green eyes shining, Scarlett gazed down on the lovers from her dais, some trick of the light making her look for a moment as if she were amused.

⌀

A Note to the Reader

Thank you very much for reading *Ripples*. I hope that you enjoyed it. I welcome your perspectives on the story and hope that you will help me spread the word about my first novel by writing a brief review on the *Ripples* page of amazon.com.

Happy reading and best wishes!
Jennifer Lew

www.ingramcontent.com/pod-product-compliance
Lightning Source LLC
Chambersburg PA
CBHW020239200626
46816CB00001BA/40